J. R supportive husband and he
After graduating from law ... working
in health care in Boston and spent many years as
ief of staff for one of the premier academic medical
tres in the nation.

sit her at www.jrward.com

Praise for J. R. Ward:

'[A] raw, gritty tour de force'
Booklist

'Tautly written, wickedly sexy, and just plain fun'
Lisa Gardner

'Ward pulls no punches in this dark, dangerous,
and at times tragic series. Waiting for successive
instalments is getting harder and harder'
Romantic Times

COVE✝

A NOVEL of the FALLEN ANGELS

piatkus

PIATKUS

First published in the United States in 2009 by New American Library,
A Division of Penguin Group (USA) Inc., New York
First published in Great Britain as a paperback original in 2009 by Piatkus
This paperback edition published in 2011 by Piatkus
Reprinted 2012

A CIP catalogue record for this book
is available from the British Library.

ISBN 978-0-7499-5558-8

Printed and bound by CPI Group (UK) Ltd, Croydon, CR0 4YY

Papers used by Piatkus are from well-managed forests
and other responsible sources.

MIX
Paper from
responsible sources
FSC
www.fsc.org   FSC® C104740

Piatkus
An imprint of
Little, Brown Book Group
100 Victoria Embankment
London EC4Y 0DY

An Hachette UK Company
www.hachette.co.uk

www.piatkus.co.uk

For Our Theo

ACKNOWLEDGMENTS

With thanks to:
Kara Cesare, Claire Zion, Kara Welsh, Leslie Gelbman,
and everyone at NAL. As always.

Thank you also to Steven Axelrod, my voice of reason.

With love to Team Waud: Dee, LeElla, K, and Nath—
without whom none of this would be possible.
Thank you also to Jen and Lu and
all our Mods and Hall Monitors.

And with total gratitude to Doc Jess
(aka Jessica Andersen), Sue Grafton, Suz Brockmann,
Christine Feehan and her wonderful family,
Lisa Gardner, and Linda Francis Lee.

And with all love to my husband, my mother,
the better half of WriterDog, and my whole family.

Prologue

Demon was such a nasty word.

And so damned old-school. People heard *demon* and they conjured up all kinds of Hieronymus Bosch helter-skelter—or worse, Dante's stupid-ass *Inferno* crap. Honestly. Flames and tortured souls and everyone wailing.

Okay, maybe Hell was a little toasty. And if the place had had a court painter, Bosch would have been at the head of the pack.

But that wasn't the point. The Demon actually saw itself as more of a Free-Will Coach. Much better, more modern. The anti-Oprah, as it were.

It was all about influence.

The thing was, the qualities of the soul were not dissimilar to the components of the human body. The corporeal form had a number of vestigial parts, like the appendix, the wisdom teeth, and the coccyx—all of which were at best unnecessary, and at worst capable of compromising the functioning of the whole.

Souls were the same. They, too, had useless baggage that impeded their proper performance, these annoying, holier-than-thou bits dangling like an appendix waiting for infection. Faith and hope and love ... prudence, temperance, justice, and fortitude ... all this useless clutter just packed too much damn morality into the heart, getting in the way of the soul's innate desire for malignancy.

A demon's role was to help people see and express their inner truth without their being clouded by all that bullshit, diverting humanity. As long as people stayed true to their core, things were going in the right direction.

And lately, that had been relatively true. Between all the wars on the planet, and the crime, and the disregard for the environment, and that cesspool of finance known as Wall Street, as well as the inequalities far and wide, things were okay.

But it wasn't enough and time was running out.

To go with a sports analogy, Earth was the playing field and the game had been going on since the stadium had been built. The Demons were the Home Team. Away was made up of Angels pimping that chimera of happiness, Heaven.

Where the court painter was Thomas Kincaid, for fuck's sake.

Each soul was a quarterback on the field, a participant in the universal struggle of good against evil, and the scoreboard reflected the relative moral value of his or her deeds on earth. Birth was kickoff and death was game-over—whereupon the score would be added to the larger tally. Coaches had to stay on the sidelines, but they could put different complements of players on the field with the human to influence things—and also call time-outs for pep talks.

Commonly known as the "near-death experience."

Here was the problem: Like a spectator who had been watching a postseason game in a cold seat with one too many hot dogs in his belly and a screamer sitting right behind his ear, the Creator was eyeing the exit.

Too many fumbles. Too many time-outs. Too many ties that had led to too many unresolved overtimes. What had started out as a gripping contest had evidently lost its appeal, and the teams had been given their notice: Wrap up the play, boys.

So both sides had to agree on one particular quarterback. One quarterback and seven plays.

Instead of an endless parade of humans, they were down

to seven souls in the balance between good and evil . . . seven chances to determine whether humanity was good or bad. A tie was not possible and the stakes were . . . everything. If Team Demon won, it got to keep the facility and all the players that had ever been or ever would be. And the Angels became slaves for eternity.

Which made torturing human sinners seem like nothing but a bore.

If the Angels won, the entire Earth would be nothing but one giant Christmas frickin' morning, a choking wave of happiness and warmth and caring and sharing taking over everything. Under that hideous scenario, the Demons would cease to exist not just in the universe, but in the hearts and minds of all of humanity.

Although considering all the happy-happy, joy-joy, that was the best outcome in that scenario. Short of getting stabbed repeatedly in the eye with a pole.

The Demons couldn't bear losing. It just wasn't an option. Seven chances were not a lot, and the Away Team had won the metaphysical coin toss—so they got to approach the quarterback who was going to drive the seven "balls," as it were.

Ah, yes . . . the quarterback. Not surprisingly the choice of that key position had led to a lot of heated discussion. Eventually, though, one had been selected, one who both sides found acceptable . . . one who both coaches expected to rock the plays according to their values and goals.

Poor fool didn't know what he was in for.

The thing was, though, the Demons weren't prepared to leave such a momentous responsibility on the shoulders of a human. Free will was malleable, after all—which was the basis of the whole game.

So they were sending someone onto the field as a player. It was against the rules, of course, but true to their nature— and also something the opponent was incapable of doing.

This was the edge the Home Team had: The one good thing about the Angels was they always colored within the lines.

They had to.

Suckers.

CHAPTER

1

"She wants you."

Jim Heron lifted his eyes from his Budweiser. Across the crowded, dim club, past bodies that were clad in black and hung with chains, through the thick air of sex and desperation, he saw the "she" in question.

A woman in a blue dress stood beneath one of the few ceiling lights in the Iron Mask, the golden glow floating down over her Brooke Shields brown hair and her ivory skin and her banging body. She was a revelation, a stand-out slice of color among all the gloomy, neo-Victorian Prozac candidates, as beautiful as a model, as resplendent as a saint.

And she *was* staring at him, though he questioned the wanting part: Her eyes were set deep, which meant as she looked over, the yearning that stalled out his lungs could just be a product of the way her skull was built.

Hell, maybe she was simply wondering what he was doing in the club. Which made two of them.

"I'm telling you, that woman wants you, buddy."

Jim glanced over at Mr. Matchmaker. Adrian Vogel was the reason he'd ended up here, and the Iron Mask was definitely the guy's scene: Ad was dressed in black from head to toe and had piercings in places most people didn't want needles anywhere around.

"Nah." Jim took another swig of his Bud. "Not her type."

"You sure about that."

"Yup."

"You're a fool." Adrian dragged a hand through the black waves on his head and the stuff eased back into place like it had been trained well. Christ, if it weren't for the fact that he worked construction and had a mouth like a sailor, you'd wonder whether he trolled the women's mousse and spray aisles.

Eddie Blackhawk, the other guy with them, shook his head. "If he's not interested, that doesn't make him foolish."

"Says you."

"Live and let live, Adrian. It's better for everyone."

As the guy eased back on the velvet couch, Eddie was more Biker than Goth in his jeans and shitkickers, so he looked as out of place as Jim did—although given the hulking size of the guy and those weird-ass red-brown eyes of his, it was hard to imagine him fitting in with anyone but a bunch of pro wrestlers: even with his hair in that long braid, nobody razzed him at the construction site—not even the meathead roofers who gave the biggest lip.

"So, Jim, you don't talk much." Adrian scanned the crowd, no doubt looking for a Blue Dress of his own. After focusing on the dancers who writhed in iron cages, he flagged their waitress. "And after working with you for a month, I know it's not because you're stupid."

"Don't have a lot to say."

"Nothing wrong with that," Eddie murmured.

This was probably why Jim liked Eddie better. The SOB was another member of the Spare Club for Men, a guy who never used a word when a nod or a shake of the head could get his point across. How he'd gotten so tight with Adrian, whose mouth had no neutral on its stick shift, was a mystery.

How he roomed with the fucker was inexplicable.

Whatever. Jim had no intention of going into all their hows, whys and wheres. It was nothing personal. They were actually the kind of hardheaded smart-asses he would have been friends with in another time, on another planet, but here and now, their shit was none of his business—and he'd only gone out with them because Adrian had threatened to keep asking until he did.

Bottom line, Jim lived life by the code of the disconnected and expected other people to leave him to his I-am-an-island routine. Since getting out of the military, he'd been vagabonding it, ending up in Caldwell only because it was where he'd stopped driving—and he was going to hit the road after the project they were all working on was finished.

The thing was, given his old boss, it was better to stay a moving target. No telling how long it was going to be before a "special assignment" popped up and Jim got tagged again.

Finishing off his beer, he figured it was a good thing he owned only his clothes, his truck, and that broken-down Harley. Sure, he didn't have much to show for being thirty-nine—

Oh, man . . . the date.

He was forty. Tonight was his birthday.

"So I gotta know," Adrian said, leaning in. "You have a woman, Jim? That why you're not picking up Blue Dress? I mean, come *on*, she's smokin' hot."

"Looks aren't everything."

"Yeah, well, they sure as hell don't hurt."

The waitress came over, and while the others ordered another round, Jim shot a glance at the woman they were jawing about.

She didn't look away. Didn't flinch. Just slowly licked her red lips like she'd been waiting for him to make eye contact again.

Jim refocused on his empty Bud and shifted in the booth, feeling like someone had slipped lit coals into his shorts. It had been a long, long time for him. Not a dry spell, not even a drought. Sahara Desert was more like it.

And what do you know, his body was ready to end that stretch of nuthin' but left-handers.

"You should go over there," Adrian said. "Introduce yourself."

"I'm cool where I am."

"Which means I may have to reassess your intelligence." Adrian drummed his fingers on the table, the heavy silver ring he wore flashing. "Or at least your sex drive."

"Be my guest."

Adrian rolled his eyes, clearly getting the picture that there was no negotiating when it came to Blue Dress. "Fine, I'll lay off."

The guy sat back into the sofa so that he and Eddie were striking similar sprawls. Predictably, he couldn't stay silent for long. "So did you two hear about the shooting?"

Jim frowned. "There another one?"

"Yup. Body was found down by the river."

"They tend to turn up there."

"What is this world coming to," Adrian said, throwing back the last of his beer.

"It's always been this way."

"You think?"

Jim leaned back as the waitress planted freshies in front of the boys. "Nope, I know."

"Deinde, ego te absolvo a peccatis tuis in nomine Patris, et Filii, et Spiritus Sancti. . . ."

Marie-Terese Boudreau lifted her eyes to the confessional booth's lattice window. On the other side of the screen, the priest's face was in profile and heavily shadowed, but she knew who he was. And he knew her.

So he was very aware of what she did and why she had to go to confession at least once a week.

"Go, my child. Be well."

As he closed the panel between them, panic nailed her

in the chest. In these quiet moments when she laid out her sins, the degrading place where she'd ended up was exposed, the words she spoke shining a brilliant spotlight on the horrible way she spent her nights.

The ugly images always took a while to fade. But the choking feeling that came from knowing where she was headed next was just going to get worse.

Gathering her rosary together, she put the beads and links in her coat pocket and picked her purse up off the floor. Footsteps right outside the confessional stopped her from leaving.

She had reasons for keeping a low profile, some of which having nothing to do with her "job."

When the sound of heavy heels dimmed, she pulled open the red velvet curtain and stepped out.

Caldwell's St. Patrick's Cathedral was maybe half the size of the one down in Manhattan, but it was big enough to inspire awe in even the casually faithful. With gothic arches like the wings of angels and a lofty ceiling that seemed only inches away from Heaven, she felt both unworthy and grateful to be under its roof.

And she loved the smell inside. Beeswax and lemon and incense. Lovely.

Walking down by the chapels of the saints, she weaved in and out of the scaffolding that had been erected so that the clerestory's mosaics could be cleaned. As always, the racks of flickering votive candles and the dim spotlights on the still statues calmed her, reminding her that there was an eternity of peace waiting at the far end of life.

Assuming you were allowed past the pearly gates.

The cathedral's side doors were closed after six p.m., and as usual, she had to go out the main entrance—which seemed like a waste of the thing's effort. The carved panels were much better suited to welcoming the hundreds who came for services each Sunday . . . or the guests of important marriage ceremonies . . . or the virtuous faithful.

No, she was more of a side-door kind of person.

At least, she was now.

Just as she leaned all her weight on the thick wood, she heard her name and looked over her shoulder.

No one was there, as far as she could see. The cathedral was empty even of people praying in the pews.

"Hello?" she called out, voice echoing. "Father?"

When there was no reply, a chill licked up her spine.

On a quick surge, she heaved herself against the left side of the door and burst out into the cold April night. Holding the lapels of her wool coat together, she moved fast, her flats making a *clip*, *clip*, *clip* sound down the stone steps and over the sidewalk as she hustled to her car. The first thing she did as she got in was lock all the doors.

As she panted, she looked around. Shadows curled on the ground beneath leafless trees, and the moon was revealed as thin clouds drifted. People moved around in the windows of the houses across from the church. A station wagon went by slowly.

There was no stalker, no man in a black ski mask, no attacker lurking. Nothing.

Reining in her tailspin, she coaxed her Toyota into starting and gripped the steering wheel hard.

After checking her mirrors, she eased out into the street and headed deeper into downtown. As she went along, lights from streetlamps and other cars flared in her face and flooded the inside of the Camry, illuminating the black duffel bag on the passenger seat. Her god-awful uniform was in there, and as soon as she got out of this nightmare, she was burning it along with what she'd had to put on her body every night for the last year.

The Iron Mask was the second place she'd "worked." The first had blown up about four months ago. Literally.

She could not believe she was still in the business. Every time she packed that duffel, she felt as if she were getting sucked back into a bad dream, and she wasn't sure whether the confessions at St. Patrick's were making things better or worse.

Sometimes she felt like all they did was stir up crap that

was better left buried, but the need for forgiveness was too strong to fight.

As she made a turn onto Trade Street, she started past the concentration of clubs, bars, and tattoo parlors that made up the Caldie Strip. The Iron Mask was toward the far end, and like the others, it was hopping every night with its perpetual wait line of wannabe zombies. Ducking into an alley, she bumped over the potholes by all the Dumpsters, and came out into the parking lot.

The Camry fit nicely in a spot along the brick wall that was marked STAFF ONLY.

Trez Latimer, the owner of the club, insisted that all the women who worked for him use the designated spaces that were closest to the back door. He was as good as the Reverend had been about taking care of his employees, and they all appreciated it. Caldwell had a seedy side, and the Iron Mask was right in the thick of it.

Marie-Terese got out with her duffel and looked up. The bright lights of the city dulled the few stars that twinkled around the patchy clouds, and the heavens seemed even farther away than they were.

Closing her eyes, she took long, deep breaths and drew the collar of her coat in tight. When she went into the club, she would be in the body and mind of someone else. Someone she didn't know and wouldn't care to remember in the future. Someone who disgusted her. Someone she despised.

Last breath.

Just before she cracked her lids, that panic flared again, sweat breaking out under her clothes and over her brow in spite of the cold. As her heart beat like she was running from a mugger, she wondered how many more nights of this she had left in her. The anxiety seemed to be getting worse with every week, an avalanche picking up speed, sweeping over her, covering her in icy weight.

Except she couldn't stop. She was still paying off debts . . . some financial, some that felt existential. Until she was back where she started, she needed to stay where she didn't want to be.

And besides, she told herself that she didn't want to *not* go through this shocking anxiety. It meant she hadn't surrendered to the circumstances completely and that at least some part of her true self still survived.

Not for much longer, a small voice pointed out.

The back door to the club swung open and an accented voice said her name in the most beautiful way. "You okay, Marie-Terese?"

She flipped open her eyes, put her mask on, and strode with calm purpose over to her boss. Trez had no doubt seen her on one of the security cameras; God knew they were everywhere.

"I'm fine, Trez, thanks."

He held the door open for her, and as she walked by him, his dark eyes scanned her. With coffee-colored skin and a face that seemed Ethiopian in its smooth bones and perfectly balanced lips, Trez Latimer was a looker—although his manners were the most attractive thing about him, as far as she was concerned. The guy had gallantry down to a science.

Although you didn't want to cross him.

"You do that every night," he said as he shut the door behind them and cranked the bar bolt in place. "You stand by your car and look at the sky. Every night."

"Do I?"

"Anybody bothering you?"

"No, but if someone was, I would tell you."

"Any*thing* bothering you?"

"Nope. I'm good."

Trez didn't look convinced as he escorted her down to the ladies' locker room and left her at the door. "Remember, I'm available twenty-four/seven, and you can talk to me anytime."

"I know. And thank you."

He put his hand to his heart and gave her a little bow. "My pleasure. You take care of yourself."

The locker room was walled with long metal compartments and broken up by benches that were screwed down into the floor. Against the far wall, the lighted showgirl mirror had a six-foot-long counter that was littered with makeup, and there were hairpieces and skimpy clothes and stilettos everywhere. The air smelled like girl sweat and shampoo.

As usual, she had the place to herself. She was always the first to come in and the first to leave, and now that she was in work mode, there were no hesitations, no hiccups in the routine.

Coat went into her locker. Street shoes were kicked off. Scrunchie was pulled free of her ponytail. Duffel bag was yanked open.

Her blue jeans and her white turtleneck and her navy blue fleece were traded for a set of clothes she wouldn't be caught dead wearing on Halloween: microscopic Lycra skirt, halter top that came down to the bottom of her ribs, thigh-highs with lace tops, and pimpish pumps that pinched her toes.

Everything was black. Black was the Iron Mask's signature color, and it had been the other club's as well.

She never wore black when she was away from work. About a month into this nightmare, she'd thrown away every thread of clothing she had with any black in it—to the point where she'd had to go out and buy something to wear to the last funeral she'd gone to.

Over at the lighted mirror, she hit her five tons of brunette hair with some spray and then weeded through the palettes of eye shadows and blushers, picking out dark, sparkly colors that were about as girl-next-door as a *Penthouse* centerfold. Moving quickly, she went Ozzy Osbourne on the eyeliner and glued on some fake eyelashes.

The last thing she did was go to her bag and take out a tube of lipstick. She never shared lipsticks with the other girls. Everyone was properly screened each month, but she wasn't taking chances: She could control what she did and how scrupulous she was when it came to safety. The other girls might have different standards.

The red gloss tasted like plastic strawberry, but the lipstick was critical. No kissing. Ever. And most of the men knew that, but with a coating of the grease, she cut short any debate: None of them wanted their wives or girlfriends to know what they were doing on their "guys' night out."

Refusing to look at her reflection, Marie-Terese turned away from the mirror and headed out to face the noise and the people and the business. As she went down the long, dim hall to the club proper, the bass of the music grew louder and so did the sound of her heart pounding in her ears.

Maybe it was one and the same.

At the end of the corridor, the club sprawled out before her, its deep purple walls and black floor and bloodred ceiling lit so sparsely it was like walking into a cave. The vibe was all about kinked-out sex, with women dancing in wrought-iron cages and bodies moving in pairs or threesomes and trippy, erotic music filling the thick air.

After her eyes adjusted to the darkness, she sifted through the men, applying a data screen she wished she'd never acquired.

You couldn't tell whether they were prospects by the clothes they wore or who they were with or whether they had a wedding ring on. It wasn't even a case of where they looked at you, because all men did the breast-to-hip sweep. The difference with the prospects was that they stared at you with something more than greed: As they ran their eyes over your body, the deed had already been done as far as they were concerned.

It didn't bother her, though. There was nothing that any man could do to her that was worse than what had already happened.

And there were two things she knew for sure: Three a.m. was going to come eventually. And like the end of her shift, this phase of her life wasn't going to last forever.

In her saner, less depressive moments, she told herself that this rough patch was something she was going to get through and come out of, kind of like her life had the flu: Even though it was hard to have faith in the future, she had to believe that one day she would wake up, turn her face to the sun, and revel in the fact that the sickness was gone and wellness had returned.

Although that was assuming it was just the flu. If what she was putting herself through was more like a cancer . . . maybe a part of her would always be gone, lost to the disease forever.

Marie-Terese shut off her brain and walked forward, into the crowd. Nobody ever said life was fun or easy or even fair, and sometimes you did things to survive that would seem utterly and completely incomprehensible to the home-and-hearth part of your brain.

But there were no shortcuts in life and you had to pay for your mistakes.

Always.

CHAPTER
2

Marcus Reinhardt Jewelers, est. 1893, had been housed in the same gracious brick building in downtown Caldwell since the mortar in its deep red walls had been set. The firm had changed hands in the Depression, but the ethos of the business had remained the same and prevailed into the Internet era: high-end, important jewels offered at competitive prices and paired with incomparable personal service.

"The ice wine is chilling in the private room, sir."

"Excellent. We're almost ready." James Richard Jameson, great-grandson of the man who had bought the store from Mr. Reinhardt, straightened his tie in one of the mirrored displays.

Satisfied with how he looked, he turned to inspect the three staff members who he'd chosen to stay after hours. They all had on black suits, with William and Terrence sporting gold-and-black club ties marked with the store's logo and Janice wearing a gold-and-onyx necklace from the 1950s. Perfect. His people were as elegant and discreet as everything in the showroom, and each was capable of conversing in English and French.

For what Reinhardt had to offer, customers were willing to travel up from Manhattan or down from Montreal, and north or south, it was always worth the trip. All around the showroom, sparkling flashes twinkled at the eye, a galaxy come home to roost, and the angles of the direct lighting and the arrangement of the glass cases were calibrated to decimate the distinction between want and need.

Just before the grandfather clock by the door chimed the tenth hour, James flashed over to a pocket door, whipped out an Oreck, and ran the vacuum across the footprints on the antique Oriental rug. On the return to the broom closet, he backed his way over his own path so there was nothing to mar the nap.

"I think he's here," William said by one of the barred windows.

"Oh . . . my God," Janice murmured as she leaned in beside her colleague. "He certainly is."

James slid the vacuum out of sight and snapped his suit jacket back into place. His heart was alive in his chest, beating fast, but on the outside he was calm as he walked toe-heel, toe-heel over to look into the street.

Customers were welcome in the store from ten a.m. to six p.m. Monday through Saturday.

Clients got to come privately after hours. On any day and time that suited them.

The gentleman who stepped out of the BMW M6 was solidly in client territory: European-cut suit, no overcoat in spite of the chill, stride like an athlete, face like an assassin. This was a very smart, very powerful man who probably had some shady in him, but it wasn't as though Mafia or drug money was discriminated against at Marcus Reinhardt. James was in the business of selling, not judging—so as far as he was concerned, the man coming to his door was a paragon of virtue, upstanding in his pair of Bally loafers.

James released the lock and opened the way before the bell was rung. "Good evening, Mr. diPietro."

The handshake was firm and short, the voice deep and sharp, the eyes cold and gray. "Are we ready?"

"Yes." James hesitated. "Will your intended be joining us?"

"No."

James shut the door and indicated the way to the back, studiously ignoring how Janice's eyes clung to the man. "May we offer you a libation?"

"You can start showing me diamonds, how about that."

"As you wish."

The private viewing room had oil paintings on the walls, a large antique desk, and four gold chairs. There was also a microscope, a black velvet exhibition pad, the chilling ice wine, and two crystal glasses. James nodded at his staff and Terrence came forward to remove the silver bucket while Janice took away the globlets with a bit of a fluster. William remained in the doorway, at the ready for any requests.

Mr. diPietro took a seat and put his hands on the desk, a platinum Chopard watch flashing from beneath his cuff. Those eyes of his, which were the same color as the watch, didn't so much as focus on James as bore right through to the back of his skull.

James cleared his throat as he sat opposite the man. "Pursuant to our conversation, I have pulled a selection of stones from our collection as well as called in a number of diamonds from Antwerp directly."

James took out a gold key and inserted it into a lock in the top drawer of the desk. When he dealt with a client who had yet to do a viewing or purchase, as he was now, he had to make a call whether they were the type who wanted to see the top range of their options first or build up to the most expensive choices.

It was clear which category Mr. diPietro fit into.

There were ten rings in the tray that James put out on the blotter, all of which had been steam-cleaned for presentation. The one he plucked from the black velvet crease was not the largest, although only by a fraction of a carat. It was, however, by far the best.

"This is a seven-point-seven-carat emerald-cut, D in

color, internally flawless. I have both the GIA and EGL certifications for your perusal."

James stayed silent as Mr. diPietro took the ring and bent down to inspect it. There was no reason to mention that the polish and the symmetry of the stone were exceptional or that the platinum setting had been handmade for the diamond or that it was the kind of thing that came onto the market very infrequently. The reflected light and fire spoke for themselves, the flashes radiating upward so brilliantly one had to wonder if the stone itself weren't magical.

"How much?" Mr. diPietro demanded.

James put the certificates on the desk. "Two million, three hundred thousand."

With men like Mr. diPietro, the more expensive the better, but the truth was, it was a good deal. For Reinhardt to stay in business, one had to balance volume and margin: too much margin, not enough volume. Besides, assuming Mr. diPietro stayed out of jail and/or bankruptcy, this was the kind of man James wanted to have a long relationship with.

Mr. diPietro handed the ring back and studied the certs. "Tell me about the others."

James swallowed his surprise. "Of course. Yes, of course."

He proceeded from right to left through the tray and described the attributes of each ring, all the while wondering whether he had misread his client. He also had Terrence bring in six more, all over five carats.

An hour later, Mr. diPietro sat back in the chair. The man had not stretched or wavered in his attention and there had been no quick checks of his BlackBerry or jokes to break the tension. He hadn't even glanced in passing at Janice, who was lovely.

Total and complete absorption.

James had to wonder about the woman whose finger would bear the ring. She'd be beautiful, naturally, but she'd have to be very independent and not very emotional. Generally speaking, even the most logical and successful man got a glint in his eye when he bought a ring like one of these for his woman—whether it was the thrill of surprising her with something over the top or the pride that came with being able to afford something that only .01 percent of the population could, the men usually showed some emotion.

Mr. diPietro was as cold and hard as the stones he regarded.

"Is there something else I might show you?" James said, deflating. "Some rubies or sapphires, perhaps?"

The client reached inside his suit jacket and brought out a thin black wallet. "I'll take the first one you showed me for two million even." As James blinked, Mr. diPietro put a credit card on the desktop. "If I'm giving you my money, I want you to work for it. And you will be discounting the stone, because your business needs repeat clients like myself."

James took a moment to catch up with the fact that a transaction might actually occur. "I . . . I appreciate your discerning eye, but the price is two million, three hundred thousand."

Mr. diPietro tapped the card. "That's debit. Two million. Right now."

James quickly did some math in his head. At that price he was still making about three hundred and fifty thousand on the piece.

"I believe I can do that," he said.

Mr. diPietro did not sound surprised. "Smart of you."

"What about sizing? Do you know what size your—"

"The seven-point-seven carats is the only size she's going to care about. We'll take care of the rest later."

"As you wish."

James typically encouraged the staff to engage with a client as he went back to set a purchase into its box and print out the valuation for insurance purposes. Tonight, though, he shook his head at them as Mr. diPietro palmed a cell phone and started dialing.

As James worked in the back office, he heard Mr. diPietro talking on the phone. There was no teasing, "Darling,

I have something for you," or suggestive, "I'm coming to see you." No, Mr. diPietro was not calling his soon-to-be fiancée, but rather someone named Tom about some kind of land issue.

James swiped the card. As he waited for authorization, he steam-cleaned the ring again, periodically checking the green digital readout on the card machine. When he was told to call the bank's twenty-four-hour line directly, he was not surprised given the purchase amount, and as soon as he got on with them, the representative requested to speak to Mr. diPietro.

Transferring the call to the phone on the desk in the viewing room, James put his head through the door. "Mr. diPietro—"

"They want to talk to me?" The man extended his right hand, flashing that watch, and picked up the receiver. Before James could come and take the line off hold, Mr. diPietro did it himself and started talking.

"Yes, it is. Yes, I am. Yes. Yes. My mother's maiden name is O'Brian. Yes. Thanks." He looked up at James as he put the call on hold again and the phone back in its seat. "They have an authorization code for you."

James bowed and went back to the office. When he reappeared, he was carrying a sleek red bag with satin handles and an envelope with the receipt in it.

"I hope you will call on us again if we may be of service."

Mr. diPietro took what he now owned. "I plan on getting engaged only once, but there will be anniversaries. Plenty of them."

The staff stepped back to get out of his way and James had to hustle to open the store's door before Mr. diPietro came to it. After the man breezed through, James relocked the thing and looked out the window.

The man's car was gorgeous as it took off, its engine growling, the bright lights of the street lamps reflecting off black paint as glossy as still water.

As James turned away, he caught Janice leaning into another window, her eyes sharp. One could be quite sure she wasn't measuring the car as he had, but focusing on the driver instead.

Odd, wasn't it. That which you could not have always seemed more valuable than what you did, and maybe that was why diPietro was so removed: He could afford all of what had been shown, so to him the transaction was no different from buying a newspaper or a can of Coke to the average person.

There was nothing that the truly wealthy could not have, and how lucky they were.

"No offense, but I think I'm going to take off."

Jim put down his empty and grabbed for his leather jacket. He'd had his two Buds, and one more was going to put him into DUI territory, so it was time to pull out.

"I can't believe you're leaving alone," Adrian drawled, his eyes going over to Blue Dress.

She was still standing beneath that ceiling light. And still staring. And still breathtaking. "Yup, just me, myself, and I."

"Most men don't have your kind of self-control." Adrian smiled, the hoop in his lower lip glinting. "Kind of impressive actually."

"Yeah, I'm a saint, all right."

"Well, drive home safe so you can keep polishing that halo. We'll see you tomorrow at the site."

There was a round of palm slapping and then Jim was making his way through the crowd. As he went, he drew looks from the black-chained and spike-collared, probably in the same way all these Goths did when they were out at a mall: *What the hell are you doing here?*

Guess Levi's and a clean flannel shirt offended their leather-and-lace sensibilities.

Jim chose a path that kept him far away from Blue Dress, and once he was outside, he took a deep breath like he'd passed some kind of test. The cold air didn't bring quite the relief he wanted, though, and as he walked around to the back parking lot, his hand went to the pocket of his shirt.

He'd quit smoking, and yet a year later, he was still reaching for the Marlboro Reds. His frickin' habit was like having an amputated limb with phantom pain.

As he made the corner and walked into the lot, he went past a row of cars that were parked grilles-in to the building. All of them were dirty, their flanks spackled with salt from the road treatments and months-old white-snow grime. His truck, which was way down at the end of the third row in, was exactly the same.

He looked left and right as he went. This was a bad part of town, and if he were going to get jumped, he wanted to see what was coming at him. Not that he minded a good fight. He'd gotten into a lot of them in his younger years, and then been trained properly in the military—plus, thanks to his day job, he was in rock-hard shape. But it was always better to—

He stopped as a flash of gold winked at him from the ground.

Crouching down, he picked up a thin gold ring—no, it was a hoop earring, one of those guys that plugged into itself. He cleaned the grunge off and glanced over at the cars. Could have been dropped by anyone, and it wasn't very expensive.

"Why did you leave without me?"

Jim froze.

Shit, her voice was as sexy as the rest of her.

Straightening to his full height, he pivoted on his work boot and stared across the trunks of the cars. Blue Dress was about ten yards away, standing under a security light—which made him wonder if she always chose spots that illuminated her.

"It's cold," he said. "You should go back inside."

"I'm not cold."

True enough. *Hot as fuck* would cover it. "Well ... I'm leaving."

"Alone?" She came forward, her high heels tracking across the pitted asphalt.

The closer she got, the better-looking she became. Shit,

her lips were made for sex, deep red and slightly parted, and that hair of hers . . . All he could think about was it falling over his bare chest and thighs.

Jim shoved his hands into the pockets of his jeans. He was much taller than she was, but the way she walked was a sucker punch to the solar plexus, immobilizing him with hot thoughts and vivid plans: Staring at her fine pale skin, he wondered if it was as soft as it seemed. Wondered a whole hell of a lot about what was under that dress. Wondered what she would feel like beneath his naked body.

As she stopped in front of him, he had to take a deep breath.

"Where's your car?" she said.

"Truck."

"Where is it?"

At that moment a cold breeze rolled in from the alley and she shivered a little, raising thin, lovely arms to wrap herself in a hug. Her dark eyes, which had been seductive in the club, abruptly became pleading . . . and made her nearly impossible to turn away from.

Was he going to do this? Was he going to fall into this warm pool of a woman, if only for a short time?

Another gust came barreling in, and she stamped one stiletto, then the other.

Jim took off his leather jacket and closed the distance between them. With their eyes locked, he encircled her with what had warmed himself. "I'm over here."

She reached for his hand and took it. He led the way.

Ford F-150s were not exactly great for hooking up, but there was enough room if you needed it—and more to the point, the truck was all he had to offer. Jim helped her inside and then went around and got behind the wheel. The engine started quick and he turned the fan off, halting the blast of frigid air until things heated up.

She moved across the seat to him, her breasts rising above the tight bands of her dress as she got closer. "You're very kind."

Kind was not he way he saw himself. Especially not now, given what was on his mind. "Can't have a lady cold."

Jim ran his eyes all over her. She was huddled in his beat-to-shit leather jacket, her face turned down, her long hair falling over her shoulder and curling up into her cleavage. She might have come across as a seducer, but the truth was she was a good girl who was in over her head.

"Do you want to talk?" he said, because she deserved better than what he wanted from her.

"No." She shook her head. "No, I want to do ... something."

Okay, Jim was definitely not kind. He was a man who was a palm's reach away from a beautiful woman, and even though she was giving off vulnerable vibes, playing therapist with her was not the sort of horizontal he was after.

As her eyes lifted, they were orphan sad. "Please ... kiss me?"

Jim held back, her expression putting the brakes on him and then some. "You sure about this?"

She swept her hair over her shoulder and tucked it behind her ear. When she nodded, the dime-size diamond in her lobe flashed. "Yes ... very. Kiss me."

When she held his stare and didn't look away, Jim leaned in, feeling ensnared and not minding in the slightest. "I'll go slow."

Oh ... God ...

Her lips were every bit as soft as he'd imagined, and he stroked her mouth carefully with his own, afraid he would crush her. She was sweet, she was warm, and she trusted him to set the careful pace, welcoming his tongue inside of her, then later shifting back so that his palm could ease down from her face to her collarbone ... to her full breast.

Which changed the tempo of things.

Abruptly, she sat up and took off his jacket. "Zipper's in the back."

His rough workman's hands found it quick, and he worried about marring the blue dress as he drew the fastening downward. And then he stopped thinking as she took the top from her breasts herself, revealing a satin-and-lace bra that probably cost as much as his truck.

Through the fine material, her nipples were peaked, and in the shadows thrown by the dim light of the dash, they were feast-for-the-starved spectacular.

"My breasts are real," she said softly. "He wanted me to get implants, but I . . . I don't want them."

Jim frowned, thinking that whatever pig asshole had come up with that one deserved an eye operation— performed by a tire iron. "Don't do it. You're beautiful."

"Really?" Her voice wavered.

"Truly."

Her shy smile meant too much to him, piercing through his chest, going too deep. He knew all about the ugly side of life, had been through the kinds of things that could make a single day feel like it lasted a month, and he wished her none of that. Seemed, though, she'd had plenty of hard cracks herself.

Jim reached over and turned the heater on to warm her.

When he eased back, she swept aside one of the bra's cups and framed herself with her hand, offering the nipple to him.

"You're amazing," he whispered.

Jim bent down and captured her flesh with his lips, sucking on her gently. As she gasped and thrust her hands into his hair, her breast cushioned his mouth and he had a moment of raw lust, the kind that turned men into animals.

Except then he remembered the way she'd looked at him, and he knew he wasn't going to have sex with her. He was going to take care of her, here in the truck cab, with the heater going and the windows fogging up. He was going to show her how beautiful she was and how perfect her body looked and felt and . . . tasted. But he wasn't taking anything for himself.

Hell, maybe he wasn't all bad.

You sure about that? his inner voice cut in. *Are you re-ally sure about that?*

No, he wasn't. But Jim laid her down on the seat and wadded his leather jacket into a pillow for her head and vowed to do the right thing.

Man . . . she was drop-dead gorgeous, a lost, exotic bird who'd found a chicken coop for shelter. Why on God's green earth did she want him?

"Kiss me," she breathed.

Just as he braced his weight on his heavy arms and leaned over her, he caught sight of the digital clock on the dash: 11:59. The very minute he had been born forty years before.

What a happy birthday this had turned out to be.

CHAPTER
3

Vin diPietro sat on a silk-covered sofa in a living room decorated in gold, red and creamy white. The black marble floors were covered with antique rugs, the bookcases were filled with first editions, and all around his collection of crystal, ebony, and bronze statuary gleamed.

But the real showstopper was the view of the city over to the right.

Thanks to a glass wall that ran the entire length of the room, Caldwell's twin bridges and all of its skyscrapers were as much a part of the decorations as the drapes and the floor coverings and the objets d'art. The sprawling vista was urban splendor at its best, a vast, glimmering landscape that was never the same, even though the buildings didn't change.

Vin's duplex in the Commodore took up all of the twenty-eighth and twenty-ninth floors of the luxury high-rise, for a total of ten thousand square feet. He had six bedrooms, a maid's suite, an exercise room, and a movie theater. Eight bathrooms. Four parking spaces in the underground parking garage. And inside everything was exactly as he wanted it, every square of marble, slab of granite, yard of fabric, plank of hardwood, foot of carpet—all of it had been hand-picked from the best of the best by him.

He was ready to move out.

With the way things were going, he figured he'd be ready to hand over the keys to its next owner in another four months. Maybe three, depending on how fast the crews were at the construction site.

If this condo was nice, what Vin was building on the banks of the Hudson River was going to make the duplex look like subsidized housing. He'd had to buy up a half dozen old hunting lodges and camps to get the kind of acreage and shoreline he wanted, but everything had fallen into place. He'd razed the shacks, cleared the land, and dug a cellar hole big enough to play football in. The crew was framing now and working on the roof; then his fleet of electricians would install the house's central nervous system and his plumbers would put in the arteries. Finally, it would be the detail crap with the counters and tiles, the appliances and fixtures, and the decorators.

It was all coming together, just like magic. And not only about where he would live.

In front of him, on the glass-topped table, was the velvet box from Reinhardt's.

As the grandfather clock in the hall struck midnight, Vin sat back into the sofa cushions and crossed his legs. He was not a romantic, never had been, and neither was Devina—which was only one of the reasons they were perfect together. She gave him his space, kept herself busy, and was always ready to hop on a plane when he needed her to. And she didn't want children, which was a huge plus.

He couldn't go there. Sins of the fathers and all that.

He and Devina hadn't known each other for all that long, but when it was right, it was right. Kind of like buying land to develop. You just knew as you stared over the ground that *here is where I need to be building*.

Looking out at the city from a perch high above so many others, he thought of the house he'd grown up in. Back then, his view had been of the crappy little two-story next door, and he'd spent a lot of nights trying to see past where he was from. Over the din of his mother and father's drunken fighting, the only thing he'd wanted was out. Out from under his parents. Out of that pathetic lower-middle-class neighborhood. Out of himself and what separated him from everyone else. And what do you know, that was exactly what had happened.

He infinitely preferred this life, this landscape. He'd sacrificed a lot to get up here, but luck had always been with him—like magic.

But then, the harder you worked, the luckier you got. And damn everything and everyone, this was where he was going to stay.

When Vin checked his watch again, forty-five minutes had passed. And then another half hour.

Just as he reached forward and palmed the velvet box, the click and release of the front door brought his head around. Out in the hall, stilettos clipped on the marble and came down toward him. Or passed him was more like it.

As Devina walked by the living room's archway, she was taking off her white mink, exposing a blue Herve Leger dress she'd bought with his money. Talk about knockout: Her body's perfect curves were showing those fabric bands who was in charge, her long legs had better lines than the red-soled Louboutins she had on, and her dark hair gleamed brighter than the crystal chandelier over her head.

Resplendent. As always.

"Where have you been?" he asked.

She froze and looked over at him. "I didn't know you were home."

"I've been waiting for you."

"You should have called." She had spectacular eyes, almond shaped and darker than her hair. "I would have come if you'd called."

"Thought I'd surprise you."

"You . . . don't do surprises."

Vin got to his feet and kept the box hidden within his palm. "How was your night?"

"Good."

"Where did you go?"

She folded the fur over her arm. "Just to a club."

As he came up to her, Vin opened his mouth, his hand tightening on what he'd bought for her. *Be my wife.*

Devina frowned. "Are you okay?"

Be my wife. Devina, be my wife.

He narrowed his eyes on her lips. They were puffier than usual. Redder. And for once she had no lipstick on.

The conclusion he slammed into teed off a brief, vivid memory of his mother and father. The pair of them were screaming at each other and throwing things, both drunk off their asses. The subject was what it always had been, and he could hear his father's raging voice clear as day: *Who were you with? What the hell you been doing, woman?*

After that, the next thing on the agenda would be his mother's ashtray banging off the wall. Thanks to all the practice she got, she'd had good arm strength, but the vodka tended to throw off her aim, so she hit his father's head only one out of every ten shots.

Vin slipped the ring box into the pocket of his suit coat. "You have a good time?"

Devina narrowed her eyes like she was having trouble judging his mood. "I just went out for a little bit."

He nodded, wondering whether her hair's tousled effect was styling or another man's hands. "Good. I'm glad. I'm just going to go do some work."

"Okay."

Vin turned and walked through the living room and into the library and down to his study. All the while, he kept his eyes on the walls of glass and the view.

His father had believed two things about women: You could never trust them; and they would walk all over you if you gave them the upper hand. And as much as Vin didn't want any legacy from that son of a bitch, he couldn't shake the memories he had of his dad.

The guy had always been convinced his wife was cheating on him—which had been hard to believe. Vin's old lady had bleached her hair only twice a year, sported circles under her eyes the color of thunderclouds, and had a wardrobe limited to a housecoat that she cleaned with the same frequency the Clairol box made it home. The woman never left the house, smoked like a bonfire, and had alcohol breath that could melt paint off a car.

Yet his father somehow thought men would be attracted to that. Or that she, who never lifted a finger unless there was a cigarette to light, regularly summoned the gumption to go out and find joes whose taste in chicks ran toward ashtrays and empties.

They'd both beaten him. At least until he'd gotten old enough to move faster than they could. And probably the kindest thing they did for him as parents was killing each other when he was seventeen—which was pretty fucking pathetic.

When Vin got to his study, he took a seat behind the marble-topped desk and faced off at his office away from the office. He had two computers, a phone with six lines on it, a fax, and a pair of bronze lamps. Chair was bloodred leather. Carpet was the color of the bird's-eye maple paneling. Drapes were black and cream and red.

Tucking the ring between one of the lamps and the phone console, he swiveled away from business and resumed his watch over the city.

Be my wife, Devina.

"I've changed into something more comfortable."

Vin looked over his shoulder and got a load of his woman, who was now draped in see-through black.

He swiveled his chair around. "You certainly did."

As she came over to him, her breasts swayed back and forth beneath the sheer fabric and he could feel himself harden. He'd always loved her breasts. When she'd told him she wanted implants, he'd nixed that idea fast. She was perfect.

"I'm really sorry I wasn't here when you wanted me," she said, sweeping that translucent robe out and easing down onto her knees in front of him. "I truly am."

Vin lifted his hand and ran his thumb back and forth over her full lower lip. "What happened to your lipstick?"

"I washed my face in the bathroom."

"Then why is your eyeliner still on."

"I reapplied it." Her voice was smooth. "I had my phone with me the entire time. You told me you had a late meeting."

"Yes, I did."

Devina put her hands on his thighs and leaned in, her breasts swelling over the bodice of her gown. God, she smelled good.

"I'm sorry," she moaned before she kissed his neck and dug her nails into his legs. "Let me make it up to you."

She closed her lips on his skin and sucked.

As Vin let his head fall back, he looked at her from under his lids. She was any man's fantasy. And she was his.

So why the fuck couldn't he get those words out?

"Vin . . . please don't be angry at me," she whispered.

"I'm not."

"You're frowning."

"Am I." Exactly when did he ever smile? "Well, why don't you see what you can do to improve my mood."

Devina's lips lifted as if this were precisely the kind of invite she'd been angling for, and in quick succession, she undid his tie, opened his collar and popped free the buttons of his shirt. Kissing her way down to his hips, she unbuckled his belt, pulled out his shirttails and scraped her nails and her teeth across his skin.

She knew he was into the rough stuff and didn't have a problem with that in the slightest.

Vin swept her hair back from her face as she freed his arousal, and knew full well he wasn't the only one likely to get a view of what she was going to do to him: Both of the desk lamps were on, which meant if anybody in those skyscrapers was still at their office and had a pair of binocs, they were about to get one hell of a show.

Vin didn't stop her or turn off the lights.

Devina liked an audience.

As her mouth parted over the head of his cock, he groaned and then gritted his teeth as she swallowed him down into her throat. She was very good at this kind of thing, finding a rhythm that swept him away, staring up at him as she worked him out. She knew he liked it a little dirty, so at the last moment she pulled back so that her perfect breasts were what he came on.

With a low laugh, she looked at him from under her brows, all naughty girl not yet sated. Devina was like that, changeable depending on the situation, able to be a proper woman one moment and a slut the next, her moods masks that she wore and discarded at will.

"You're still hungry, Vin." Her beautiful hand drifted down the sheer bustier to her thong and stayed there as she stretched out on her back. "Aren't you."

In the light, her eyes were not deep brown, but dense black, and they were full of knowledge. She was right. He did want her. He had since the moment he'd seen her at a gallery opening and taken both a Chagall and her home.

Vin shifted off his chair and knelt between her legs, spreading them wider. She was ready for him, and he took her right on the carpet next to his desk. The sex was fast and hard, but she was crazy into it and that turned him on.

As he orgasmed into her, she said his name as if he had given her exactly what she after.

Dropping his head to the fine silk carpet, he breathed hard and didn't like the way he felt. With the passion gone, he was more than spent; he was barren.

Sometimes it was as if the more he filled her, the emptier he got.

"I want more, Vin," she said in a deep, guttural voice.

In the locker room shower at the Iron Mask, Marie-Terese stepped under the hot spray and opened her mouth, letting the water wash into her as well as over her. On a stainless-steel dish, there was a golden bar of soap, and she reached for it without having to look over. The Dial imprint was nearly washed smooth, which meant the thing was going to last only another two or three nights.

As she washed every inch of her body, her tears joined

the sudsy water, following its path into the drain at her feet. In some ways, this was the hardest part of the night, this time alone with the warm steam and the rotgut soap— worse even than the post-confession blues.

God, it was getting so that even the smell of Dial was enough to make her eyes water, proof positive Pavlov didn't just know about dogs.

When she was done, she stepped out and grabbed a rough white towel. Her skin tightened up in the cold, shrinking, becoming like armor, and her will to keep going performed a similar retraction, pulling in her emotions and holding them secure once more.

In the cubicle outside, she changed back into her jeans and her turtleneck and her fleece, stuffing her work clothes into the duffel. Her hair took about ten minutes of blow-drying before she was ready to go out into the chilly night with it, and the extra time at the club made her pray for summer.

"You almost ready to go?"

Trez's voice came through the locker room's closed door and she had to smile. Same words every night, and always at the very moment she put the hair dryer down.

"Two minutes," she called out.

"No worries." Trez meant that, too. He always made a point to escort her to her car, no matter how long it took her to get ready to leave.

Marie-Terese put the dryer down, drew her hair back, and wrapped a scrunchie around the thick waves—

She leaned in closer to the mirror. Sometime during the shift, she'd lost an earring and God only knew where the thing was. "Damn it."

Shouldering her duffel, she left the locker room and found Trez out in the hall texting on his BlackBerry.

He put the phone in his pocket and looked her over. "You all right?"

No. "Yup. Was an okay night."

Trez nodded once and walked with her to the back door. As they went outside, she prayed he didn't hit her with one of his lectures. Trez's opinion about prostitution was that women could choose to do it, and men could choose to pay, but it had to be handled professionally—hell, he'd fired girls for skipping condoms. He also believed that if there was even a hint that a female was uncomfortable with her choice, she should be given every opportunity to rethink what she was doing and get out.

It was the same philosophy the Reverend had had at ZeroSum, and the irony was that because of it, most of the girls didn't want to leave the life.

As they came up to her Camry, he stopped her by putting his hand on her arm. "You know what I'm going to say, don't you."

She smiled a little. "Your speech."

"It's not rhetoric. I mean every word."

"Oh, I know you do," she said, taking her keys out. "And you're very kind, but I'm where I need to be."

For a split second, she could have sworn his dark eyes flashed with a peridot light—but it was probably just a trick of the security lights that flooded the back of the building.

And when he just stared at her, like he was choosing his words, she shook her head. "Trez . . . please don't."

Frowning hard, he cursed under his breath, then held out his arms. "Come here, girl."

As she leaned forward and stood in the lee of his strength, she wondered what it would be like to have a man like this, a good one who might not be perfect, but who was honorable and did right and cared about people.

"Your heart isn't in this anymore," Trez said softly in her ear. "It's time for you to go."

"I'm fine—"

"You lie." As he pulled back, his voice was so sure and certain, she felt like he could see right through into her heart. "Let me give you the money you need. You can pay it back interest-free. You aren't meant for this. Some are. You are not. Your soul's not doing well here."

He was right. He was so very, very right. But she was done relying on anyone else, even somebody as decent as Trez.

"I'll get out soon," she said, patting his huge chest. "Just a little longer and I'll be caught up. Then I'll stop."

Trez's expression tightened and his jaw went rigid—evidence that he was going to respect her decision even if he didn't agree with it. "Remember my offer about the money, okay?"

"I will." She arched up on her tiptoes and kissed his dark cheek. "Promise."

Trez settled her in the car, and after she backed out of her spot and started off, she glanced in the rearview mirror. In the glow of her taillights, he was watching her, his arms crossed over that heavy chest . . . and then he was gone as if he'd just disappeared.

Marie-Terese hit the brakes and rubbed her eyes, wondering if she had lost it . . . but then a car came up from behind her, its headlights flashing in the rearview and blinding her. Shaking herself, she hit the gas and shot out of the parking lot. Whoever was on her bumper turned off at the next street, and the trip home was about fifteen minutes long.

The house she rented was tiny, just a little Cape Cod that was in okay shape, but there were two reasons why she'd picked it over the other ones she'd looked at when she'd come to Caldwell: It was in a school zone, so that meant there were a lot of eyes around the neighborhood, and the owner had allowed her to put bars on all the windows.

Marie-Terese parked in the garage, waited for the door to trundle shut, and then got out to enter the darkened back hall. Going through the kitchen, which smelled like the fresh apples she always kept in a bowl, she tiptoed toward the glow in the living room. On the way, she tucked her duffel bag into the coat closet.

She'd empty it and repack it when there was no one around to see her.

As she stepped into the light, she whispered, "It's just me."

CHAPTER
4

He slept with her.
  The following morning, Jim's first thought was a real shitkicker, and to try to get away from it, he rolled over on his bed. Which just made his wakey-wakey worse. Dawn's early light was kicking the ass of the curtain next to him, and as the brightness barged into his skull, he wished the frickin' window were made out of Sheetrock.

Man, he couldn't believe he'd slept with that gorgeous, vulnerable woman in his truck—like she was some kind of whore. The fact that he'd then come back here and drunk himself into a Corona-tose state was a little more believable. But what it all added up to was that he still felt bad about what he'd done *and* he was going to have to hammer nails all day with a hangover.

Great. Planning.

Throwing off the blanket, he looked down at the jeans and flannel shirt he'd worn to the club. He'd passed out before he'd had a chance to get naked, so everything was rumpled, but he was going to wear the Levi's to work. The shirt, on the other hand, he had to save from twelve hours of construction. It was his only "good" one—which meant no paint specks, no holes, no missing buttons, and no frayed cuffs. Yet.

Jim stripped down and dumped the shirt into the leaning tower of dirty laundry by the bed. As he walked his headache into the stall shower, he was reminded of why not having a lot of furniture was a good thing. Short of his two piles of clothes, the clean and the needed-to-be-cleaned, all he had was the rattan couch that the studio had come with and a table with two chairs—all of which were mercifully out of the path to the bathroom.

He shaved fast and showered quick; then it was boxers and the Levi's and four aspirin. Undershirt was next, followed by socks and boots. On the way to the door, he grabbed his tool belt and his work jacket.

His rental was on top of a garage-like outbuilding, and he paused at the top of the stairs, squinting so hard he bared his teeth. Goddamn ... all that eye-piercing light made it seem like the sun had decided to return the Earth's attraction and move a little closer to seal the deal.

Down the creaking wooden steps. Across the gravel drive to the cold truck. All the way with an expression like he had a spike through his foot.

As he opened the driver's-side door, he caught a whiff of perfume and cursed. Images came back to him, all of them carnal as hell, each one of them another source of inspiration for the headache.

He was still cursing and squinting as he drove out the lane and past the white farmhouse, the owner of which was his elderly landlord, Mr. Perlmutter. No one had lived in the big place for as long as Jim had been a renter, its windows boarded up on the inside, its porch perennially empty of wicker anything.

That nobody-home routine along with the thirty days' notice to get out were his two favorite parts about where he stayed.

On the way to work, he pulled into a gas station and bought a large coffee, a turkey sub, and a Coke. The quick mart smelled like old shoes and laundry softener, and there was a probability that the sandwich had been made last week *in* Turkey, but he'd been eating the same thing for the last month and was still upright in his boots, so the shit obviously wasn't killing him.

Fifteen minutes later he was steaming up Route 151N, drinking his coffee, wearing his sunglasses, and feeling marginally more human. The job site was on the western shore of the Hudson River, and when he got to the turnoff for it, he recapped the Styrofoam mug and ten-and-two'd the wheel. The lane that went down the peninsula was pothole central, thanks to all the heavy-duty machinery that had barreled across its bare back, and the truck's shock absorbers bitched and moaned the whole way.

At some point there was going to be manicured lawn everywhere, but for the moment the rolling earth resembled the skin of a fifteen-year-old boy. There were countless tree stumps across the shaggy winter-brown grass—pimples on the face of the land that had been created by a team of guys with chain saws. And that wasn't the worst of it. Four whole cabins had been torn down, their footings and the bald plots beneath their first floors all that was left of structures that had been there for over a hundred years.

But everything had to go. That was the command from the general contractor.

Who was his own client.

And about as much fun as a hangover on a cheery, chilly morning.

Jim pulled into the line of pickups that was forming as more of the workers came in. He left the sandwich and the Coke behind on the floor of the cab to stay cool and crossed the tire-chewed dirt tracks toward the gestating house. With its skeleton of two-by-fours erected, its skin was now going up, the particleboard sheets being nailed onto the bone structure of the frame.

Fucking thing was a monster, so big it was capable of making those McMansions in town seem the size of dollhouses.

"Jim."

"Chuck."

Chuck, the foreman, was a six-foot guy with square shoulders, a round gut, and a perpetual cigar stub shoved in his mouth—and that was about it for conversation with him. Thing was, Jim was clear which part of the house he was working on and what he was going to do, and both men knew it. With a crew of about twenty carpenters on the project, there were varying degrees of skill and commitment and sobriety, and Chuck knew the drill with everybody. If you had half a brain and could throw a hammer well, he left you alone, because fuck knew he had enough on his plate with the jackholes.

Jim braced himself and headed for the supplies. The nail boxes were kept stacked in a lockable cabinet on the six-car garage's concrete slab, and next to them, lined up in a row, were the gas-powered electrical generators that were already going at a roar. Wincing at the noise, he stepped over the snakes of extension cords that ran out to the table saws and the nail guns and filled up the pouch on the left side of his tool belt.

It was a relief to head for the southern side of the house—which, considering the floor plan, was practically in the next county. Setting to work, he began hefting six-foot-by-four-foot sections of particleboard and locking them in place against the framers. He used a hammer instead of a nail gun because he was just that flavor of old school—and because even with the manual stuff he was one of the fastest carpenters around.

The sound of a pair of Harleys coming down the dirt drive brought his head up.

Eddie and Adrian pulled their bikes in together and dismounted in sync, removing their leather jackets and their black sunglasses in the same rhythm too. As they approached the house, they came gunning in his direction and Jim groaned: Adrian was looking at him with a whole lot of what-the-hell-happened-with-the-hottie on his pierced face.

Which meant the guy had noticed that Blue Dress disappeared about the same time Jim did.

"Shit," he muttered.

"What?"

Jim shook his head at the guy next to him and refocused on what he was doing. Positioning one of the sheets against the frame, he held it with his hip, unhooked his hammer from his belt, got a nail, and pounded. Repeat. Repeat. Repeat—

"Have fun last night?" Adrian said as he came up.

Jim just kept on pounding.

"Ah, come on, I don't need all the details—but you could spare me a few." Adrian glanced at his roommate. "Back me up, would ya?"

Eddie just walked by and knocked his shoulder into Jim, which was his version of a good morning. Without being asked, he took over bracing the particleboard, which freed Jim up to hammer twice as fast. They were a great team, although Adrian balanced out the pace. He was less than industrious, preferring to spend his time fucking around and running his mouth. It was a wonder he hadn't gotten fired in the four weeks he'd been on the site.

Ad leaned against a naked doorjamb and rolled his eyes. "You aren't going to tell me whether you got a birthday present or not?"

"Nope." Jim positioned a nail and creamed the head of it. Two hits and the top was flush with the board and then he got another fresh shot at imagining Adrian's face on a target.

"You suck."

Yes, he certainly had last night—not that it was any business of that friendly neighborhood gum-flapping mother-fucker with a metal fetish.

Things fell into their usual rhythm, and the other guys got out of Jim and Eddie's way as they went around, closing the gap from where they'd stopped the day before, sealing things up from the spring rains that were just starting. The house was going to be about fifteen thousand square feet in size, so to get it battened down tight in just one week was a tall order. Still, Jim and Eddie were busting ass, and the roofers were already halfway across the rafters. By the end of the weekend, they weren't going to have to worry about the cold drizzle or the freezing wind anymore, and thank God for it. Yesterday had been a suckfest of wet and nasty, and there were still puddles here and there that splashed up onto his jeans.

Lunchtime came quickly, which was what happened when he worked with Eddie, and while the other guys propped themselves on the edge of the house facing the sun, Jim went back to his truck and ate alone sitting in the cab.

The sandwich was still cold, which always improved the taste, and the Coke was spectacular.

As he sat on his own and chewed, he glanced over to the empty seat next to him . . . and remembered dark hair spilling over the upholstery and the arch of a female neck in the dash lights and the feel of a soft body beneath his.

He was such a shit, taking advantage of her like that, and yet, after it was all done, she'd smiled up at him as if he'd given her exactly what she'd wanted. Except that couldn't be true. Sex between strangers was just a temporary reprieve from loneliness. How could that be enough for someone like her? Christ, he didn't even know her name. When the deep breathing had passed, she'd kissed him and lingered on his lips; then she'd pulled the top of her dress up and the bottom of it down, and left him.

With a curse, Jim threw open the driver's-side door and took his lunch around to the back bumper. It was warmer out in the sun, but more to the point, the air smelled like fresh pine boards, not perfume. As he turned his face to the sky and tried to wipe clean his mind, he lost interest in the sandwich, putting it aside on its Saran Wrap and focusing on the Coke instead.

The dog appeared a moment later, peeking out from behind a stack of felled trees that were due for removal. The thing was the size of a small terrier and had a coat that looked like mottled steel wool. One ear was flopped over and it had some kind of scar on its muzzle.

Jim lowered his Coke bottle as the two of them locked stares.

Damn animal was frightened and using the grizzled stumps as cover because they were far, far larger than he was, but he was also starved: Going by the way that little black nose was sniffing the breeze, clearly the smell of the turkey was calling him.

The dog took a tentative step out. And then another. And another.

It walked with a limp.

Jim reached to the side slowly, putting his hand on the sandwich. Popping off the top of the roll, he pushed aside the languid lettuce and the Styrofoam tomato, and picked up a slice of turkey.

Leaning down, he extended the meat. "Don't taste like much, but it won't kill you. Promise."

The dog circled, closing in with that gimpy front paw, the spring wind lifting its wiry coat and showing sharp ribs. The thing had its head extended as far as the neck would allow, and its back legs were trembling as if they were ready to leap into a retreat at any second. Hunger, however, pushed it to go where it didn't want to be.

Jim stayed still and let the animal inch closer to him.

"Come on, son," Jim said roughly. "You need this."

Up close, the dog looked exhausted, and when it took the turkey it was with a swift snap and a back-away. Jim got another piece ready, and this time the animal came more quickly and didn't move away so fast. The third piece was accepted with a delicate mouth, as if the animal's innate nature were not what its experiences had turned it into.

Jim fed the thing the roll, too. "That's it."

The dog planted its butt in front of Jim, curling into a sit and tilting its head to one side. There were smart eyes on the thing. Smart, old, tired eyes.

"I'm not a dog person."

Evidently, the dog didn't understand English. In a leap that was surprisingly graceful, it propelled itself up into Jim's lap.

"What the . . ." Jim lifted his arms out of the way and stared down. "Jesus, you don't weigh much."

Duh. Probably hadn't eaten in days.

Jim put a tentative hand on its back. Christ. All he felt was bones.

The whistle blown meant lunch was over, so Jim gave the dog one stroke before putting it back on the ground. "Sorry . . . like I said, not a dog person."

He grabbed his tool belt out of the cab and strapped it back on as he walked away. The look over his shoulder was a bad idea.

Shit, the dog was under the truck, behind the back tire, and those old eyes were on Jim.

"I don't do pets," Jim called out as he went off.

The purring sound of a car approaching rolled across the job site, and when the men who were lined up on the lip of the house looked over, their expressions fell into a collective *fuck-me*—which meant Jim didn't have to pull another over-the-shoulder to know exactly who it was.

The general contractor/owner/pain in the ass was here again.

Son of a bitch showed up at all different times of the day, like he didn't want to set a schedule the crew could depend on so his spot inspections would be more accurate. And it so didn't take a genius to figure out what he was looking for: lax workers, sloppy construction, mistakes, theft. Made you feel like you were dishonest and lazy even if you weren't, and for a lot of the guys that was an insult they were willing to let pass only because they were always paid on time on Friday.

Jim stepped up his pace as the BMW M6 pulled up right next to him. He didn't look at the car or the driver: He always stayed out of the guy's way, not because he had anything to apologize for in terms of performance, but because he was a grunt, pure and simple: When the general came to inspect the troops, the chain of command mandated that the asshole was Chuck the foreman's problem, not Jim's.

Thank you, Jesus.

Jim hopped up onto the flooring, and headed back over to where he'd been working. Eddie, ever ready to pitch in, followed and so did Adrian.

"Holy . . . shit."

"Okay . . . wow."

"Madre de Dios . . ."

The comments bubbling up from the workers made Jim glance back.

Oh, hell, no . . . talk about your *fuck-me-and-a-halfs*: A stunningly beautiful brunette was stepping out of the car with the grace of a flag unfurling in a calm breeze.

Jim squeezed his eyes shut. And saw her in the cab of his truck, stretched out with her perfect breasts bare to his mouth.

"Now, that is a helluva woman," one of the workers said.

Man, there were times in life when disappearing was a great idea. Not because you were a pussy, but because you really didn't need the hassle of dealing.

This was one of them. And then some.

"Well, shit, Jim . . ." Adrian dragged a hand through his thick hair. "That's . . ."

Yeah, he knew. "Got nothing to do with me. Eddie—you ready with that board?"

As Jim went to turn away, the brunette looked up and their eyes met. Her lovely face flickered with recognition, just as her man walked over to her and wrapped his arm around her waist.

Jim took a step back without looking where he was going.

It happened in an instant. Faster than the strike of a match. Quicker than a gasp.

The heel of Jim's boot landed on a piece of two-by-four that was lying across an extension cord and gravity took hold of his body, sweeping him off balance. As he fell, he split the cord from its joining with another, and sent the live end popping free and flipping into one of the puddles.

Jim hit the flooring in a loose sprawl of limbs . . . which

ordinarily would have just left him with some bruises on his ass and his shoulders.

But his bare hand landed in the water.

The electrical shock blared up his arm and slammed directly into his heart. As his spine jacked for the sky and his teeth locked together, his eyes flew wide and his hearing shorted out, the world receding until all he knew was the wild, consuming pain in his body.

The last image he had was of Eddie's long braid swinging wide as the guy lunged forward to help.

Vin didn't see the guy fall. But he heard the hard landing of a big body and then the scramble of boots and the shouted curses as people ran over from all directions.

"Stay here," he told Devina as he took out his cell phone.

He punched in 911 as he rushed toward the commotion, but didn't hit *send* yet. Jumping up onto the floorboards, he jogged over—

His thumb hit a button and the call was made.

The workman on the ground had eyes that were fixed and unseeing on the bright blue sky overhead, and his limbs were stiff as a corpse's. The live extension cord remained in the puddle, but the man's spasms had carried him away from the source of the deadly charge.

Vin's ring was answered. "Nine-one-one, what kind of emergency is this?"

"A man's been electrocuted." Vin dropped the phone from his mouth. "Turn off the fucking generators!" Lifting the cell back up, he said, "Job site address is Seventy-seven Rural Route one-fifty-one N. He appears to be unconscious."

"Is someone administering CPR?"

"They will be right now." Vin handed the phone off to Chuck the foreman and pulled guys out of the way.

Dropping to his knees, he yanked the workman's jacket open and put his head down on a muscled chest. No heartbeat and a hover over the mouth revealed no breathing, either.

Vin yanked the guy's head back, did an airway check, pinched the nose, and blew two breaths deep into those frozen lungs. Moving to the chest, he linked his hands together, positioned his palms over the guy's heart, and stiff-armed ten compressions. Two more breaths. Thirty more compressions. Two more breaths. Thirty more compressions. Two more breaths ...

The color in the guy's face wasn't good and only got worse.

The ambulance took about fifteen minutes to come, although not because they weren't hauling ass. Caldwell was nearly ten miles away, and that was the kind of geography no amount of pedal-to-the-metal was going to improve. The second they arrived, the EMTs didn't waste any time getting up into the house, and they took over from Vin, doing a vital statistics check before one continued what Vin had started and the other went racing back for the gurney.

"Is he alive?" Vin asked when the workman was lifted from the floor.

He didn't get an answer because the medics were moving too fast—which maybe was a good sign.

"Where are you taking him?" Vin said as he hopped off the foundation and hustled along with them.

"St. Francis. You got a name, age, anything on his medical history?"

"Chuck! Get over here—we need information."

The foreman ran up. "Jim Heron. I don't know much more than that. Lives alone down on Pershing Lane."

"You got an emergency contact?"

"No, he's not married or anything."

"I'm the contact," Vin said, taking out a card and giving it to the medic.

"Are you kin?"

"I'm his boss and all you've got at the moment."

"Okay, someone from St. Francis will be in touch." The medic disappeared Vin's info into his jacket and the workman was shoved into the ambulance. A split second later, the double doors were shut, and the vehicle took off with lights and sirens going.

"Is he going to be okay?"

Vin looked back at Devina. Her dark eyes were glossy with unshed tears and her hands were up around the collar of her fur coat, as if in spite of all the white mink she was freezing cold.

"I don't know." He went over and loosely took her arm. "Chuck, I'll be right back. I'm going to take her home first."

"You do that." Chuck took his hard hat off and shook his head. "Damn it. Damn it to hell. He was one of the good ones."

CHAPTER
5

"Nigel, you are a sod."

Jim frowned in the darkness that surrounded him. The English voice came from over on the right, and the immediate temptation was to open his eyes, lift his head, and see what was doing.

Training overrode the impulse. Thanks to being in the military, he'd learned that when you came to and didn't know where you were, it was better to possum it until you had some intel.

Moving imperceptibly, he flattened his hands out and felt around. He was on something soft, but it was springy, like a deep-napped rug or . . . grass?

Inhaling deep, his nose confirmed his palms' observation. Shit, fresh grass?

In a rush, his accident at the job site came back to him—except, what the hell? Last thing he knew he'd had one hundred and twenty volts of electricity sizzling through his body—so it seemed logical to assume that if he could still string two thoughts together he must be alive and therefore in a hospital. Except as far as he knew, hospital beds were not covered in . . . sod.

And in the States most nurses and doctors didn't sound like British lords or call each other lawns.

Jim opened his eyes. The sky overhead was dappled with cotton-puff clouds, and though there was no sun to see, the glow was all summer Sunday—not just bright and stormless, but relaxing, as if there were nothing urgent to do, nothing to worry about.

He looked over to the voices . . . and decided he was dead.

In the shade of a castle's great stone walls, four guys with croquet mallets were standing around a bunch of wickets and colored balls. The quartet was dressed in whites, and one had a pipe and another a pair of round, rose-tinted glasses. The third had his hand on the head of an Irish wolfhound. Number four had his arms crossed over his chest and an expression like he was bored.

Jim sat up. "Where the hell am I?"

The blond who was lining up his shot glared over and talked around his pipe. Which made his accent even more high brow. "One moment, if you please."

"I say you keep talking," his cross-armed, dark-haired buddy muttered—in the same dry voice that had woken Jim up. "He's cheating anyway."

"I knew you would come around," Round Glasses chirped in Jim's direction. "I knew it! Welcome!"

"Ah, you're awake," the one next to the wolfhound chimed in. "How lovely to meet you."

Goddamn, they were all good-looking, with the no-care-in-the-world vibe that resulted from not just being rich, but coming from generations of wealth.

"Are we done with the chatter, lads?" Pipe Guy, who was evidently named Nigel, looked around. "I should like some silence."

"Then why don't you stop telling us what to do?" the dark-haired one said.

"Pop off, Colin."

With that, the pipe was shifted around to the other

side of the mouth, the shot was taken with a crack, and a red-striped ball rolled through a pair of wickets and struck a blue one.

The blond smiled like the prince he no doubt was. "Now it's time for tea." He glanced over and met Jim's eyes. "Well, come on, then."

Dead. He was definitely dead and in Hell. Had to be it. Either that or this was some weird-ass dream because he'd passed out in front of the TV and there'd been a *Four Weddings and a Funeral* marathon on.

Jim got to his feet as the lads and the wolfhound headed for a table set with silver and china, and without a lot of options, he followed them over to "tea."

"Won't you have a seat?" Nigel said, indicating the vacant chair.

"I'll stand, thanks. What am I doing here?"

"Tea?"

"No. Who are—"

"I am Nigel. This rather acerbic fool"—the blond nodded at the dark-haired guy—"is Colin. Byron is our resident optimist and Albert is the dog lover."

"I go by Bertie to friends," Mr. Canine said as he stroked the wolfhound's ruff. "So, please, by all means. And this is the darling Tarquin."

Byron pushed his rose-colored roundies higher on his straight nose and clapped. "I just know this tea is going to be fabulous."

Sure it was. Absolutely.

It's finally happened, Jim thought. I've finally lost my damn mind.

Nigel picked up a silver pot and started pouring into porcelain cups. "I can imagine you are a bit surprised to be here, Jim."

Ya think? "How do you know my name, and what is this place?"

"You've been chosen for an important mission." Nigel put down the pot and hit the sugar cubes.

"A mission?"

"Yes." Nigel lifted his tea with his pinkie extended, and as he looked over the rim, it was hard to pin down his eye color. It was neither blue nor gray nor green . . . but it wasn't brown or hazel either.

Good God, it was a color Jim had never seen before. And all of them had it.

"Jim Heron, you are going to save the world."

There was a long pause. During which the four lads looked at him with straight faces.

When no one else started laughing, Jim picked up the slack, throwing back his head and belly-rolling it so hard, tears spiked into his eyes.

"This is not a joke," Nigel snapped.

When Jim caught his breath, he said, "It sure the hell is. Man, what a fucked-up dream this is."

Nigel put his cup down, got to his feet, and walked over the bright green grass. Up close, he smelled like fresh air, and those weird eyes of his were positively hypnotic.

"This. Is. Not. A. Dream."

The bastard punched Jim in the arm. Just balled up his smooth hand into a fist and fired the thing hard.

"Fuck!" Jim rubbed the sting—which was considerable. Pipe Guy might have been built lean and long, but he packed a punch all right.

"Permit me to repeat myself. You are not dreaming and this is not a joke."

"Can I hit him next?" Colin said with a lazy grin.

"No, you have horrid aim and you might strike him somewhere delicate." Nigel returned to his seat and took a small sandwich off a wheel of perfect little snackie-poos. "Jim Heron, you are the tiebreaker in the game, a man agreed upon by both sides to be on the field and settle the score."

"Both sides? Tiebreaker? What the hell are you talking about?"

"You are going to have seven chances. Seven opportunities to influence your fellow man. If you perform as we believe you will, the outcomes shall save the souls in question and we shall prevail over the other side. As long as that win occurs, humanity will continue to thrive and all shall be well."

Jim opened his mouth to shoot off some shit, but the expressions of the lads stopped him. Even the smart-ass in the group was looking serious.

"This has to be a dream."

No one got up to punch him again, but as they stared at him with such gravity, he began to get the creeping suspicion this might be something other than his subconscious talking while he was out cold.

"This is very real," Nigel said. "I realize it is not where you saw yourself going, but you have been chosen and that is the way of it."

"Assuming you're not full of shit, what if I say no?"

"You won't."

"But what if I do."

Nigel looked out over the distance. "Then everything ends as it stands now. Neither good nor bad wins and we are all, including yourself, over. No Heaven, no Hell, all that has gone before wiped clean. The mystery and the miracle of creation over and done and dusted."

Jim thought back on his life . . . the choices he'd made, the things he'd done. "Sounds like a good plan to me."

"It isn't." Colin drummed his fingers on the tablecloth. "Think about it, Jim. If nothing exists anymore, than all that went before was meaningless. So therefore your mother doesn't matter. Are you prepared to say that she is nothing? That her love for you, her darling son, is not valuable?"

Jim exhaled as if he'd been hit again, the pain of his past ricocheting through his chest. He hadn't thought of his mother for years. Maybe decades. She was always with him, of course, the only warm spot in his cold heart, but he did not allow himself to think of her. Ever.

And yet suddenly, and from out of nowhere, he had an image of her ... one so familiar, so vivid, so achingly real, it was as if a piece of the past had been implanted into his brain: She was cooking him eggs over the old stove in their ancient kitchen. Her grip on the iron pan handle was strong, her back straight, her dark hair cut short. She'd started out as the wife of a farmer and ended up as the farmer herself, her body as wiry and tough as her smile had been soft and kind.

He'd loved his mother. And although she had given him eggs every morning, he remembered that particular breakfast. It was the last she'd ever made—not just for him, but for anybody.

She'd been murdered come nightfall.

"How do you know ... about her," Jim asked with a voice that cracked.

"We have a vast knowledge of your life." Colin cocked an eyebrow. "But that begs the question. What say you, Jim? Are you prepared to relegate everything she did and everything she was to—as you would put it so bluntly—shit?"

Jim didn't like Colin very much.

"That's all right," Nigel murmured. "We don't care for him ourselves."

"Untrue," Bertie piped up. "I adore Colin. He hides behind his gruffness, but he is a wonderful—"

Colin's voice sliced through the compliment. "You are such a fairy."

"I'm an angel, not a fairy, and so are you." Bertie glanced over at Jim and resumed playing with Tarquin's ear. "I know you're going to do the right thing, because you loved your mother too much not to. Do you recall how she used to wake you up when you were small?"

Jim closed his eyes hard. "Yeah."

His bed growing up had been a small twin in one of the farmhouse's drafty upstairs rooms. He'd slept in his clothes most nights, either because he was too exhausted from working out in the cornfields to change or because it was too cold to lie down without multiple layers.

On school days, his mother had come in singing to him. . . .

"You are my sunshine, my only sunshine. . . . You make me happy when skies are gray. . . . You'll never know, dear, how much I love you. . . . Please don't take my sunshine away."

Except he wasn't the one who had left her, and when she had gone away, it hadn't been voluntarily. She had fought like a wildcat to stay with him, and he'd never forget the look in her eyes right before she'd passed. She'd stared out of her beaten face and spoken to him with her blue eyes and her bloody lips, because she'd had no more air left in her lungs to carry her voice.

I love you forever, she had mouthed. *But run. Get out of the house. Run. They're upstairs.*

He had left her where she lay, half-naked, bloody, and violated. Ducking out the back door, he'd raced to the truck he wasn't old enough to drive, and his feet had barely touched the pedals as he'd started the thing.

They had come after him, and to this day, he had no idea how he'd managed to get that old truck to go that fast down that dusty dirt road.

Bertie spoke up quietly. "You must accept this as both reality and your destiny. For her sake if for no one else's."

Jim opened his eyes and looked at Nigel. "Is there a Heaven?"

"We are on the edge of it right now." Nigel nodded over his shoulder at the castle wall, which ran off into the distance. "On the far side of our gracious manse, the souls of the good tally in fields of flowers and trees, their hours spent in sunshine and warmth, their cares and worries no more, their pain forgotten."

Jim stared at the footbridge over the moat and the double doors that were each the size of an RV. "Is she there?"

"Yes. And if you do not prevail, she will be ever gone as if she never was."

"I want to see her." He took a step forward. "I have to see her first."

"You may not enter. The quick are not welcome therein, only the dead."

"Fuck that and fuck you." Jim walked and then ran for the bridge, his boots thundering across the grass, then echoing on the wooden planks over the quicksilver river. When he got to the doors, he grabbed onto the great iron pulls, yanking so hard his back muscles screamed.

Fisting up one of his hands, he pounded at the oak, then pulled again. "Let me through! Let me through, you son of a bitch!"

He needed to know for himself that she wasn't hurt anymore and that she didn't suffer and that she was okay. Needed that reassurance so badly, he felt like he was shattering as he fought to get past the barrier, his battering fists driven by the memory of his beloved mother on the linoleum in the kitchen, the stab wounds in her chest and her neck bleeding out onto the floor, her legs spread, her mouth gaping open, her eyes terrified and imploring him to save himself, save himself, save himself. . . .

The demon in him came out.

Everything went white as rage took over. He knew he was hitting something hard, that his body was going wild, that when someone put a hand on his shoulder he took them down to the ground and pummeled them.

But he heard nothing and saw nothing.

The past always unwrapped him, which was why he made a point of never, ever thinking about it.

When Jim regained consciousness for the second time, he was in the same position he'd been in for the first coming-around: flat on his back, grass beneath his palms, eyes closed.

Except this time there was something wet on his face.

Popping his lids, he found Colin's face right above his own, and as the guy's blood dripped onto Jim's cheeks, the "rain" was explained.

"Ah, you're awake, well-done." Colin pulled back a fist and cracked Jim right in the puss.

As pain exploded, Bertie let out a cry, Tarquin whimpered, and Byron rushed over.

"Right, now we're even." Colin hopped off and shook out his hand. "You know, taking human form has its benefits, indeed. That felt rather nice."

Nigel shook his head. "This is not going well."

Jim had to agree as he sat up and accepted the handkerchief Byron held out. While he stemmed the bleeding from his nose, he couldn't believe he'd exploded like that at those castle doors, but then he was always shocked afterward.

Nigel eased down on his haunches. "You want to know why you were chosen, and I believe you have a right to know."

Jim spat out the blood in his mouth. "Now there's an idea."

Nigel reached over and took the bloody handkerchief. The instant the cloth made contact with his hands, the stain disappeared, the white fibers as pristine as they had been before they'd been used to stop a red geyser.

He gave it back for further use. "You are the two halves together, Jim. The good and the bad in equal measure, capable of great reserves of kindness and profound depths of depravity. Thusly, both sides found you acceptable. We and ... the other ... both believe that when you are presented with the seven opportunities, you will influence the course of events according to our values. We for the good, they for the evil—with the outcome determining the fate of humanity."

Jim stopped mopping up his face and focused on the Englishman. He could dispute nothing of what had been said about his character, and yet his brain remained scrambled. Or maybe he had a concussion, thanks to Colin, the knuckle-cracking motherfucker.

"So do you accept your destiny?" Nigel said. "Or does all end here?"

Jim cleared his throat. Begging wasn't something he was

used to. "Please . . . just let me see my mother. I . . . I need to know she's okay."

"I'm so sorry, but as I said, only the dead may pass to the other side." Nigel's hand came to rest on Jim's shoulder. "What say you, man?"

Byron came in close. "You can do it. You're a carpenter. You build things and you rebuild things. Lives are constructions just the same."

Jim looked at the castle and felt his heartbeat in his busted nose.

If he took everything at face value, if everything were true, if he were some kind of savior, then . . . if he walked away, the only peace his mother knew was gone. And as attractive as he might find the emptiness and timelessness of nonexistence, that was a cold exchange for where she was now.

"How does it work?" he asked. "What do I do?"

Nigel smiled. "Seven deadly sins. Seven souls swayed by these sins. Seven people at a crossroads with a choice that must be made. You enter their lives and affect their path. If they choose righteousness over sin, we prevail."

"And if they don't . . ."

"The other side wins."

"What is the other side?"

"The opposite of what we are."

Jim glanced over at the table with its white linens and sparkling silver. "So . . . we're talking about a bunch of ass-scratchers sitting on Barcaloungers watching *Girls Gone Wild* and drinking beer."

Colin laughed. "Not hardly, mate. Although that is an image, indeed."

Nigel glared at his buddy and then looked back at Jim. "The other side is evil. I shall let your mind summon the appropriate reference, but if you should want a place to start, you have but to think of what was done to your mother and know that those who hurt her enjoyed it."

Jim's gut clenched so hard, he leaned to the side and

dry-heaved. When a hand smoothed over his back, he had a feeling it was Bertie. And he was right.

Eventually, Jim's gag reflex cut the crap and he got his breath back. "What if I can't do this?"

Colin spoke up. "I shall not lie—it is not going to be easy. The other side is capable of everything. But you shall not be without resources."

Jim frowned. "Wait, the other side thinks I'm going to be a bad influence? During the crossroads of these people?"

Nigel nodded. "They have the same faith in you that we have. But we had the advantage of reaching out to you."

"How'd you manage that?"

"Coin toss."

Jim blinked. Right, because . . . that's how they did it at the Super Bowl.

Focusing on the gates, he tried to see his mom not as how he'd left her on that kitchen floor, but as these princes said she was. Happy. Relieved of burden. Whole.

"Who are the seven people?"

"For the identification of this first one, we shall give you a bit of help and make it obvious," Nigel said, getting to his feet. "Good luck."

"Hold on a minute—how will I know what to do?"

"Use your head," Colin cut in.

"No," Bertie said, cradling his wolfhound's face, "your heart."

"Just believe in the future." Byron pushed his tinted glasses up on his nose. "Hope is the best—"

Nigel rolled his eyes. "Just tell people what to do. It cuts down on the conversation, freeing up time for more worthwhile pursuits."

"Such as cheating at croquet?" Colin muttered.

"Will I see you again?" Jim asked. "Can I come to you for help?"

He didn't get an answer. Instead, he got another jolt that sure as shit felt like two-forty . . . and abruptly found himself shooting through a long, white hallway, the light blinding him, the wind blasting him in the face.

He had no idea where he was going to end up this time. Maybe it was back in Caldwell. Maybe it was Disneyland.

With the way things appeared to be going, who the fuck knew.

CHAPTER
6

A s night fell, Marie-Terese gripped the handle of the nonstick pan and slid a spatula around the edges of a perfectly round pancake. The thing was just ripe for the flipping, a pattern of little bubbles forming on its creamy surface.

"You ready?" she said.

Her son smiled from his supervisory stool on the other side of the countertop. "We're going to count, right?"

"Yup."

Their voices joined together in the three, two ... one. Then with a flick of the wrist, she sent the pancake flying and caught it dead in the center.

"You did it!" Robbie said as the sizzle rose up.

Marie-Terese smiled through a stinging sadness. Seven-year-olds were spectacular with approval, capable of making you feel like you were a miracle worker over the simplest of victories.

If only she deserved the praise on the big stuff.

"Would you get the syrup, please," she said.

Robbie slid off the stool and padded over to the fridge in his slippers. He was wearing a Spider-Man T-shirt, a pair of jeans, and a Spider-Man hoodie. His bed had Spider-

Man sheets and a Spider-Man duvet, and the lamp he read his Spider-Man comics by had a Spider-Man shade on it. His previous obsession had been SpongeBob, but back in October, as he'd prepared to leave six years old in the dust, he'd declared that he was a grown-up and that henceforth gifts should be of the webbed-crusader variety.

Right. Got it.

Robbie pulled open the fridge door and grabbed the squeeze bottle. "Do we always gots to do as much grammar as we did today?"

"That would be 'have to' and yes, clearly it's needed."

"Can't we do more math?"

"Nope."

"At least I gots pancakes for dinner." As Marie-Terese glanced over at him, he smiled. "Have pancakes."

"Thank you."

Robbie hopped back on the stool and changed the channel on the little TV next to the toaster. The mini-Sony was allowed to be on during breaks from schooling, and the biggie Sony, which was in the living room, could be on Saturday and Sunday afternoons and nights after dinner until bedtime.

Sliding the pancake onto a plate, she fired up another one, pouring the Bisquick in with a ladle. The kitchen was too small for a table, so they used the overhang off the counter as one, tucking stools beneath it and sitting at the stretch of Formica for every meal.

"Ready to flip number two?"

"Yup!"

She and Robbie counted it down together, and she executed another Flying Wallenda with the pancake . . . and her beautiful angel of a son smiled up at her like she was the sun in his world again.

Marie-Terese delivered his plate to him and then took a seat in front of the salad she'd made herself earlier. As they ate, she glanced over at the stack of mail on the counter and knew without opening it what the bills would add up to. Two of them were big boys: She'd had to put both the private investigator she'd used to find Robbie and the law firm she'd hired to get a divorce on a payment plan, because $127,000 wasn't the kind of thing she could write a check for. Naturally, payment plans involved interest, and unlike credit cards, default wasn't an option: She was taking no chances that P.I. or those lawyers would try to find her. As long as she paid on time, there was no reason for her current location to come to light.

And she always sent money orders that were mailed from Manhattan.

After eighteen months, she was about three-quarters through what she owed, but at least Robbie was safe and with her, and that was all that mattered.

"You are better than her."

Marie-Terese refocused. "Excuse me?"

"That waitress just dropped all the food on her tray." Robbie pointed to the little TV screen. "You would never do that."

Marie-Terese looked over at an ad featuring a harried woman having a bad day working at a diner. Her hair was a frizz bomb, her uniform spackled with ketchup, her name tag off-kilter.

"You're a better waitress, Mom. And cook."

Abruptly, the scene changed so that Harried Waitress was now in a pink bathrobe on a white sofa, submerging her aching feet in a vibrating pool. The expression on her face was pure bliss, the product obviously relieving her aching soles.

"Thanks, baby," Marie-Terese said roughly.

The commercial flipped into order-now mode, an eight-hundred number appearing under the price of $49.99 as an announcer said, "But wait! If you call now, it will cost you only $29.99!" While a red arrow started to flash next to the price, he demanded, "Isn't this a steal?" and the happy, relaxed waitress came back on and said, "Yes, it is!"

"Come on," Marie-Terese cut in. "Time for a bath."

Robbie slid off the stool and took his plate to the dishwasher. "I don't need help anymore, you know. I can take my own bath."

"I know." God, he was growing up fast. "Just make sure you—"

"—do behind the ears. You tell me alla time."

As Robbie hit the stairs, Marie-Terese turned the TV off and went to clean the pan and bowl. Thinking back on that ad, she wished like hell she were just a waitress . . . and that all it would take to make her stress go away was a tub you plugged into the wall.

That would be absolute heaven.

Three tries were a charm.

Finally, Jim woke up in a hospital bed: He was stretched out on white sheets, with a thin white blanket pulled up to his chest and little handrails jacked up on either side of him. And the room fit the bill, too, with bland walls, a bathroom in the corner and a TV mounted on the ceiling that was on, but muted.

Of course, the IV in his arm was the real giveaway.

He'd only been dreaming. That shit about those four dainty wing nuts and the castle and everything had just been a weird dream. Thank. God.

Jim lifted his hand to rub his eyes—and froze. There was a grass stain on his palm. And his face hurt like he'd been punched.

Abruptly, Nigel's aristocratic voice sounded in his head so clearly, it was more than a memory: *Seven deadly sins. Seven souls swayed by these sins. Seven people at a crossroads with a choice that must be made. You enter their lives and affect their path. If they choose righteousness over sin, we prevail.*

Jim took a deep breath and looked toward the window that had a gauze curtain pulled across it. Dark out. Perfect for nightmares. But as much as he wanted to go with the whole it's-only-a-dream thing, the shit was so vivid, so fresh . . . and men might get hairy palms if they were pumping themselves off, but grassy?

Besides it wasn't like he'd been master of his domain with any great frequency.

Especially not the night before, thanks to that brunette. Hello.

Trouble was, if this was the new reality, if he'd been to a parallel universe where everyone was a cross between Simon Cowell and Tim Gunn, if he'd accepted some kind of mission . . . how the hell did he proceed—

"You're awake."

Jim glanced over. Stepping up to the foot of the bed was none other than Vin diPietro, the general contractor from Hell . . . who was evidently the boyfriend of the woman Jim had . . . yeah.

"How you feeling?"

The guy was still wearing the black suit that he'd had on when he and the woman had shown up, and also the same bloodred tie. With his dark hair combed back and just a dusting of beard across his hard face, he presented himself to be exactly who he was: rich and in charge.

Surely it wasn't possible that Vin diPietro was the first assignment.

"Hello?" DiPietro waved. "You in there?"

Nah, Jim thought. Can't be. That would be above and beyond any call of duty.

Over the guy's shoulder, the commercial that was on the TV suddenly showed a price of $49.99—no, $29.99, with a little red arrow that . . . considering where Vin was standing, pointed right at his head.

"Shit, no," Jim muttered. This was the guy?

On the TV screen, some woman in a pink bathrobe smiled up at the camera and mouthed, *Yes, it is!*

DiPietro frowned and leaned over the bed. "You need a nurse?"

No, he needed a beer. Or six. "I'm cool." Jim rubbed his eyes again, smelled fresh grass, and wanted to curse until he ran out of breath.

"Listen," diPietro said, "I'm assuming you don't have health insurance, so I'll cover all your bills. And if you need to take a couple of days off, I won't dock your wages. Sound good?"

Jim let his hands flop down on the bed and was grateful to see that the grass stains had magically disappeared. DiPietro, on the other hand, was evidently going nowhere. At least not until he had a sense of what Jim might sue him for. It was so frickin' obvious that the guy was not bedside offering up his no doubt limitless credit card because he gave two shits about how Jim was feeling. He didn't want a workers'-comp action against his corporation.

Whatever. The accident was not even on Jim's radar; all he could think of was what had happened the night before in his truck. DiPietro was exactly the kind of man who'd have a Blue Dress on his arm, but the coldness in that stare meant he was also the type who could find imperfection in a perfectly beautiful woman. God knew the SOB saw faults in everything that happened at the site, from the way the cement settled in the basement foundation to the tree clearing to the grading of the acres to the position of the nail heads on the framing boards.

No wonder she'd sought out someone else.

And if Jim had to handicap which of the seven sins diPietro was guilty of, there wasn't much of a contest: Avarice was stamped all over not only the guy's designer wardrobe but his car, his woman, and his taste in real estate. He liked his money, this one.

"Listen, I'm going to get a nurse—"

"No." Jim pushed himself up on the pillows. "I don't like nurses."

Or doctors. Or dogs. Or angels . . . saints . . . whatever those four lads were.

"Well, then," diPietro said smoothly, "what can I do for you?"

"Nothing." Thanks to the way destiny had reached up and nailed Jim in the balls, the question was what he could do for his "boss."

What was it going to take to turn this guy's life around? Did Jim just berate him into a massive donation to a soup kitchen? Would that be enough? Or, shit, was he going to have to get this silk-suited, M6-driving, misogynistic motherfucker to renounce everything material and turn his ass into a monk?

Wait . . . crossroads. DiPietro was supposed to be at some kind of crossroads. But how the hell was Jim supposed to know what that was?

He winced and massaged his temples.

"You sure you don't want a nurse?"

Just as frustration put him on the verge of an aneurysm, the images on the TV switched and two chefs appeared on screen. And what do you know. The one who had dark hair looked like Colin and the blond guy next to him sported the exact same bossy expression Nigel had. The pair were leaning into the camera with a covered silver tray, and when the lid was popped off, a dinner plate with some kind of itty-bitty fancy food on it was revealed.

Goddamn it, Jim thought as he glared at the TV. Don't make me do that. By all that's holy—

DiPietro put his face in Jim's field of vision. "What can I do for you?"

As if on cue, the chefs on TV grinned, all *ta-da!*

"I think I . . . want to have dinner with you."

"Dinner?" DiPietro's eyebrows rose. "As in . . . dinner."

Jim resisted the urge to flip off the chefs. "Yeah . . . but not like *dinner*, dinner. Just food. Dinner."

"That's it."

"Yeah." Jim shifted his legs around so they hung off the edge of the bed. "That's it."

Reaching over to the IV in his arm, he peeled the tape off the insertion and popped the needle free of his vein. As saline or whatever was in the bag by the bed started to leak onto the floor, he went under the sheets and grunted as he pulled the catheter out of his cock. The electrical pads on his chest were next, and then he leaned to the side and quieted the monitoring equipment.

"Dinner," he said gruffly. "That's all I want."

Well, that and a clue about what he should be doing with the guy. But hopefully a side order of here's-an-idea would come with the meal.

As he stood up, the world spun and he had to use the wall for balance. After a couple of deep breaths, he lurched for the bathroom—and knew when the hospital johnny broke open because diPietro said *fuck* under his breath.

Clearly the guy was getting a look-see of what was all over Jim's back.

Pausing at the door, Jim looked over his shoulder. "Is 'fuuuuuuck' the way rich people say yes?"

As their eyes met, diPietro's suspicious stare narrowed even further. "Why the hell do you want to have dinner with me?"

"Because we have to start somewhere. Tonight's good for me. Eight o'clock."

When all that came back at him was tense silence, Jim smiled a little. "Just to help you along, it's either dinner or I file a workers'-comp action against you that will make your checkbook bleed. Your choice and I'm good with either outcome."

Vin diPietro had dealt with a lot of SOBs in his lifetime, but this Jim Heron guy was high on the list. It wasn't the outright threat, necessarily. Or the two hundred pounds on that big frame. Or even all that attitude.

The real trouble was the guy's eyes: Anytime a stranger looked at you like he knew you better than family, you had to wonder what the angle was. Had he done his research? Did he know where your bodies were buried?

What kind of threat was he to you?

And dinner? The bastard could have squeezed him for cash, but all he wanted was meat and two veg?

Unless the real ask was going to come outside of the hospital.

"Dinner at eight," Vin said.

"And because I'm a fair guy, I'll let you pick the place."

Well, hell, that was easy. If there was going to be trouble, a public peanut gallery was not the kind of condiment Vin was after. "My duplex at the Commodore. You know the building?"

Heron's eyes went to the window over the bed and then returned. "What floor?"

"Twenty-eighth. I'll tell the doorman to let you up."

"See you tonight then."

Heron turned away, flashing that back of his again.

Vin swallowed another curse as he got a second gander at the black tattoo that covered every inch of skin Heron was showing. Against the vista of a graveyard, the Grim Reaper stared out of that muscled back, a hood shielding its face, its eyes glowing through the shadow created by the robe. One bony hand was locked on its scythe, and the body was leaning forward, its free palm reaching out as if in a moment it was going to snatch your soul. Equally as creepy, there seemed to be a tally at the bottom: Underneath the fringe of the Reaper's robes, there were two rows of little line marks grouped in fives.

You added that shit up and you got to a hundred pretty damn easy.

The bathroom door shut just as a nurse came rushing in, her crepe-soled shoes squeaking on the floor. "What . . . where is he?"

"He unplugged himself. I think he's taking a piss and then leaving."

"He can't do that."

"Good luck changing his mind."

Vin headed out and walked down to the waiting room. Leaning inside, he got the attention of the two workmen who had insisted on hanging around until Heron woke up. The one on the left had piercings on his face and the hard-ass, kinked-out air of someone who enjoyed pain. The other was huge with a long, dark braid over the shoulder of his leather jacket.

"He's ready to go home."

Pierced got to his feet. "The doctors are releasing him already?"

"Got nothing to do with the docs. He made the decision himself." Vin nodded down the hall. "He's in room six sixty-six. And he's going to need a ride home."

"We're on it," Pierced said, his silver eyes serious. "We'll get him where he needs to go."

Vin good-bye'd the pair and went over to catch an elevator down to the first floor. As he stepped inside the car, he took out his BlackBerry and called Devina to let her know they were having a guest for dinner. When he got voice mail, he kept it short and sweet and tried not to wonder what the hell she was doing while he was leaving his message.

Or who, as was the case.

Halfway down, the elevator bumped to a halt and the doors opened to let a pair of men in. As the trip downward resumed, the two traded affirming noises, like they'd just concluded a conversation satisfactorily and were reinforcing the fact. They were both dressed in slacks and sweaters, and the one on the left was balding at the crown, his brown hair pulling away like it was afraid being on top of the mountain. . . .

Vin blinked. And then blinked again.

A shadow bloomed all around the balding man, the glimmering, shifting aura the color of pencil lead and the consistency of heat waves on pavement.

It couldn't be . . . oh, God, no . . . after all these years of quiet, it couldn't be back.

Curling his hands into fists, Vin closed his eyes and willed away the vision, kicking it out of his brain, denying it access to his neurons. He did not just see that. And if he had, it was a misread of the overhead lighting.

The shit was not back. He'd gotten rid of it. *It was not back.*

He cracked a lid, looked over at the guy . . . and felt like he'd been punched in the gut: The translucent shadow was as obvious as the clothes the man was wearing and as tangible as the person standing next to him.

Vin saw dead people, all right. Before they died.

The double doors opened at the lobby, and after the pair filed out, Vin dropped his head and walked as fast as he could for the exit. He was making good time, running from the side of himself he'd never understood and didn't want anything to do with, when he slammed into a white coat

who was carrying an armful of files. As paperwork and manila folders took flight like startled birds, Vin helped steady
the woman and then dropped down to help her clean the
mess up.

The balding man who'd stood ahead of him in the elevator did the same.

Vin's eyes locked on the guy and refused to budge.
The smoke was emanating from the left side of the man's
chest . . . boiling up into the air from a specific spot.

"Go see a doctor," Vin heard himself say. "Go see one
right away. It's in your lungs."

Before anyone could ask him what the hell he was talking about, Vin scrambled to his feet and tore out of the
building, heart in his throat, breath coming in short blasts.

His hands were shaking by the time he got to his car, so
it was a good thing BMWs let you get inside and start the
engine without plugging the key into anything.

Gripping his steering wheel, he shook his head back and
forth.

He'd thought he'd left all that freaky bullshit behind. He
thought that second-sight crap was solidly in his past. He'd
done what he'd been told to do, and even though he hadn't
believed in the actions he'd taken, they had appeared to
work for almost twenty years.

Ah, shit . . . he couldn't go back to the way it had been
before.

Just couldn't.

CHAPTER

7

When Jim came out of the bathroom, diPietro was gone and a nurse with a lot to say had taken his place. While she went on about ... shit, whatever the hell it was ... Jim focused over her shoulder in hopes of cutting short the tirade.

"Are you done?" he asked when she took more than a single breath.

Crossing her arms over her large bosom, she looked at him like she was hoping she'd be the one to put his catheter back in. "I'm going to call the doctor."

"Well, good for you, but it's not going to change my mind." He glanced around, figuring the private room he'd gotten was diPietro's influence. "What happened to my things?"

"Sir, you were nonresponsive up until about fifteen minutes ago, and you were dead when they brought you in. So before you take off like you had the common cold, you should—"

"Clothes. That's really all I'm interested in."

The nurse stared at him with a kind of hatred, like she was so done with patients giving her lip. "Do you think you're immortal?"

"At least for the time being," he muttered. "Look, I'm through with arguing. Get me something to wear and tell me where my wallet is, or I'm walking out in this and making the hospital pay for my taxi home."

"Wait. Here."

"Not. For. Long."

As the door eased shut, he paced around, energy burning through him. He'd woken up logy, but that was all gone now.

Man, he could remember this feeling, back when he'd been in the service. Once again, he had a goal, and as before, that gave him the power to throw off exhaustion and injury and anyone who threatened to divert him from his target.

Which meant that nurse had better get out of his way.

Not surprisingly, when she came back a couple of minutes later, she brought not one, but three reinforcements. Which was not going to help her. While the doctors formed a circle of rational thinking around Jim, he just watched their mouths move and their eyebrows go up and down and their elegant hands gesticulate.

As he thought about his new job—because he sure as hell wasn't listening to the MD brigade—he wondered how he was going to know what to do. Yeah, he had a date with diPietro . . . but then what? And, holy hell, was that girlfriend going to be there?

Talk about "guess who's coming to dinner."

He focused on the peanut gallery. "I'm done. I'm leaving. Can I have my clothes now, thanks."

Crickets in the background. Then everyone walked out in a huff, proving that they thought he was stupid, but not mentally compromised—because adults who had their marbles were allowed to make bad choices.

As the door was shutting, Adrian and Eddie stuck their heads in the room.

Ad smiled. "So you tossed the white coats out on their asses, huh?"

"Yup."

The guy chuckled as he and his roommate stepped inside. "Why does this not surprise me—"

The whistle-blower nurse barged past them with a pair of hospital scrubs and a large Hawaiian shirt draped over her forearm. Ignoring Eddie and Adrian as if they weren't even there, she tossed the threads onto the bed and presented Jim with a clipboard. "Your things are in that closet and your bill's been taken care of. Sign this. It's a form stating that you are releasing yourself AMA. Against medical advice."

Jim took the black Bic from her and drew an X on the signature line.

The nurse looked down at the mark. "What is that?"

"My signature. An X is legally sufficient. Now will you excuse me?" He untied the neck ribbon on the johnny and let the thing drop from his body.

Full-frontal got her out of the room without further conversation.

As she took off at a dead run, Adrian laughed. "Not much on the words, but you know how to get things done."

Jim turned around and drew on the scrub bottoms.

"Hell of a tat you got there," Adrian said softly.

Jim just shrugged and reached for the ugly-ass shirt. The color combination was red and orange on a white background, and he felt like a frickin' Christmas present with the damn thing on.

"She gave you that because she hates you," Adrian said.

"Or maybe she's just color-blind." More likely it was the former, though.

Jim went to the closet and found his boots lined up on the bottom and a plastic bag with the St. Francis Hospital seal hanging on a hook. He put his bare feet into his Timberlands and took his jacket out of the bag, covering up the damn shirt. His wallet was still in his coat's inside pocket, and he went through the folds. Everything was there. His fake driver's license, his false social security card, and the VISA debit card that linked to his Evergreen Bank account. Oh, and the seven dollars that was change from his having bought the turkey sandwich and the coffee and the Coke that morning.

Before life had FUBAR'd out big-time.

"Any chance either of you didn't come on a motorcycle?" he asked the roommates. "I need a ride back to the site to pick up my truck."

Although to get out of here, he'd hop on the back bump of a Harley if he had to.

Adrian grinned and swept a hand through that gorgeous hair of his. "Brought my other wheels. Figured you'd need transport."

"I'll take a clown car at this point."

"Give me a little more credit than that."

The three of them left, and when they passed by the nursing station, no one got in their way, even though all the staff stopped what they were doing and glared.

The trip from St. Francis to diPietro's nascent temple took about twenty minutes in Adrian's Explorer, and he had AC/DC playing the entire time. Which wouldn't have been a problem, except for the fact that the guy sang every word of every song and was *never* going to be the next American Idol: Fucker wasn't just tone-deaf—he had white-boy rhythm and way too much enthusiasm.

As Eddie stared out the window like he'd turned to stone, Jim cranked the volume even louder in hopes of drowning out the wounded badger behind the wheel.

When they finally turned onto diPietro's dirt drive, the sun had set and the light was draining from the sky, the tree stumps and the raw patches casting sharper shadows because of the angle of illumination. The hacked-up land was utterly stark and unappealing, and contrasted badly with the unrazed opposite shore, but no doubt diPietro was going to replant it with specimen everything.

He was definitely the type who had to have the best.

As they pulled up to the house, Jim's truck was the only one left, and he was ready to jump out at it before the Explorer rolled to a stop.

"Thanks for the ride," he shouted.

"What?" Adrian went for the volume and turned it all the way down. "What you say?"

In the acoustic vacuum, Jim's ears rang like church bells, and he resisted the urge to try to shake the vibration out of his skull by slamming his forehead into the dashboard.

"I said, thanks for the ride."

"No problem." Adrian nodded at the F-150. "You okay to drive?"

"Yeah."

After he got out, he and Eddie pounded knuckles, and then he walked over to his truck. As he went, his right hand searched out the pocket of the shirt the hospital had given him. No Marlboros. Damn it. But come on, like coffin nails were going to be a parting gift when you pulled out of St. Francis?

While Adrian and Eddie waited for him, he filled his cigaretteless hand with his keys and unlocked his—

A flash of movement by the back tire caught his eye.

Jim looked down as the dog he'd shared his lunch with limped out from under the security of the transmission system.

"Oh . . . no." Jim shook his head. "Listen, I told you . . ."

There was the sound of a car window going down and then Adrian's voice: "He likes you."

The mutt did that curled-sit thing and stared up at Jim.

Shit. "That turkey I gave you sucked. You have to know that."

"If you're hungry, everything tastes good," Adrian cut in.

Jim glanced over his shoulder. "Why are you still here? No offense."

Adrian laughed. "None taken. Later."

The Explorer reversed, its tires crunching over the cold ground, its headlights swinging around and hitting the half-done house before sweeping across the cleared acreage and the river beyond. As the illumination headed off down the lane, Jim's eyes adjusted in the darkness, and the mansion presented itself as a jagged beast, the enclosed first floor its belly, the ragged second story framing its thorned head, the scattered piles of stacked brush and logs the bones of its victims. Its arrival had consumed the peninsula, and the more it gathered strength, the more it would dominate the landscape.

God . . . you were going to be able to see it for miles in all directions, from land and water and sky. It was a real temple to greed, a monument to everything Vin diPietro had obtained in his life—which made Jim willing to bet that the guy had come from nothing. People who had money inherited old houses this size; they didn't build them.

Man, derailing diPietro from this shit was going to be a hard sell. Very hard. And somehow, the threat of eternal damnation just didn't seem like enough of a motivator. Guy like this wasn't going to believe in life in the hereafter. No fucking way.

As a cold wind rolled across the property, Jim looked back down at the dog.

The thing seemed to be waiting for an invitation. And prepared to sit it out for eternity.

"My apartment's a pit," Jim said as they stared at each other. "About on a level with that sandwich. You come with me and it ain't no lap-of-luxury gig."

The dog pawed at the air as if a roof and four walls were all it was looking for.

"You sure about this?"

More with the pawing.

"Okay. Fine."

Jim unlocked the cab's door and bent down to pick up the thing, hoping he'd read the conversation correctly and wasn't going to lose the tip of a finger. All was cool, though. The dog just lifted its butt and gave its body up to the palm that encircled its belly.

"Damn, we need to put some weight on you, boy."

Jim settled the animal on the passenger seat and got behind the wheel. The truck started up quick, and he turned the blowers off so that the little guy didn't catch a chill.

Flipping his headlights on, he eased the engine into gear and followed the path Adrian and Eddie had forged, turning around and going out the lane. When he got to Route 151N, he hit the left-hand blinker and—

The dog ducked under his arm and sat in his lap.

Jim glanced down at the animal's boxy head and realized he had nothing to feed the thing. Or himself.

"You want more turkey, dog? I can hit the Citgo on the way home."

The thing wagged not only its tail, but its entire bony butt.

"Okay. That's what we'll do." Jim hit the gas and eased out of diPietro's driveway, his free hand stroking the dog's back. "Ah, just one thing . . . any chance you're housebroken?"

CHAPTER
8

Darkness brought with it, among many blessings, the benefit of prevalent shadow. Which made it far more useful than daylight.

As the man sat behind the wheel of the taxi, he knew that both he and his vehicle were invisible to the one he watched. She couldn't see him. She did not know he was there or that he had taken pictures of her or that he had been trailing her for weeks. And this confirmed the power he had over her.

Through the bars on her window, he watched her as she sat on the couch with the boy. He couldn't see them clearly, as there was a gauze curtain in the way, but he recognized the shapes of them, the larger and the smaller, nestled close together on the sofa in the living room.

He'd made it his business to learn her schedule. During the week, she schooled the boy until three in the afternoon, whereupon on Mondays through Thursdays she took him to the YMCA for his swimming and basketball lessons. While the boy was at the facility, she never left him—whether he was in the pool or on the court, she was perpetually seated on the benches where the children left their warm-ups and their little bags. When the boy was finished, she waited right outside the locker room for him, and after he got changed, she drove him straight home.

Careful. She was so very careful—except for the fact that the rhythms of her life never changed: Every night except Sundays, she made the boy dinner at six; then the babysitter showed up at eight o'clock and she took off, going to St. Patrick's either for confession or prayer group. After which she went to that godforsaken club.

He hadn't been inside the Iron Mask yet, but that was going to change tonight. His plan was to trail her for hours while she worked as a waitress or a bartender or whatever she was, learning more about her and how she lived. God was in the details, as they said, and he needed to know *everything*.

Glancing into the rearview mirror, he fussed with the wig and the mustache he was using as a disguise. They weren't sophisticated, but they hid his features well enough, and he needed them for a variety of reasons.

Plus he relished the feeling he got when he was invisible to her; the thrill of watching her when she was unaware of it was downright sexual.

At seven forty, a sedan pulled up in front of the house and an African-American woman got out. She was one of three babysitters he'd seen this week, and after following one of them home and seeing where she went the next morning, he'd learned they all came from a social service called the Caldwell Center for Single Mothers.

Ten minutes after the sitter went inside, the garage door trundled up and he ducked lower in his seat—because two could play at the extra safe game.

Seven fifty. Right on time.

His woman backed out into the driveway and waited as the door shut tight, as if she were worried that one of these times it wouldn't make it all the way down. When it was finished doing its thing, her red brake lights went out and the car reversed into the street and took off.

He started the cab and was just putting it in gear when the dispatcher's voice broke through the silence. "One forty—where are you, one forty? One forty, we need your goddamn car back."

No way, he thought. He didn't have time to drop off the cab and catch up with her. St. Patrick's would be the next stop, and by the time he checked out of work, she'd be done at the church.

"One forty? Goddamn you—"

He curled up a fist, prepared to punch the radio into silence and it was hard to tame his temper. Always had been. But he reminded himself that he would have to return the taxi at some point, and busted equipment meant he'd have to deal with the dispatcher.

He *had* to avoid conflicts because they never ended well for him or the other person. That much he'd learned.

And he had big plans.

"Coming in now," he said into the receiver.

He'd just have to see her at the club, even though he felt cheated because he'd miss her at St. Pat's.

Marie-Terese sat in the basement of St. Patrick's Cathedral in a plastic chair that made her butt hurt. To her left was a mother of five who always cradled her Bible in the crook of her arm like it was a baby. To her right was a guy who must have been a mechanic: His palms were clean, but there was always a black line beneath each of his fingernails.

There were twelve other people in the circle and one empty chair, and she knew everybody in the room as well as the person who was missing tonight. After having listened to them all go on about their lives for the past couple of months, she could recite the names of their husbands and wives and children, if they had them, knew the critical events that had shaped their pasts, and had insight into the darkest corners of their inner closets.

She'd been going to the prayer group since September, and she'd found out about it from a notice posted on the church bulletin board: *The Bible in Daily Life, Tuesdays and Fridays, 8 p.m.*

Tonight's discussion was on the book of Job, and the extrapolations were obvious: Everyone was talking about the vast struggles they were dealing with, and how they were certain that their faith would be rewarded and God would see them through to a prosperous future—as long as they kept believing.

Marie-Terese didn't say anything. She never did.

Unlike when she went to confession, down here in the basement she was looking to do something other than talk. The thing was, there was no other place in her life where she could be around normal-ish people. She certainly wasn't finding them at the club, and outside of work, she had no friends, no family, no anyone.

So every week she came here and sat in this circle and tried to connect in some small way to the rest of the planet. As it was now, she felt like she was on a distant shore, staring across a raging river at the Land of the Worried Well, and it wasn't that she begrudged or belittled them. On the contrary, she tried to take strength from being in their company, thinking that maybe if she breathed the same air they did, and drank the same coffee, and listened to their stories . . . maybe someday she would live among them once again.

As a result, these meetings weren't a religious thing to her, and unlike the fecund mother hen next to her with the obvious Bible, Marie-Terese's Good Book stayed in her purse. Heck, she brought it only in case someone asked her where it was and it was a good thing it was only the size of a palm.

With a frown, she tried to remember where she'd picked it up. It had been somewhere south of the Mason-Dixon, in a convenience store . . . Georgia? Alabama? She'd been on the trail of her ex-husband and had needed something, anything to get her through the days and nights without losing her mind.

That was what, three years ago?

Seemed like three minutes and three millennia at the same time.

God, those horrible months. She'd known getting away

from Mark was going to be awful, but she'd had no idea how bad it would really get.

After he'd beaten her up and abducted Robbie, she'd spent two nights in the hospital getting over what he'd done to her, and then she'd found a private investigator and headed after them. It had taken all of that May, June, and July to locate her son, and she still to this day had no clue how she'd gotten through those horrible weeks.

Funny, she hadn't had her faith back then and things had still worked out, the miracle she had been praying for being granted even though she hadn't really believed in who she was asking things of. Clearly, all the entreaties had worked, though, and she could remember with total clarity the sight of the PI's black Navigator pulling up to the Motel 6 she'd been staying in. Robbie had opened the SUV's door and stepped into the Florida sunshine, and she had meant to run toward him, but her knees had failed. Sinking down onto the sidewalk, she had held her arms out as she'd wept.

She'd thought he was dead.

Robbie had turned toward the choking sound ... and the instant he'd seen her, he'd bolted across the distance as fast as he could go. As he'd slammed into her arms, his clothes had been dirty and his hair shaggy and he'd smelled like burnt macaroni and cheese. But he lived and breathed and was in her arms.

He hadn't cried then, however. And he hadn't cried since.

Hadn't spoken of his father or those three months, either. Even to the therapists she'd taken him to.

Marie-Terese had assumed that the worst part of the experience had been not knowing whether the son she had birthed and loved was alive or not. His coming home was just another hell, though. She wanted to ask him if he was all right every minute of every day, but obviously she couldn't do that. And every once in a while, when she cracked and put the question out there, he just told her he was fine.

He was not fine. Could not possibly be fine.

The details the PI had been able to give her were

sketchy. Her husband had taken Robbie across the country, going from rental car to rental car, and living off of a host of aliases and a massive cash stash. It had turned out that he'd kept a low profile for a couple of reasons—because it wasn't just Marie-Terese who'd been looking for him.

And to keep Robbie from trying to escape, it was likely that Mark had bullied him. Which made her want to kill her ex-husband.

After she'd gotten Robbie back and filed for divorce, she'd run as far away from where they'd lived as she could, surviving on money she'd taken from Mark and jewelry he'd bought her. Unfortunately, it hadn't been enough to live off of for long, not after the lawyers' fees, the PI's bill, and the cost of reinventing herself.

What she had ended up doing for money made her think about Job. She was willing to bet when the tide had turned against him he hadn't known what hit him: One minute he was fine and dandy; the next he'd been stripped of everything that had defined him and been taken so low that surely he'd thought of doing things to survive that once would have been incomprehensible.

She was the same. She never would have seen this coming. Not the descent downward or the hard landing as she'd bottomed out and turned to prostitution.

But she should have known better. Her ex had been shady from the start, a man with cash everywhere except in bank accounts. Where the hell had she thought the money came from? People who were in legitimate businesses had credit cards and debit cards and maybe a couple of twenties in their wallets. They didn't keep hundreds of thousands of dollars in Gucci briefcases hidden in the closets of their Las Vegas hotel suites.

Of course, she hadn't known about all that in the beginning. When it had all started, she'd been too snowed by the presents and the dinners out and the plane rides. Only later had she started to question things, and by then it was too late: She had a son she loved and a husband she was terrified of, and that had shut her up quick.

If she was brutally honest with herself, the mystery of Mark had been the true attraction in the beginning. The mystery and the fairy tale and the money.

She had paid for that attraction. Dearly . . .

The sound of chairs skidding across the floor brought her out of her own head. The meeting was over and the participants were standing up and doing the supportive huggy thing—which meant she needed to get out fast before she became entangled.

It was one thing to listen to them; another to feel them against her.

That she couldn't handle.

Rising to her feet, she slung her bag onto her shoulder and beelined for the door. On the way out, she said some quick, detail-less things to the others, and as always, got those looks Christians bestowed on the less fortunate, all *poor, dear girl.*

She had to wonder whether they would have been so generous with the support if they knew where she went and what she did after these meetings. She wanted to believe it would have been no different. Couldn't help but doubt it, though.

Out in the hall, there were others gathering for the next meeting of the night, which she'd heard was a Narcotics Anonymous group that had recently started congregating at St. Patrick's. Everyone was cordial, the two sets of troubled mingling as the room handoff occurred.

Searching in her purse to find her car keys, she—

Slammed into a wall of a man.

"Oh, I'm so sorry!" She looked up, way up, into a pair of lion's eyes. "I, er . . ."

"Easy, there." The man steadied her and gave her a small, gentle smile. His hair was as spectacular as that yellow stare, all different kinds of colors that flowed onto his huge shoulders. "You okay?"

"Ah . . ." She'd seen him before, not only out in the hallway but also at ZeroSum, and had marveled at his unreal looks, thinking maybe he was a model. And naturally, part of her worried that he knew what she did for a living, but he never seemed awkward with her or skeevy in the slightest.

Besides, if he was attending NA, he had some demons of his own to confront.

"Ma'am? Hello?"

"Oh . . . God, sorry. Yes, I'm fine—I just really need to watch where I'm going."

With a smile back to him, she ducked into the stairwell, headed up to the cathedral's first floor and left through those big double doors in front. Out on the street, she hustled past the rows of cars that were parallel-parked and wished she'd gotten a better spot. Her Camry was down quite a way, and she was biting on her molars from the cold by the time she jumped in and started the ritual of getting the engine to turn over.

"Come on . . . come on . . ."

Finally she got a wheeze and a *vroom* and then she was doing an illegal U-turn over the double yellow line that ran down the middle of the street.

Caught up in her own head, she failed to notice the pair of headlights that slipped into her wake . . . and stayed there.

CHAPTER
9

As Jim parked his truck a half a block from the Commodore, he thought, Yup, he could see Vin having a crib there. The outside of the building was stark, nothing but glass bezel set into thin steel girders, but that was what would give each of the condos such incredible views. And just from what he could see of the lobby from the street, the inside was pure decadence, all flood-lit, bloodred marble, with a flower arrangement the size of a fire truck smack in the middle of the space.

Also made sense that Blue Dress would live in a place like this.

Shit, he should have suggested just he and diPietro go out somewhere together to eat: With what had happened the night before still so vivid, being in the same enclosed space with that woman was not the brightest idea. And then, hello, there was the complication of his having to save her fucking boyfriend from eternal damnation.

Killing the engine, he rubbed his face and for some reason thought of Dog, who he'd left at home all curled up on the messy bed. The little guy had been out like a light, his thin flank rising and falling, his full belly a ball his little legs had to splay around.

How in the hell had he managed to pick up a pet?

Putting his keys into his leather jacket, he left the truck and went across the street. As he pushed his way into the lobby, what had looked lush from the street was magnificent up close, but there was going to be no loitering to admire the place. The instant he walked in, the guard behind the desk looked up with a frown.

"Good evening—are you Mr. Heron?" The guy was fiftyish and dressed in a black uniform, his eyes neither slow nor stupid. Chances were good he was armed and knew how to handle what he was packing.

Jim had to approve. "Yeah, I am."

"May I see some identification, please?"

Jim got out his wallet and flipped it open to the New York State driver's license he'd bought about three days after he'd arrived in Caldwell.

"Thank you. I'll call Mr. diPietro." The guard was two seconds on the phone, and then he swept his arm toward the elevators. "Go right up, sir."

"Thanks."

The ride to the twenty-eighth floor was smooth as silk, and Jim amused himself by locating the mostly hidden eyes of the security cameras: The things were positioned in the upper corners where the gold mirrored panels came together, and they were made to look like decorations. With the four of them, no matter which way someone was facing, there'd be a clean shot at his or her face.

Nice. Very nice.

The *bing* that announced Jim's arrival was just as discreet, and as the doors parted, Vin diPietro was right there, standing in a long ivory hallway, looking like he owned the whole frickin' building.

DiPietro put out his palm. "Welcome."

Guy had a solid handshake, firm and quick, and he looked great—also not a surprise. Whereas Jim was in his second-best flannel shirt and sporting a fresh shave, Vin was in a different suit than he'd had on a mere three hours ago at the hospital.

Probably just wore the things once and threw them away.

"You mind if I call you Jim?"

"Nope."

DiPietro led the way over to a door and opened the way into ... Shit, the place was right out of the Donald Trump collection, nothing but black marble, gold curlicues, crystal crap, and carved statutes. From the floors of the front hall, to the stairs that led up to a second level ... and then, yeah, what was laid down in the living room, there was so much cut and finished stone, Jim had to wonder how many quarries had been stripped to kit the place out. And the furniture ... Christ, the sofas and chairs looked like jewelry, with all of their gold leafing and gemstone-colored silk.

"Devina, come meet our guest," diPietro called over his shoulder.

As the sound of high-heeled shoes came toward the living room, Jim stared out at a truly stunning view of Caldwell ... and tried not to think of when he'd seen the woman last.

She had on the same perfume she'd worn the night before.

And how fitting her name was. She'd certainly felt divine.

"Jim?" diPietro said.

Jim waited a moment longer, to give her time to look at the side of his face and compose herself. Seeing him from far away was one thing; having him in her home, close enough to touch, was another. Was she in blue again?

No, red. And diPietro had his arm around her waist.

Jim nodded at her, refusing to let even one memory enter his head. "Nice to meet you."

She smiled at him and extended her hand. "Welcome. I hope you like Italian food?"

Jim shook her palm quickly and then stuffed his hand in the pocket of his jeans. "Yeah, I do."

"Good. The cook is off for the next week, and Italian is pretty much all I can do."

Shit. Now what.

In the silence that followed, the three of them stood around as if they were all wondering the same thing.

"If you'll excuse me," Devina said, "I'll just go check on dinner."

Vin dropped a kiss on her mouth. "We'll have drinks here."

As the clipping of those high heels receded, diPietro went over to a wet bar. "What's your poison?"

Interesting question. In Jim's old line of work, he'd used cyanide, anthrax, tetrodotoxin, ricin, mercury, morphine, heroin, as well as some of the new designer nerve agents. He'd injected the stuff, put it in food, dusted it on doorknobs, sprayed it on mail, contaminated all manner of drink and medications. And that was before he'd gotten really creative.

Yup, he was as good with all that as he was with a knife or a gun or his bare hands. Not that diPietro needed to know it.

"Don't suppose you have any beer?" Jim said, glancing at all of the top-shelf liquor bottles.

"I've got the new Dogfish. It's fantastic."

Right, Jim had been thinking a Bud, and God only knew what that was—neither dogs nor fish were something you wanted brewing with hops. But whatever. "Sounds good."

DiPietro fired up two long glasses and opened a panel that turned out to be a mini-fridge. Grabbing a pair of bottles, he popped off the caps and poured out a dark beer with a head so white it looked like ocean foam.

"I think you'll like this."

Jim accepted one of the glasses along with a little linen napkin that had the initials V.S.dP. on it. A single sip . . . and all he could say was, "Damn."

"Good, right?" DiPietro took a draw and then lifted the beer to the light as if inspecting its character. "It's the best."

"Straight from Heaven." As Jim savored what was passing over his tongue, he looked around with fresh eyes at all the fancy-dancy. Maybe the rich did have a something going on. "So, this is a hell of a place you got."

"The bluff house is going to be even more magnificent."

Jim wandered over to the banks of glass and leaned into the view. "Why would you want to leave this?"

"Because where I'm going is better."

A subtle doorbell-like chiming went off, and Jim glanced down at a phone.

Vin looked over as well. "That's my business line and I have to take it." With his beer in his hand, he headed for a doorway on the opposite side of the room. "Make yourself at home. I'll be right back."

As the guy walked off, Jim laughed to himself. Home here? Riiiiiiight. He felt like he was part of one of those children's quizzes where the kid had to pick out the object that didn't belong: carrot, cucumber, apple, zucchini. Answer: apple. Silk-covered sofa, fine woven rug, workman, crystal decanters. Answer: duh.

"Hi."

Jim closed his eyes. Her voice was still lovely. "Hi."

"I . . ."

Jim pivoted around and was not surprised to find that her eyes were still sad.

As she struggled for words, he held up his hand to stop her. "You don't have to explain."

"I've . . . I've never done anything like last night before. I just wanted . . ."

"Something that was very not him?" Jim shook his head as she grew agitated. "Oh . . . shit . . . look, don't cry."

He put down the beer diPietro had poured for him and came forward holding out the napkin. He would have dabbed at her tears himself, but he didn't want to smudge the makeup.

Devina's hand trembled as she took what he offered. "I'm not going to tell him. Ever."

"And he's not finding out from me."

"Thank you." Her eyes drifted over to the phone console, where a light was flashing next to the word *study*. "I love him. I do. . . . It's just . . . he's complicated. He's a . . . complicated man, and I know he cares for me in his own way, but sometimes I feel invisible. And you? You actually saw me."

Yeah, he had. He couldn't deny it.

"The truth is," she murmured, "although I shouldn't have been with you, I don't regret it."

He wasn't so sure of that, given the way she stared up at him like she was waiting for words of wisdom or . . . absolution. Which he really couldn't give her. He'd never been in a relationship before, so it wasn't like he could offer advice about her and Vin—and he only knew from one-night stands, so what might be shocking to her was all he had experience with when it came to sex.

One thing was clear, though. As this spectacular woman looked at him with those dark, luminescent eyes, he saw the love she had for the man she was with: It was in her heart, radiating out of her.

Man, Vin diPietro was a full-load idiot to fuck this up.

Jim lifted his hand to her face and brushed off one of her tears. "Listen to me. You're going to forget it ever happened. You're going to lock it away and never think about it again, okay? If you don't remember it, it's not real. It didn't happen."

She sniffled a little. "Okay . . . all right."

"Good girl." Jim tucked a strand of her soft hair behind her ear. "And don't worry, everything's going to be okay."

"How can you be so sure."

And that was when it dawned on him. Maybe this was Vin's crossroads—right here in front of the man, wanting to love him, hoping to get the chance, but losing the fight to stay connected. If the guy could just see what he had, and not as in his real estate or his cars or his statues and marble, but what *really* mattered, maybe he'd turn his life and soul around.

Devina blotted at one of her tears. "I'm running out of faith, it seems."

"Don't. I'm here to help." Jim took a deep breath. "I'm going to make it okay."

"Oh, God ... you're making me cry more." Devina laughed and clasped his hand. "But thank you so much."

Damn ... those eyes of hers made him feel as if she'd reached in past his ribs and taken his heart into her delicate palm.

"Your name," he whispered, "suits you."

A blush flared in her cheeks. "In school, I used to hate it. I wanted to be Mary or Julie or something normal."

"No, it's perfect. I can't imagine you being called anything else." Jim glanced down at the phone and saw that the light was off. "He's ended the call."

She dabbed under both eyes. "I must be a mess. Here ... let me give you some *amuse-bouche*. Take them to him and keep him busy in the study while I go fix myself."

As he waited for her to come back from the kitchen, Jim finished his beer and wondered how in the hell he'd found himself in the role of Cupid.

Man, if those four lads even *thought* about getting him to wear the wings and a diaper while he nocked his arrow, he was so renegotiating his employment contract. And not with words.

Devina returned with a silver tray of bite-size somethings. "The study's down that way. I'll come get you both when I don't look so weepy."

"Roger that." Jim took the tray, prepared to act the waiter and babysit diPietro. "I'll keep him in there."

"Thank you. For everything."

Before he said too much again, Jim took off, carrying the tray with both hands through an endless spread of rooms. When he got to the study, the door was open and diPietro was sitting behind a big marble desk that had a lot of computers on it. The guy wasn't staring at the machines, though. He was turned around and focused on the bank of windows and the twinkling view.

Something small and black was buried in his palm.

Jim knocked on the jamb. "I got some amusements for your mouth."

Vin pivoted around in his chair and tucked the ring box next to the phone. As Heron stood in the study's doorway with a tray in his hands, the guy made an unlikely waiter, and not because of the flannel shirt and the jeans. He simply wasn't the kind to be anyone's servant.

"You know French?" Vin murmured as he nodded at the *amuse-bouche*.

"She told me what they were."

"Ah." Vin got to his feet and went over. "Devina's a great cook."

"Yeah."

"You try one already?"

"Nah, I'm just going by the smells coming out of your kitchen."

They both took a stuffed mushroom cap. And a tiny sandwich with paper-thin slices of tomato and leaves of basil. And a flat-bellied spoon with caviar and leeks on it.

"So have a seat," Vin said, nodding at the one across from his desk. "Let's talk. I mean, I know you want food . . . but there's something else, isn't there."

Heron put down the tray but didn't take a load off. Instead, he went over to the windows and looked out at Caldwell.

In the silence, Vin resettled in his leather throne and measured his "guest." Bastard had a jaw like a two-by-four, hard and straight, and he was playing his cards close to the chest: There was no tell in his face whatsoever.

Which suggested the territory they were going to head into was dark and tricky.

As Vin twirled a gold pen around on his blotter and waited for the ask, he wasn't worried about dark and tricky. Most of his money had been made in construction, but he hadn't started out in the legitimate land of boards and nails—and his contacts with the black-market side of Caldwell were still good.

"Take your time, Jim. Money is easier to ask for than ... other things." He smiled a little. "You want something that isn't readily available at the local Hannaford, by any chance?"

Heron's eyebrow twitched, but that was about it as he continued searching the lights of the city. "What exactly are you talking about."

"What exactly are you looking for."

There was a pause. "I need to know about you."

Vin sat forward in his chair, not sure he'd heard right. "Know about me how?"

Heron turned his head and stared downward. "You're about to make a decision. Something significant. Aren't you."

Vin's eyes shot to the black velvet square he'd hidden.

"What's in there?" Heron demanded.

"None of your business."

"A ring?"

Vin cursed and reached for what he'd bought at Reinhardt's. As he tucked the box into a drawer, he started to lose his patience. "Look, stop bullshitting around and tell me what you want. It's not dinner and it's not to get to know me. Why don't you assume that there is nothing in this town that is unavailable to me and let's get this over with. What the fuck do you want."

The soft words that came back at him seemed so wrong: "It's not what I want—it's what I'm going to do. I'm here to save your soul."

Vin frowned ... and then busted out laughing. This guy with the Grim Reaper tat on his back and the tool belt wanted to *save* him? Yeah, that made sense.

And PS: Vin's "soul" wasn't drowning.

When he took a break to do some deep breathing, Heron said, "You know, that's exactly how I reacted."

"To what?" Vin said as he rubbed his face.

"Let's just say the call to duty."

"You some kind of religious freak?"

"Nah." Heron finally went around and sat in the chair,

his knees falling to the sides, his hands resting loosely on his thighs. "Can I ask you something?"

"Sure, why the hell not." Vin found himself echoing Heron's pose, just easing on back and relaxing. At this point, the whole thing was getting so weird, he was beginning to think it didn't matter. "What do you want to know?"

Heron glanced around at the first-edition books and the artwork. "Why do you need all this shit? And I'm not being nasty. I'm never going to live like you, so I'm kind of wondering why anybody has to have it all."

Vin was tempted to blow off the question, and later he would wonder why he didn't. But for some reason he answered truthfully.

"It gives me weight and grounds me. I feel safe with beautiful things around my home." The instant the words were out, he wanted to take them back. "I mean . . . shit, I don't know. I didn't come from money. I was just an Italian kid over on the north side of town, and my parents were always scraping to get by. I fought my way up because I wanted much better than where I'd been."

"Well, you're waaaaaay up, all right." Heron glanced at the computers. "So you must work a lot."

"All the time."

"Guess that means you've earned this amazing view."

Vin swung his chair around. "Yeah. Been looking at it a lot lately."

"You going to miss it when you move?"

"I'll have the river to stare out at. And that house you and your boys are building is going to be spectacular. I like spectacular things."

"That beer was probably the best one I've ever had."

Vin focused on the guy's reflection in the darkened glass. "Is Heron your real name?"

The guy smiled a little. "Of course it is."

Vin glanced over his shoulder. "What other languages do you know aside from French?"

"Who says I know it?"

"The fact that you don't have a clue about exotic beer

makes me doubt you're a foodie and into gourmet lingo. And Devina wouldn't have translated *amuse-bouche* because it would be rude to think you didn't know what it meant. Therefore, I assume you know the language."

Heron drummed his fingers on his knee as he seemed to think things over. "Tell me what's in that box you hid in the drawer and maybe I'll answer you."

"Anyone ever say they had to drag things out of you?"

"All the time."

Figuring it was no real revelation—because, really, when was Heron going to have anything to do with Devina?— Vin got the Reinhardt box back out and popped the lid. As he turned the thing around so Heron could see what was in it, the guy let out a low whistle.

Vin just shrugged. "Like I said, I'm into beautiful things. I bought it last night."

"Christ, what a sparkler. When you going to pop the Q?"

"Don't know."

"What are you waiting for?"

Vin snapped the box shut. "You've asked more than one question. My turn. French? *Oui ou non?*"

"*Je parle un peu. Et vous?*"

"I've done some real estate deals north of the border, so I speak it. Your accent is not Canadian, though. It's European. How long were you in the military?"

"Who said I was?"

"Just a guess."

"Maybe I went to college overseas."

Vin regarded the guy steadily. "Not your style, I wouldn't think. You don't take orders well, and I can't imagine you'd be content behind a school desk for four years."

"Why would I go into the service if I don't take orders?"

"Because they let you do something on your own." Vin smiled as the guy's face remained utterly closed. "They let you work by yourself, didn't they, Jim. What else did they teach you?"

Silence expanded to fill not just the room, but the whole duplex.

"Jim, you do realize that the more you stay quiet, the more I make up my own mind about your military haircut and that tattoo on your back. I showed you what you wanted to see—seems only fair you return the favor. More to the point, those are the rules of the game."

Jim leaned in slowly, his pale eyes as dead as stone. "If I tell you anything, I'd have to kill you, Vin. And that would be a buzz kill for the both of us."

So that tat wasn't just something the guy had seen on a wall in some two-bit piercing and body art parlor and gotten it inked onto himself because he thought it was cool. Jim was the real deal.

"I am so curious about you," Vin murmured.

"I suggest you get over that."

"Sorry, my friend. I'm a tenacious motherfucker. Lest you think I just won the lottery to get all this crap you're gawking at."

There was a pause, and then Jim's face broke into a small smile. "So you want me to think you have balls, do you."

"Believe it, my man. And word to the wise, they're as big as church bells."

Jim settled back in his chair. "Oh, really. Then why are you sitting on that ring?"

Vin narrowed his eyes, anger flaring. "You want to know why."

"Yeah. She's an incredibly gorgeous woman and she looks at you like you're a god."

Vin tilted his head to one side and spoke what had been banging around his head since the night before. "My Devina went out last evening wearing a blue dress. When she came home, she immediately changed out of it and took a shower. This morning, I pulled the thing out of the dry-cleaning hamper and there was a black smudge on the back of it—like she'd been sitting somewhere other than on a neat and tidy chair in a bar. But more than that, Jim, when I lifted the dress to my nose, I smelled something on the fabric that was a lot like men's cologne."

Vin measured every single one of the guy's facial muscles. Not one of them moved.

Vin sat forward in his chair. "I don't need to tell you that it wasn't my cologne, do I. And it might interest you to know that it smells a hell of a lot like yours—*not* that I think you were with her, but a man wonders when his woman's clothes smell like someone else, doesn't he. So you see, it's not because I don't have balls. It's because I wonder who else's she's been touching."

CHAPTER

10

Well, wasn't this a fucking party.

As Jim stared across the desk at his host, he realized it had been a long, long time since he'd met a man he'd been impressed by—but Vin diPietro did the trick. SOB was calm, cool, collected. Smart as shit, and not a pussy.

And it was evident that the guy truly believed Jim hadn't been with his girlfriend—at least, that was what Jim's instincts were telling him, and as they rarely were wrong, he was inclined to trust them. But how long would that last?

Christ, if only he could go back to the night before and leave Devina in that parking lot. Or . . . shit, just walk her inside where it was warm and let her find some other guy to work out her confusion and sadness with.

Jim shrugged. "You can't be sure she was with someone."

A shadow passed over Vin's face. "No. I can't."

"You ever cheat on her?"

"Nope. I don't believe in that shit."

"Neither do I." Strange . . . for once, lying sent a shaft through Jim's chest. In truth, he hadn't cared at the time that Devina was with someone else.

As silence flared again, Jim knew the guy was waiting

for another revelation so he sifted through his life, looking for ready-for-prime-time details. Eventually, he said, "I also speak Arabic, Dari, Pashto, and Tajik."

Vin's smile was part Cheshire, part respect. "Afghanistan."

"Among other places."

"How long did you serve?"

"A while." He hadn't been kidding about having to kill the guy if the information exchange went any further on his part. "And let's end the conversation there, if you don't mind."

"Fair enough."

"So, how long you been with your woman?"

Vin's eyes went over to an abstract drawing that hung on the wall by the desk. "Eight months. She's a model."

"Looks it."

"You ever been married, Jim?"

"Fuck, no."

Vin laughed. "Not looking for Ms. Right?"

"More like I'm the wrong kind of man for that sort of thing. I move around a lot."

"Do you. You get bored easily?"

"Yeah. That's it."

The sound of high heels on marble brought the guy's eyes to the study's doorway. It was obvious when Devina made her appearance, and not just because that faint, flowery perfume wafted into the air: Vin's stare went slowly down and then up, like he was seeing her for the first time in a while.

"Dinner is ready," she said.

Jim looked into the bank of glass across the room and studied her reflection. She was, yet again, poised under a light, the radiant glow making her stand out against the backdrop of the night view—

He frowned. An odd shadow floated behind her, like a black flag waving in the wind . . . as if she were being trailed by a ghost.

Jim whipped around and blinked hard. As his eyes searched the space behind her . . . they found a whole lot of absolutely nothing. She was just standing beneath a light, smiling at Vin as the guy came up to her and kissed her mouth.

"You ready to eat, Jim," the man said.

How about a head transplant first, then the frickin' pasta. "Yeah, that'd be good."

The three of them walked down through the various rooms to yet another marble table. This one was big enough to seat twenty-four, and if there were any more crystal hanging from the ceiling above, it you'd have sworn you were in an ice cave.

The flatware was gold. And no doubt solid.

Are you kidding me, Jim thought as he sat down.

"As the cook's on vacation," Vin said as he settled Devina in her chair, "we'll just serve ourselves."

"I hope you like what I made." Devina picked up her damask napkin. "I kept it simple, just some Bolognese sauce over homemade linguine. And the salad is nothing but microgreens, artichoke hearts, and red peppers with an ice wine vinaigrette that I whipped up."

Whatever it was, the stuff smelled amazing, and looked even better.

After big bowls with gold on their edges were passed around and plates were filled, everyone started eating.

Okay, Devina was a spectacular cook. Period. That micro-whatever with the ice-la-di-da dressing was flat-out amazing . . . and don't get him started on the pasta.

"So the work on the bluff house is coming along well," Vin said. "Don't you think, Jim?"

This launched an hour-long discussion on the construction, and Jim was once again impressed. In spite of Vin's digs and his flashy wardrobe, he'd clearly had firsthand experience with the job Jim and the boys were doing—as well as everything the electricians and the plumbers and the siders and the roofers got up in the morning for. The guy knew tools and nails and boards and insulation. Hauling and waste removal. Blacktopping. Permits. Regulations. Easements.

Which made all his attention to detail seem not like that of a nitpicking asswipe owner, but a fellow workman with high standards.

Yup, he'd definitely been a rough palm, at one point.

". . . so that's going to be an issue," Vin was saying. "The weight on the load-bearing walls in that four-story cathedral foyer is going to be over code. The architect is worried about it."

Devina spoke up for once. "Well, couldn't you just make it shorter? Like, closer to the ground?"

"Ceiling height's not the issue—it's the steep angle and the weight of the roof. I think we can solve the problem by upgrading to steel beams, though."

"Oh." Devina wiped her mouth as if she were embarrassed. "That sounds like a good idea."

As Vin went off on another tangent about the house, Devina took a special interest in folding the napkin in her lap.

Shit, the guy might know from construction, but you had to wonder: If you'd asked him what his woman's favorite color was, would he have said the right one?

"So this was a great meal," Vin said eventually. "To the chef."

As he lifted his wineglass and gave Devina a nod, she ate up the attention, positively glowing with happiness. Then again, he'd just spent the balance of the meal talking about something she wasn't familiar with, relegating her to a shut-out observer seemingly without a care.

"I'll clear and bring in dessert," she said, getting to her feet. "No, please, sit. It won't take a moment."

Jim lowered himself back into his chair and focused on Vin. In the quiet that bloomed while Devina went in and out of the butler's door with the dishes, you could practically smell the wood burning between the guy's ears.

"What's on your mind," Jim asked.

"Nothing." A quick shrug was followed by a sip of wine. "Nothing whatsoever."

Dessert was homemade cherry-and-chocolate-chip ice cream and coffee so strong it could put hair on your chest. The combination was sublime, and yet it wasn't sweet or savory enough to clear the frown from Vin's eyebrows.

When the dessert plates were empty, Devina got to her feet again.

"Why don't you two go back to the study while I clean up in the kitchen?" She shook her head before Jim could offer to help. "It won't take a minute. No . . . honestly, let me do it. You two go back and talk."

"Thank you for dinner," Jim said as he got out of his chair. "Best meal I've had in ages."

"I second that," Vin murmured while tossing his napkin onto the table.

When they were in the study once again, Vin went to the wet bar in the corner. "Hell of a cook, isn't she."

"Yeah."

"Brandy?"

"Nah, thanks." Jim paced around, looking at the leather-bound books on the shelves, and the paintings and drawings and framed U.S. stamps. "So you build things up in Canada, too?"

"I'm all over the country, actually."

Vin picked up a fat glass and poured himself a couple of inches, then sat down behind the desk. While he swirled the brandy sniffer, he swept a wireless mouse around and the planes of his face lit up as the screen saver on his computer flickered off.

Jim stopped in front of the drawing Vin had fixated on when he'd been thinking of Devina. The depiction was of a horse . . . sort of. "This artist do a lot of acid?"

"It's a Chagall."

"No offense, but it's weird."

Vin laughed and regarded the piece of art . . . or shit, depending on your taste . . . with grave appreciation. "It's relatively new. I got it the night I met Devina. God, I haven't looked at it for a while. Reminds me of a dreamscape."

Jim thought about the life the guy must live. Work, work, work . . . come home . . . not see all the expensive stuff he owned.

"Do you see your girlfriend?" Jim said abruptly.

Vin frowned and took a sip of his brandy.

Well, wasn't that the answer.

"It's none of my business," Jim murmured. "But she really sees you. You're a lucky man."

Vin's brows drew together, and as the silence expanded, Jim knew he was running out of time for tonight. Chances were good he was going to be shown the door in another fifteen or twenty minutes, and although he had a feeling he'd ID'd Vin's problem, he wasn't even close to the goal line, so to speak.

He thought of the little television hanging from the ceiling in that hospital room and of the two chefs who had gotten him into this dinner-from-Hell situation.

"So . . . you got a TV around here?" he asked.

Vin blinked and seemed to come back into focus. "Yeah, check this out."

Getting to his feet, he picked up a remote and came around the desk while punching buttons. All at once, the shelving split across the way and a flat-screen the size of a twin bed came forward.

"Man, you love your toys, huh," Jim said with a laugh.

"I so do—I'm not going to lie."

The two of them parked it in the chairs in front of the desk as Vin played with more buttons. While the channels switched, Jim felt like a schizoid as he prayed for a clue from what was shown—looking for guidance from the television? Next thing he knew he was going to think satellites were tracking his every move.

Oh, wait . . . been there, done that.

As the screen flashed, he took note of the various shows: *Who Wants to Be a Millionaire?* Vin had and he now was. *Lost?* Well, duh, that made two of them—though Jim was the only one who knew it. *Home Improvement?* Plenty of that to go around on both sides—but it was hardly a newsflash.

The channel changing stopped on Leonardo DiCaprio in some kind of movie.

"There's actually a better model coming out this year," Vin said, putting the remote to the side. "It's going in the new house."

Jim tried to read into what was going on in the movie, but it was just Leo dressed like something out of a renaissance fair emoting to a chick in a similar wardrobe.

Shit, no help.

"Jim, I got to be honest." Vin's cool gray eyes were clear. "I don't know what the hell you're playing at here, but I like you, for some reason."

"Ditto."

"So where does this leave us?"

Just what Jim was wondering.

Up on the screen, things were abruptly not going well for Leo. Medieval-esque "bad guys" were doing a snatch-and-drag of the poor bastard. "What the hell movie is this?"

Vin fired up the remote and an info strip popped up at the bottom of the screen:

The Man in the Iron Mask. Leonardo DiCaprio, Jeremy Irons (1998).

Only got two stars, evidently—

Oh, fuck him. The Iron Mask? Damn it, the last place he wanted to be was back in that club. Especially with—

Devina appeared in the doorway of the study. "I don't suppose you two would like to go out?"

Well, if that wasn't an opening.

Jim cursed to himself as he tried to imagine being there with her again—only this time under the watchful, suspicious eyes of her boyfriend. And he'd thought this whole dinner thing had been awkward?

Except the movie had to be a sign, right? The four lads said he'd have help.

"Yeah, let's head downtown," he muttered. "To the . . . How about the Iron Mask."

Devina's eyes flared as if she were shocked by his choice of club.

Schmega dittos there.

There was some conversation at that point and Vin got to his feet. "Okay, if that's what you two want, I'm game." He went over to his woman, and like he was trying to make an effort, leaned in and kissed her. "I'll get your coat."

Devina turned away with him and followed her man down the hall. Jim, left behind in the study, dragged a hand through his hair while wishing he could rip the stuff out of his head.

Maybe he had to stop thinking TVs were sending him messages. Because this was a dumb fucking idea.

CHAPTER

11

Marie-Terese saw the man first.

As she stood by the bar closest to the Iron Mask's front door, she was inspecting the crowd when he walked into the club. It was, as they say, right out of the movies: Everyone else disappeared the instant he came in, the other people fading into dim, blurry shadows while she focused on him and him alone.

Six-three-ish in height. Dark hair and pale eyes. Suit like something out of a Fifth Avenue window display.

On his arm was a woman in a red dress and a white fur coat, and beside him was a taller guy with a brush cut and a military manner. None of them fit in among the crowd of leathered and laced and chained, but that wasn't why she stared.

No, the staring thing was all about the man himself. He was eye-catching in the same sharp, hard way her ex had been: a wealthy man with a shot of gangster in him, a guy who was used to being in charge of whatever was going on around him . . . and someone who was probably about as warm and caring as a meat locker.

Fortunately, shutting down her instant attraction was easy: She'd already made the mistake of assuming wealth and power made guys like that some kind of modern-day dragon slayer.

Very bad assumption. Sometimes dragon slayers ... were just slayers.

Gina, another one of the working girls, came up to the bar. "Who *is* that by the door?"

"A customer."

"Of mine, I hope."

Marie-Terese wasn't so sure of that. Going by the looks of that brunette with him, he had no reason to buy sexual companionship—wait ... that woman ... she'd been here the night before, hadn't she, and so had the other guy. Marie-Terese remembered them for the same reason they stood out tonight—they didn't belong here.

As the trio sat down in a dark corner, Gina adjusted her wing-and-a-prayer bustier and pushed at her now-red hair. Last month it had been white and pink. Month before that jet-black. She kept this up and she was going to be sporting a Telly Savalas, thanks to all the chemical warfare on her roots.

"I think I'll just go over and introduce myself. Laters."

Gina sauntered off, her black latex skirt and stiletto boots the kind of thing she wore with pride. Unlike Marie-Terese, she got off on what she did for a living and even had ambitions to become what she referred to as a "major mul-timedia erotica star" along the lines of Janine Lindemulder or Jenna Jameson. Whoever they were. Marie-Terese knew their names only because Gina talked about them like they were the Bill Gates of porn.

Marie-Terese hung back and watched the drive-by. As Gina sauntered up, the woman in the white fur took one look at what was so obviously for sale and her stare went blade sharp. Which was unnecessary. Her businessman boy-friend didn't give Gina a glance—he was too busy talking to his buddy. And all the back-off-that's-my-man did was encourage the come-on: Gina positively preened in front of that territorial hatred, lingering until the man finally looked up.

He didn't focus on what was in front of him, though. He gaze shifted past Gina's latex buffet and trained on Marie-Terese.

Instant. Cosmic. Attraction. The kind you couldn't hide from other people and you couldn't bottle up and you couldn't turn off if you ever got the chance to act on it. With their stares locked, they were both naked and in each other's arms, not for hours, but for days.

Which meant she wasn't going anywhere near him and not because he had a possessive girlfriend. If what she'd felt at first around her ex had been trouble, this moment between her and that stranger had the potential for catastrophe.

Marie-Terese turned away and wound through the crowd, seeing nothing in front of her or around her. Those steel gray eyes of that man consumed her, and though she knew he couldn't see her anymore, she could have sworn she felt him staring at her still.

"Hey, honey."

Marie-Terese glanced over her shoulder. A pair of college boys dressed in hip-riding jeans, Affliction T-shirts, and skulled-out accessories—i.e., the bell-bottoms of the twenty-first century—had come up behind her and were once-overing her body. Given the sly way they looked at her, it was pretty clear they had pockets full of their daddies' money and heads vacant of everything but the confidence typical of big, dumb football players.

She also got the impression they were on something: Their eyelids twitched rather than blinked, and both had lines of sweat over their upper lips.

Great. Just what she needed.

"How much for me and my friend?" the one who'd spoken up said.

"I think you'd better go see someone else." Gina had no problems with threesomes, for instance. Or video cameras. Or camera phones. Or other women. Hopefully she drew the line at the Catherine the Great equine stuff, but you couldn't be sure—it was entirely possible that a lusty whinny meant "suck harder" to her.

Mr. Talker got in close. "We don't want anyone else. We want you."

Taking a step back, she looked them both right in the eye. "Find someone else."

"We have money."

"I'm a dancer. That's all I get paid to do."

"Then why haven't you been up in any of the cages?" He leaned in again and she got a whiff of his cologne: eau de beer. "We've been watching you."

"I'm not for sale."

"Bullshit, baby doll."

"If you continue to harass me, you're going to get banned from this club. All it takes is one word from me to management. Now back the hell off."

Marie-Terese walked away, knowing damn well they were pissed and not caring in the slightest—thank you very much, Trez. As much as she hated asking for help from the man, she would in a heartbeat if it meant keeping herself safe.

Over at the bar in the back, she ordered a Coke with extra ice and regrouped. It was still early, only about ten thirty, which meant she had another four or so hours.

"Those two steakheads giving you trouble?"

She looked up at Trez and smiled. "Nothing I couldn't handle." She eyed the leather coat in his hand. "You off?"

"Just over to my brother's for a meeting. Listen, the bouncers are all tight and I should be back in about an hour, two at the most. But you call me if you and the girls need anything, 'kay? Phone's going to be on the whole time. I can be back in the blink of an eye."

"Will do. Drive carefully."

He gave her hand a squeeze and strode through the crowd, his height dwarfing everyone in the club.

"That your pimp? Maybe we should just talk to him."

Marie-Terese glared over her shoulder at the college guys. "He's my boss, and his name's Trez. Why don't you go and introduce yourselves to him?"

"You think you're too good for us?"

She turned and faced them. "Do yourself a favor and leave me alone. Unless you want to be taken out of here in an ambulance."

The one who had been doing all the talking smiled, revealing sharp white teeth. "Do *us* a favor and stop thinking that whores like you have the right to an opinion."

Marie-Terese recoiled—but only on the inside. "Does your mother know you talk to women like this?"

"You are not a woman."

Marie-Terese's throat closed up hard. "Leave me alone," she said hoarsely.

"Make us."

Vin scanned the crowd for the dark-haired woman and got frustrated when he couldn't find her. They'd made eye contact for one electric moment and then she'd disappeared into the sea of bodies like a ghost.

He'd seen her before. He couldn't place where ... but he'd definitely seen her before.

"Who are you looking for?" Devina said in a low voice.

"No one." Vin nodded at a waitress, who came over quickly.

After drinks had been ordered, Devina edged closer and eased in, her breasts pushing against Vin's biceps. "Let's go back."

"Back where?"

"To the private bathrooms."

Vin frowned as a dark-haired woman in the far corner turned. . . . No, it wasn't the one. Maybe ... no, not her either.

Black hair, blue eyes, heart-shaped face that he wanted to take into his hands. Who was she?

"Vin?" Devina pressed her lips behind his ear. "Let's go ... I'm hungry."

Unlike the night before, this do-me-now stuff annoyed more than tempted him. He knew damn well that the seduction routine was less about sex between the two of them, and more about that prostitute coming over and pulling a whole lot of how-about-some-of-this. The thing was, Devina didn't mind including other women as long as it was on her terms—and evidently those didn't include half-dressed ladies of the night making like they wanted to mount him and ride him off to an orgasm in public.

Nope, the women had to be more attracted to Devina than him for her to be cool with it.

"I want some privacy," she purred.

"We have a guest."

"It won't take long." Her tongue licked up the side of his neck, making him feel like he was a fence post getting pissed on. "I promise you that. I'm hungry, Vin."

"Sorry." His eyes searched the crowd. "I'm full at the moment."

Devina dropped the act and sat back in the seat. "Then I want to go home."

At just that moment, the waitress came over with a beer for Jim, a shot of Patrón for Vin, and a Cosmo for Devina.

"We can't leave now," Vin murmured as he gave the woman a hundred and told her to keep the change.

"But I want to go home." Devina crossed her arms over her chest and pegged him right in the eye with the demand. *"Now."*

"Come on, Devina. Enjoy your drink—"

Before he could tell her there'd be plenty of privacy as soon as they got back to the duplex, Devina cut him off with, "Maybe I'll just go buy that red head for myself then, since you're not going to take care of me."

Right, okay. Wrong thing to say. Absolutely wrong button to hit.

Easing to the side, Vin took the keys to the M6 out of his pocket. "Do you want me to walk you to the car? Or do you need cash for the prostitute?"

Devina's eyes flashed black in the silence that erupted between them. But she should have known not to play hardball with him.

After a moment, she snatched the key out of his hand.

"Oh, I wouldn't dream of troubling you. Jim will walk me out. That way you can stay and enjoy the view some more."

With a small nod, Vin glanced at the other man. "Jim, would you mind doing the honors?"

The guy slowly lowered his beer. "Look, if she wants to go—"

"Then she's free to. And she wants you to escort her to the car."

The poor bastard looked as if he'd rather have his fingers filed into stubs than get in the middle of things, and Vin didn't blame him.

Uncrossing his legs, Vin stood up. "Ah, hell, man, you just relax here and I'll—"

Devina shot to her feet. "Jim, please take me to his car. Now."

Vin shook his head. "No, I'm going to—"

"The hell you are," Devina snapped. "I don't want you taking me anywhere."

"It's cool," Jim muttered. "I'll do it."

The man got up, but he left his leather jacket, as if he were not expecting to be gone long. "I'm just taking her to the car. We clear on that?"

"Thanks, man." Vin sat down again and swallowed his Patrón on a oner. "I'll be here waiting."

Jim indicated the way to the door, and Devina walked off, her chin up and her shoulders back, her fur in her arms.

As Vin watched them go, it was times like this that made him question the ring thing. He'd done nothing to encourage the prostitute—he hadn't even looked at her.

But you had been staring at someone, an inner voice pointed out.

Vin resumed scanning the crowd, all of whom seemed to have black clothes and dark hair. Damn it ... why did she have to be in a club like this, where everyone was a brunette?

Except ... well, the *why* had been pretty obvious: She hadn't been dressed as a customer.

With a curse, he glanced up at one of the cages, where a woman was aglow in blue light, writhing as if she'd lost a cold penny down the front of her thong and wasn't allowed to use her hands to get it out. Was his dark-haired woman a dancer . . . or what that first female had been?

Oh, who the hell was he kidding. No doubt you could buy what was in the cages as well.

Still, prostitute or not, that had been some kind of moment when they'd locked eyes—the pull had been undeniable, even though it made no sense. It wasn't that he'd ever judge a woman for being a professional, but he couldn't imagine being with one who'd done that for a living. Was *doing* it for a living.

Nope. No way. Even if she were as safe as she could be, even if she chose to do it because she liked it, his mind was not hard-wired to share. There's was too much of his father in him, and the paranoia would kill him.

Cursing, Vin wondered how in the hell he'd gone from taking one look at the woman across a club to trying her on for a relationship. When he was already in one. And had a diamond the size of a grape waiting at home for his—

Abruptly, his dark-haired woman burst through the crowd in the back. She was walking fast, her shoulders knocking into people as she went, her face grim and tight. And right on her tail were a pair of guys who had necks larger than their heads and nasty expressions.

Like they were ten-year-olds about to pick the wings off a butterfly.

Vin frowned . . . and got to his feet.

CHAPTER
12

As Jim walked around the back of the Iron Mask, he was not cool with what was doing on so many levels. And his outlook did not improve as Devina slipped her arm through his and pressed herself close to him.

"It's chilly again," she said in a low voice.

Yeah, it was, but he wasn't going to warm her up like he had last night. "Let me help you put your coat on, then."

"No . . ." She stroked the fur that was over her arm. "I don't want to wear this right now."

Which, gee, wow, probably meant Vin had bought it for her.

This was *really* not a good turn of events.

Jim got her over to the BMW, and the moment she killed the security alarm with the electronic key, he opened the driver's-side door.

"I'm not good at stick shifts," she said, staring into the interior of the M6. "I really can't drive them." She waited like she expected him to say something. "Jim—"

"Let's get you into that car."

She glanced over at his truck, which was parked two spaces down. Although she didn't come out and say it, given the way she angled her head, she was asking him a question.

"I can't." Jim took a step back. "I'm sorry."

Devina hugged that white mink closer to her chest. "Didn't you like last night?"

"Of course I did. But I know him now, and no matter what you say in this moment, you will regret it later."

There was a long, tight moment; then Devina nodded and slowly sank into the bucket seat. Instead of closing the door or pulling the belt across herself, though, she just stared out over the steering wheel, the lights of the dash illuminating her gorgeous face.

"I'm sorry, Jim. I don't know why I asked. . . . It's not fair to you or him or me. I'm just so empty that I'm making bad choices and not acting right."

Shit, he knew exactly what that was like. "It's okay. People do that."

He crouched down so he could look into her eyes, and as he did, he got pissed with Vin. Didn't the guy know what he had? For fuck's sake, no one was perfect, and the spat they'd just had in the club proved that on both sides. But come *on*.

"Look, Devina, have you talked to him? Tried to explain . . ." Goddamn it, Jim couldn't believe the f-word was about to come out of his mouth. "Have you tried to explain how you're feeling?"

"He's always so busy." Her eyes were dark and deep as she looked over. "But maybe you would speak to him for me? Tell him that I love him and I want to be with him—"

"Wait . . . whoa . . ." Okay, that was almost as bad an idea as their having sex again. "I'm not the kind of guy—"

"Please. Jim, please. It's clear he likes you, and believe me, that doesn't happen all that often. You could just tell him that you and I talked out here and that I miss him even though he's in my life. I mean, I'm not a fool. I know what kind of man he is. Making money is always going to be important to him, and there are benefits to being with someone like that. But there has to be more." Her eyes seemed to flash. "Don't you think there has to be more to life, Jim?"

As he felt that ensaring pull reach out and grab onto him, he got to his feet. "Yeah, but you need to be saying those things yourself."

For a moment he thought he saw something hard flash in her eyes, but then she nodded again and stretched the seat belt across her breasts.

"Vin is not who I thought he was." Devina started the engine and put the M6 in gear. "I've been waiting for him to warm up and trust me and love me, but it hasn't happened, and I'm losing the strength to hang on, Jim, I really am."

"He's bought you a ring."

As her head whipped around, Jim was totally aware he'd not just overstepped his bounds, but bombed the shit out of them. Keeping her in Vin's life was the important thing, though.

"He has?" she breathed.

"Just hold on a little longer." Christ, maybe he could talk to Vin tonight. God knew Jim was a good liar, and in this case, for once his motivations were good: He could try and argue that marriage is something worth believing in. "Look, let me sit down with him, okay?"

"Oh, thank you." She reached out and squeezed his hands. "Thank you so much. I really do want this to work."

She blew him a kiss and shut the door. Stepping to the side, he watched her ease out of the parking lot and accelerate down Trade Street, the engine going through its gears slick as shit through a goose.

Jim frowned and thought that if that was what she classed as not knowing how to work a stick shift, he wanted to know exactly what proficient would be.

Man, he needed a cigarette.

With a rattle and a whir, a car pulled up to the brick wall of the club and parked under one of the staff-only signs.

Two barely dressed women with *Playboy* breasts and legs as thick as toothpicks got out and stopped when they saw him.

"Hey," the blonde said with a sexy smile. "You coming into the club?"

Her friend had an Amy Winehouse beehive and a necklace that spelled out SLUT in diamonds. "Yeah, how'd you like to *come* with us through the back door?"

The innuendo was way too obvious for Jim's taste, and that dangler around her neck meant he was far more interesting in going if she were involved—but if it saved him a trip all the way around the club in the cold night? Fine and dandy, thank you, ma'am.

Jim walked over as a bouncer opened the door for the ladies.

"He's with us," Blondie said to the guy. "He's my cousin."

"'Sup, man." The bouncer put out his knuckles and Jim gave them a pound. "Good to meet you."

After they were inside, the guy relocked the door and talked into the Bluetooth clipped on his ear. "Up front? Okay. Coming. Shit, girls, we got a rumble in general population. You're gonna wanna hang here till it's over."

"Oh, we'll find something to do," the blonde quipped.

"Or somebody," the beehive cut in, taking Jim's arm and rubbing up on him.

He disengaged himself. "I got a friend waiting for me."

"Male or female?" the blonde asked.

"Male."

"Perfect for a double date. Club's that way—see you in a bit."

The one with the beehive leaned up to his ear. "You think I look good now, wait'll you see my work clothes."

They hustled off through a door marked LADIES' LOCKER ROOM, leaving him in the dark hall thinking that if they were changing into something smaller than what they had on, the pair were going to come out dressed in postage stamps.

As he started down for the club proper, a dark-haired working woman turned the corner up ahead and came toward him. He recognized her instantly as the one Vin had actually been staring at when Devina's latex nemesis had been begging him for attention, and Jim was not happy to see who was on her tail: That pair of big, young guys were way too close, and they had looks on their faces like they'd chased her into this dim, secluded hallway because they wanted something she clearly wasn't interested in giving them.

Jim glanced up and back. The corridor was a good forty feet long and about ten feet wide, and aside from a door marked OFFICE, which was way far down by the exit, the locker room was the only shot she had at losing them.

And the bouncers were already busy with some kind of disturbance.

Jim planted his feet and got ready to intervene . . . when from out of nowhere, Vin appeared in the archway at the club end of things, looking like he'd come to the same this-ain't-right conclusion.

Striding down, Vin closed the distance fast, but the drama reached Jim first.

"I said no," the woman snapped over her shoulder.

"Your kind of female doesn't get to say no."

Okay, so the wrong thing to say, right there. Jim stepped into the path of the guys and spoke to the woman over his shoulder. "You all right?"

As she turned to him, it was clear by her hard face and her terrified eyes that she was keeping it together by force of will only. "Yup. Just taking a break."

"Why? Is your mouth tired already?"

Jim faced off at the guy who'd spoken. "Why don't you back the fuck off."

"Who are you? Another one of her pimps?" The SOB reached around and grabbed her wrist. "Why don't you let her do—"

Vin diPietro, who had closed the distance, moved like the street was still in his blood. Before Jim took action, he was on the unwelcome contact, catching the biceps of that arm and breaking the guy's hold on the woman by snapping the kid around. He didn't say a thing. Didn't have to. He was ready to pop the motherfucker, gray eyes no longer cool, but volcanic.

"Let go of my goddamn arm!" the punk yelled.

"Make. Me."

Jim glanced at the woman. "My buddy and I are gonna handle this. Why don't you grab a cup of coffee and tell those other two girls to hang with you. I'll give you a shout when the attitude adjustment is finished."

Her eyes drifted over to Vin. It was clear she didn't like accepting the help, but she wasn't stupid. Given the buzz in the college kids' eyes, there wasn't just booze fueling them, but some coke or meth, too. Which meant the chances of things going downhill fast were high.

"I'll call for a bouncer," she muttered as she opened the locker room door.

"Do me a favor," Vin said, still vapor-locked on his boy. "Don't call anyone."

She shook her head a little and ducked out of the hall.

And that was when the knife appeared in the quiet kid's hand.

Leaving Vin to deal with the chatty Cathy of the pair, Jim stepped forward and anticipated which direction the lunge with the blade was going to come from. Ah, yes, fidiot with the sharpie was going to cruise in from the right because he was right handed, so it was just a case of waiting—

Jim grabbed the guy in midcharge, snagging his wrist, whipping him around, and applying pressure to the joint until the weapon dropped to the floor. And just as he introduced the bastard's face to the wall, Vin broke into a fistfight, ducking a wide punch, then coming up with his bare knuckles like a boxer. His impact was a cracking stunner . . . but the trouble with illicit stimulants was that they carried, in addition to the possibility of felony and addiction, the certainty of anesthetic properties.

So the kid with the ugly, and now bloody, mouth didn't seem to feel a thing. He slammed a return hook into Vin's face and it was on. The pair of them went hog wild, turning the hallway into an MMA octagon—and check that shit out: Vin was both the aggressor and the punisher of the pair.

To give him plenty of room for the beat-down he was delivering, Jim dragged his deadweight out of the way, prepared to keep things civil as long as his load of crap kept the trouble and the opinions to a minimum.

Fucker had to open his mouth, though. Just had to: "Why do you give a shit what some whore does? She's just a heartbeat and a hole, for fuck's sake."

Jim's vision flickered on and off, but he got ahold of himself and glanced up at the ceiling. Sure enough there were pods at regular intervals—which meant this was all being recorded. Then again . . . he and Vin had been smart enough to let their opponents throw the first punch and take out the weapon, so legally they could argue self-defense.

But more to the point, two college-aged fuck-twits who'd been doing illegal drugs weren't going to want to report shit to the police.

So no reason not to finish this.

Jim tightened his hold on that wrist, secured another grabber on the upper arm, and yanked the kid back so he could whisper in his ear. "I want you to take a deep breath. Come on, now . . . concentrate. Calm down and take a deep breath for me. That's it . . ."

Jim squeezed and squeezed some more until pain cut off any struggle. And when there was plenty of compliance with the even breathing, he dislocated that arm right from its shoulder socket with a quick twist. The resulting scream was loud, but the music from the dance floor drowned out the echo. Which was why, all things considered, clubs were not a bad place for throw-downs.

As the kid sagged onto the floor, Jim knelt in front of him. "I hate hospitals. Just out of one myself. You know what they're going to do to someone with your kind of injury? They're going to put the arm back where it belongs. Here, let me show you."

Jim took the flopping limb and didn't bother telling the guy to breathe deep. He just applied the appropriate pressure so that the bone popped back into its home. No screaming this time—the SOB just passed out cold.

In the wake of his stab at being an ortho doc, Jim glanced up to see how things were going with the other half of the altercations—and got an eyeball full of Vin working his opponent's liver like it was bread dough. College Boy was wilting badly and looking royally licked, his hands up not to throw punches, but to ward them off . . . and his knees knocking together like his balance was going fast.

Which would have been great except for the fact they had trouble.

At the end of the hall, they were attracting attention, a clubgoer peering down the corridor.

The lights were dim, but not that dim.

They had to clear the fuck out.

"Vin, we got to go," Jim hissed.

The newsflash didn't register, and that wasn't a surprise, given the brutal focus Vin was bringing to his fight. Shit, screw the peanut gallery; if he was allowed to keep this up, he was going to kill the guy. Or at least turn the fool into a linebacker-size vegetable.

Jim stood up, prepared to intervene with more than words.

CHAPTER
13

Vin was having a fucking ball.

It had been years since he'd thrown punches at more than a bag of sand in the gym, and he'd forgotten how good it felt to physically express his opinion of an asshole—directly in the guy's face. Man, it all came back, the stance, the power, the focus.

He still had it. He could still fight.

The trouble was, like all good things, the party had to come to an end and it turned out not to be of the knocked-out-opponent variety—although given the way the college kid's pins were wobbling, if Vin had just a little longer . . .

But no, Jim broke up the fun, locking a heavy hand on Vin's shoulder and yanking him out of range. "We've got an audience."

Panting like an f'in bull, Vin glanced up the hallway. Sure enough, a guy with glasses and a mustache was staring at them all, his expression like he'd been witness to a car accident.

Before anyone could react, however, the back door to the club swung open and an African-American man came striding down toward the melee, looking like he was capable of tearing the front fender off a car. With his teeth.

"What the *hell* is going on in *my* house?"

Vin's dark-haired woman stepped out from the locker room. "Trez, the two in the skull shirts are the problem."

Vin blinked like a dummy at the beautiful sound of her voice, but then he refocused and muscled his kid face-first into the wall. "Feel free to finish what I started here," he said to the club's owner.

Jim pulled his loose bundle of frat boy off the floor. "This one had the knife."

The Trez guy looked the kids over. "Where's the weapon?" Jim kicked the thing over and the owner bent down and picked it up. "Police been called?"

Everyone glanced at the woman, and as she shook her head, Vin found himself unable to look away. From across the club she'd made his heart pound; up close she made the thing stop dead: Her eyes were so blue they reminded him of a summer sky.

"I think these boys are done," Trez said with approval. "Nice work."

"Where do you want them?" Jim asked.

"Let's take 'em out back."

Look at me, Vin thought at the woman. *Look at me again. Please.*

"Roger that," Jim said, and began hauling his load down the hall.

After a moment, Vin followed the example, pushing his guy along. When they came to the door, Trez opened the way like a perfect gentleman and stepped to the side.

"Anywhere you like," the owner said.

Jim 'liked' the brick wall to the left, whereas Vin preferred the opposite side—

Just as he dropped the kid on his ass, he froze.

The security lights around the door shone down over the heads of the boys, casting a solid blanket of illumination all the way to their feet. So their shadows should have been on the asphalt. They weren't. Both of them had dark halos on the brick behind their heads, a twin pair of smoky gray crowns that weaved ever so slightly.

"Oh . . . Christ," Vin whispered.

The one he'd been beating on glanced up with eyes that were more tired than hostile. "Why are you looking at us like that."

Because you're going to die tonight, he thought.

Jim's voice registered from a distance: "Vin? What's up?"

Vin shook himself, and prayed those damn shadows disappeared. No luck. He tried to rub his eyes in hopes of wiping them away—and found that his face hurt too much from the punches it took to handle that kind of attention.

And the shadows prevailed.

Trez nodded over his shoulder to the club. "If you two can head in, I'm going to have a word with this pair of shit-heads. Just so that they're perfectly clear on where things stand."

"Yeah. Cool." Vin forced himself to get moving, but as he came up to the door, he glanced over at the kids. "Be careful . . . watch yourselves."

"Fuck you," was what came back at him. Which meant they were taking it not as advice, but a threat.

"No, I mean—"

"Come on," Jim said, muscling him back into the building. "Let's go."

God, maybe he was wrong. Maybe he just needed to get his eyes checked. Maybe he was going to get a migraine in another twenty minutes. But whatever the explanation, he couldn't go back to where he'd been with this shit. He just couldn't handle that.

In the hallway, Jim took his arm. "You get knocked in the head bad?"

"Nope." Although, given how much his face was flaring up, that wasn't entirely true. "I'm fine."

"Whatever. Let's give the owner a minute out back and when he comes in again, I'll take you to my truck."

"I'm not leaving until I see that—"

Woman. There by the locker room door.

Vin headed for her, shutting all of his paranoid, wing-nut head spins down and concentrating on her. "Are you okay?"

She'd put a fleece on over her revealing getup, and the thing fell to her thighs, making her seem like the kind of woman you wanted to take into your arms and hold through the whole night.

"Are you all right?" he repeated when she didn't answer.

Her eyes, those stunning blue eyes of hers, finally swung over to his face . . . and he felt it again, that high-bore charge barreling through him, enlivening him.

Her lips lifted in a small smile. "The question is more . . . are you?" As Vin frowned, she made a motion around his face. "You're bleeding."

"It doesn't hurt."

"I think it's going to—"

Two other women bubbled out of the locker room like a pair of yappy dogs, talking a mile a minute, hands waving like tails, the gold chains around their waists bouncing and chiming like tags on a collar. Fortunately, they were all over Jim, but then again, they could have popped skirt and mooned Vin and he wouldn't have noticed.

"I'm sorry about those guys," he said to the dark-haired woman.

"It's okay."

God, her voice was lovely. "What's your name?"

The rear door to the club opened and the Trez guy strode over. "Thanks again for taking care of things."

Conversation sprang up, but Vin wasn't interested in anyone but the female in front of him. He was waiting for her to answer him. Hoping she would.

"Please," he said softly, "tell me your name."

After a moment, the dark-haired woman turned to the owner. "Mind if I clean him up in the locker room?"

"Go right ahead."

Vin glanced back at his comrade in harm. "You okay to hang out, Jim?"

The guy nodded. "Especially if it means you won't bleed all over my truck."

"I won't take long with him," the woman said.

Not a problem, Vin thought. As far as he was concerned, she could take forever—he stopped himself. Devina might have stormed off, but she was in his house, in his bed at this very moment. He owed her more than the way he was going on about this other female.

At least, you think you know where Devina is, his inner voice pointed out.

"Come on," the woman said to him as she opened the locker room door.

Vin looked back at Jim for some reason—and the expression he met was all about the watch-yourself-my-man.

Vin opened his mouth, prepared to be reasonable and get a grip.

"I'll be right back, Jim," was all that came out.

Slut. Whore. Prostitute.

He couldn't believe it. She was whoring herself out. Selling her body to men who used her for sex. The reality was incomprehensible.

At first, he hadn't been able to fathom what appeared to be going on. Bad enough if she'd been a bartender or a waitress or, God forbid, a caged dancer in a club like this—but then he'd seen her walking around with her breasts on display and her thighs bared to the eyes of other men.

And she got what she deserved for doing what she did: Those two young guys had tracked her like prey, treating her exactly as men treated women like her.

He'd followed along as the pair had trailed her into the hallway, and watched as that fight had erupted. He'd been unable to move, so great was his shock. Of all the things he had pictured her doing, of all the assumptions he had made about what her life here in Caldwell was like, this was not it.

This was not happening.

As the harassers got pounded in the corridor, he backtracked through the crowd and tore out of the front of the club in an urgent haze, having no idea what he was doing or where he was going. The chilly night air didn't clear his head or his confusion, and he went around to the parking lot with no plan whatsoever. When he got into his nondescript car, he shut himself in and breathed hard.

That was when the anger hit. Great waves of fury poured through his body, making him sweat and shake.

He knew his temper had gotten him in trouble before. He knew this boiling rage was a problem, and he remembered what he'd been taught in prison. Count to ten. Try to calm down. Call to mind the safety image—

Movement by the back of the club brought his head around.

A door opened and the two kids who'd been stalking her were dropped like bags of garbage onto the pavement by the ones who'd come to her rescue. A black man stayed out in the cold and spoke to both of the offenders for a moment and then returned into the club.

From behind the wheel, he stared hard at the young guys.

The lightning strike hit him as it always did, wiping everything out of the way: His rage condensed and then crystallized, locking on the pair by the back door, all the anger and the sense of betrayal and the fury and the confusion that woman had created getting trained on those two.

Moving in a daze, he double-checked that the false mustache and the glasses were where they were supposed to be. Chances were very good there were security cameras on the back of the club, and having been caught by the likes of them before, even in his rage he knew enough not to do this in front of prying lenses even with a disguise.

So he waited.

Eventually, the college kids got stiffly to their feet, one of them spitting out blood, the other holding his arm as if he were afraid it was going to drop off his torso. Facing each other, they argued, whatever harsh words they shared nothing but mute theatrics because he was too far away to hear what they were saying. But the fight didn't last long. They fell silent fairly quickly, as if they'd lost their collective will, and after some looking around, they lurched into the parking lot like drunks.

Probably because their heads were spinning from the beatings they'd taken.

When they passed by his car, he got a good look at them. Fair skinned, light eyed, both had an earring or two. Their faces were the kind you'd see in the newspaper, not in the criminal section, but under the header *College Sports*.

Healthy, young, with a lot of life ahead of them.

There was no conscious thought at all as he reached under the seat and then got out from behind the wheel. He shut the car door quietly and fell in behind the young men.

As he moved silently, he was action and nothing more.

The pair went to the last row in the parking lot and took a right ... going into a tight alley. With no windows.

If he had asked them to find some privacy, they couldn't have possibly been more accommodating.

He tracked them until they were halfway down the buildings, right in the middle of the double block. With smooth control, he leveled the muzzle at the strong, young back in front of him and paused with his finger on the trigger.

They were up ahead a good ten yards, their sloppy strides cutting through the slush, their shifting torsos presenting moving targets.

Closer would be better, but he didn't want to wait or risk spooking them.

He pulled the trigger, the loud *pop!* followed by a messy scramble and a thump onto the ground. The second of the pair wheeled around.

Which meant the kid got dropped by a bullet right through the front of the chest.

Satisfaction made him soar, though his feet stayed on the asphalt. The free expression of his anger, the prickling, orgasmic release, made him smile so wide that the frigid wind registered on his front teeth.

The joy didn't last. The sight of the two lying side by side and moaning doused everything that had bonfired his brain, leaving a whole lot of rational horror: He'd just fucked himself. He was on parole, for God's sake. What had he been thinking?

He paced around as they writhed in slow motion and bled red. He'd sworn he'd never find himself in this situation again. Sworn to it.

As he stopped, he realized both his victims were looking up at him. Given that they were still breathing, it was hard to be sure whether they were going to die or not, but more gunshots were not going to help the situation.

He tucked his gun into the small of his back and took off his parka, wadding it up into a pillow of Gor-Tex and down. He went over to the taller one first.

CHAPTER
14

He was beautiful, Marie-Terese thought.

The man who'd protected her was absolutely beautiful. Thick dark hair. Warm brown-toned skin. Face that even with its bruises was stunningly attractive.

Flustered by so much, Marie-Terese pulled out one of the stools in front of the makeup counter and got ahold of herself. "If you sit here, I'll get a washcloth."

The man who'd thrown down for her looked around, and she tried to ignore what he was seeing: the kicked-off, scratched-up stilettos, the torn miniskirt hanging from the bench, the towels strewn here and there, the pair of thigh-highs draped on the edge of the lighted mirror, the bags on the floor.

Given how amazing his black pin-striped suit was, this kind of cheap chaos was clearly not what he was used to.

"Please sit," she said.

The man's gray eyes came to rest on her. He was about eight inches taller than she was, and the width of his shoulders was easily two of her. But she wasn't uncomfortable around him. And she wasn't scared.

Man, his cologne was delicious.

"Are you okay," he said again.

Not a question, but a quiet demand. As if he wasn't going to let her do anything about the shape his face was in until he was certain she wasn't hurt.

Marie-Terese blinked. "I'm . . . fine."

"What about your arm? He locked on pretty damn hard."

Marie-Terese tugged up the sleeve of the fleece she'd put on. "See . . . ?"

He leaned in and his palm was warm as it wrapped around her wrist. Warm and gentle. Not grabbing. Not demanding. Not . . . owning.

Kind.

Abruptly, she heard that college kid's voice in her head: *You are not a woman.*

The nasty crack had been said to be cruel and to wound, and it had . . . but mostly because it had become what she felt about herself. Not a woman. Not . . . anything. Just empty.

Marie-Terese pulled her arm away from the man's touch and tugged the sleeve back in place. She couldn't handle his compassion. In some weird way, it was harder to bear than the insult.

"You're going to have a bruise," he said softly.

What was she doing? Oh . . . right. Washcloth. Clean him up. "Sit down here. I'll be right back."

Going into the shower room, she took a white towel from a stack by the sinks, grabbed a small bowl, and got some hot water running. As she waited for the stream to warm up, she looked at herself in the mirror. Her eyes were wide and a little crazy, but not because of the pair who'd been so grossly inappropriate and disrespectful. It was the ass kicker with the gentle hands sitting on the stool outside . . . the one who looked like an attorney, but fought like Oscar De La Hoya.

When she came back to the makeup counter, she was a little calmer. At least until she met his eyes. He was staring at her as if absorbing what she looked like into his body, and what made her uncomfortable was not how he regarded her, but how she felt as he did.

Not quite so empty.

"Have you seen yourself?" she asked, just to say something.

He shook his head and didn't seem to care enough to turn away from her to the mirror behind him.

She put the bowl down and snapped on latex gloves before stepping up to him and dipping the washcloth. "You have a gash on your cheek."

"Do I."

"Brace yourself."

He didn't, and he didn't flinch as she touched the open wound.

Dab ... dab ... dab ... Then back to the bowl, a little tinkling sound as she rinsed the cloth out. Dab ... dab ...

He closed his eyes and parted his lips, his chest rising and falling evenly. Up this close, she saw the five-o'clock shadow over his straight jaw and each of his long, black eyelashes and all of his trimmed, thick hair. He'd had his ear pierced at one point, but only on the right side, and it had obviously been years since he'd worn anything in the hole.

"What's your name?" he asked, his voice guttural.

She never gave johns her real fake name, but he wasn't just a john, was he. If he hadn't come along when he had, things could have gotten ugly for her: Trez had been away from the club, the bouncers had been breaking up a skirmish out by the bar, and the hall led directly into the parking lot. Work of a moment and those two beefy college types could have had her in a car and ...

"You have blood on your shirt," she said, going back to the bowl.

Great conversationalist, she thought.

His lids lifted, but he didn't look down at himself. He looked at her. "I have other shirts."

"I'll bet."

He frowned a little. "Does that kind of thing happen to you often?"

With anyone else, she would have shut the question down with a quick *of course not*, but she felt as though, given what he'd done in the hall for her, he deserved something more truthful.

"Any chance you're undercover?" she murmured. "Not that you'd necessarily tell me, but I have to ask."

He reached into the breast pocket of his coat and took out a card. "There's no way I'm a cop. I'm not as illegal as I used to be, but I wouldn't be eligible for a badge even if I wanted one. So ironically, you can trust me."

She looked over what he gave her. *The diPietro Group.* Address here in downtown Caldwell. Very expensive card stock, very flashy professional logo, and a lot of numbers and e-mail addresses to reach him at. As she put the thing down on the counter, her instincts told her the part about his not being with the Caldwell PD was right. But the trust thing? She didn't trust men anymore.

Especially ones she was attracted to.

"So does that happen a lot?" he said.

Marie-Terese went back to work, wiping off his face, working her way down his cheek to his mouth. "Most people are okay. And management looks out for us. I've never been hurt."

"Are you ... a dancer?"

For a moment, she entertained a fantasy where she told him that all she did was hang out in one of those cages, showing off some moves, being nothing but eye candy. She could guess what he would do. He'd take a deep breath of relief and start relating to her as if she were just any other woman who'd caught his eye. No complications, no implications, nothing but some flirting between two people that might lead to bed.

Her silence made him take a breath, and it wasn't the oh-good kind. As he exhaled, the muscles that ran up his neck tightened into stark cords, like he had to fight back a wince.

This was the thing: She was never again going to have a

normal get-to-know-you with a man. She had a dark secret, the kind that you had to gauge how many dates could pass before you had to reveal it—otherwise you were a liar by omission.

"How bad are your hands?" she said to fill the void.

When he held them out, she inspected his knuckles. The right ones were bruised and bleeding, and as she put the washcloth to use on them, she asked, "Do you come to the rescue of women a lot?"

"No, I really don't. You're missing an earring, by the way."

She touched her lobe. "Yeah, I know. I meant to put another pair on today. But . . ."

"I'm Vin, by the way." He put his palm out and waited. "Nice to meet you."

Under other circumstances, she would have smiled at him. Ten years and a lifetime ago, she would have had to smile as she put her palm in his and they shook. Now, she just felt sadness.

"Nice to meet you, too. Vin."

"Your name?"

She took her hand from his and ducked her head to concentrate on his knuckles. "Marie-Terese. My name . . . is Marie-Terese."

She had such lovely eyes.

Marie-Terese of the lovely French name had absolutely lovely eyes. And she was gentle with her hands, carefully cleaning him up with that warm washcloth as if his nicks and scratches were something important.

Shit, he wanted to get into another fight just so she could nurse him again.

"You should probably go to the doctor," she said, patting the little towel across his cracked knuckles.

Absently, he noted that the terry cloth had started off white but now was pink from his blood, and he was glad that she'd put on the latex—not because he was HIV positive, but because he hoped the gesture generalized and meant she protected herself in what she did for a living.

He'd hoped all she did was dance. He really had.

She rinsed out the washcloth. "I said, you should see your doctor."

"I'll be fine." But would she? What would have happened if he and Jim hadn't come along?

God, there were so many questions he had all of a sudden. He wanted to know why someone like her was in this line of work. He wanted to know what harshness had brought her to the place she was at. He wanted to know ... what he could do to help, not just tonight, but tomorrow and the day after that.

Except none of that was any of his business. More to the point, he had a feeling that if he pressed her for details, she would close up on him.

"Can I ask you something?" he said, because he couldn't help it.

She paused with the cloth. "Okay."

He knew he shouldn't do what he was about to, but he could not fight the overwhelming draw of her. It had nothing to do with his mind and everything to do with his ... okay, *heart* was too stinkin' melodramatic. But whatever was driving him came from the center of his chest.

So fine, maybe his sternum was really into her.

"Will you have dinner with me?"

The door to the locker room swung wide, and the flame-haired prostitute who'd triggered Devina's exit strode in.

"Oh! Excuse me ... I didn't know anyone was in here." As she stared at Vin, her bright red lips widened into a false smile that suggested she'd known exactly who was in the locker room.

Marie-Terese moved away from him, taking her warm cloth and her bowl of water and her soft hands with her. "We were just leaving, Gina."

Vin took the cue and stood up. As he cursed the red-head's interruption, he caught an eyeball full of all the makeup on the counter and reminded himself that she had more of a right to be here than he did.

Marie-Terese went into the bathroom, and he imagined her cleaning out the bowl and rinsing the washcloth off, then snapping free the gloves. She was going to come out of there and he was going to say good-bye and . . . she was going to take off that fleece and go back into the crowd.

Staring at the door she'd gone through, while the prostitute next to him chattered away, the strangest feeling came over Vin. It was like a fog had gathered on the floor and sent tendrils up his legs and over his chest and all the way to his brain. He was suddenly hot on the outside and cold on the inside. . . .

Shit, he knew what this was. He knew exactly what was happening. It had been years, but he knew where this constellation of sensation went.

Vin grabbed onto the stool and let his ass fall back upon it. *Breathe. Just breathe, you big dumb bastard. Breathe . . .*

"So I saw your girlfriend left," the redhead was saying as she sidled up to him. "You want some company?"

Hands with blood-colored nails as long as talons reached out and drifted up his stained lapel.

He brushed her off him with a sloppy palm. "Stop it. . . ."

"You sure?"

Oh, God, he was even hotter on the outside, even colder on the inside. He had to stop this . . . because he didn't want to know the message that was coming to him. He didn't want the vision, the communication, the look-see into the future, but he was the telegraph who was powerless to deny receipt of the letters sent to him.

First the man in the elevator, then the two outside . . . now this.

He'd exorcised the dark side from himself years ago. Why was it back now?

The redhead rubbed herself against his arm and leaned into his ear. "Let me take care of you—"

"Gina, give it a rest, would you?"

Vin's eyes moved toward Marie-Terese's voice and he opened his mouth to try and speak. Nothing came out.

Worse, as he stared at her, she became a vortex into which his sight was sucked, everything but her going blurry. He braced himself for what was coming next—and sure enough, the trembling started at his feet, just as the fog had, and moved up his body, taking over his knees and his stomach and his shoulders. . . .

"Whatever, I don't need to beg," Gina said as she headed for the door. "Have fun with him—he looks too strung out to party anyway."

"Vin?" Marie-Terese came over. "Vin, can you hear me? Are you all right—"

The words bubbled up out of him, the voice not his own, the possession overcoming everything such that he knew not what he spoke because the message was not for him, but for the one he was addressing.

His ears heard only nonsense: "*Theio th lskow . . . Theio th lskow . . .*"

She blanched and stepped back, hand lifting up to her throat. "Who."

"*Theio . . . th . . . lskow . . .*

Vin's voice was deep and dark and senseless to him, even as he tried to hear the syllables correctly, tried to unscramble in his head what he was telling her: This was the very worst part of his curse—he could do nothing to affect the future, because he didn't know what he foretold.

Marie-Terese backed away from him until she smacked against the door, her face pale and her eyes popping wide. With shaking hands, she fumbled to open the thing and then burst out of the locker room, desperate to get away from him.

Her absence was what brought Vin back to reality, snapping the hold that had been clamped onto him, breaking the strings that had turned him into the puppet of . . . he didn't know what. He'd never known what. From the very first time he'd been taken over, he'd been clueless as to what it was or what he spoke of or why, of all the people on the planet, it had to be him who chose to bear this terrible burden.

Good God, what was he going to do? He couldn't function in his business or his life with intrusions like this. And he didn't want to go back to his years as a young kid when people thought he was crazy.

Besides, this shouldn't be happening. He'd taken care of this.

Planting his palms onto his knees, his let his head sag on his shoulders, his breathing shallow, his locked elbows all that held him upright.

That was how Jim found him.

"Vin? What's doing, big man? You got a concussion?"

If only that were the case. He'd so choose a brain hemorrhage over the speaking-in-tongues thing.

Vin forced his eyes over to the other man. And because his mouth evidently wasn't through with its independent streak, he heard himself say, "Do you believe in demons, Jim?"

The guy frowned. "Excuse me?"

"Demons . . ."

There was a long pause; then Jim said, "How 'bout we get you home? You don't look right."

Jim's pointed pass on the question was a reminder of the polite way people dealt with the freaky in life. There were a lot of other reactions, though, from Marie-Terese's taking off at a dead run to outright cruelty—which was what he'd gotten as a kid.

And Jim was right. Home was exactly where he needed to go, but damned if he didn't want to find Marie-Terese and tell her . . . what? That between the ages of eleven and seventeen he'd had these "spells" happen to him regularly? That they'd made him lose friends and gotten him labeled a freak and forced him to learn how to fight? That he was sorry she'd gotten scared twice tonight?

More to the point, that she needed to take whatever he'd spoken as the gospel truth and protect herself? Because he was never wrong. Fuck him to hell and back . . . but whatever he said always happened.

Which was how he knew it was never good news. Later,

someone on the periphery, or maybe the person him- or herself, would tell him what he'd said and what it meant. God, how the aftermath of the truth had horrified him. When he'd been young and had scared easier, he would go to his bedroom and shut the door and huddle under the covers, a shaky mess.

Just like he saw dead people, he foretold the future. The bad, bloody, destructive kind.

So what kind of trouble was Marie-Terese in?

"Come on, Vin. Let's go."

Vin looked toward the locker room door. Probably the kindest thing he could do for the woman was leave quietly— all that explaining was only going to draw her in deeper and frighten her more. But that wasn't what was going to help her avoid whatever trouble was coming her way.

"Vin . . . let me take you out of here."

"She's in danger."

"Vin, look at me." The guy pointed to both of his own eyes. "*Look at me*. You are going home now. You got your head knocked around in that hall, and apparently you just gave passing out some serious consideration. I get the no-doctor bit, fine. But you're talking out your ass if you think I'm going to let this shit go on any longer. Come with me—now."

Damn it, this fuzzy aftermath, with the disorientation and confusion, with his fear about what he'd said and his feeling out of control—shit, even the WTF expression on Jim's face . . . he remembered all of this. So many times . . . Vin had been through this so many times, and he hated it.

"You're right," he said, trying to let it all go. "You're absolutely right."

He could always come back and talk to her later, when things weren't so fresh. Like tomorrow. He'd come back tomorrow as soon as the club opened. It was the best he could do.

Getting off the stool carefully, he went over to where she'd left his business card on the makeup counter. Taking his pen out, he wrote two words on the back and then looked at all the bags. He knew exactly which duffel was hers. Out of the pink-and-purple Ed Hardys and the Gucci and the two identical Harajuku Lovers . . . there was a plain black one with not so much as a Nike logo on it.

After tucking the card inside that one, he strode for the door, his shoulders aching, his right hand starting to pound, his ribs sending him a sharp shooter every time he took a breath. The real shitkicker, though, was the headache between his temples that had nothing to do with the fight. He always had one after . . . whatever the hell that was.

Out in the hall, he looked both ways and saw no sign of Marie-Terese.

For a moment, the compulsion to find her struck strong and hot, but when Jim took his arm, he put his faith in the other man's rationality and allowed himself to be led over to the rear exit of the club.

"Wait here."

Jim knocked on the manager's door, and when the guy came out, there was another round of thank-yous and then Vin found himself breathing cold, clear air.

Christ . . . what a night.

CHAPTER
15

In the club's parking lot, Vin walked through rows of cars, but he wasn't tracking much ... at least not until he caught sight of the guy with the mustache and glasses who'd witnessed the fight from the head of the corridor. Fortunately, as they all passed each other, the man ducked his eyes like he didn't want any trouble and continued pulling on his parka, like he'd gone out to a car to get the thing.

When they got to the truck, Vin slid into the passenger seat and carefully rubbed his aching face.

Letting his head fall back, he despised the spinning, twirling tangle of pain that was making his skull scream. And the headache got even worse as it dawned on him that whereas he was headed back home, Marie-Terese had returned to work. Which meant she was with other men at this very moment, giving them—

He had to stop going there before he went totally mad.

Looking out the window, he watched streetlights flare and fade as Jim took lefts and rights and stopped at intersections on the way to the Commodore.

When they rolled to a halt in front of the high-rise, Vin released the seat belt and popped the door open. He had no idea whether Devina was going to be at the duplex or whether she'd have headed over to the place she still kept in the old meatpacking district of Caldie.

As he hoped she wasn't in his bed, he felt like a bastard.

"Thanks," he said to Jim as he stepped out. Before he shut the door, he leaned in. "Life is too frickin' crazy sometimes, it really is. . . . You never know what's going to happen, do you."

"You got that right." The guy ran his rough hand through his hair. "Listen, go be with your woman. Make up with her, okay?"

Vin frowned as something dawned on him. "Is this it? For you and me? Are we done now?"

Jim exhaled like he was disappointed his relationship advice was being ignored. "No, not hardly."

"Why won't you just tell me what you want?"

Jim just braced his forearm on the top of his steering wheel and stared across the seat. In the silence, his pale blue eyes seemed ancient. "I told you why I'm here. Go be nice to Devina and then get some sleep before you fall on your ass."

Vin shook his head. "Drive safe."

"I will."

The truck took off and Vin went up the graduated steps to the Commodore's lobby entrance. With the swipe of a pass card, he opened one of the doors and walked into the marble lobby. Over at the sign-in desk, the older, overnight security guard glanced up, caught a look at Vin's puss, and dropped the pen he was holding.

Guess the swelling was kicking in. Which would explain why one of Vin's eyes was having trouble blinking.

"Mr. diPietro . . . are you—"

"Hope you have a quiet night," Vin said as he strode to the elevator doors.

"Thank . . . you."

On the way up the building, Vin got a good gander at what the security guard had gone penless over. In the darkened mirrors of the elevator, he stared at his busted nose and the scratch on his cheek and the beginnings of the shiner he was going to have in the morning—

All at once, his face started to pound with the beat of his heart. Which made him wonder if he hadn't seen his reflection whether it would have stayed quiet.

Up on the twenty-eighth floor, he stepped out into the hall and got his key ready. While he worked the lock, he had the sense that his life had taken a beating tonight along with that college kid. Everything felt off. Dislocated.

He hoped it wasn't the start of a trend.

Vin opened his door, took a listen, and got hit with a whole lot of exhaustion. There was no security alarm to deactivate, and from the second floor, he could hear the television mumbling: She was home. Waiting for him.

Shutting himself in, he turned the lock, engaged the alarm, and eased back against the wall. When he could stand it, he looked up the marble staircase and watched the blue flicker of whatever show was on.

It sounded like an old movie, some kind of Ginger Rogers–Fred Astaire flying-hoof special.

Guess he had to go up and face the music, so to speak.

As forties-era standards rippled out of the bedroom, he pictured Devina propped up on the Frette pillowcases, wearing one of her wispy chiffon nightgowns. When he walked in, she would be shocked at his face and would try to nurse him—and she'd want to apologize for bailing from the club in the same way she'd made up for being unreachable the night before.

Or she would try to. He didn't feel like having sex tonight.

At least . . . not with her.

"Shit," he muttered.

Damn him to hell, but he wanted to drive right back to that club, but not to try to rehab Marie-Terese's opinion of him. He wanted to pull out five hundred dollars and buy some time with her. He wanted to kiss her and pull her against his body and run his hands up the insides of her thighs. He wanted his tongue in her mouth and his chest against her breasts and he wanted her gasping and wet. He wanted her to let him take her.

The fantasy got him instantly hard—but it didn't last, neither the hot images nor the erection.

What killed the fantasy was the memory of her in that fleece. She'd been so small. So ... fragile. Not an object to be bought, but a woman in a brutal business, leveraging her body for cash.

No, he didn't want to be with her like that.

As the raw mechanics of the way she earned her money tackled him, Vin thought, of course she was in danger. Look at what had happened tonight. Men couldn't be trusted when their cocks were involved, and he himself was guilty of that kind of penile thinking. Just now, for example.

Desperate for a drink, Vin headed for the bar in the living room. Devina had turned the lights off, but the electric fireplace was on and the flames flickered around the walls, turning them liquid and making the shadows move like they were tracking his stride through the room.

With his fucked-up punching hand, he poured himself a bourbon, and as he drank it, his lip hurt on one side.

Looking around, he measured everything he had bought with money he'd made, and in the shifting illumination it seemed to melt around him, the wallpaper dripping off in oozing sheets, the shelves sagging, the books and the paintings morphing into Dalí-esque figments of their normal selves.

Amidst the distortion, his eyes went to the ceiling and he imagined Devina up above him.

She was just one more thing he'd purchased, wasn't she: He paid for her with clothes and travel and jewelry and spending money.

And he'd bought that diamond yesterday not because wanted her to have the stone as a token of love—it was just one more part of an ongoing transaction.

The fact was, he'd never told Devina he loved her ...

not because he was emotionally repressed, but because he didn't feel that way about her.

Vin shook his head until his brain sloshed around enough so that the room returned to normal. Tossing back the rest of the bourbon, he performed a refill. Which he drank.

'Nother refill. 'Nother polish-off. More of the pouring.

He had no idea how long he stood in front of the bar drinking on his feet, but he was able to measure the way the level in the bottle dropped. And after four inches, he decided to just finish what was in the thing, and took the Woodford Reserve with him over to the couch that faced the view.

Staring out over the city, he got really fucking drunk. Saturated. Plowed. Messed the fuck up until he couldn't feel his legs or his arms and he had to let his head fall back against the pillow because he couldn't hold it up anymore.

Sometime later, Devina appeared naked behind him, her reflection in the glass looming in the archway of the living room.

Through the haze of his numbed-out state, he realized that there was something wrong about her ... about the way she moved, about the way she smelled.

He tried to lift his head to see more clearly, but it was as if the damn thing were Velcroed to the back of the sofa, and though he strained until his breath jammed in his throat, he got nowhere.

As the room degraded once more, everything looking like a bad acid trip, he was powerless. Frozen. Both alive and dead.

Devina didn't stay behind him.

She moved around the couch, and his eyes stretched wide as she came in front of him. Her body was decayed, her hands twisted into claws, her face nothing but a skull with strips of gray flesh hanging from the cheeks and chin. Trapped inside his paralyzed body, he struggled to get away, but there was nothing he could do as she approached.

"You made the bargain, Vin," she said in a dark voice. "You got what you wanted and a deal is a deal. You can't go back on it."

He tried to shake his head, tried to speak. He didn't want her anymore. Not in his house, not in his life. Something had changed when he'd seen Marie-Terese, or maybe it was Jim Heron—although why that guy would matter he hadn't a clue. But whatever the cause, he knew he didn't want Devina.

Not in her beautiful form and certainly not in this one.

"Yes, you do, Vin." Her horrible voice wasn't just in his ears; it vibrated through his body. "You asked me to come to you and I gave you what you wanted and more. You made a bargain and you've taken everything I brought into your life, you've eaten it, drank it, fucked it—I'm responsible for it all and you owe me."

Up close, she didn't have eyes, just raw sockets that were black holes. And yet she saw him. Just as Jim had said, she *saw* right into him.

"You have what you wanted, including me. And there is a price and a payment for everything. My price . . . is you and me together forever."

Devina mounted him, putting a skeletal knee on each side of his thighs, planting her horrible, shredded palms on his shoulders. The stench of her rotten flesh clawed into his sinuses, and the hard edges of her bones cut into him. Ugly hands went for his fly and he shrank back inside his skin.

No . . . no, he didn't want this. He didn't want her.

As Vin struggled to open his mouth and couldn't budge his jaw, she smiled, her waxy lips parting from teeth anchored by black gums. "You're mine, Vin. And I always take what is mine."

Devina sprang his cock, which was hard with terror, and stood it up between her parted legs.

He didn't want this. He didn't want her. No . . .

"Too late, Vincent. It's time for me to claim you, not just in this world but the next."

With that, she took him, her decomposing body encompassing his, fisting his flesh in a cold, scratching grip.

The only thing that moved on him, apart from her, was his tears. They ran down his cheeks and onto his throat, getting absorbed by the collar of his shirt. Caged under her, taken against his will, he tried to scream, tried to get a—

"Vin! Vin—wake up!"

His eyes flashed open. Devina was right in front of him, her beautiful face drawn in panicked lines, her elegant hands reaching out to him.

"No!" he hollered. Yanking her out of the way, he lunged to his feet and overshot his mark, falling face-first into the carpet, landing as his glass did with a hard bounce.

"Vin . . . ?"

He jacked himself onto his back and brought his hands up to fight her off—

Except she wasn't coming after him anymore. Devina was sprawled on the couch where he had been, her glossy hair on the cushions he'd been leaning against, her perfect pale skin set off by an ivory satin nightgown. Her eyes were as his had been, wide, terrified, confused.

As he panted, he clutched his pounding chest and tried to decipher what was real.

"Your face," she said eventually. "God . . . your shirt. What happened?"

Who was she? he asked himself. The dream or . . . what he saw now?

"Why are you looking at me like that?" she whispered, covering the base of her throat with her hand.

Vin glanced down at his fly. It was closed and his belt was done up, his cock soft in his boxer briefs. Glancing around the room, he found everything was as it always appeared, in perfect, luxurious order, the flames from the fire setting the scene off to gorgeous effect.

"Shit . . ." he groaned.

Devina sat up slowly, like she was afraid of spooking him again. Staring down at the liquor bottle on the floor next to the couch, she said, "You're drunk."

True enough. Dead drunk. To the point where he wasn't sure he could stand . . . to the point where he could start to hallucinate . . . to the point that maybe none of that had just happened. Which would be a blessing.

Yeah, the idea that it was all nothing but a bourbon-fueled nightmare calmed him more than any amount of deep breathing.

With a surge, he went to stand up, but his balance was shot, so he lurched around and slammed into the wall.

"Here, let me help you."

He held up his hand to stop her. "No, stay . . ." *Away.* "I'm all right. I'm cool."

Vin collected himself and, when he'd steadied out, he searched her face. All he saw was love and concern and confusion. Hurt, too. She appeared to be nothing other than a spectacularly attractive woman who cared about the man she was looking at.

"I'm going to go to bed," he said.

Vin headed out of the room, and she followed him upstairs in silence. As he tried not to feel stalked, he reminded himself that she wasn't the problem. He was.

When he came to the doorway to the master bath, he said, "Gimme a minute."

After shutting himself in, he turned on the shower, took off his clothes, and got under the hot water. He couldn't feel the spray, even on his busted face, and took it as evidence that however drunk he thought he was, he should be a little more generous in his assessment.

When he stepped out, Devina was waiting with a towel for him. He didn't let her dry him off, even though she no doubt would have done a better job, and he put a pair of pajama bottoms on even though he normally slept naked.

They settled into bed, side by side but not touching, the television's flickering like that of a fireplace with blue flames. In a moment of madness, he wondered if the walls were going to melt up here, too, but no. They stayed the same.

On the TV, Fred and Ginger were dancing around, her gown swinging wide, his tails doing the same.

Either Vin hadn't been out for very long or this was a marathon on whatever channel she'd chosen.

"Won't you tell me what happened?" Devina said.

"Just a bar fight."

"Not with Jim, I hope?"

"He was on my side."

"Oh. Good." Silence. Then, "Do you need to go to the doctor?"

"No."

More silence. "Vin . . . what were you dreaming about?"

"Let's go to sleep."

When she reached for the remote to turn the TV off, he said, "Leave it on."

"You never sleep with the television on."

Vin frowned as he watched Fred and Ginger moving in sync, their eyes locked as if they couldn't bear to look away. "Tonight's different."

CHAPTER
16

Pounding on his door woke Jim up the next morning.
Even though he'd been dead asleep, he was instantly
conscious . . . and pointing the muzzle of a forty across the
studio. With the blinds drawn across the big window in the
front and the two small ones down over the kitchen sink,
he had no idea who it could be.

And considering his past, it might not be a friend.

Dog, who was tucked in beside him, lifted his head and
let out a ripple of inquiry.

"Not a clue who it is," Jim said, throwing the covers off
and going buck naked to the far side of the front drapes.
Parting them ever so slightly, he saw the M6 parked in his
driveway.

"Vin?" he called out.

"Yeah," came the muffled response.

"Hold on."

Jim put the gun back in the holster that hung on the
bedpost and pulled on a pair of boxers. When he opened his
door, Vin diPietro was standing on the other side, looking
like a hot mess. Although he'd had a wash and a shave and
changed into rich-guy casual clothes, his face was bruised
and his expression was grim as hell.

"You see the news yet?" he said.

"No." Jim backed up so the guy could come in. "How'd you find me?"

"Chuck told me where you lived. I would have called, but he didn't have your number." Vin went to the television and turned the thing on. As he flipped through the channels, Dog went over and gave him a sniffing.

Guy must have passed, because the animal sat on his loafer.

"Shit . . . I can't find it . . . it was all over the local news," Vin muttered.

Jim glanced at the digital clock by his bed. Seven seventeen. The alarm should have gone off at six, but he'd obviously forgotten to set the thing. "What's on the news?"

At that moment, the *Today* show turned it over to a local update, and the Caldwell station's almost beautiful announcer looked into the camera with gravity.

"The dead bodies of two young men that were found in the eighteen hundred block of Tenth Street early this morning have been identified as Brian Winslow and Robert Gnomes, both aged twenty-one." Pictures of the college meatheads he and Vin had taken care of flashed on the screen to the right of the blonde's head. "The two were the apparent victims of gunshot wounds, their bodies found by a fellow clubgoer about four o'clock this morning. According to a CPD spokeswoman, the pair were roommates at SUNY Caldwell and were last seen headed out to the Iron Mask, a local hot spot. No suspects have been named as yet." The camera angle changed and she turned into the new lens. "In other news, another peanut-butter recall has been . . ."

As Vin glanced over his shoulder, his demeanor was focused and calm, which suggested he was not unfamiliar with having his ass in a crack with the police. "That guy with the mustache and glasses who looked down the hall when we were fighting could be a problem. We didn't kill them, but chances are good it's going to get complicated for us."

True enough.

Turning away, Jim went over to the cupboards and took out the instant coffee. Only half an inch of grounds were left in the jar, not enough for one, much less two cups. Which was fine; it tasted like swill anyway.

He put the jar back and went to the fridge even though there was nothing in it.

"Hello? You there, Heron?"

"Heard what you said." And he wished like hell someone hadn't shot those two idiots. Getting into a fistfight was one thing. Being implicated in a shooting was another entirely. He was confident enough in his false identity on a local level—after all, it had been created by the U.S. government. But what he didn't need was his old bosses up in his face again, and getting flagged for murder by the CPD was going to pop him onto their radar immediately.

"I'd like to keep this as quiet as possible," he said, closing the refrigerator door.

"Myself as well, but if that club's owner wants to find me, he can."

That was right; Vin had given the prostitute they'd rescued his card. Assuming the black duffel had been hers, and she didn't toss the info, the link was there.

Vin leaned down and gave Dog a scratch behind the ears. "I doubt we're going to be able to keep totally out of this. I have excellent lawyers, though."

"I bet." Crap, Jim thought. He couldn't just bolt out of town—not with Vin's future hanging in the balance here in Caldwell.

Well, wasn't this complication just what the situation needed.

Jim nodded at his open bathroom. "Listen, I'd better get showered and go to work. The guy whose house I'm building can be an asshole."

Vin looked up with a half smile. "Funny, I feel the same way about my boss—except I work for myself."

"Least you're self-aware."

"More so than you. It's Saturday. So you don't have to go to the site."

Saturday. Damn, he'd forgotten what day of the week it was. "I hate the weekends," he muttered.

"Me, too—so I work my way through them." Vin glanced around and focused on the two laundry piles. "You could always neaten this place up."

"Why bother? The one on the left is the clean, the right is dirty."

"Then you should do your laundry, 'cuz there's a mountain-molehill thing going on that doesn't bode well for fresh socks."

Jim picked up the pair of jeans he'd had on the night before and tossed them onto the "mountain" of dirties.

"Hey, something dropped...." Vin bent down and picked up the little gold earring that had been in the front pocket since Thursday night. "Where did you get this?"

"In the alley behind the Iron Mask. It was on the ground."

Vin's eyes locked on the thing like it was worth more than the two bucks it had probably cost to make and the fifteen it had cost to buy. "Mind if I keep it?"

"Not at all." Jim hesitated. "Was Devina home? When you got back?"

"Yeah."

"Did you work things out?"

"Guess so." The guy disappeared the gold hoop into his breast pocket. "You know, I saw you handle that kid last night."

"You don't like to talk about Devina."

"My relationship with her is no one else's business but mine." Vin's eyes narrowed. "You've been trained to fight, haven't you. And not by some strip-mall martial-arts academy."

"Keep me posted if you hear anything from the police." Jim went into the bathroom and cranked on the shower. As the pipes groaned and rattled, an anemic spray arched out and fell onto the plastic floor of the stall. "And don't worry about locking the door behind you. Dog and I will be fine."

The guy met Jim's eyes in the little mirror over the sink. "You are not who you say you are."

"Who is."

Abruptly, a shadow passed over Vin's face, like he was remembering something horrible.

"You okay?" Jim frowned. "You look like you've seen a ghost."

"I had a bad dream last night." Vin dragged a hand through his hair. "Haven't quite shaken it."

Abruptly, Jim heard the guy's voice in his head: *Do you believe in demons?*

As Dog whimpered and started limping back and forth between the two of them, the hairs on the back of Jim's neck tingled. "Who was the dream about."

Not a question.

Vin laughed tightly, put a business card on the coffee table and went for the door. "No one. I didn't know who it was about."

"Vin . . . talk to me. What the fuck happened when you got home?"

Sunlight poured into the studio as the guy stepped out onto the stairwell's landing. "I'll let you know if I get contacted by the police. You do the same. I left my card."

There was no pushing the subject, clearly. "Okay, fine, you do that." Jim recited his cell number and wasn't surprised when Vin memorized it without writing it down. "And listen, you might want to stay away from that club."

Christ knew adding a set of jail bars to this equation was not going to make things easier. Plus, Vin had looked at that dark-haired prostitute the way he should have been staring at Devina—which meant the less time he was around her, the better.

"I'll be in touch," Vin said, before shutting the door.

Jim stared at the wooden panels as heavy footsteps went down the stairs and then a powerful engine started up. After the M6 crackled down the gravel drive, he went over and let Dog out and then hit the shower before his half-gallon hot-water tank had nothing but cold to offer.

As he soaped himself up, the question Vin had asked the night before echoed again.

Do you believe in demons?

Across town, Marie-Terese sat on her sofa and stared at a movie she wasn't watching. It was her . . . fourth in a row? Fifth? She hadn't slept the night before. Hadn't even tried to put her head on the pillow.

Vin was in her mind . . . in her mind and speaking in that strange voice: *He's coming for you. He's coming for you.*

When he'd gone into that bizarre trance in the locker room, the message that had come out of his mouth had been terrifying, but his fixated eyes had been even worse. And her first response? It hadn't been, *What the hell are you talking about?* No, she'd thought to herself, *How do you know?*

Having had no idea what to do or how to handle herself, much less him, she'd bolted out of the locker room and told his friend to go in there.

She looked down at the business card in her hand. Turning it over for the hundredth time, she stared at what he'd written: *I'm sorry.*

She believed that—

The ring tone that lit off beside her scared the hell out of her, making her jerk so badly the card flipped from her hand and went flying.

Catching her breath, she reached for the cell phone that was next to her on the sofa, but the call failed before she could see who it was and answer it. Just as well—she didn't feel like talking to anyone and it was likely just a wrong number.

The little Nokia was the only phone she had. The one in the kitchen that was wired into the wall didn't have a dial tone because she had never activated the line. The thing was, however private you could make a residential phone number, people could still penetrate the identity shield more easily than they could a mobile, and she was all about anonymity—which was why she had looked only at rentals that had utilities included in the monthly rate: It meant that the bills remained in her landlord's name, instead of being switched to hers.

As she put her phone down, she thought of the past, to the way things had been before she'd tried to leave Mark. Back then, her son's name had been Sean. Her name had been Gretchen. Their last name had been Capricio.

And she was actually a real, live redhead. Unlike Gina at the club.

Marie-Terese Boudreau was a total lie, with the only thing she'd kept true being her Catholic faith. That was it. Well, that and the debt with the lawyers and the private investigator.

At the time, after everything had gone down, she'd had the option of entering into the witness-protection program. But cops could be bought—God knew her ex and his capos had taught her that. So she'd done what she'd had to with the district attorney, and when Mark had pled out, she'd been officially free to run east, getting as far away from Las Vegas as she could.

God, she'd hated having to explain to her son that they were going to change the names they went by. She'd been worried that he wouldn't understand . . . except when she'd started to explain, he'd stopped her. He knew exactly why it had to happen and had told her it was so no one could know who they were.

That facile knowledge had broken her heart.

As her cell whistled again at her, she picked it up. There were few who had the number: Trez, each of the sitters, and the Center for Single Mothers.

It was Trez and the connection was bad, suggesting he was traveling.

"Everything okay?" she asked.

"Did you see the news?"

"I've been watching HBO."

As Trez started talking, Marie-Terese grabbed for the remote and went to the local NBC station. Nothing but the *Today* show—

The local update chilled her straight to the bone.

"Okay," she said to him. " All right. Yes, of course. When? Okay, I'll be there. Thanks. Bye."

"What's wrong, Mama?"

Before she looked over at her son, she gathered the reins of her face and reeled her expression in. When she finally turned toward him, she thought he seemed closer to three than seven in his pj's with his blanket dragging on the floor.

"Nothing. Everything's fine."

"You always say that." He walked over and shuffled up onto the couch. When she handed him the remote, he didn't change the channel to Nickelodeon. Didn't even glance at the TV. "Why are you looking like that?"

"Like what?"

"The bad time is back."

Marie-Terese reached over and kissed his head. "It's going to be okay. Listen, I'm going to have Susie or Rachel or Quinesha come over and sit with you for a while. I have to go in to work for a minute."

"Right now?"

"Yes, but I'll get you breakfast first. Tony the Tiger?"

"When will you be back?"

"Before lunch. Just after, at the latest."

"Okay."

As she went into the kitchen, she dialed the Center for Single Mothers' babysitter service and said a prayer as the ringing started up. When she got voice mail, she left a message and went through the motions of filling up a bowl with Frosted Flakes.

Her hands trembled so badly, they actually helped the cereal out of the box.

Those two college kids from the club were dead. Shot in the alley behind the parking lot. And the police wanted to talk to her because the clubgoer who'd found the bodies had reported seeing the pair harass her.

As she took out the milk, she told herself that it was just a coincidence. People got violently mugged downtown all the time, and those kids had clearly been on drugs. Maybe they'd been trying to make a buy and the transaction had gone south.

Please let it not have anything to do with her, she thought. Please let her old life not be catching up with her.

Vin's voice rippled through her head. *He's coming for you. . . .*

Resolutely shutting that part of things out so she didn't lose her mind with fear, she focused on the fact that in less than a half hour she was going to be sitting down with the police. Trez had seemed confident that her cover was going to stick, that the whole I'm-just-a-dancer was ironclad. But God . . . what if she were arrested for what she did?

See, this was another thing she'd learned from her husband: If you lived a life with a shaky foundation, the walls could cave in on you pretty damn quick once the cops got to asking questions.

It had turned out that was really why he'd had to hit the road. He and his "friends" had killed one too many of their "clients" in the "building" trade and the feds as well as the locals had come after them. The one saving grace for her was that as a mere wife, she hadn't had a clue about the way the mob had worked. His mistress, on the other hand, had known much more and been brought up on charges as an accomplice.

What a mess it had been. What a mess it still was.

Marie-Terese took the bowl of cereal to her son and got him one of their two TV trays. As she walked around, her heart was pounding so hard it was a wonder Robbie couldn't hear the thing, but she did her best to remain calm on the surface.

Clearly, he didn't buy the act. "Are we going to move again, Mama?"

She paused in the process of flipping open the tray's

legs. She didn't lie to her son—okay, not about the majority of things—but she wasn't sure how to coach her words.

But then there was no way to do that, was there.

As her phone rang again, she looked at him before she accepted the call from the sitters. "I don't know."

CHAPTER
17

As Vin drove through Caldwell's outer reaches, his efficiency was autopilot more than awareness, and it was hard to know what was riding him harder: the shit with those dead boys or that hideous dream about Devina.

The cops were absolutely going to show up at the Iron Mask for a hi-how're-ya-what-the-fuck, and if anyone said a peep about what had gone down in the hallway, they were going to want to see what those security cameras had caught. Which wouldn't be good news. Sure, neither he nor Jim had thrown the first punch or pulled a knife, but then, they were still breathing whereas the other two had had a matching set of lead pacemakers implanted in their chests.

And that horrible nightmare . . . it had been so real, he could still feel those bony hands locked onto his shoulders. Hell, as he thought about it, his cock shriveled behind his fly like the thing wanted to hibernate in his lower intestine.

You made a bargain and you've taken everything I brought into your life, you've eaten it, drank it, fucked it—I'm responsible for it all and you owe me.

Bargain? What bargain? As far as he knew, he'd made nothing of the sort with her. Or anybody else.

Whatever, he was arguing about what had been in a dream. Which was nuts.

Bottom line, he was going to end things with Devina as fast as he could—and not because his subconscious clearly had issues with her. The thing was, their relationship wasn't based on love and it wasn't even based on passion. Passion was sex with soul, and no matter how many times she'd made him come, only his body had been in it.

He'd thought that would be enough. He'd assumed that was what he wanted. But his first clue that something was off was when he couldn't even ask her the big question.

And then looking into Marie-Terese's eyes had sealed the deal.

Of course, it didn't mean that he and Marie-Terese were going to ride off into the sunset together; his reaction to her just told him there was a whole lot missing between him and the woman he'd thought he was going to marry.

God, the past tense in that was as jarring as a slap in the face.

Refocusing on the road, he cursed when he realized where he was. Instead of driving to his office, which was what he'd intended, he'd ended up on Trade Street, and as he passed by the front entrance of the Iron Mask, he slowed. There were two cop cars parked across from the club and a uniform by the main door.

The smart thing was to keep going.

And he did. Sort of.

Vin went to the next street and hung a left, making a box around the club and heading for where the cars parked in back. Just as he came into the lot, he stopped. There were more police cars in the rear, and on the next block over, yellow crime scene tape was stretched between two buildings.

So that was where the murders had taken place.

The beep of a car horn brought his eyes to the rearview mirror. Behind him was a dark green Toyota Camry . . . and Marie-Terese was in the driver's seat.

Popping the gearshift into neutral, he pulled the parking

brake and got out. As he walked over to her car, she put down the window—which he took as a good sign.

Man, he liked the way she looked with her hair back in a ponytail and just a red turtleneck and blue jeans on. Without all the makeup, she was truly beautiful, and as he leaned in, he smelled not perfume, but dryer sheets, the kind that were like sunshine in the nose.

Vin breathed deeply and felt his shoulders ease up for the first time since . . . yeah, right, like he could remember when.

"Did they call you, too?" she asked, staring up at him.

He shook himself back to attention. "The police? Not yet. You going to talk to them now?"

She nodded. "Trez called me about a half hour ago. I was lucky I could get a sitter."

Sitter? His eyes flipped to the steering wheel where her hands were. No wedding ring, but maybe she had a boy-friend . . . although what kind of man would let his woman do what she did every night? Vin would whore himself out first if she were his.

Crap . . . how was she going to get around the inevitable question about what she did at the club?

"Listen, if you need a lawyer, I know some good ones." Well, wasn't this the day for throwing attorney cards around. "Maybe you should get one first before you talk to the police, given what you—"

"I'll be okay. Trez isn't worried, and I'm not going to be until he is."

As her eyes bounced around, he realized she already had an exit strategy, and it didn't take an Einstein to figure out what it might be. Clearly, she was just going to disap-pear if things got too hot, and for some reason that freaked him right out.

"I have to head in," she said, nodding at his car. "You're blocking the way to the parking lot."

"Oh, yeah. Sure." He hesitated.

The question he needed to ask her jammed in his throat,

blocked by a conviction of not-here-not-now, and propelled by a whole lot of but-when.

"I have to go," she said.

"What did I say to you last night? In the locker room. When I, you know . . ." As she blanched, he wanted to hit himself. "I mean—"

"I'm sorry, but I really have to go."

Shit, he shouldn't have brought it up.

With a silent curse, he bounced his fist once on the roof as a good-bye and headed for his car. Back in the M6, he put the engine in first, released the clutch, and eased out of her way, turning around slowly as she parked nose-first to the club and got out of her Camry.

The owner opened the rear door as she came up to it, and the guy scanned the parking lot, as if he were watching out for her. When his eyes got to the M6, he nodded as if he'd known all along Vin was there, and suddenly Vin felt his temples sting, pressure building in his head as if something were pushing into him. All at once, his thoughts scrambled like a deck of cards pushed off a table, flying off in all directions, scattering faces up and faces down.

As soon as it began, it was over, his mind righted, everything from his aces to his jokers back in order.

While he winced and rubbed his head, Trez smiled tightly and said something to Marie-Terese, which caused her to look over her shoulder at the M6. Before the two of them ducked inside, she raised her hand in a little wave and then the door shut behind them.

Rain started to fall and Vin's wipers came on automatically, sweeping up and down, up and down.

His corporate offices were not far from here, only five minutes, and there was plenty of work to do there: Architectural plans to review. Permit applications to approve before they were submitted. Offers to buy and sell land or houses that needed to be countered. Inspections to delegate. Pissing contests between contractors to settle.

Plenty of shit for him to do.

Except evidently, he'd rather wait here like a dog for her to come out again.

Pathetic.

Vin took off, leaving the Iron Mask and going toward the skyscrapers by the river. The building he had his offices in was one of the newest and tallest in Caldwell, and when he got to it, he swiped his access card and went down into the underground garage. After leaving the M6 in his designated space, he rode up in the elevator, passing floors of law offices and accounting firms and big-name insurance companies.

The ding for the forty-fourth floor sounded, the doors opened, and he got off and strode by the reception desk. Up high on the dense black wall behind it, done in golden letters and lit from below, was the name of his business: THE DIPIETRO GROUP.

Group. What a lie that was. Even though some twenty employees had desks here, and he had hundreds of contractors and workmen on his payroll every week, there was him and that was it.

Walking down the plush black carpet to his office, he felt stronger with every stride. This business of his was something he knew about and controlled. . . . He'd built the whole damn thing up from the ground, just like he did his houses, until the corporation was better and bigger than anything like it.

As he came into his corner office, he flipped the light switch and all of the tigerwood paneling he'd handpicked glowed like sun rays. In the middle of his black desk, there was a legal-size manila envelope on the blotter, and he thought, Ah, yes, Tom Williams always worked as hard as he did.

Vin sat down and opened the flap, sliding out the folded land study and approved plot plan of the three parcels of a hundred or so acres he had just closed on. The project that unified the separate farms was going to be a masterpiece, one hundred fifty luxury homes in what was currently horse country in Connecticut. The goal was to attract Stamford commuters who were willing to drive forty-five minutes to work so they could live like they were Greenwich high rollers.

He was going to start demolition and construction as soon as the bids from contractors were where he wanted them to be. The land was perfectly sound, with a low water table that meant owners weren't going to have to worry about their wine cellars getting a bath every spring, and he was going to run water and electric and sewer in through an interlocking underground system. First move, as was the case with the bluff property, was going to be tearing down all the old farmhouses and barns, but he'd decided to leave the stone marking walls in place to keep some character— provided they didn't get in the way.

He was feeling good about all of it, especially for the price he'd gotten everything for. Times were tough and his offers more than fair. Besides, he'd sent Tom to do the negotiating with the local Realtors, which meant those poor fuckers hadn't stood a chance.

Tom was his baby-faced killer. The guy was a Harvard MBA with a vicious drive—who happened to look like he was twelve. Sweet-as-apple-pie Tom had no problem posing as an environmental conservationist and making unactionable, verbal commitments to preserve land that was in fact going to be developed.

Well, he had no problem now. In the beginning, Vin had had to coach him into it, but as soon as the money had really started rolling in, the guy had gotten with the program and then some.

The pair of them had done the dog and pony show so many times, it was practically rote, with Tom going in and snowing the prospects with tree-hugger charm while Vin marshaled the money and got the permit and contracting side of things worked out. It was precisely how they'd gotten the property on the Hudson River, that quartet of old hunting cabins yielding the ten acres he was putting his grand house on.

When it came to his palace, he could have built anywhere, but he chose that peninsula because of the golden rule in real estate: location, location, location. Unless an earthquake shaved California off the West Coast, or every polar ice cap in Alaska melted, they weren't making more waterfront, and you had to think of resale.

Sure as shit in another couple of years, he was going to want something bigger and better than what he was building now and that was another thing he was coaching Baby-face Tom on: Tom was the one who was buying the duplex at the Commodore.

Nothing like bringing the next generation along.

Vin picked up the phone and called his lieutenant, prepared to advance the ball even farther with the Connecticut project.

"Thank you, ma'am. I think that's all we need right now."

Marie-Terese frowned and glanced at Trez, who was sitting next to her on one of the club's velvet couches. As he uncrossed his legs as if he were getting ready to stand up, he seemed utterly unsurprised at how little time the questioning had taken—almost as if he'd prepped the police officer into keeping it short and sweet.

She looked back at the cop. "That's it?"

The officer closed his notebook and rubbed his temple like it hurt. "Detective de la Cruz is in charge of the investigation and he might have more questions later, but you're not a suspect or anything." He nodded at Trez. "Thank you for cooperating."

Trez smiled a little. "I'm sorry those security cameras weren't working. Like I've said, I've been meaning to get them fixed for months now. I have a log of malfunctions that I'd be happy to show you, by the way."

"Well, I'll take a look at it, but . . ." The man rubbed his left eye. "But as you say, you have nothing to hide."

"Not a thing. Let me see her out first and then we'll go to my office?"

"Sure. I'll wait here."

As Marie-Terese walked off with Trez and they headed down the back hallway, she said quietly, "I can't believe they aren't going any further with this. I don't know why I even needed to come."

Trez opened the rear door and put his hand on her shoulder. "I told you I would take care of things."

"And you really did." Her eyes searched the parking lot and she hesitated in the doorway. "So you saw that Vin came by."

"That his name?"

"It's what he said it was."

"He makes you uneasy."

On a lot of levels. "You don't suppose he and his friend—"

"Killed those guys? Nope."

"How can you be so sure?" She got her car keys out of her pocketbook. "I mean, you don't know them. They could have gone back and . . ."

Except even as she said the words, she didn't believe them: She couldn't imagine Vin and his friend being the killer or killers. They'd fought with those boys, sure, but they'd done that to protect her and had stopped before they seriously hurt them. Besides, Vin had been with her right afterward in the locker room.

Although God only knew exactly when the shootings had occurred.

Trez leaned in and gently stroked her cheek. "Stop it. You don't have to worry about Vin or his buddy. I get feelings about people and I'm always right."

She frowned. "I don't believe those security cameras are broken. You'd never put up with that—"

"Those two guys took care of you when I wasn't here. And so I take care of them." Trez put his arm around her and walked her over to her car. "You see your Vin again, tell him not to worry about anything. I've got his back."

Marie-Terese blinked in the bright cold sunlight. "He's not mine."

"Of course not."

She stared up at Trez. "How can you be so certain—"

"Stop worrying and trust me. When it comes to you, that man's heart is not dark."

After everything she had been through, Marie-Terese had learned not to put her faith in what was said to her. What she listened to was the security alarm in the center of her chest—and as she looked into Trez's eyes, her inner warning bell was utterly silent: He knew exactly what he was talking about. She didn't have a clue how, but then Trez had ways, as they said . . . ways of finding things out and fixing problems and taking care of business.

So yeah, the police weren't going to see anything he didn't want them to. And Vin hadn't killed those two boys.

Unfortunately that pair of convictions gave her only a measure of relief.

He's coming for you. . . .

Trez unlocked her door for her and then gave her back her keys. "I want you to take tonight off. This is tough stuff."

She got in, but before starting the engine, she glanced up and spoke her greatest fear. "Trez, what if those killings have something to do with me. What if someone saw them with me, someone other than Vin? What if . . . they were shot because of me."

Her boss's eyes grew sharp, like he knew every single thing she had never told him. "And who in your life would do such a thing."

He's coming for you. . . .

God, Trez knew about Mark. He had to. And yet Marie-Terese forced herself to say, "No one. I don't know anyone who would do that."

Trez's stare narrowed like he didn't appreciate the lie, but was willing to respect it. "Well, you decide to answer that in a different way, you can come to me for help. And even if you decide to pull out of town, I need to know if that's the why."

"Okay," she heard herself say.

"Good."

"But I'll be back at ten tonight." She pulled her seat belt across her chest. "I need to work."

"I won't argue with you, but I don't agree with you. Just remember, you see your Vin, you tell him I got his back."

"He's not mine."

"Right. Drive carefully."

Marie-Terese shut her door, forced the Camry to start, and turned around. As she came out on Trade, she put her hand in the pocket of her fleece.

Vin diPietro's card was exactly where she'd put it after she'd found it tucked in her duffel, and as she got his information out, she thought of the way he'd looked this morning with his beaten up face and his smart, concerned eyes.

It felt odd to realize she was frightened more by what he might know, and not of what he might be.

The thing was, she was a Scully kind of girl, a nonbeliever in all that *X Files*–esque stuff. She didn't believe in horoscopes, much less . . . much less whatever could turn a grown man into some kind of channel for . . . yeah, whatever. She didn't believe in that.

At least, not usually.

The trouble was, after having spent most of the night replaying what had happened in the locker room with him, she wondered if it was possible that something you didn't believe in could in fact be real: He'd been terrified in the midst of that trance, and unless he'd pulled off an Oscar-worthy performance today, he honestly had no clue what he'd said to her and he was honestly worried about what it all meant.

Taking her cell phone out of her purse, she dialed the number at the bottom of his card that didn't have *cell* or *fax* written next to it. Except as the ringing started, she remembered it was Saturday, and if this was the office number, she was going to get voice mail. What could she say?

Hi, I'm the prostitute Mr. diPietro helped out last night and I'm calling to reassure him that my pimp is going to take

*care of everything. He doesn't have to worry about those two
dead bodies in the alley.*

Perfect. Just the kind of a Post-it note he'd want his assistant sticking to his desk.

She dropped the phone from her ear and put her thumb
over the *end* button—

"Hello?" came a male voice.

She scrambled to get the cell back into place. "Hello?
Ah ... I'm looking for Mr. di—"

"Marie-Terese?"

Oh, that deep voice was dangerous. Caught up in the
sound of it, she almost said, *No, it's Gretchen.* "Ah, yes. I'm
sorry to bother you, but—"

"No, I'm glad you called. Is there anything wrong?"

She frowned and hit her directional signal. "Well, no. I
just wanted you to know—"

"Where are you? Still at the club?"

"I just left."

"You have breakfast yet?"

"No." Oh, God.

"You know the Riverside Diner?"

"Yes."

"I'll see you there in five minutes."

She glanced at the clock on the dash. The babysitter was
supposed to be at the house until noon, so there was plenty
of time, but she had to wonder what kind of door she was
opening. A big part of her wanted to run from Vin because
he was too handsome and too much her type and she was
an idiot if she didn't learn from the past.

But then she reminded herself she could bolt. At the
drop of a hat. Hell, she was on the verge of pulling out of
Caldwell completely anyway.

He's coming for you. . . .

Remembering the words he'd spoken to her gave her
the impetus to meet with him. Attraction concerns aside,
she wanted to know what he'd seen and why he'd said
those things.

"Okay, I'll see you there." She ended the call, flicked her

directional signal to the other side, and headed for one of Caldwell's landmarks.

The Riverside Diner was just two miles away and so close to the Hudson's shoreline, the only way it could get any nearer was if the booths were anchored by buoys and floating in the current. The dining car had been rolled onto its blocks in the 1950s, before the EPA laws, and still had original everything, from the Naugahyde twirling stools at the Formica counter, to the jukebox extensions at each table, to the soda fountain from which the waitresses still pulled Cokes for customers.

She'd been there once or twice before with Robbie. He liked the pie.

When she walked in, she saw Vin diPietro right away. He was sitting in the last booth over on the left, and facing the door. As their eyes met, he got to his feet.

Even with the shiner, the bruise on his cheek, and the swelling on his lower lip, he was stunningly sexy.

Boy . . . as she walked over, she wished she had a thing for accountants, podiatrists, or chess players. Maybe even florists.

"Hi," she said as she sat down.

On the table's countertop, there were a pair of menus, two sets of stainless-steel silverware on paper napkins, and a pair of thick ceramic mugs.

It was all so down to earth, homey, cute. And in his black cashmere sweater and his toffee suede jacket, Vin looked like he should have been at a fancy café, instead.

"Hi." He lowered himself slowly into his seat, his eyes locked on her. "Coffee?"

"Please."

He lifted his hand and a waitress with a red apron and a red-and-white uniform came over.

"Two coffees, thanks." As the woman left to go get the pot, Vin tapped his red-and-white menu. "I hope you're hungry?"

Marie-Terese opened hers and looked at all the choices,

thinking that every single one of them was appropriate for a Fourth of July picnic. Okay, maybe not all the breakfast items, but this was the kind of place where the word *salad* always had a modifier like *chicken*, *potato*, *egg*, or *macaroni*, and lettuce was only for sandwiches.

It was glorious, actually.

"See anything you like?" Vin asked.

She did not take the opportunity to look across the table at him. "I'm not a big eater, generally. I think for now I'll just stick with coffee."

The waitress came back and poured. "You know what you want?"

"You sure you won't do breakfast?" he asked Marie-Terese. When she nodded, he took both menus and handed them to the other woman. "I'd like the pancakes. No butter."

"Hash browns?"

"No, thanks. The pancakes are quite enough."

As the waitress headed for the kitchen, Marie-Terese smiled a little.

"What?" he asked as he offered her the sugar.

"No, thanks, I take it black. And I'm smiling because my son . . . he likes pancakes, too. I make them for him."

"How old is he?" Vin's spoon made a clinking sound as he stirred.

Although the question was casual, the way he waited for her answer was anything but. "Seven." She glanced at his bare ring finger. "Do you have kids?"

"No." He took a test sip and sighed like it was perfect. "Never been married, no children."

There was a pause as if he were expecting her to quid pro quo the info.

She picked her mug up. "The reason I called you was because my boss . . . he wanted to let you know he's taking care of everything. . . ." She hesitated. "You know, about what the security cameras might have caught last night or . . . things like that."

Although she was worried he might not appreciate

someone obstructing justice on his behalf, Vin just nodded once, like he was the kind of man who'd handled things in the same way Trez did. "Tell him I appreciate it."

"I will."

In the silence that followed, Vin ran his thumb up and down his mug's thick handle. "Listen, I didn't do anything to those two guys last night. Well, other than what you saw me do to them. I didn't kill them."

"That's what Trez said." She took a sip and had to agree with him: The coffee was superb. "And I didn't mention anything about you or your friend when I spoke with the police. I didn't tell them about the fight at all."

Vin frowned. "What did you say?"

"Just that the two guys had been harassing me. That Trez spoke with them, and when that didn't work, they were escorted from the club. Turns out that was what the two other witnesses who'd come forward maintained as well so it all matched."

"Why did you lie for me?" he said softly.

To avoid his eyes, she looked out the window next to them. The river, which seemed close enough to touch, was sluggish and opaque, thickened by the rain they'd had earlier in the week.

"Why, Marie-Terese?"

She took a deep drink from her mug and felt the coffee warm its way down into her belly. "For the same reason Trez did. Because you protected me."

"That's dangerous. Given what you do."

She shrugged. "I'm not worried."

From the corner of her eye, she saw Vin rub his face and wince as if the bruising hurt. "I just don't want you risking more trouble down the line for my sake."

Marie-Terese hid a smile. Funny, some things a man could say made you feel warm all over—not because the words were sexual, but because they went beyond that lowest common denominator and into more important, more meaningful territory.

Fighting the pull of his voice, his eyes, his savior routine, she said, "I'm sorry I left so quickly last night. You know, from the locker room. I was just . . . rattled."

"Yeah . . ." He exhaled on a curse. "And I apologize for flipping out like that—"

"Oh, no, it's okay. It . . . didn't appear you had much control over it."

"Try none." There was another long pause. "I hate to bring it up again, but what did I say to you?"

"You don't know?" He shook his head. "Was that a seizure?"

His voice grew tight. "Guess you could call it that. So . . . what did I say?"

He's coming for you. . . .

"What did I say?" Vin reached across and put his hand lightly on her arm. "Please tell me."

She stared at where he touched her, and thought . . . yes, and sometimes it wasn't even what a man said that made you warm—just the feel of his palm resting above your wrist was enough to heat your entire body.

"Your pancakes," the waitress said, breaking the moment. As they both sat back, the woman put down a plate and a little stainless-steel pitcher with a flop top. "More coffee?"

Marie-Terese glanced in her half-empty mug. "For me, please."

Vin got busy with syrup, pouring out a thin amber stream over three big, fat golden circles.

"Mine aren't that high," Marie-Terese said. "When I make them . . . they're not that golden or that high."

Vin let the lid on the syrup bounce shut and picked up his fork, cleaving through the stack, carving out a forkful. "I'm sure your son doesn't complain."

"No . . . he doesn't." Thinking of Robbie made her chest burn, so she tried not to remember how he'd looked at her with such love and awe when she'd flipped those home-made flapjacks for him.

The waitress returned with her pot of coffee, and after she'd poured and left, Vin said, "I'm really hoping you'll answer my question."

For no good reason, she thought even more of Robbie. He was an innocent that she'd ended up dragging into a harsh life thanks first to the bad husband she'd picked and then the way she'd chosen to clean up the financial mess she'd found herself in. Vin was not dissimilar. The last thing he needed was getting sucked into the black hole she was trying to get out of—and he'd already proven he had a come-to-the-rescue complex. At least where she was concerned.

"It was just nonsense," she murmured. "What you said was nonsense."

"So if it doesn't matter, there's no reason not to tell me."

She stared out the window at the river again ... and called forth all her strength. "You said, 'Rock, paper, scissors.'" As his eyes shot to her face, she forced herself to meet his stare and lie. "I have no idea what it means. To be honest, it was more what you looked like than what you said that made me nervous."

Vin's eyes bored into hers. "Marie-Terese ... I have a track record with those kind of things."

"Track record how?"

He resumed eating, as if he needed to do something to cut the tension. "In the past, when I've gone into that state and said stuff ... it comes true. So if you're keeping whatever it was from me for privacy's sake, I understand that. But I strongly urge you to take whatever it was very seriously."

Her cold hands squeezed her hot mug. "Like you're some kind of fortune-teller?"

"You're in a dangerous line of work. You need to be careful."

"I am always careful."

"Good."

There was another long period of quiet, during which she stared at her coffee and he focused on his food.

It was pretty easy to guess that the "careful" thing was

not just about creeps chasing after her. It was about other aspects of the job.

"I know what you're wondering," she said quietly. "How can I do it in the first place, and why don't I stop altogether."

When he eventually spoke, his voice was low and respectful, like he wasn't judging. "I don't know you, but you don't seem like ... well, some of those other women at the club. So I'm guessing something must be pretty damn wrong for you to be in that line of work."

Marie-Terese looked out the window again and watched a branch float on by. "I'm not like most of my colleagues. And let's just leave it at that."

"All right."

"Was that your girlfriend last night?"

He frowned and lifted his mug to his lips. After he took a deep sip, he cocked an eyebrow. "So you're allowed to keep secrets, but I can't?"

She shrugged and thought, damn it, she needed to keep her mouth shut. "You're right. That's not fair."

"Yes, she's my girlfriend. At least ... well, she was last night."

Marie-Terese actually bit her own lip to keep from pressing him for details. Had the pair of them broken up? And if so, why?

Vin resumed eating, but his broad shoulders did not relax. "Can I say something I shouldn't?"

She stiffened as he stared over at her. "Okay."

"Last night I fantasized about being with you."

Marie-Terese slowly lowered her mug. Yeah, okay ... and there were some things a man could say that made you hotter than hell. And some looks that were as tangible as touches. And both of those together, coming from the man across from her ...

In a stunning rush, her body responded, her breasts tingling at the tips, her thighs tightening, her blood racing ... and the effect shocked her. It had been so long—forever, actually—since she'd felt anything remotely sexual toward a man. And yet here she was in this diner, sitting across from a huge no-no in a cashmere sweater, experiencing for real something she'd been faking every night with strangers.

She blinked quickly.

"Shit, I shouldn't have said anything," he muttered.

"Oh, it's not you. Honest." It was her life. "And I don't mind."

"You don't?"

"No." Her voice was a little too deep.

"Well, it wasn't right."

Her heart stopped in her chest. Okay, that little comment was better than a gallon of ice to get rid of those warm fuzzies.

"Well, if you're feeling guilty," she said roughly, "I think you're confessing to the wrong woman."

Maybe that was why he'd hit a bad patch with the girlfriend.

Except Vin shook his head. "It wasn't right because I imagined paying for you and I . . . didn't like how that felt at all."

Marie-Terese put her mug down on the table. "And why is that."

Although she knew the answer: because someone like him could never be with somebody like her.

As Vin opened his mouth, she held up one palm and reached for her purse at the same time. "Actually, I already know. And I think I'd better get go—"

"Because if I were with you, I would want you to pick me." His eyes flashed up to hers and held on. "I would want you to choose me. Not be with me because I paid for it. I would want you . . . to want me and want to be with me."

Marie-Terese froze with her body halfway out of the booth.

He continued softly. "And I'd want you to enjoy it as much as I know I would."

After a long moment, Marie-Terese eased back down into her seat. Picking up her mug again, she swallowed hard and heard herself talking—although it wasn't until after she'd spoken that she realized what she'd said: "Do you like redheads?"

He frowned a little and shrugged. "Yeah. Sure. Why?"

"No reason," she murmured from behind her coffee.

CHAPTER
18

A crossroads meant you went left or you went right, Jim thought as he lay stretched out on the garage floor, a wrench in his hand.

When you came to a crossroads, by definition, you had to pick a course, because going straight on the path you were on was no longer an option: You got on the highway or stayed on the surface road. You passed this car on the dotted line or stayed behind him to keep safe. You saw an orange light and either sped through or started to slow.

Some of these decisions didn't matter. Others, unbeknownst to you, put you in the path of a drunk driver or kept you out of his way.

In Vin's case, that ring he was sitting on was the equivalent of a right hand turn that took him out of the way of an eighteen-wheeler that was just about to hit a patch of black ice: What the guy did now meant everything to his life and he had to hit that direction signal and get onto the new road fast. The SOB was running out of time with his woman and had to pull the trigger on that all important question before she—

"Fuck!"

Jim dropped the wrench that had slipped and shook out

his hand. All things considered, he probably needed to pay a little more attention to what he was doing; assuming he wanted to keep his knuckles where they were. Trouble was, he was consumed with the whole Vin thing.

What the hell did he do with the guy now? How did he motivate him to ask for that woman's hand in marriage?

In his old life, the answer would have been easy: He'd have just put a gun to Vin's head and dragged the fucker to the altar. Now? He needed to be a little more civilized.

Sitting back on the cool concrete floor, Jim glared at the piece-of-shit motorcycle that he'd been carting around since he'd landed back in the States. It hadn't worked then and it didn't now, and going by his half-assed rehabbing job this morning, its future didn't require shades. Christ, he had no idea why he'd bought the thing. Dreams of freedom, maybe. Either that or, like any guy with a set of balls, he was into Harleys.

Dog looked up from the patch of sunlight he'd been snoozing in, his shaggy ears pricking.

Jim sucked on the knuckle he'd skinned. "Sorry I cursed."

Dog didn't seem to care as he put his head on his paws, his bushy eyebrows up like he was prepared to keep listening, whether it was curses or something folks could say in mixed company.

"Crossroads, Dog. Do you know what that means? You got to choose." Jim picked up the wrench again and had another go at a bolt that was so encased in old oil, you couldn't tell it was hexagonal. "You got to choose."

He thought of Devina looking up at him from the driver's seat of that fancy-ass BMW. *I've been waiting for him to warm up and trust me and love me, but it hasn't happened, and I'm losing the strength to hang on, Jim, I really am.*

Then he thought of the way diPietro had stared at that dark-haired prostitute.

Yeah, there was a crossroads, all right. The problem was, diPietro, the fidiot, had come up to the signpost and instead of going to the right, where the arrows pointed to Happyville, he was gunning for Work-yourself-into-an-early-grave-and-be-mourned-by-no-one-but-your-accountant-opolis.

Jim hoped that telling Devina about the ring would buy some time, but how long would that last?

Man, on some levels, his last job had been easier, because he'd had much more control: Get the target in his sights, drop the bastard, take off.

Making Vin see what was so obvious, though . . . much harder. Plus, before Jim had had training and support. Now? Nada.

The growling sound of two Harleys brought his head around. Dog's too.

The pair of bikes rolled up the gravel to the garage, and Jim envied the SOBs who were gripping those handlebars. Adrian's and Eddie's rides gleamed, the chrome fenders and pipes catching the sunlight and winking like the Harleys knew they had the goods and would be damned if they'd hide the pride.

"Need some help with your hog?" Adrian said as he kicked out his stand and dismounted.

"Where's your helmet?" Jim balanced his arms on his knees. "New York has a law."

"New York has a lot of laws." Adrian's boots crunched over the driveway, then stomped on the concrete as he came up to give Jim's DIY project a look-see. "Man, where did you find that thing? A landfill?"

"No. I got it at a scrap yard."

"Oh, right. That's a step up. My bad."

The men were nice to Dog, giving him pats as he wagged around. And the good news was that limp of his seemed a little better today, but Jim was still taking him to a vet on Monday. He'd already left messages at three different places and whoever could get them in first won.

Eddie glanced up from doing the pet and coo thing to shake his head at the bike. "Think you need more than one person on this."

Jim rubbed his chin. "Nah, I'm good."

All three of them, Adrian, Eddie, and Dog, looked over at him with identical expressions of doubt . . .

Jim slowly dropped his hand, his nape tightening sure as if a cold palm had settled on it.

None of them cast a shadow. As they stood backlit by the brilliant sunlight, in the midst of the spindly dark trails thrown by the bare branches of the trees around the garage, it was as if they had been Photo-shopped in—in the landscape, but not of it.

"Do you know . . . an English guy named Nigel?" As soon as the words left Jim's mouth, he knew the answer.

Adrian smiled a little. "Do we look like people who'd hang out with a Brit?"

Jim frowned. "How did you know where I lived?"

"Chuck told us."

"He tell you it was my birthday Thursday night?" Jim slowly got to his feet. "He tell you that, too? Because I didn't, and you knew yesterday when you asked if I'd had myself a birthday present."

"Did I." Adrian's big shoulders shrugged. "Lucky guess on my part. And you never did answer that question of mine, did you."

As the two of them went nose-to-nose, Adrian shook his head with a curious sadness. "You did her. You had her. At the club."

"You sound disappointed in me," Jim drawled. "Hard to believe, considering you were the one who pointed her out to me in the first place."

Eddie stepped in between them. "Relax, boys. We're all on the same team here."

"Team?" Jim stared at the other guy. "Didn't know we were on a team."

Adrian laughed tightly, the piercings at his eyebrow and lower lip catching the light. "We aren't, but Eddie's a peacekeeper by nature. He'll say anything to chill people out, won't you."

Eddie just fell into silence and stayed right where he

was. Like he was prepared to physically break things up if it came to that.

Jim leveled his stare on Adrian. "Englishman. Nigel. Hangs out with three other pantywaists and a dog the size of a donkey. You know them, don't you."

"Already answered the question."

"Where's your shadow? You're standing in sunlight and throwing a whole lot of nothing."

Adrian pointed to the ground. "Is this a trick question?"

Jim looked down and frowned. There on the concrete was the black reflection of Adrian's wide shoulders and tight hips. As well as Eddie's huge body. And Dog's scruffy head.

Jim cursed to himself and muttered, "I need a fucking drink."

"You want me to beer you?" Adrian asked. "It's five o'clock somewhere in the world."

"Like England," Eddie cut in. As Ad glared at him, he shrugged. "Scotland, too. Wales. Ireland—"

"Beer, Jim?"

Jim shook his head and planted his ass back on the floor, figuring that if his brain wasn't working right, he wasn't about to chance his knees anymore in the event they decided to take up the fad. As he stared out at the pair of Harleys in the drive, he realized he was in a rat-piss kind of mood and clearly paranoid. Neither of which was a newsflash.

Unfortunately, beer was only a short-term answer. And head transplants had yet to be approved by the FDA.

"Any chance you know how to work a socket wrench?" he said to Adrian.

"Yup." The guy took off his leather jacket and cracked his knuckles. "And I got nothing better to do than get this piece of junk back on the road."

As Vin stared across the table at Marie-Terese, the cascading daylight filtering through the diner window transformed her into a vision, the echoes of which resounded in the back of his mind.

Where did he know her from? he thought once again. Where had he seen her before?

God, he wanted to touch her hair.

Vin forked up the last bite of his pancakes, and wondered why she had asked him if he liked redheads. Then he remembered. "I don't like red hair enough to be with Gina, if that's what you want to know."

"No? She's beautiful."

"To some . . . probably. Look, I'm not the kind of guy who—"

The waitress came up to the table. "More coffee? Or do you want the ch—"

"—fucks around with other women."

Marie-Terese blinked and so did the waitress.

Shit. "What I mean is . . ." Stopping himself, Vin glanced up at the other woman, who seemed to be ready to hang around. "Are you pouring? Or what?"

"I—ah, I could do with some more coffee," Marie-Terese said, holding up her mug. "Please."

The waitress topped slowly, looking back and forth between them like she was hoping to hear the rest of the story. When Marie-Terese's mug was full, the woman went to work on his.

"More syrup?" she asked him.

He pointed to his clean plate. "I'm finished."

"Oh. Right." She cleared what was in front of him and walked away with the same alacrity with which she'd worked the pot: Molasses moved faster.

"I don't cheat," he repeated when there was some privacy. "After watching my parents, I learned more than enough about what not to do in relationships, and that's pretty much rule number one."

Marie-Terese held out the sugar to him, and when he stared down at the bowl like he didn't know what it was, she said, "You know, for your coffee. You put sugar in yours."

"Yeah . . . I do."

As he doctored up his java, she said, "So your parents' marriage wasn't a good one?"

"Nope. And I'll never forget what it was like to watch them rip each other apart."

"Did they divorce?"

"No. They killed each other." As she recoiled back in her seat, he wanted to curse. "Sorry. I probably shouldn't be so blunt, but that's what happened. One of their fights got really out of control and they fell down the stairs. Didn't end well for either of them."

"I'm so sorry."

"You're very kind, but that was a long time ago."

After a moment, she murmured, "You look exhausted."

"Just need a little more coffee before we go." Hell, on that theory, he'd keep drinking the stuff until his kidneys floated if it meant they had more time together.

The thing was, as she stared across at him, her warm concern made her . . . precious. Utterly precious and therefore susceptible to loss.

"Are you safe on the job?" he blurted. "And I'm not talking about from violence." During the long pause that followed, he shook his head, feeling like both his loafers had just served as pancake chasers. "I'm sorry, it's none of my business—"

"Do I practice safe sex, you mean?"

"Yeah, and I'm not asking because I want to be with you." As she jerked back again, he cursed himself. "No, I mean, I want to know because I hope you're taking care of yourself."

"Why would that matter to you?"

He stared into her eyes. "It just does."

She turned away and looked out over the river. "I'm safe. Always. Which makes me very different from loads of so-called 'honorable' women who sleep around without using anything. And you can stop searching my face like you're trying to solve some deep mystery. Anytime. Now would be good."

He resigned himself to staring down into his mug. "How much do you cost?"

"I thought you said you didn't want to be with me like that."

"How much?"

"What, because you want to pull a *Pretty Woman* and buy me out of my horrible life for a week?" She laughed in a short, hard burst. "The only thing I have in common with Julia Roberts in that movie is that I get to pick who I'm with. As for how much, that's none of your business."

He still wanted to know. Because, hell, maybe he hoped that if she was very expensive the quality of men would be better—although if he was honest with himself, that was a crock of shit. He *did* want to pull a Richard Gere, except he didn't want to buy a week. Years was more like it.

Even though that was never going to happen.

As the waitress trolled by with the pot of coffee and both her ears open, Marie-Terese said, "The check would be great now."

The waitress put the pot on the table and fished around in her apron for her pad. Ripping free a page, she put the thing facedown. "Take care, you two."

As she went off, he reached across and touched Marie-Terese's arm. "I don't want this to end on a bad note. Thanks for keeping me out of it with the police, but I want you to come clean about me if you get any heat, okay?"

She didn't pull away, just looked down at where they were linked. "I'm sorry, too. I'm not great company. At least . . . not for the civilized."

There was pain in her voice—just a sliver of it, but he heard the note as clearly as a bell struck on a still night.

"Marie-Terese . . ." There was so much he wanted to say, but none of it was his right . . . and none of it would be received well. ". . . is such a lovely name."

"You think?" When he nodded, she said something under her breath that he couldn't quite catch but that sounded a lot like, *That's why I picked it.*

She broke their contact by taking the check and holding it as she opened her purse. "I'm glad you liked the pancakes."

"What are you doing? Here, let me get that—"

"When was the last time someone bought you breakfast?" When she glanced up, she smiled a little. "Or anything, for that matter?"

Vin frowned and considered the question as she fanned out a ten and a fiver. Funny . . . he couldn't remember Devina ever paying for anything. Granted, he was always front and center with the cash, but still.

"I usually pay," he said.

"Not a surprise." She started scooting out of the booth. "And I don't mean that in a bad way."

"Don't you need change?" he said, thinking he'd do anything to keep her with him a little longer.

"I leave big tips. I know how bad it can be, working in a service industry."

As he followed her out of the diner, he put his hand into his pocket to get his keys and felt something small and out of place. With a frown, he realized it was the gold earring he'd taken from Jim's.

"Hey, you know what? I think I have something of yours," he said as they closed in on her car.

She unlocked her door. "You do?"

"I think this belongs to you?" He held out the hoop.

"My earring! Where did you find it?"

"My buddy Jim picked it up in the parking lot outside the club."

"Oh, thank you." She pushed her hair out of the way and put it on. "I didn't want to lose these. They're not worth much, but I like them."

"So . . . thanks for the pancakes."

"You're welcome." She paused before she got behind the wheel. "You know, you should take a day off. You look really tired."

"Probably just the bruises on my face."

"No, it's the ones behind your eyes that make you seem worn down."

As she slid in and started the car, Vin caught a flash from over on the left and he looked across the river—

The instant the sun hit his retinas, his body seized up and tingled all over.

There was no gradual, fogging possession this time. The hateful trance claimed him between one second and the next, as if what had happened the night before had been just a warm-up and this was the real deal.

Sagging against Marie-Terese's hood, he went for his coat, opening it so he got some air—

When the vision struck him, it was more sound than image and it replayed over and over: A gunshot. Ringing out and echoing. Someone falling. A body dropping on a thunderous bounce. A gunshot. Ringing out and echoing. Someone falling. A body dropping on a thunderous bounce ...

As his knees buckled and he sank down onto the asphalt, he struggled to stay conscious, holding on mentally to anything he could—which turned out to be the memory of when he'd had his first attack. He'd been eleven and the trigger had been a watch, a ladies' watch that he'd seen in the window of a jeweler's downtown. He'd been on a field trip with his classmates to the Caldwell Art Museum, and as he'd passed by the store, he'd looked at the display.

The watch had been a silver one, and when the sunlight had hit it, his eye had focused on the flash and he'd stopped in his tracks. Blood on the watch. There had been bright red blood on the watch.

Just as he'd struggled to understand what he was seeing and why he suddenly felt so strange, a female hand had reached into the display and picked the thing up. Behind her, there had been a man standing with happy expectation in his face, a customer. ...

Except the guy couldn't buy the watch—whoever wore it next was going to die.

With the kind of strength that came only with full-bodied panic, Vin had broken the hold of the trance and bolted into the store. He hadn't been fast enough, though. One of the parent chaperones had raced in and caught him before he'd been able to say anything, and when he'd fought to get to the man and the watch, he'd been dragged out by the collar and condemned to wait in the bus while the others continued on to the museum.

Nothing came of the vision.

At least, not right away. Seven days later, though, Vin had been in school and seen one of the teachers in the cafeteria with what appeared to be the watch on her wrist. She'd been showing it off to her colleagues, talking about a birthday dinner she'd had the night before with her husband.

In that instant, a flash of sunlight on the playground slide had come through the window and captured Vin's eye . . . and then he'd seen the blood on the timepiece again, as well as much, much more.

Vin had collapsed on the linoleum of the cafeteria, and as the teacher had rushed over and leaned down to help, he saw with great clarity the car crash she was going to be in: Her head was hitting the steering wheel, her delicate face splitting open on impact.

Gripping the front of her dress, he'd tried to tell her to wear a seat belt. Get her husband to pick her up. Take another route. Take a bus. A bicycle. Walk home. But as his mouth had moved, nothing but random syllables had come out as far as he knew—although the horror dawning on the faces of the other teachers and the students suggested they were understanding what he was saying.

In the aftermath, he'd been sent to the nurse's office, and when his parents had been called, they'd been told he needed to go see a child psychiatrist.

And the teacher . . . the lovely young teacher with the thoughtful husband had died that afternoon on the way home from school with her new watch on her wrist.

Car accident. And she hadn't been wearing her seat belt.

When Vin had heard the next morning in his classrom, he'd burst into tears. Of course, a lot of kids had started crying too, but it was different for him. Unlike the rest of them, he'd been in a position to do something to prevent the outcome.

Everything had changed after that. Word had gotten out that he'd predicted the death—which made the teachers nervous around him and his peers either avoid him or ridicule him as spooky.

His father had started having to beat him to get him to go to school.

Abruptly, Vin lost his train of thought, the past getting submerged by the seizure's command of his mind and body, his consciousness ebbing more than it was flowing. . . .

A gunshot. Ringing out and echoing. Someone falling. A body dropping on a thunderous bounce. A gunshot. Ringing out and echoing. Someone falling. A body dropping on a thunderous bounce . . .

Just before he passed out, the vision crystallized in his mind's eye, no longer just sounds but bona fide images . . . a sand castle being formed by the wind instead of worn away by it: He saw Marie-Terese with her hands up as if she were trying to protect herself, her eyes wild with terror, her mouth opening in a scream.

And then he heard the shot going off.

CHAPTER
19

About an hour after Adrian and Eddie showed up and made their hands available, Jim slung his leg over the old bike and turned the key. Planting the sole of his work boot on the strike pedal and slamming his weight down, he didn't have any real faith the thing was going to—

That trademark Harley growl sprang to life immediately.

As he cranked the throttle, the engine vibrated between his legs and he had to shout over the din. "Christ, Ad, you did it."

Adrian grinned as he wiped his greasy palms on a red chamois cloth. "No problem. Let's take her for a spin and check the brakes."

Jim rolled the bike out of the garage and into the sunlight. "Let me get my helmet."

"Helmet?" Adrian mounted his hog. "Never thought you were an Eagle Scout."

Jim came back out with his black-and-hard. "Avoiding head injury is not a pussy move."

"But you gotta think about the wind in your hair, my man."

"Or the electrical plugs that'll keep you alive afterward."

"I got the dog," Eddie said, as he got on his own and held out his hands. The instant the opportunity presented itself, the little guy took a flying leap and parked it on the leather wrap over Eddie's tank.

Jim frowned, thinking he wasn't loving that. "What if you get into an accident?"

"I won't." As if the laws of physics didn't apply to him.

Jim was about to kibosh the deal when he saw how psyched Dog was to be on board, his claws curled into the cowhide like bliss was making his toes tingle, his tail going as fast as his butt would allow.

Plus, as the big man took the handlebars, his arms bracketed the animal.

"Just be careful with my damn dog. That animal gets hurt and you and I are having words."

Well, wasn't he turning into a good owner.

Strapping on his helmet, he drew on his leather jacket and straddled his bike. As he cranked the gas, his ride gave out a nasty, low cursing sound, and the power of all those horses rumbled up through his body.

Man, however much of a pain in the ass Adrian could be, he knew what he was doing with engines. Which might finally explain why Eddie could handle living with him.

On an unspoken we're-out-of-here, all three of them took off into the sunshine, Adrian in the lead, and Eddie in the rear with Dog.

Turned out, Jim's bike was straight-up magic, a beast with no manners at all, and as they went through farm country, he started to get a feel for the thing.

And whatever, you didn't need wind in your hair to be free.

Adrian ended up taking them down by the Hudson, heading toward town, and when they started to hit the traffic lights by the city's riverside parks, Jim took to praying for reds—just because accelerating was so frickin' satisfying.

As they pulled up to the intersection of Twelfth and River streets, he shouted up to Adrain, "I need gas."

"There's an Exxon up here, right?"

"Yeah, two blocks."

When the light changed, they roared off, the sounds of their engines exploding into the air and being amplified as they went beneath the overpasses of the highway. At the gas station, they pulled up to the pumps and Jim hit the high-test.

"How're the brakes?" Adrian asked as he eyed a blonde getting out of a beater. The woman headed into the quickie mart with a hip swivel and a half, the fringe of her long hair tickling the tattoo at the small of her back.

Jim had to laugh. The mouthy bastard was instantly distracted and clearly considering the merits of trailing her inside and asking her if she wanted to play with his screwdriver—which, given the way she kept looking over her shoulder at him, was going to be one big, fat *yes*.

"Why do I get the feeling mine are better than yours," Jim murmured as he pulled the nozzle out of his tank.

"You mean brake-wise?" Adrian's head swiveled around. "You think? 'Cuz I do believe you were the one getting laid Thursday night, not me."

"And to think I'd decided your company was worth your grease skills." Jim crammed the nozzle back into its place on the pump. "Musta been out of my damn mind."

He remounted and put his helmet back on. "So you want to head back—"

"I'm sorry."

Jim stopped in the process of buckling up the strap under his chin. Adrian was standing in front of him, the guy's face grim, his eyes focused on the sky above the gas station. He was dead serious.

Jim frowned. "What are you sorry about what?"

"Pointing her out to you at the club. I was thinking this was all sort of a game, but it's not. I shouldn't have encouraged you down that road. It wasn't right."

That Adrian was so bothered by what was actually just normal guy shit was a surprise, but maybe there was some marshmallow under that crispy exterior.

Jim put out his palm. "It's cool. We're cool."

Adrian took what was offered. "I'll try not to be an ass-hole all of the time."

"Let's not get ahead of ourselves."

Adrian smiled. "Yeah, maybe I'll just alternate with being a dickhead."

"Also something you could easily pull off." Jim started up his hog and curled his fist on the accelerator to pump the fresh gas right into those big, hungry pistons. "Shall we, gentlemen?"

"Abso," Adrian said as he hopped on his own bike. "You go first this time."

"Dog okay there, Eddie?" Jim asked while eyeing the animal—who seemed thrilled with the adventure.

"We're rock steady."

As Jim headed them back in the direction they'd come from, he took in the yellow of the sunlight and the bright white of the clouds and the blue of the sky and the gray of the road. Over to the left, the river paralleled the road, as did the walking path that had been built along the shore. Here and there, fledgling trees that looked like pencils poked into the earth forced the asphalt to wind around as did flower beds that would no doubt be sprouting tulips and daffodils in a couple of weeks.

The Riverside Diner was another shoreline marker, an old lady of a dive that was the kind of place Jim would feel comfortable in and something he'd been meaning to check out. Word was it had pancakes to die for—

Jim eased up on the throttle. In the parking lot, a BMW M6 that looked a hell of a lot like Vin's was parked next to a green Toyota Camry.

And there was a pair of legs sticking out between the cars, as if a man were lying out on the ground.

Major U-ey action. Lot of gas.

Because Jim had no doubt who belonged to those two shiny loafers.

Whipping into the parking lot, he gunned for the woman who was crouched down by the . . . yup, it was Vin diPietro who was spread out belly to the heavens. The guy wasn't moving and had a face like someone had stuck a wax mold of his bruised features on the free end of his spine.

"What happened?" Jim hit the kickstand and got off the bike.

The woman from the club looked up at him. "He just went down. Like last night."

"Shit." Jim crouched down as Adrian and Eddie pulled up. Before they could get off their Harleys, he waved for them to stay put, thinking the fewer people involved in this situation, the better.

"How long has he been out?" he asked the woman.

"Only about five minutes or so— Oh, my God . . . hi."

She leaned down as the other guy's eyes opened slowly. At first, they locked on Marie-Terese, then on Jim.

"Wakey-wakey," Jim murmured as he checked to see whether those pupils responded to the light in the same way. When they did, he was only marginally relieved. "How about we get you to a doc."

Vin grunted, and as he struggled to sit up, Marie-Terese tried to get him to stay put. "There's nothing wrong with me," the guy said gruffly, "and no, I don't have a concussion."

Jim frowned, thinking that even hardheaded assholes tended to take notice when they back-flatted it out in public, but Vin wasn't surprised—or worried. He was . . . resigned.

He'd had experience with this before, hadn't he.

As the guy started to look around, Jim glanced over at Adrian and Eddie and nodded his head at the road, giving them a signal to head off. The pair took the hint, backing their bikes up and palming a wave before leaving.

"Shit . . ." Vin said as he rubbed his face. "That wasn't fun."

"Yeah, I think that's self-evident." Jim glanced over at the dark-haired woman and wondered why the two had met up. If Vin wanted to keep things quiet about having any connection with those dead bodies, hooking up with her was not the brightest idea—even if it was just for coffee.

"I don't know what happened," she said. "We just had breakfast—"

"You only had coffee," Vin muttered, indicating that his short-term memory was working. Assuming she hadn't had French toast, too.

The woman lifted her hand as if she wanted to soothe him, but then dropped her arm. "He ate and we talked and we came out here and—"

"I'm okay now." Vin pushed himself up off the ground and steadied himself on the Camry's hood. "Just fine."

Jim grabbed the guy's elbow. "We're going to the doc now."

"The hell we are." Vin pulled his arm back. "I'm going home."

Well, shit. Given the hard angle of the guy's jaw, the only shot Jim had at helping was playing chauffeur and taking him back to the Commodore.

"I'll drive you across town, then."

Vin opened his mouth to argue, but the woman put her hand on his shoulder. "What if that happens again while you're behind the wheel?"

As their eyes made contact and held, the sun broke through the dappling clouds and a shaft of liquid warmth shot down from the sky and bathed them in a glow.

Jim frowned, and glanced up at the heavens, half expecting to see a live-action Michelangelo moment, with the hand of God pointing at the two. But no, just clouds and sky and sun . . . and a flock of Canadian geese honking their way south.

Jim refocused on the pair of them. What had been painfully lacking over dinner when Vin had looked at Devina was totally and completely showing now: His eyes were locked on the woman in front of him, and Jim was willing to bet his left nut that if he'd asked the guy anything from what she was wearing to how tall she was to what, if any, perfume she wore, the answer coming back would have been one hundred percent accurate.

Jim frowned more deeply. . . . What if he was wrong? What if Devina wasn't Vin's right path?

"Please, Vin," the woman said. "Let him take you back."

Whatever. There was time to worry about that stuff later. Right now, he had to get Vin home. "Give me your keys, my man."

"Please," the woman prompted.

Vin actually did it. Palmed up the ringle-jingle, or in the M6's case the black fob, and handed it over to Jim.

"How will you get back to your bike?" Vin asked.

Jim clapped his ass pocket, thinking he'd cab it—and found that he'd been as illegal as Adrian. No wallet. Which meant no license and no cash for a taxi.

Shit, the bike wasn't registered or insured either.

Jim's expression seemed to speak for itself as Vin laughed a little. "No plate on that Harley you rolled in on. No license for you, either?"

"Hadn't expected to come this far on it. But don't you worry. I'll obey all traffic laws."

"Is your car a stick?" the woman asked Vin. When he nodded, she shook her head. "That's a shame, because I can't drive a manual. But maybe I can follow you both and drive you"—she nodded at Jim—"back to wherever you live."

"Here will be fine."

"You're going to call a flatbed for the bike?" the woman said. "Because you are way illegal."

"Yeah. A flatbed. I'll get one of those."

Okay, it was time for the kind of good-bye that didn't require an audience.

Vin pointed to his car. "Considering you have the key, you mind warming that up?"

Jim's brow rose. "I might be acting like your chauffeur, but I'm not wearing a cap and uniform. So if you want some privacy, just ask for it." The guy turned and gave Marie-Terese a nod. "I'll meet you out in front of the Commodore."

She nodded back. "See you there."

Vin watched the guy get behind the wheel of the M6 and shut the door. A moment later, the engine turned over and a thumping vibrated. Stereo was on. Nice touch.

Marie-Terese shook her head. "You really need to go to the doctor."

"Would you feel better if I told you I've been doing that since I was eleven?"

"No."

"Well, it hasn't killed me yet." Abruptly, he thought of his vision of the gun and the sound of the shot, and it took all he had not to sound as desperate as he felt. "Listen, I don't know what's doing in your background. . . ." As her face tightened up, he knew better than to take that one any further. "I realize the owner of that club is making you feel protected, but that's only at the Iron Mask. What if someone follows you home?"

"If you saw my house, you'd understand why I'm not worried."

Vin frowned, thinking that at least she seemed prepared. "I promise I'm not going to pry, but if you know who might come after you, go to the police. And if you can't go to them, have your manager take care of it privately."

"Ah . . . thanks for the advice."

Man, he hated this. If only he knew what he'd said to her in the trances, except . . . well, shit, the gun told him enough, didn't it.

"Where do you live?" he said softly.

As she opened her mouth, he thought for a moment that she was going to answer him. But then she caught herself. "Where exactly is the Commodore? In case I get separated from you guys."

He gave her directions. "I'm on the twenty-eighth and twenty-ninth floors."

"Both?"

"Both."

"I'm not surprised." Shit, he could feel her closing herself off from him, unplugging the connection. "I'll follow you guys over there."

As she turned away, he touched her elbow. "What's your cell number?"

There was a long pause. "I'm sorry . . . I just can't."

"All right. I understand. But you have all mine. Call me, please. Anytime." He leaned to the side and cranked her door even wider so she could get in, and he waited to shut it until she had the seat belt drawn across her chest. After a couple of tries, her car wheezed into a semblance of an idle, and she glanced up like she was waiting for him to get a move on.

The sound of one of the M6's windows going down made him want to curse. And so did Jim's voice: "Textbook way of getting a ride home is you sit in the car. Unless you want to jump on the front bumper?"

Vin stalked around the BMW, got in and parked it in the passenger seat. "Don't lose her."

"I won't."

And he didn't. Jim handled the M6 perfectly. He was fast, nimble . . . but not so quick that Marie-Terese couldn't keep up.

Against the backdrop of classic rock, Vin didn't feel the need to explain why he and Marie-Terese had been at the diner alone. Not in the slightest.

At all.

"Just answer me one thing," Jim said, as if he read minds.

"Marie-Terese met with the cops and so did the owner." Vin looked across the car. "They didn't say anything about us and have no intention to."

Jim's eyes shot across the seats. "Not what I was going to ask, but good to know. What about the security cameras?"

"Taken care of."

"Nice."

"Don't get too excited. I told Marie-Terese that if she was going to get compromised, or if there was any pressure on her, she needed to serve us up like a steak."

"Answer me one thing."

"What."

"What are you going to do about Devina?"

Vin crossed his arms over his chest. "Just because I have breakfast with someone—"

"Bull. Shit. And don't front. What are you going to do."

"Why do you care?"

There was a long pause. So long that they went through two red lights.

As they accelerated after the second, Jim looked over. His eyes were arresting, positively glowing. "I care, Vin, because I've come to believe in demons."

Vin whipped his head around, and Jim went back to focusing on the road as he continued. "I wasn't kidding when I said I was here to save your soul. I'm beginning to think I got it wrong, though."

"Got what wrong?"

"Tell me about this fucking Victorian vapors thing you've got going on."

"Wait, what did you get wrong?"

"I don't think you're supposed to end up with Devina." The guy slowly shook his head and glanced up into the rearview mirror. "My job is to help you get through this part of your life and end up in a better place. And I'm coming to believe that means you need to be with that woman who . . . yup, just ran a red light to keep up with us."

"You should have stopped," Vin snapped, taking hold of the mirror and yanking it around so he could see Marie-Terese behind the wheel.

She was ten-and-two'ing her hands, and focusing on the M6, concentration tightening her brows. Her lips were moving slightly, as if she were singing a song or talking to herself, and he wondered which one it was.

"So what about this passing-out thing?" Jim prompted. "You're not surprised about it, are you."

Vin reangled the mirror. "You ever hear of a medium?"

Jim looked over. "Yeah."

"Well, I see the future and sometimes I talk when I do. And there's some other shit, too. So . . . there you go. And lest you think it's a fucking party, let me assure you it's not. I did my best to get it out of me and thought I'd licked it. Guess not."

When there was just the rising and falling of the M6's massive engine, he said roughly, "You get points for not laughing."

"You know what? I might have a couple of days ago." Jim shrugged. "Now I'm not inclined to at all. You always been like that?"

"Started when I was a kid."

"So . . . what did you see about her?" When Vin couldn't bring himself to reply, Jim muttered, "Okay, I'm guessing it wasn't candlelit dinners and romantic walks on the beach."

"Not hardly."

"What was it, Vin. And you might as well tell me. You and I are in this together."

Anger spiked, hard and hot. "Right, I showed you mine. Now you show me yours. What the fuck are you doing—"

"I died. Yesterday afternoon . . . I died and I've been sent back to help people. You're my first."

Now it was Vin's turn to get good and silent.

"Looks like you get points for not laughing, too," Jim muttered. "Tell you what, let's stipulate that we both have some of the WTF going for us and move along. I need to save your ass from yourself and like I said, I have a feeling the solution is not Devina, but the woman behind us in that Camry. So why don't you cut the shit and tell me what you saw about her—because I'm not going to fail on my first trip out of the park, and the more I know the better."

Jim Heron did not seem delusional, and considering where Vin was coming from when it came to the freaky shit, he figured he could give at least marginal credence to what the guy said. Even if it didn't make any more sense than . . . well, medium trances, for example.

"I saw . . . a gun go off."

Jim's head slowly swiveled around. "Who was hit? You or her?"

"I don't know. I'm assuming her."

"You ever been wrong?"

"No."

The guy's hands cranked on the steering wheel. "Well. There you go."

"Sounds like we have more to talk about."

"Yup."

Instead, they didn't say another thing: They sat side by side in the car, and Vin couldn't ignore the metaphor, the two of them belted in on some kind of ride, with God only knew what outcome waiting for them.

As he looked into the rearview mirror again, he prayed that Marie-Terese wasn't the one who got hurt. Better him. Much better.

When they finally got to the Commodore, they pulled into the garage, and as Marie-Terese waited in front, Vin thought maybe that was a good thing: He'd just end up trying to say good-bye to her again, and enough was enough.

"I'm spot number eleven over there."

After the M6 was parked, Vin got out of the car, took the key from his new buddy, and they went their separate ways, with Jim heading over to the stairwell that would lead him up to the street.

Vin walked off in the opposite direction to the elevator, and when its doors opened wide for him, he stepped in and turned around. Jim was almost to the exit, his stride closing the distance quickly.

Vin blocked the elevator doors from shutting and called out, "I'm going to break up with Devina."

Jim stopped and looked over his shoulder. "Good. But go easy on her. She's in love with you."

"She certainly makes it appear that way." But underneath all that "loving" exterior, there was something hollow about her—and it had been part of the reason he'd wanted her around: He'd rather have dealt with the calculation, because self-interest he trusted more than love.

Not anymore. Shifts were occurring in him, shifts he could no more control than he could stop the imposition of those visions. On a usual day, he was ninety-nine percent about business. In the past twenty-four hours? He was pulling a fifty percent, if that: His mind had been consumed with other, more important things . . . things that had a lot to do with Marie-Terese.

"I'll keep you posted," he told Jim.

"You do that."

Vin let the doors close, and hit the button for his floor. He had to talk to Devina, and he needed to get that conversation over with. It wasn't only the fair thing to do . . . he had some sense of urgency about it that had nothing to do with the fact that he wasn't looking forward to hurting her.

That horrible dream was still with him . . . like it had stained his brain permanently.

On the twenty-eighth floor, the elevator let out a discreet *bing*, and he stepped out and went up to his door. As he opened the way into the duplex, Devina rushed down the stairs, a huge smile on her face.

"Look what I found while I was tidying your study." She extended her open palms, holding out the Reinhardt's box. "Oh, Vin! It's perfect!"

She rushed forward and threw her arms around his neck, her perfume choking him even more than her hold did. As she went on about how she shouldn't have opened it but couldn't help herself, and how it even fit her finger, Vin closed his eyes and saw echoes of the nightmare he'd had.

A conviction lit off in the center of his chest, one that was as undeniable as his own reflection in a mirror.

She was not who she said she was.

CHAPTER
20

When Jim got into the green Camry, he leaned over and extended his hand. "Jim Heron. Figured we might as well introduce ourselves."

"Marie-Terese."

The woman's smile was slight, but warm, and as he waited for a last name, he had a feeling one wasn't coming.

"Thanks for the ride back," he said.

"Not a problem. How's Vin doing?"

"For a guy who just trouted it in a parking lot, he seems all right." Jim looked over at her as he did up his seat belt. "You holding up okay? Talking to the cops is not a party."

"Did Vin tell you? You know about the security tapes and . . ."

"Yeah, he did, and thanks."

"You're welcome." She put on her directional signal, checked her mirrors, and pulled out after an SUV went by. "Can I ask you something?"

"Sure."

"How long have you been sleeping with his girlfriend?"

Jim tightened his shoulders and narrowed his eyes. "Excuse me?"

"The night before last, I saw you leave with his girl-friend after she'd spent about an hour staring at you. Same thing last evening. No offense, but I've been watching people do stuff like that for a while now, so I doubt there was only a lot of hand-holding going on in the parking lot."

Well, well, well . . . she was smart. This Marie-Terese was smart.

"What do you think of Vin?" he asked.

"Not going to answer me? I don't blame you."

"What's your last name?" He smiled grimly as silence reigned. "Not going to answer me? I don't blame you."

As she flushed, he eased off with a curse. "Look, I'm sorry. Been a rough couple of days."

She nodded. "And it's none of my business, actually."

He wasn't so sure about that.

"Just out of curiosity, what do you think of him?" As Jim waited for her to answer, he thought, Jesus, since when had he turned into a modern-day, dick-swinging Ann Landers? Next thing he knew, he'd be getting facials and ironing his clothes.

Or . . . cleaning his clothes.

Whatever.

"Well, anyway," he said, aware she hadn't replied, "I don't know him all that much, but Vin's a good guy."

She glanced over. "How long have you known him?"

"I work for him. He's into construction and I have a hammer. Match made in Heaven." Jim thought of the Four Lads and rolled his eyes. "Literally."

As they came up to a stoplight, she said, "I'm not looking for him. For anyone."

Jim glanced up at the sky through its frame of sky-scrapers. "You don't have to be searching to find what you need."

"I'm not going to be with him, so . . . yeah. That's it."

Great. One step forward. Two steps back. Vin appeared to be on board; Marie-Terese was not interested—in spite of the fact that she was clearly attracted to the guy *and* that she cared about him enough to worry how he was going to make it back home safely.

As they went along with the traffic, they passed by a couple who were walking side by side, their hands linked. They weren't young lovers, though; they were old. Very old.

But only in the skin, not in the heart.

"You ever been in love, Marie-Terese?" Jim asked softly.

"Hell of a question to ask a prostitute."

"I haven't. Been in love, that is. Just wondered if you had." He touched the glass, and the old woman caught the gesture and clearly thought he'd waved at her. As she lifted her free hand, he wondered if maybe he had.

He smiled at her a little and she smiled back and then they resumed their separate ways.

"Why is that relevant," Marie-Terese said.

He thought of Vin in that cold, beautiful duplex, surrounded by inanimate beautiful objects.

And then he thought of Vin, looking at Marie-Terese in the sunlight.

The guy's soul had been fed at that moment. He had been transformed. He had been truly alive.

"It's relevant because I'm beginning to think," Jim murmured, "love might be everything."

"I used to believe that," Marie-Terese said hoarsely. "But then I married the man I did, and that whole fantasy stuff got blown out the window."

"Maybe that wasn't love."

Her choked laugh told him he was on the right track with that one. "Yeah, maybe."

They pulled into the parking lot of the diner and headed over to his Harley.

"Thanks again for the ride," he said.

"I'm happy to help."

He got out of the car, closed the door and watched her turn around. As she took off, he memorized her license plate.

When he was sure she was gone, he put on his helmet,

started his bike, and took off. Considering his list of crimes, an unregistered Harley wasn't even a blip on his radar.

Besides, the stiff wind on his chest and arms peeled off some of the stress and blew his brain more clear—although what was revealed made him ill. It was pretty obvious what he needed to do next, and though he hated it, sometimes you had to suck shit up: He had a woman he needed to keep alive, Vin's vision of a gunshot, and two obnoxious college boys who were now dead, thanks to having been popped. What the situation required was information, and there was only one way he knew to get it.

He didn't like whoring himself out, but you had to do what you had to do . . . and he was willing to bet that mantra was something Marie-Terese knew all about, too.

As soon as he pulled into his studio's gravel drive, Dog came out from under the truck and limped with joy over to the bike, all wags as he escorted the way into the garage. After Jim took off his helmet, he leaned down for a proper hello and Dog's tail got going so fast, it was a damn miracle the little guy could stay on his paws.

Odd to have someone to welcome him home.

Jim picked the dog up, hooked him over his arm, and went up the stairs to unlock the door. Inside, he did the petting thing while he found his cell phone in the messy bed.

Sitting down on the mattress and feeling Dog's small, warm body curl up around his hip, Jim thought long and hard before dialing. It felt like a step backward, and the familiarity of it sickened him, which was kind of interesting.

Christ, had he been trying to make a fresh start of things here?

Looking around, he saw what Vin had seen: two piles of clothes, a twin bed that no one bigger than a twelve-year-old could be comfortable in, furniture that had Goodwill stamped all over it, and a single ceiling light with a crack through its cover.

Not exactly fresh-start material, but then again, compared to where he'd been and what he'd been doing, sleeping on a park bench would have counted.

As he stared at the phone, the ramifications of what would happen if that old, familiar voice came on the line were very clear.

Jim punched in the eleven digits and hit *send* anyway.

When the ringing stopped and there was no voice mail, he said one word: "Zacharias."

The reply was nothing but the laconic laugh of a man for whom life held no more surprises. "Well, well, well . . . never thought I'd get that name again."

"I need some information."

"Do you."

Jim's grip cranked down hard on the cell. "It's just a license plate trace and an identity search. You could do it in your fucking sleep, you piece of shit."

"Yes, clearly that is the way to get me to do anything for you. Absolutely. You always were such a diplomat."

"Fuck you. You owe me."

"Do I."

"Yes."

There was a long silence, but Jim knew damn well that the call hadn't gotten dropped: The kind of satellites that the government used for people like his former boss were powerful enough to beam a signal down into the center of the frickin' Earth.

That low laugh came again. "Sorry, my old friend. There's a statute of limitations on obligation and yours has passed. Don't ever call me again."

The phone went dead.

Jim stared at the thing for a moment, then tossed it back on the bed. "Guess that's a deadend, Dog."

Christ, what if Marie-Terese was some kind of con artist and Vin was just getting snowed?

Stretching out on the rumpled sheets, he arranged Dog on his chest before reaching over to the little table and snagging the TV remote. As he stroked Dog's rough coat, he pointed the thing at the tiny TV across from the head of the bed, his thumb hovering over the red button marked POWER.

I could use some help, lads, he thought. *Which way am I supposed to be going with all this?*

He pushed down and the picture came forward, summoned out of the glass screen, blooming into a clear image. A woman in a long red gown was being led by a guy in a tuxedo from a limousine to a jet airplane. He didn't recognize the movie, but considering he'd spent the last twenty years of his life in the hard-core military, there hadn't been a lot of time for going to the damn pictures.

When he hit *info*, Jim had to laugh. *Pretty Woman* was evidently about a prostitute and a businessman falling in love. He glanced up at the ceiling. "Guess I got it wrong the first time, huh, boys."

That evening, when Marie-Terese walked into St. Patrick's Cathedral, her feet were slow and the aisle down to the altar seemed a mile long. As she passed by the chapels of the saints, heading for the confessionals, she paused at the fourth bay in. The life-sized figure of a pious Mary Magdalene had been removed from its pedestal, the white marble statue no doubt having been taken to be cleaned of dust and incense residue.

The empty space made her realize that she'd decided to leave Caldwell.

It was all getting to be too much. She just was not in a place in her life where she could afford to get emotionally attached to a man, and that was happening with Vin already. Those dead college boys aside, more time around him was not going to help her, and she was a free agent, able to hit the road at any moment—

The creaking of a door behind her pricked her nerves, but when she looked over her shoulder, no one was close by. As usual, the church and all of its pews were essentially empty, with just two women in black veils praying up front and a man wearing a Red Sox baseball cap settling on his knees in the far back.

As she continued down the aisle, the weight of her decision to pull out of town exhausted her. Where would she go? And how much would it cost to think up another identity? And work. What would she do about that? Trez was unique in the business, and the Iron Mask was the only place she could imagine doing what she did.

Except how would she cover the bills?

At the pair of confessionals, there were a couple of people before her, so she waited with them, smiling once in greeting and then keeping her eyes elsewhere, as they did. Which was always the way it went. The guilty tended not to want to make conversation when they were about to unload, and she wondered if the others were practicing what they would say, just as she was.

No matter what their issues were, she figured she could lap them in the sin contest. Easy.

"Hello."

She glanced behind her and recognized a guy from the prayer group. He was a quiet one like her, a regular attendee who rarely opened his mouth.

"Hello," she said.

He nodded once and then stared at the ground, clasping his hands together and keeping to himself. For no particular reason, she noticed that he smelled like incense, the kind that was used in the church, and she was comforted by the smoky, sweet scent.

Together they moved up two paces when someone else went in ... then another two paces ... and then Marie-Terese was up next.

After a lady with red-rimmed eyes came out from behind the thick velvet curtain, it was Marie-Terese's turn to go in, and she gave the prayer group guy a smile of goodbye before stepping up to the cubicle.

When she'd shut herself in and taken a seat, the wooden

panel slid back and the priest's profile was revealed on the far side of the brass screen that separated them.

After making the sign of the cross, she said softly, "Forgive me, Father, for I have sinned. It has been two days since my last confession."

She paused, because even though she'd said the words many, many times, they were hard to get out.

"Speak to me, my child. Unburden yourself."

"Father, I have . . . sinned."

"In what manner."

Even though he knew. But the point of confession was the vocalized recitation of evil deeds; without that there could be no absolution, no relief.

She cleared her throat. "I have . . . been with men unlawfully. And I have committed adultery." Because some of them had had wedding rings on. "And . . . I took the Lord's name in vain." When she'd seen Vin hit the ground by the diner. "And I . . ."

It was a while before her list dried up and the priest's profile nodded gravely when she fell silent. "My child . . . surely you know the errors of your ways."

"I do."

"And the transgressions against God's ways cannot go . . ."

As the priest's voice continued, Marie-Terese closed her eyes and took the message deep inside. The pain of how far she had sunk and what she was doing to herself squeezed her lungs until she couldn't draw in any air at all.

"Marie-Terese."

She shook herself and looked at the screen. "Yes, Father?"

". . . and therefore, I shall . . ." The priest paused. "Excuse me?"

"You said my name?"

A frown appeared on his profile. "No, my child. I did not. But for your sins, I shall decree that . . ."

Marie-Terese looked around, even though there was

nothing to see but the wood paneling and the red velvet curtain.

"... *te absolvo a peccatis tuis in nomine Patris et Filii et Spiritus Sancti. Amen.*"

Dropping her head, she thanked the priest, and after he'd closed the partition, she took a deep breath, picked up her bag, and stepped out of the confessional. Next to the one she'd been in, she could hear the voice of the other sinner. Soft. Muffled. Utterly indistinct.

As she walked down the side aisle, paranoia had her eyes going all around the cathedral. The pair of women with veils were still there. The man who'd been praying was gone, but two others had come in and taken his place at the back.

She hated looking over her shoulder and wondering whether she was hearing her name and worrying if she were being followed. But ever since she'd pulled out of Las Vegas, she'd been hypervigilant and she had a feeling she would always be like that.

Outside, she jogged over to her car and she didn't breathe easy until she was locked in. For once, the Camry turned over on the first try, as if her adrenaline were being transmitted to the engine, and she drove off to the club.

By the time she pulled into the parking lot of the Iron Mask and got out with her duffel, her paranoia was irritating the hell out of her. No cars had followed hers. No dark shadows were moving in for the kill. Nothing was out of the ordinary—

Her eyes went to the alley where the bodies had been found . . . and she was reminded of precisely why she worried all the time.

"How you doing?"

Marie-Terese spun around so fast, her duffel bag slammed into her. But it was only Trez, waiting by the back door. "I'm . . . good." As his eyes narrowed, she put up her palm. "Don't prod me. Not tonight. I know you mean well, but I can't handle it right now."

"Okay," he murmured, stepping back so she could pass by him. "I'll give you the space you need."

Fortunately, he was true to his word, leaving her off at the locker room so she could change. When she was in her god-awful uniform, with her hair fluffed out and her lids caked with eye shadow and her mouth all greasy, she walked down the long hall to the club proper, completely dissociated from who and where she was.

As she trolled the fringes of the crowd, it didn't take long to find business. A little eye contact, some hip, a slight smile and she had her first candidate of the night.

The guy was an utter civilian—in other words, he would have looked absolutely fine anywhere else but here in Gothlandia. He was over six feet tall, with brown hair and brown eyes, and he smelled of Calvin Klein's Eternity for Men—an old-school favorite that suggested he wasn't all that suave, but at least had a good enough nose. His clothes were nice, but not over-the-top, and he didn't have a wedding band.

The conversation about the transaction was stilted and awkward, and he blushed the entire time, so it was clear he'd not only never done this before, but had never pictured himself in the position of exchanging money for sex.

Join the club, she thought.

He followed her into one of the bathrooms, and in a characteristic warping of reality, she felt as if she were disembodied and walking two steps behind, watching the pair of them go behind the closed door.

Inside the cramped space, she took the money he offered, tucking it into the hidden pocket inside her skirt, and then she stepped into him, her body cold as ice, her hand trembling as it brushed up his arm. Stretching her lips into a fake smile, she braced herself for him to touch her, forcing her body to stay where it was, praying that her self-control was enough so that she didn't run out screaming.

"My name's Rob," the john said in a nervous voice. "What's yours?"

All at once the bathroom closed in, the deep purple and black walls going trash-compactor on her and squeezing her tight, making her want to yell for help so someone, any-one would stop them.

Swallowing hard, Marie-Terese gathered herself and blinked fast in the hope that clearing her eyes would help cleanse her brain and get her back on track.

When she leaned in, the man frowned and pulled away.

"Changed your mind?" she said, wishing that he had, even though it would just mean she'd have to head out and find another one.

He seemed perplexed. "Ah . . . you're crying."

Recoiling, she looked around his shoulder at the mirror over the sink. Good Lord . . . he was right. Tears were roll-ing down her cheeks in a slow stream.

Raising her hands, she brushed them off.

The man turned to face the mirror as well, and his face was as sad as she felt. "You know what?" he said. "I don't think either one of us should be doing this. I'm trying to get back at someone who doesn't care who I sleep with, and I just didn't want anyone else getting hurt. That's why I came to . . ."

"A whore," she finished for him. "That's why you came to me."

God, her reflection looked awful. Her heavy eyeliner was melting off and her cheeks were paper white and her hair was frizzed out.

As she stared at her face, she realized she was done. The moment had finally come. She had been inching toward this for some time, with all those gearing-up pauses before she could come into the club and those Dial-scented crying jags in the shower and those panic attacks in the confessionals, but the approach was no longer.

The arrival was here.

She wiped her hand on her skirt and took out the folded bills. Taking the man's palm, she put the money into it. "I believe you're right. Neither of us should be doing this."

The guy nodded and squeezed the money hard, looking hopeless. "I'm such a pansy."

"Why?"

"It's just so typical of me. I always choke in these situations."

"For what it's worth, you didn't choke. I did. You were . . . kind."

"That's me. The nice guy. Always the nice guy."

"What's her name?" Marie-Terese murmured.

"Rebecca. She's in the cubicle next to me at work and she's really . . . perfect. I've been trying to impress her for about four years now, but all she does is talk about her love life. I thought maybe if I could tell her about a date of mine where I get lucky . . . Trouble is, I never get lucky and I'm a rotten liar."

He tugged at the sleeves of his shirt as if he were trying to spiff himself up in the face of his reality.

"Have you asked her out?" Marie-Terese asked.

"No."

"You think maybe she's hoping to impress you with all those dates of hers?"

The guy frowned. "But why would she do that."

Marie-Terese reached up and turned his face back to the mirror. "Because you're actually good-looking and you're nice, and maybe you're reading the situation wrong. The thing is, if you ask her and she blows you off, you don't want to go there anyway. There's no reason to be one of many."

"God, I can't imagine how to ask her for a date."

"How about . . . 'Rebecca, what are you doing Thursday night?' Make sure you go for one of the weekdays. Too much pressure for a weekend."

"You think?"

"What do you have to lose?"

"Well, she is next to me at work and I see her every day."

"But you're not exactly having a good time now, are you? At least you can have some closure."

He met her eyes in the mirror. "Why were you crying?"

"Because . . . I can't do this anymore."

"You know, I'm glad. I picked you because you don't seem like the kind of woman who . . ." He flushed. "Ah—"

"Who should be doing this. I know. And you're right."

The guy turned to her and smiled. "This actually worked out okay."

"It did." On impulse she reached out and gave him a hug. "Best of luck. And remember when you're asking that woman out that you're a catch and she'd be lucky to have you. Trust me. I've learned the hard way that a good man is hard to find."

"You think?"

Marie-Terese rolled her eyes. "You have *no* idea."

He smiled even more widely. "Thank you—I mean that. And I think I will ask her. What the hell, right?"

"You only live once."

He was beaming and full of purpose while he left the bathroom, and as the door eased shut, Marie-Terese went back to staring at herself. In the light that shone down on her from above, all the smudged black makeup made her look like a bona fide Goth.

How ironic that on her last night in the club, she finally looked like a regular.

Leaning to one side, she snapped free a paper towel, thinking she'd tidy her eyeliner. Instead, she ended up rubbing her lipstick off, just ripping the glossy coat from her mouth. Never again. She wasn't ever wearing that horrible gooey stuff again . . . or any of the rest of the makeup . . . or the ridiculous slutty clothes.

Done. This chapter of her life was done.

God, it was amazing how light she felt. Amazing and insane. She had *no* idea what she was going to do next or where she was going to go, so by all that was rational, she should have been panicked.

But all she could think of was how relieved she felt.

Turning away from the mirror, she reached for the wrought-iron doorknob and realized that she had gone from tears to smiling. Opening the way out, she—

Looked up into the grim face of Vincent diPietro.

He was leaning against the wall right across from the private bathroom, his arms crossed over his chest, his big body tensed up in spite of what should have been a relaxed pose.

His expression was of a man who'd just had his gut slit open.

CHAPTER
21

The problem was, he had no reason and no right to feel sucker punched.

As Vin stared at Marie-Terese, taking note of the flush on her cheeks and the fact that she didn't have any lipstick left on her mouth, he shouldn't have felt a thing. Same deal when that guy had come out of the bathroom with a smile on his face and his shoulders set like he was so the man—there should have been nothing unusual going on in the center of Vin's chest.

This was not his woman. This was not his business.

"I need to go," he said, standing up from the wall and turning away. One look at the thick crowd and he headed for the back of the club, for the hallway that, thanks to last night, he knew had a door at the end of it.

All the way along, his father's drunken voice dogged him: *You can never trust a woman. They're sluts, every one of them. Give them a chance and they'll fuck you every time—and not in a good way.*

Marie-Terese caught up with him about a third of the way to the exit, her high-heeled shoes clipping over the tiled floor. Grabbing his arm, she tugged him to a halt. "Vin, why are you—"

"Behaving like this?" Damn it, he couldn't look at her. Just couldn't do it. "You know, I don't have an answer for that."

She seemed nonplussed. "No, I was asking ... why did you come? Is there something wrong?"

God, where to start with that one. "Everything is fine and dandy. Just frickin' perfect."

As he started to walk off again, he heard her say loud and clear, "I wasn't with him. That man in there. I was *not* with him."

Vin glanced over his shoulder; then marched back up to her. "Yeah, right. You're *with* men for a living—or do you think I've forgotten what a prostitute does for money."

While he watched her pale, he felt like a total bastard. But before he could backpedal, she filled the silence.

Lifting her chin, she said, "It's the truth, and whether or not you choose to believe it is your problem. Not mine. Now if you'll excuse me, I'm going to change."

As she brought up her hand to push her hair over her shoulder, he saw that she had something gripped in her fist ... a rumpled paper towel with smudges of red all over it.

"Wait." He stopped her and glanced at the thing. "You took off your lipstick."

"Of course I— Wait, I guess you assumed that man kissed it off me, right?" She pivoted around and beelined for the locker room door. "Good-bye, Vin."

Now it was his turn to drop a newsflash: "I broke up with Devina this afternoon. My girlfriend is now an 'ex.' That's what I came to tell you."

Marie-Terese halted, but did not face him. "Why did you do that?"

He traced the back of her with his eyes, from her small shoulders to the proud set of her spine to the dark hair that fell below her shoulder blades. "Because when I looked at you across that table at the diner, no one else existed. And whether or not anything happens between you and me, it took meeting you to show me what I was missing."

She looked over her shoulder, her spectacular blue eyes astonished.

"It's the truth," he said. "The God's honest truth. And it's why I was so upset outside of that bathroom. I'm not saying you're mine... I just wish you were."

As the moody, depressive music from the club filled the air between them, he scrambled to put together the magic combination of words that would keep her from taking off on him.

Although not channeling his father was probably the first place to start, he thought.

She turned around and he felt the measure of her stare. "I'm going to go get changed and tell Trez I'm quitting. Will you wait for me?"

What ... had he heard that right? "You're quitting?"

She held up the paper towel. "I've known for a while I couldn't keep doing this ... I just didn't know tonight was the end. And it is."

Vin stepped forward and wrapped his arms around her, holding her carefully so she could pull back if she wanted to. She didn't though. As their bodies met, she took a deep breath ... and hugged him back.

"Yes ... yes, I will wait for you," he whispered. "Even if it takes hours."

As if he knew precisely the right time to appear, Trez walked out of his office at the far end of the corridor and strode toward them.

He extended his hand to Vin. "So, you taking her out of here?"

Vin lifted his brows as they clapped palms. "If she'll let me."

Trez looked down at Marie-Terese, his brown eyes impossibly kind. "You should let him."

Marie-Terese blushed the color of a Valentine's Day card. "I ... ah ... listen, Trez I'm not going to come in anymore."

"I know. And I'll miss you, but I'm glad." When the man held out his huge arms, the two of them hugged briefly.

"I'll tell the rest of the girls, and please don't feel like you have to keep in touch—sometimes a clean break is the best. Just remember, if you need something, anything— money, place to stay, shoulder to lean on—I am always here for you."

Okay, Vin liked this guy. A lot.

"I will." She glanced at Vin. "I won't be long."

After she ducked into the locker room, Vin dropped his voice, even though it was arguably unnecessary, as no one was in the hall with them. "Listen, she told me about how tight you're being with the police. I appreciate it, but if it costs you or her anything, you open right up, okay?"

The guy smiled a little, his self-confidence palpable. "You don't worry about the cops. You just take care of your girl and everything'll be cool."

"She's not my girl, really." Although if he had half a chance . . .

"Can I give you a piece of advice?"

"Yeah, sure."

As the guy stepped in close, it was unusual for Vin to have other men meet him square in the eyes given how tall he was, but Trez sure as shit didn't have a problem with that.

"Listen to me carefully," the man said. "There's going to come a time, maybe sooner rather than later, that you're going to have to trust her. You're going to have to have faith that she's who you know her to be and not what you fear. She did what she had to here, and maybe she'll tell you the whys. But this kind of shit, it doesn't get left behind in either of your minds for a long time . . . if ever. Let me assure you of what you already suspect, though. She's not like some of the other girls here. If life hadn't been what it was, she never would have been here, got it?"

Vin totally saw the guy's point—except he wondered just how much the club owner knew. Given how he was looking at Vin, it was as if he saw . . . everything. "Yeah, okay."

"Good. Because if you do a head job on her"—the guy put his mouth right next to Vin's ear—"I'm going to make a meal out of the meat on your bones."

As Trez straightened and flashed another one of his small smiles, Vin wasn't fooled in the slightest as visions of hot-dog rolls, hamburger buns, and BBQ sauce swirled in his head.

"You know," Vin murmured, "you're okay, big man, you really are."

Trez bowed a little. "Feel the same way about you."

When Marie-Terese came out about ten minutes later, her face was free of makeup, she had on jeans and another fleece, and her duffel bag was nowhere in sight.

"I just threw out my stuff," she said to Trez.

"Good."

They all walked down to the exit, and when they got to the door, she hugged her boss again. "Trez, about the police—"

"If they show up here looking for you, I'll let you know. But I don't want you to worry about it, okay?"

She smiled up at him. "You take care of everything, don't you."

A dark shadow passed over the man's face. "Almost everything. Now run along, you two. And don't take this the wrong way, but I hope I never see you again."

"Bye, Trez," Marie-Terese whispered.

He reached out and brushed her cheek softly. "Goodbye, Marie-Terese."

As the owner opened the back door, Vin put his arm around her waist and led her out into the night air.

"Can we go somewhere and talk?" he said as their footfalls echoed around in the stillness.

"The diner?"

"I was thinking . . . somewhere else. Actually, I have this place I want to take you to."

"Okay. I can follow you?"

"How about I just drive us both?" As she glanced back

at the club, he shook his head. "Actually, follow me, please. You'll feel safer with your own car."

There was a pause, as if she were testing her instincts. Then she shrugged.

"No ... that's not necessary." She looked up at him. "I really don't think you'll hurt me."

"You can bet your life on that."

Vin escorted her over to the M6, and after she was settled in the passenger seat, he got in behind the wheel. "We're going to the Wood."

"What's that?"

"A residential part of town where every single street ends with 'wood.' Oakwood, Greenwood, Pinewood." He started the engine. "It's like the city planners just ran out of inventive names at that point, and you have to wonder why there isn't a Woodwood Avenue over there."

She laughed. "I've been here for about a year and a half. I should probably know where it is."

"It's not far. Just about ten minutes."

Five blocks over from the club, he eased onto the Northway and went up one exit, getting off at Caldie's northern suburbs. As they passed street after street of postage-stamp lots, the houses were small and became even smaller as he went on.

He had memories of these neighborhoods, but not the Norman Rockwell, squeaky-clean, happy-family kind. More like him sneaking out of the house to get away from his parents and hooking up with his friends to go and drink and smoke and fight. Anything was better than being home back in those days.

God, how he'd prayed for them to go away. Or for him to leave.

And he'd gotten his wish, hadn't he.

"Almost there," he said, although Marie-Terese seemed perfectly content next to him, her body relaxed, her head back against the seat rest as she looked out the window.

"I feel like you could just keep driving for hours," she

murmured, "and I'd be happy just to sit here and watch the world go by."

He reached over and took her hand, giving it a squeeze. "When's the last time you had a vacation?"

"Forever."

"Ah. I know how that one is."

When he got to 116 Crestwood Avenue, he pulled into the driveway and up to a tiny two-bedroom with aluminum siding and a concrete walkway to the front door.

The place where he'd grown up had never looked so good, the bushes around the foundation trimmed and the big oak tree free of dead branches—and when there was grass growing on the ground, it would be mowed every week. He'd also replaced the roof two years ago and had the siding redone and the driveway resurfaced. It was the best-kept house on the street, if not in all of the Wood.

"What is this?" she said.

He was abruptly embarrassed, but then that was the point. Devina had never been here. No one who worked with him even knew about the place. Ever since he'd started making it, he'd shown people only what he'd been proud of.

He opened his door. "This . . . is where I grew up."

Marie-Terese was out of the car by the time he came around, and her eyes were going over every inch of the house, from stoop to flashing.

He took her arm and led her up to the front door. As he unlocked and opened the way, the scent of artificial lemon rolled out like a welcome mat, but it was a false greeting, as fake as the chemicals that were approximating the smell.

Together, they stepped through the jambs and he flipped on the hall light, then closed the door and cranked the heat on.

Cold. Damp. Disordered. In contrast to the exterior, the house inside was a mess. He'd left it exactly as it had been the day his parents had fallen down the stairs together: an artifact of ugliness.

"Yup, this is what I grew up in," he said roughly, looking

down at the only fresh stretch of rug in whole the house—
which was at the foot of the staircase. Where they'd landed
after they'd fallen from the top landing.

As Marie-Terese looked it all over, he went into the
living room and clicked on a lamp so she could also see
the ratty sofa with the bald patches on the arms . . . and
the low coffee table with the cigarette burns . . . and the
bookshelves that were still filled more with his mother's
empty vodka bottles than anything you could read.

Man, the light was not kind to the orange-and-yellow
drapes that hung with wilted exhaustion from their wrought-
iron rods or the faded rug that had a worn track leading
from the couch into the kitchen.

His skin was crawling as he walked over to the archway
and hit the light switch for the fixture over the stove.

What should have been Betty Crocker awesome was
even worse than the living room: The Formica countertops
were stained with circles left by cans that had sat for weeks,
bleeding rust onto the surface. The refrigerator with its loose
handle was harvest gold, or probably had been when it had
been bought—now it was hard to tell how much had been in-
tentional color choice and what was decay and dust. And the
pine cabinets . . . what a mess. Originally they'd been glossy,
but they were now dull, and the section of them that was
under the old leak in the ceiling had strips of varnish bubbling up from the wood like streaks of poison ivy on skin.

He was so ashamed of it all.

This was his real estate Dorian Gray, the rotting reality
he kept locked in his proverbial closet while to the rest of
the world he presented only beauty and wealth.

Vin glanced over his shoulder. Marie-Terese was wan-
dering around, her mouth slightly parted, as if she were
watching a scene in a movie that had shocked the shit out
of her.

"I wanted you to see this," he said, "because it's the truth
and I never show it to people. My parents were both al-
coholics. My dad worked as a plumber . . . my mom was a
professional smoker and that was about it. They fought a

lot and died in this house, and to be honest, I don't miss them and I'm not sorry. If that makes me a bastard, I'm okay with it."

Marie-Terese walked over to the stove. Sitting on the cooktop, between the gas burners, there was an old spoon cradle which she picked up and dusted off. "'The Great Escape . . .'"

"An amusement park up north. Ever heard of it?"

"No. As I said, I'm not from here."

He came over, looking at the cheap, touristy thing with the red logo on it. "I bought that on a school field trip. I thought maybe if the other kids saw me getting something homey for my mother, they wouldn't guess what she really was like. For some reason, the lie was important to me. I wanted to be normal."

Marie-Terese put the thing back with more care than it deserved and stayed where she was, staring at the thing. "I go to a prayer group every Tuesday and Friday night. At St. Patrick's."

Her revelation caught his breath . . . and he had to force himself to be cool. "You're Catholic? Me, too. Or at least my parents were married in a Catholic church. I'm lapsed and then some."

She tucked some of her hair behind her ear and took a shuddering breath. "I go . . . I go to the meetings because I want to be around the normal people. I want to be . . . like them again someday." Her eyes flashed up and met his. "So I understand. I understand . . . all of this. Not just the house, but why you don't bring people here."

Vin's heart thundered in his chest. "I'm glad," he said hoarsely.

Her eyes drifted around. "Yes . . . every bit of this, I get."

He held out his hand. "Come with me. Let me show you the rest of the place."

She took what he offered, and the warmth of her palm in his was transformative, lighting up his whole body, showing him just exactly how cold and numb he usually was. He'd been hoping she'd accept him even with this in his background. Praying.

And now that he saw she did, for some reason he wanted to thank God.

As they went up the stairs, the steps squeaked under the fetid carpet cover and the banister was about as steady as a drunk on a boat. At the top landing, he bypassed his parents' room, went down past the single bathroom, and paused in front of a closed door.

"This was where I slept."

After he opened it up, he turned on the overhead light. Tucked under the eave of the attic, his old twin bed was still covered with a navy blue quilt, and the single pillow at the head was still flat as a slice of bread. The desk where he'd done his homework, when he'd actually worked on the stuff, was still under the window, the goosenecked lamp he'd studied by cranked up to the ceiling. Over on the bureau, his Rubik's Cube and his black Ace comb and the 1989 *Sports Illustrated* Swimsuit Edition with Kathy Ireland on the cover were where he'd left them last.

Above the dresser, his mirror had various ticket stubs, pictures, and other shit tucked into its cheapo, fake-wood frame, and as he stepped forward and caught his reflection, he wanted to curse.

Yup, still the same. He was still staring at a face with bruises on it.

Of course, this trip, his father hadn't been the one who'd put them there.

Vin walked over to the window, and as he cracked the thing to let some air in, he felt like talking. So he did.

"You know, I took Devina to Montreal on our first date. Flew her there in my plane and we stayed in a suite at the Ritz-Carlton. She was as impressed as I meant her to be, and even today, she doesn't know where I come from. Most of that was my choice, but the thing was, she never cared about the past. She never asked about my parents after I told her they were both dead, and I never volunteered." He turned around. "I was going to marry her. Had the ring all bought—and what do you know, she even found the diamond this afternoon."

"Oh ... my God."

"Great timing, right? After Jim dropped me off, I went up to my place, opened the door, and there she was, all thrilled, the box in her hand."

Marie-Terese put her palm up to her mouth. "What did you do?"

Vin went over and sat on the bed. As a fine spray of dust rose up, he grimaced, stood again, and gathered the quilt in his arms. "Hold on a minute."

Out in the hall, he shook the bedspread out, turning his face away from the cloud. When it wasn't throwing off as much dust, he went back into the room, covered up the bare mattress, and sat down again.

"What did I do ..." he murmured. "Well, I took her arms off my neck and stepped away. Told her that I couldn't commit to her, that I'd made a mistake and that I was sorry."

Marie-Terese came over and sat down beside him. "What did she say?"

"She took it with a glacial calm. Which if you knew her, wouldn't be a surprise. I told her she could keep the ring and she went upstairs with it. Came back like fifteen minutes later with a bunch of her clothes packed. Said she'd move the rest of her stuff out right away and leave the key behind when she did. She was totally unfazed and in control. Fact was, she didn't seem surprised. I wasn't in love with her and I never had been and she knew it."

Vin pushed his ass back so he could lean against the wall. From the heat vent overhead, warm air drifted downward onto his face, a counterbalance to the cold-and-fresh ambling in across the windowsill.

After a moment, Marie-Terese followed his example, only she curled her legs up and linked her arms around her knees. "I hope you don't mind me asking ... but if you didn't love her, why did you buy the ring?"

"It was one more thing to acquire. Just like she was." He glanced over. "I'm not proud of it, by the way. I just didn't care before. . . ."

"Before?"

He looked away from her. "Before now."

There was a long silence as the two sources of air mixed together, the heated and the cool blending into a comfortable temperature.

"My son's name is Robbie," she said abruptly.

As he glanced over, he saw that on her knees, her knuckles were white from tension.

"It doesn't have to be a quid pro quo," he murmured. "Just because I tell you things doesn't mean you have to return the favor."

She smiled a little. "Oh. I know. It's just . . . I'm not used to talking."

"That makes two of us."

Her eyes moved around the room and then stayed on the open door. "Your parents argued a lot?"

"All the time."

"Did they . . . fight? As in more than just verbal . . . you know."

"Yup. Most of the time my mother's face looked like a Rorschach test . . . although she gave as good as she got— not that that excused in *any* way my father's punches." Vin shook his head. "I don't give a shit what goes down, a man should never, *ever* raise a hand to a woman."

Marie-Terese laid her cheek down on top of her knees, and stared over at him. "Some men don't share that philosophy. And some women don't fight back like your mother did."

When a growl sounded out in the room, she sat up in surprise . . . which confirmed that, yeah, the low, dangerous sound had come from him.

"Tell me that wasn't your experience," Vin said darkly.

"Oh, no . . ." she replied quickly. "But it was rough getting out of my marriage. After I told my now ex-husband that I was leaving him, he took our son and went all around the country. I didn't know where my child was or what had happened . . . three months. Three months and a private investigator and then lawyers to get free of the marriage and away from him. Everything I did was to make sure my son was and is safe."

Now her picture was becoming clear, Vin thought. And he was relieved that however bad it had been, she hadn't been battered on top of all of that. "Must have cost a lot of money."

She nodded and put her head down again. "My ex was a lot like you. Very wealthy, powerful . . . handsome."

Okay . . . shit. It was great she found him attractive, but he didn't like where this was invariably leading. How could he convince her that he wasn't—

"Mark never would have done something like this, though," she said quietly. "He never would have let himself be this . . . exposed. Thank you for this. . . . It's actually the nicest thing a man's ever done for me, in a way."

As Vin lifted his hand, he did it very slowly, so she knew exactly where it was. And when he brought his palm to her face, he gave her plenty of time to move back.

She didn't. She just met and held his eyes.

Moments expanded into minutes, and neither of them looked away.

As the silence thickened, Vin leaned in and her lips parted, her head shifting up off her knees as if she wanted to meet his mouth as much as he wanted to meet hers.

At the last second, he just kissed her forehead, though. And then he drew her into his arms, wrapping her up close and holding her. As her head rested on his chest, he smoothed his palm over her back in slow, big circles. In response, the shudder she let out was a surrender more complete, more profound, more intimate than if she'd given her body over to him for sex, and he accepted the gift of her trust with the reverence it deserved.

Resting his chin lightly on the top of her head, Vin looked across the room . . . and had the answer to the question he'd been asking himself since he'd first seen her.

Tucked into the frame of the mirror, just one among the other things, was a picture of the Madonna on a stiff card. In the depiction, she had jet-black hair and brilliant blue eyes and she was beyond lovely, her face tilted down, her golden halo a circle above her head, the aura around her whole form glowing.

He'd gotten the card from one of those evangelical types who'd shown up at the door here a long, long time ago.

As usual, the only reason he'd answered the knock was because his drunken mother had been on the verge of doing so, and he couldn't bear the shame of anyone seeing her in her dirty housecoat and with all that ratty hair. The guy on the other side of the door had been dressed in a black suit and had looked like what Vin had wished his father did—neat, tidy, healthy, and calm.

Vin had lied about his parents being home, and when the man had looked beyond into the living room, Vin said that was not his mother, but a sick relative.

The evangelist's eyes had filled with sorrow, as if he weren't unfamiliar with the situation, and the guy had skipped his spiel, just handing over the card and telling Vin to use the number on the back if he needed shelter.

Vin had taken what was offered and gone upstairs to sit with it in his palms. He'd instantaneously loved the lady on the front because she'd looked as if she never got drunk and never yelled and never hit anyone. And to make sure she was protected, he'd hidden her picture from his mother and father by making it obvious and placing it in full view on the mirror—usually when his mother ransacked his room, she just went for the drawers and the closet and whatever was under the bed.

Now he had his answer.

As he stared at the card, he realized Marie-Terese looked exactly like her.

CHAPTER
22

Jim worked his knife over the piece of wood with care and confidence. In front of him, on the newspaper he'd laid out on the floor at his feet, a pile of wood chips was growing and Dog was right next to the whole production, watching with those big brown eyes, appearing to understand on every level why someone would choose to behave this way toward a stick.

"It's going to be part of my chess set." Jim nodded at a shoe box he'd been filling up over the last month. "I think I'll make this one. . . . Well, I'm tired of doing pawns. So this will be the queen."

He'd gotten the wood from the oak trees on the property when branches broke off in the winds and fell to the ground, and he was slow but steady with his hobby, good for a couple of pieces every now and again. The tool he used was a hunting knife he'd been given by his commanding officer long ago and talk about oldie, but goodie. The thing was a masterpiece of weaponry that was deceptively humble, with no identifying trademarks, serial numbers or initials, and nothing to tip off the fact that it had been handmade by an expert for use by an expert. And Jim knew the thing like the back of his own hand, the stainless-steel blade a vicious piece of work, the handle wrapped in leather that had been aged with his own sweat.

Lifting it up, he measured the flash of the overhead light on the blade's patinaed surface. Funny, he thought, here in this one-room apartment, being used to transform wood into a game piece, it was just a knife. In most other circumstances, it had been a deadly weapon.

The purpose was everything, wasn't it.

As he went back to work, the blade made a soft scraping sound as he used his thumb to pull the knife toward himself, his hand carefully guiding each stroke, reducing the wood by increments to reveal the chess piece trapped inside.

Over the last twenty years, he'd spent hours like this: By himself. No radio, no television. Just a piece of wood and a knife. He'd made birds and animals and stars and letters that spelled nothing. Carved faces and places. Trees and flowers.

There were many advantages to his hobby. Cheap, portable, and he'd always had his blade wherever he'd been.

Guns had come and gone. Other kinds of weapons, too. COs as well.

But the knife had always been with him.

God, the day it had been presented to him, its flank had been mirror clear, and the first thing he'd done was take it outside of his quarters and rub dirt on both sides of it: Dulling all that bright-and-shiny, like sharpening the business edges, had been part of enhancing its utility.

The weapon had never failed him. And damn if he didn't say so himself, but it cut up a nice piece of wood, too—

His cell phone went off, ringing from over on the bedspread. As he went to go see who it was, he put the oak branch down and kept the knife with him out of habit.

Flipping open the phone, he saw that it was an untraceable number and knew exactly who it was.

Pushing his thumb on the *send* button, he brought the cell to his ear. "Yeah?"

Silence. And then that deep, cynical voice: "Which piece are you working on?"

Fucker. Matthias the fucker always knew too much. "The queen."

"Old habits die hard, don't they."

As did former bosses. "Thought you said I couldn't call you anymore."

"Your fingers didn't do the walking this time, did they."

"And to think you wasted all that effort just to find out what I was doing."

There was a pause. "The license plate number. Why do you need to run it and why do you care about the vehicle's owner."

Ah, so that was the *why* of the call. "None of your business."

"We don't condone freelancing. On any level. You pull shit like that and you're not just off active duty, you're going to be retired."

Which meant there was a pine box, not a gold watch, in his future: His bosses didn't send you off into the sunset with a Rolex. You just woke up dead one morning.

"Whatever, Matthias, I know the drill, and if you called just to double-check on that, you wasted—"

"So what's the plate number?"

Jim paused, and thought, Guess the debt was still owed.

As he recited Marie-Terese's tag number and detailed what little he knew about the woman, he was confident the search wouldn't get flagged as inappropriate, even though it was going through government channels. Matthias was smooth, for one thing. For another, there was only one other guy with more power than he had.

And that SOB worked out of an oval office.

Yup, there were times when it didn't hurt to have the big dog owe you his life.

"I'll be in touch," Matthias said.

When the phone went dead, Jim looked down at his knife. Matthias had gotten one at the same time Jim had, and the guy had been damn good with it—but he'd also been excellent at "office" politics, whereas Jim, with all of his antisocial tendencies, had stayed in the field. One path took Matthias to the top; the other had landed Jim . . . in a studio over a garage.

With a new set of bosses.

Jim shook his head as he compared those four aristocratic nancies with their croquet balls and their wolfhound and their castle to Matthias and his ilk: It was like putting a bunch of ballet slippers up against hiking boots outfitted with ice spurs. No contest—at least on the surface. Jim had the distinct impression, however, that those boys on the other side had shit in their back pockets that would make all the conventional and nuclear weapons at Matthias's disposal look like toys.

He went back over and sat down on the cheapy chair next to Dog, except this time he took his cell with him. As he resumed carving, he thought about his new line of work.

Assuming that Vin followed through and broke things off with Devina, and provided the guy managed to get through Marie-Terese's shell, Jim had to wonder what the hell his own role was with the whole "crossroads" bit. Yeah, maybe he'd managed to get the pair of them in the same place on Friday night, but other than that, what had he done?

This was either the easiest gig on the planet, or he was missing something.

A little later, Jim glanced at the clock. And then a half hour after that he looked again.

Matthias worked fast. Always. And on its face, the request was a simple one: Verify the registration and owner of a five-year-old Toyota Camry and perform a criminal background check. It was the kind of thing that took two sweeps of a mouse, six strokes on a keyboard, and about a nanosecond.

Unless a national security emergency had occurred. Or something had been found in Marie-Terese's records.

*   *   *

There were reasons why people felt the need to look behind themselves in dark alleys. Good reasons why most tended to hurry along, even if it wasn't chilly. Excellent reasons why lighted streets were much preferred at night.

"Oh . . . God, no. . . . please—"

The downward sweep of the tire iron cut off the pleading and it was a sharp extinguishing, like turning off a light: One moment there was illumination, the next nothing but blackness.

One moment there was a voice, the next nothing but silence.

Blood was on both their faces now.

As he set about killing the man, rage lifted his arm more than any conscious thought did and his anger gave him the kind of strength that meant this wasn't going to take long. Just one more strike, if even that, and there would be more than a temporary silence.

Shifting his weight to get the most out of the downward trajectory, he—

At the far end of the alley, the headlights of a car swept around, the twin paths of beams hitting the brick of the building to the left and pouring down its rough wall.

No time for another strike. In a split second, he was going to be lit as clear as if he were on stage.

Wheeling around, he shot over to the opposite side of the alley, running as fast as he could. As he gunned around the corner, they were going to catch sight of his jacket and the back of his baseball cap, but there were a hundred black Gore-Tex windbreakers in Caldwell, and a black hat was a black hat was a black hat.

There was a screech of brakes and then someone yelled something.

He kept going with the hightailing for only three blocks, and when there was no more shouting and no roaring sounds of a car chasing him, he slowed his pace, then ducked into an inset doorway that had no overhead light. Shucking the windbreaker, he buried the tire iron in it, making knot after knot with the sleeves to tie the thing up while he caught his breath.

His car was not far away because he'd left it somewhere other than the Iron Mask's parking lot just to be safe. And hadn't that turned out to be the right decision.

Even after he was breathing slowly and steadily, he stayed where he was, hidden and safe. The police sirens came about five minutes later and he watched two marked cars speed by. About a minute and a half later a third one, which was unmarked and had its flashing light stuck to the dashboard, went tearing past him.

When there were no others, he took off his baseball cap, wadded it up, and shoved it into the pocket of his jeans. Then he took off his belt, pulled up his fleece, and secured the bloody tire iron and its wrapping against his rib cage. After covering himself up again, he ghosted out of the doorway and headed for his car, which was less than a quarter of a mile away.

Going along, he walked neither fast nor slow, and he looked around with his eyes but not his head. To the casual observer, he was just another pedestrian out after midnight, a young guy about to meet up with friends or maybe on his way to his girl's house: Nothing unusual, utterly unnotable as he encountered a pair of guys and a homeless woman and a pack of couples.

His car was just where he'd left it and he had to get in carefully, thanks to what was stashed under his fleece. Starting the engine, he headed out onto Trade, and when an ambulance went steaming by him, he did the right thing, ducking to the side and getting out of the way.

No need to hurry, boys, he thought. Given how hard he'd hit that guy, there was no way they'd bring him around.

Cutting down toward the river, he stayed with the flow of traffic, to the extent that there was any, but there weren't a lot of people out on the roads this late. And there were fewer and fewer as he went farther and father away from downtown.

A good fifteen miles later, he pulled over to the side of the road.

No streetlights here. No cars. Just a stretch of asphalt with trees and brush that came right up to the gravel shoulder.

Getting out, he locked his car and crunched through the woods, heading for the river. When he emerged at the Hudson's shoreline, he looked across the way. There were some houses on the other side, but they had outdoor lights on only, which meant the inhabitants were asleep—although it wouldn't matter if they were awake, lying in bed, or even walking through their kitchens, trolling for a snack. No one was going to see him. The river was wide here, wide and deep.

Lifting up his black fleece, he freed the tire iron, and with a bracing throw, pitched it along with its windbreaker bathing suit into the water. With a plunk and just a little splash, the thing sank in the blink of an eye, never to be found again: The riverbed was at least ten feet down in this part, but even better, he'd chosen a spot where there was a curve to the Hudson's course—the current would not only carry the tire iron farther away from Caldwell; it would drag the thing farther out into the middle, away from the shore.

Back at his car, he got in and kept on going.

He drove around for a while, listening to the local radio, dying to know what the police were going to report about what had happened in that alley. But there was nothing. Just hip-hop and pop rock on FM and conspiracy theorists and right-wing talking heads on AM.

As he went along, taking random lefts and rights, he thought about the way things had gone tonight. He could feel himself slipping into old ways and habits, and that was not good—although on some level, it seemed inevitable.

Hard to change who you were inside. Very hard.

The thing was, shooting those college boys the night before had been a bit of shock, but the whole tire-iron incident just now seemed like business as usual. And the trigger for the kill had been much lower. The guy hadn't even been aggressive toward her in that club. He'd had her and that was enough: One look at that self-satisfied smile when he'd come out of that bathroom they'd disappeared into and the sonofabitch was a dead man.

But things couldn't keep going like this. He was smart enough to know that if he continued to off men downtown, his chances of getting caught increased with each body he left behind. So he either needed to stop . . . or clean up his messes.

When he was satisfied he hadn't been followed, and when he could no longer fight the urge to check the TV, he headed for home—or for what had been home for the past two months.

The house was a rental on the outskirts of town, in a neighborhood full of either young families with young kids or old couples with no kids. And given the number of folks who were having a hard time in the real estate bust, it had been easy for him to find something.

Rent was a thousand a month. No problem.

Pulling into the driveway, he hit the garage door opener and waited as the panels moved upward.

Odd. The house next door had lights on in it. One in the front hall, another in the living room, and a third upstairs. The place had always been dark before.

Not his business, though—he had plenty of his own going on.

Parking in his garage, he hit the button on the remote and waited until he was shut in so no one would see him get out. Which was a habit he'd picked up thanks to watching his woman. Inside the house, he went to the back hall bathroom and turned on the light. In the mirror, he realized that the mustache he'd put on his upper lip had gone off-kilter—not good, but at least no one had looked at him funny as he'd walked to his car. Maybe it had happened while he'd been at the river.

He ripped off the stripe of fuzz, flushed it down the toilet, and thought about washing the blood off here, but figured the shower upstairs would be better. As for his clothes? His fleece had been protected by the jacket, which was now in the Hudson, but his jeans were stained.

Damn it, the pants were an issue. There was a fireplace in the living room, but he'd never used it before, had no wood, and besides, if he lit something up, there was a chance the neighbors would smell the smoke and remember it.

Better to lose them in the river after dark, just like he'd done with the tire iron.

The hat. He'd had the hat on, too.

He took the black cap out of his back pocket. There were just a few spots on it, but that was enough to put it in the land of disposal. You couldn't get fibers clean enough in these days of the CSIers. Fire or permanent disappearance were the only options you had.

Upstairs, he paused at the top of the stairwell. With both hands, he took off the wig and smoothed his hair so that it lay flat. He supposed it would be better to take a shower before he showed himself, but he couldn't wait that long. Besides, he'd have to walk through the bedroom to get to the bathroom, so she'd see him anyway.

He went to the doorway. "I'm home."

Across the way, she looked at him from the corner, as beautiful and demure and resplendent as ever, her eyes pools of compassion and warmth, her alabaster skin glowing in the dim light cast by the street lamp outside.

He waited for a response and then reminded himself one wasn't coming: The Mary Magdalene statue he'd stolen at dawn remained as quiet as it had been when he'd taken it from the church.

He'd had to take her. Now that he knew what his woman did for a living, it was his representation of his love, the thing to tide him over until he finally and permanently got her where she belonged—which was with *him*.

The statue also reminded him that he shouldn't kill her just because she was a dirty, filthy slut. She was . . . a woman misled, strayed, off the right path. Something he himself was guilty of. But he'd done his time and he was back on track now....

Well, with minor exceptions.

As he knelt in front of the statue, he reached up to cup the face in his palm. He loved being able to touch his woman and it was a little disappointing not to have her stroke him back or worship him as she should.

But that was why he needed the real thing.

CHAPTER
23

Marie-Terese had been convinced Vin was going to kiss her on the mouth.

And there was a part of her that wanted just that, but she'd been panicky, too: She might have technically been having sex at the club, but it had been three years since she'd actually been kissed. And the last time it had happened it had been forced on her as part of an act of violence.

Instead of giving her what she both wanted and feared, though, Vin had just pressed his lips to her forehead and eased her up against his chest—and here she was, in the strong arms of a man whose heart was beating close to her ear, whose warmth was leaching into her own body, whose big hand was making slow circles around her back.

Marie-Terese smoothed her palm up his pecs. Underneath the cashmere, his body was hard, suggesting that he exercised a lot.

She wondered what he looked like without his clothes on.

She wondered what his mouth would feel like on hers.

She wondered how having him skin-to-skin would be.

"I guess we should probably go," he said, his voice rumbling through his chest.

"Do we have to?"

His breath caught and then resumed. "I think we'd better."

"Why?"

Vin shrugged, the movement rubbing his sweater against her cheek. "Just think it's for the best."

Oh, man . . . how about that for a polite brush-off. Good God, what if she'd read it all wrong?

Abruptly, she shifted upward, pushing herself off of him. "Yes, I think you're right—"

In her haste, her palm slipped on the fine nap of his sweater and brushed over something that was hard below his waist. And not hard as in bone.

"Damn, I'm sorry," he said, moving his hips away. "Yeah, it's definitely time to pull out of here . . ."

She looked down. His erection was unmistakable, and what do you know, she had a roaring sexual response to it. She wanted him. Needed to have him inside of her. And all the rational reasons not to go there were suddenly nothing more than yada, yada, yada. . . .

Locking eyes with him, she whispered, "Kiss me."

Vin froze in the process of getting up. As his chest expanded, he stared at the floor and didn't say a thing.

"Oh," she said. "I understand."

His body might have wanted her, but his mind was jamming at the thought of being with a whore.

In a horrible rush, she saw the faces of the johns she had been with . . . or at least those she could recall. So many of them, more than she could count, and they crowded the space between her and this man who sat on his boyhood bed, looking as sexy as anything.

She hadn't wanted the others. Had taken pains to be as separate from them as she could, layers of latex and dissociation barriers she used to try to stay as untouched by the contact as she could.

Vin, however . . . Vin she wanted close, and he couldn't go there.

This was the real damage she had done to herself, wasn't it: she'd assumed that as long as she stayed disease-free and unharmed physically, the long-term effects were going to be limited to a store of memories she'd be desperate to forget. But this was cancer, not the flu. Because she could barely see Vin through the cast of hundreds, and he was as blinded by the anonymous, invisible crowd as she was.

Swallowing hard, she thought ... in this moment, she would have given up everything to have had a clean slate between her and Vin. Everything ... except for her son.

Marie-Terese shifted off the bed, but he caught her hand before she could shoot out of the room.

"I can't stop at just kissing you." His hot eyes locked on her. "That's the only reason I'm holding off. I'd like to tell you I'm a gentleman and could pull back or out with only a word from you, but I can't trust myself. Not tonight."

Caught up in the distance between them, all she could hear was, *Women like you don't get to say no.*

In a hoarse voice, she said, "You already know I'm a slut. So I won't stop you."

Vin's expression went cold and he dropped his hold on her.

After a moment, he rose to his feet and glared at her. "You don't ever refer to yourself like that in front of me again. We clear? Never again. I don't give a fuck who you were with or how many there were—you're not a slut to me. You want to beat yourself up, do it on your time and don't try to drag me into it."

On a survival instinct, she cringed back from him and shielded her head, expecting his hands to curl into fists and come flying at her.

She'd been trained thoroughly in what men who were furious did to women.

Except Vin just stared at her, the anger in his face draining out and leaving a pale panic behind. "He hit you, didn't he."

Marie-Terese couldn't answer that. Because even a nod would have sent her into a spiral of tears. Tonight ... as Vin himself had said, tonight was not the night for trusting herself: Whereas quitting the business had made her feel stronger, that had been temporary. Here and now, she was vulnerable as hell.

"Jesus . . . Christ," Vin murmured.

Before she knew it, she was back in his arms, back in them and up close. As they stood together, something occurred to her about the choices she'd made . . . something that she didn't want to look too closely at, so she pushed it away and locked it up tight.

Lifting her head to look up at him, she said, "Be with me. Now."

Vin went stock-still . . . and then cupped her face with his gentle palms. "You sure?"

"Yes."

After a long moment, he closed the distance between their mouths and kissed her sweet and slow. Oh . . . soft. He was so soft and careful, stroking, tilting his head to the side, stroking some more.

It was better than she remembered, because it was better than she'd ever had.

Running her palms up his arms, she felt as if the two of them were suspended in air, tethered by choice, not trapped by circumstance. Light as the contact between them was, gentle as his lips were, careful as her hands were, power sizzled between them.

Vin pulled back a little. He was breathing hard, the muscles in his neck straining. And that wasn't the only thing. As he looked at her, his body was even more ready for what was going to happen next.

He cleared his throat. "Marie-Terese . . ."

It was on the tip of her tongue to ask him to call her by her real name, but she stopped herself. "Yes?" she whispered in a voice as husky as his.

"Lie down with me."

When she nodded, he gathered her into him and pulled her onto the bed so that they ended up with her top. As their bodies adjusted to glorious effect, his hands brushed her hair from her face and lingered on her shoulders.

"I like the way you feel under me," she said.

He smiled. "And how do I feel?"

"Hard." She arched into him, rubbing herself on his arousal.

As Vin reared back into the pillow and hissed, she put her mouth on the rigid cords that lined his neck, kissing her way up them until she got to his sharp jaw. Now she was the one fusing their mouths, and he was following her, tongues sweeping in and out, hands roaming, hips moving in the ancient surging motion of raw sex.

It wasn't long before she needed so much more. Her breasts were aching, the tips straining against her bra, and she took his hand and eased it under the shirt she had on. The contact of his palm on her ribs made her suck on his tongue and to urge him onward, she guided the contact over to her—

"*Vin* . . .

As he palmed her breast, he groaned and rubbed his thumb around her nipple. "You're hell on my willpower. Total hell . . ."

With a surge, he leaned up and nuzzled at her breast through her clothes. "I need you naked."

"Just what I was thinking." Sitting back on his hips, she swept her fleece over her head and was attacked by a wave of modesty. Abruptly, she wanted her nakedness to be beautiful to him . . . she really did.

As if he read her mind, he murmured, "Would you rather do this with the lights off?"

Well, yeah. Except then she couldn't see him. "I'm not perfect, Vin."

He shrugged. "Neither am I. But I will guarantee that whatever you choose to show me I'm going to like because it's you."

Dropping her hands and holding his stare, she said, "Take my shirt off then. Please."

Sitting up so that they were face-to-face and she was in his lap, Vin unbuttoned the thing down to her navel, his mouth going to her throat and then her collarbone and finally to the front clasp of her bra. His eyes flipped to hers as he reached up and sprang the fastening.

He didn't let the two sides snap apart, but held them in place.

Inch by inch his mouth kissed its way onto her breast. As he went, he slowly exposed her flesh until he got to her nipple and then he pulled the lace cup off entirely. His whole body shuddered with lust.

"You're so wrong," he groaned. "Look at you . . . perfect."

He extended his tongue and licked her. And licked her again.

Watching him was nearly as good as feeling him, and the two together, the sight and the sensation, fired her blood up until she was panting.

Thank God they'd left the light on.

Vin shifted their positions, putting her on the bottom and rising up above her, his broad shoulders blocking out the fixture on the ceiling as he kissed her mouth again. Beneath his strength, she felt small and fragile, but powerful too: He was breathing hard because he wanted her, because his desperation was as sharp and demanding as her own, because he needed this with the same clawing drive she did.

They were in this together.

And then she stopped thinking, because he dropped his mouth onto her breast and took deep pulls while he parted her shirt all the way and swept aside the other cup of her bra.

As he continued what he was doing, she was dying to know the feel of his skin on hers, so she fisted the back of his sweater and started pulling it up. He finished the job, lifting himself to peel it from his chest.

In the mirror across the way, she watched as his back was revealed, the light from the overhead hitting the spectacular spread of muscles that filled out his shoulders and wrapped around his torso. And the view of his pecs was just as good.

He was a fantasy made real, his body nothing but ridges of strength that shifted under smooth flesh as he brought his lips down to her nipple again. With his bowed arms supporting the weight of his chest, he was a magnificent male animal ready to ditch fifty thousand years of evolution and mental development for the base mating that was to come.

Talk about perfect . . .

Marie-Terese rolled her hips and sank her fingers deep into his thick hair. Her body was fluid under his mouth and his touch, heat rolling through her and tightening the ache between her legs. When the erotic need got to be too much, she split her thighs and—

They both moaned as his erection landed in just the right place.

Vin arched against her, and her nails raked across the waistband of his slacks: Careful and gentle was all well and good, but the momentum had started to build and all of the worry of what to do was swept away.

"Can I take off your jeans?" he asked. Or groaned was more like it.

"Oh, please . . ."

She braced herself on her heels as he slipped the top button free, unzipped and swept the denim down her legs. Her panties were black and he stopped and just stared at them on her body.

"Good . . . lord," he murmured.

His hands actually shook as he reached out and ran his fingertips across her belly. She waited for him to kiss her again . . . or move over on top of her . . . or take her panties off. . . .

"Is there anything wrong?" she said hoarsely.

"No . . . not at all . . . I just can't get enough of looking at you."

Finally, he came up to her lips. Licking into her mouth, he settled on her with his full weight, his bare chest on hers, their legs intertwining. Together, they found a rhythm, an erotic arch and retreat that sexed her up until she was gasping and so was he.

"Please . . . Vin . . ."

As he kissed her, his hand eased down her hip and over her thigh, then brushed across the stretch of her panties. "I need to feel you—" he said.

She took his forearm and pushed down, moving his fingers to her core, dragging them across her covered heat. As she shuddered and let her legs fall to the sides even more, he took his mouth to her breast and suckled at her . . . while he rubbed at what covered her.

"More," she said.

Slipping under the delicate edge, he found her softness and cursed hard, his body snapping tight from head to foot, his teeth gritting, the cords in his neck tightening up starkly.

"Oh . . . Christ . . ." he said. "Oh . . . *damn*."

Abruptly, he pulled back and looked down at himself.

"What?" she asked breathlessly.

"I think I just had an orgasm."

As he flushed, she started to smile and couldn't stop. "You did?"

He shook his head at her. "Right, okay, that's not a good thing at a time like this. Five minutes from now? Perfect. At this moment? Not so hot."

"Well, it makes me feel sexy," she said, smoothing her hand down his face.

"You don't need any help with that."

Marie-Terese let her touch slide slowly over his chest and his hard stomach, then down farther, over his belt and onto his . . .

Vin threw his head back and moaned, his pecs flexing, his torso curving up. "*Shit*."

Moving her palm up and down on his erection, she tucked her face into his neck and bit down a little. "I don't think it's going to slow you up much."

His rib cage contracted, breath shooting out of his mouth. "I gotta get naked."

"I should hope so."

His hands were rough on his belt and his fly, and his

slacks hit the floor at the speed of light. Black briefs cupped his sex—barely. His erection was a long ridge crammed over to one side, the head fighting to get free of the waistband that held it in.

Before he could lie back, she reached out and tugged those briefs down his hard thighs, springing his arousal. He had orgasmed and the glossy, weeping tip of him made her even more ready for what was coming fast.

Wrapping her hand around his shaft, she stroked his sex and looked up, watching as he planted one palm against the wall and let his head fall loose. He moved with her, and she glanced across at the mirror, watching what his back looked like as his hips swung forward and back, the clenching and releasing of his torso muscles and the way his spine undulated in a wave the most erotic thing she'd ever seen . . .

Marie-Terese let go of him, took off her panties, and stretched out beside him. Ready.

Vin righted his head and stared at her from under his brows, his silvery eyes lit up bright as a flash of steel in the midday sun.

They both remembered the same thing at the same time.

"Do you have a—"

"I have a condom—"

Thank you, God, she thought as he went to his wallet and took out one of those Tiffany blue Trojan packets. She was on the Pill, courtesy of her regularly visiting a doc-in-the-box in town, and she'd just had a checkup, but no matter how attracted she was to Vin, she wasn't going to be reckless with her own body with anyone.

Safe sex was the only way.

And watching him protect them both was sexy as hell. When he was done, they resumed the position they'd been in before, her back against the duvet, him half on top of her, half to the side. The condom was chilly against her thigh, leaving a quickly cooling trail, and she wished she'd had a moment to feel his sex for real somewhere on her. But then he was fully on top of her and between her legs, the head of him nudging at the heart of her.

She stared into his eyes as she guided him in.

How right it was. How filling and spectacular the joining. How wondrous to meet his stare and see reflected in it the same things she was feeling—the glorious shock at how well they fit, the coiling need to go even further . . .

And there was another surprise for her: For once it didn't hurt because her body actually wanted this.

"Are you okay?" he asked in a guttural voice.

"More than okay."

Marie-Terese wrapped her arms around his shoulders and held him close as they began to move together. Her last sight before she squeezed her lids shut was of them in the mirror, their bodies wrapped around each other, her legs split wide, his hips doing the driving. As she met her own eyes, her reflection was a shock. Her cheeks were flushed and her hair tangled around his heavy arm and her lips parted. She looked very much like a woman with a good partner.

Which made sense. This was sex the good old-fashioned way—between two people who wanted to be together for no other reason than that it was the right thing at the right time for both of them.

When what the mirror was showing grew wavy from tears that sprang to her eyes, she closed the sight of them off and turned her face into his shoulder.

Somehow, he managed to hug her and still keep up the rhythm.

As Marie-Terese pitched over the edge of pleasure and went into the kind of free fall she had only a vague memory of, she held on to the man responsible for the way she felt and let herself go. Her climax milked another one out of his sex and she felt utter satisfaction as he shuddered and kicked—

Except then everything went wrong. For a split second, she thought of what she had been doing for money, and that was all it took to ruin it: A cold gust blew into her chest and spread out from there until all her veins were frozen and her muscles drew tight against bones of ice.

Vin stilled as if he had sensed the change in her and he lifted his head from her hair. "Talk to me."

She opened her mouth. But nothing would come out.

"It's okay," he said softly, catching her tears with his fingertips. "This has to be hard for you. Even if it felt right, it has to be hard."

She struggled to catch her breath, not from exertion, but from the effort of not flying apart. "What if it all comes back every time I'm ..."

With you, she wanted to finish, but that seemed a bit much. For God's sake, she didn't know whether she was still going to be in this town next week.

He kissed her. "Other memories will take the place of all that. It's going to take time, but it will happen."

She glanced at the mirror and thought of the way he moved. As she recalled the feel and sight of him, the cold retreated some, ushered out of her by a wave of warmth.

"I hope you're right," she said, running her hands through his hair. "I really do."

CHAPTER
24

As they lay together, Vin covered Marie-Terese up with the best blanket he had: his own body. Damn, it felt good to be all crammed on his little bed with her, although he had to be careful with his hands and where they went. With so much exposed deliciously soft female skin so close to him . . .

After two orgasms, only one of which had been on time, he was still hard. And hungry. But he was not going to pressure her in any way.

So yeah, he watched where his palms went as he stroked her slowly, and he kept his hips out of the way, and he trained his eyes across the room instead of on, say, her perfect pink nipples.

"I'm sorry about the crying," she said, as if she knew he was worried.

"Is there anything I can do for you?"

She pressed her lips to his pec. "You did plenty."

Well, if that didn't make him go all big dog in his chest. "I'd like to do it again sometime."

"Would you?"

"Soon."

The smile she gave him was bright as a rainbow. "Too bad you had only the one condom."

"Talk about tragic."

They stayed side by side until the cold breeze coming in through the window over took the hot drift from the vent above the bed.

"You're cold," he said, rubbing the goose bumps on her arm.

"I'm comfortable, though."

He reached over her and picked up her shirt off the floor. As he helped her into it, he paused to watch her breasts sway.

"You should never wear a bra. Ever."

She laughed as she did up her buttons, and after he handed her the fleece she'd worn, he picked up her panties.

Oh, for God's sakes . . . he wanted to keep them. Which made him a perv and a jerk, but that was the caveman for you: He wanted something of his woman's with him.

Except she wasn't his, was she? For fuck's sake, what woman in her right mind would sign on for a guy who'd just dumped his would-be fiancée? Yeah, real stable right there.

"I believe these are yours," he murmured, handing over the slip of black with care.

"Yes, they would be." She took them and treated him to one hell of a show as she put the things on—not because she was being deliberately erotic, but because to him she was pretty frickin' edible any way she came and no matter what she did.

The whole thing made him think about when he'd taken her jeans off. He'd stopped at that point and stared at her for so long because he'd wanted to go down on her right then and there: He'd been struck motionless by visions of moving her hips to the edge of the mattress and kneeling on the floor in front of her and taking his damn time with her.

In some ways, though, oral sex was more intimate than the whole penetration thing, and he'd been concerned that being with him would bring up bad memories for her. Which was exactly what had happened.

But hopefully there would be other times. Shortly. And a lot of them.

When he was dressed, and her bra was tucked in her pocket, they walked out of his old room, arm in arm, and as he passed the mirror, he took the picture of the Madonna with him, slipping it into his jacket.

Downstairs, he turned off the lights and lowered the heat, and when they got to the front door, he paused and looked around. "I should clean this place up."

He had a feeling he wouldn't act on the impulse, however. Even though he had a crew of men he could send over to rip out all of the old crap and demo the baths and kitchen, he had a terrible inertia problem when it came to the house.

In a lot of ways, it sucked the will to live right out of him.

On the way back to the Iron Mask, he held Marie-Terese's hand the whole time, except for when he had to shift.

Pulling into the club's parking lot, he glanced over. As she stared out her window, the line of her chin and the way her hair fell over her shoulder were incredibly beautiful.

And then he realized what she was looking at. The alley on the far side that was cordoned off with crime scene tape.

"You want me to follow you home?" he said.

She nodded, her eyes still locked on where those kids had been killed. "Would you mind?"

"I would love to." Man, trust from a woman could make a guy feel tall as a mountain.

Marie-Terese turned to face him. "Thank you ... for everything."

He leaned in slowly, in case kissing so close to where she had worked was going to be too much. She didn't move out of the way, though, and as their lips met briefly, he inhaled deep.

Clean laundry and fresh woman. That was what she smelled like.

Better than any perfume ever made.

"Can I see you again?" he asked.

Ducking her head, she picked her purse up from the floor. "I hope so."

With a last, too-quick smile, she sprang the door, got out, and went over to her car. Instead of using a security fob, she unlocked the thing using the actual key, and it took forever for the fucking thing to start.

He didn't like that Camry of hers. Way too unreliable.

And while he was at it, he didn't like how she'd avoided his eyes just now.

When her car finally decided to get with the program, she took off and he rode her bumper out of downtown and into another section of suburban houses. He knew immediately which one was hers: the little Cape Cod with the bars over every window, even those on the second floor. The car parked parallel to the curb right in front was no doubt the babysitter's.

Vin waited at the foot of the driveway while the garage door went up and she drove inside. As the panels trundled shut, he hoped he would catch another glimpse of her, but she stayed in the car.

Which was no doubt safer, and therefore a very good thing.

He waited some more.

And then there she was at the window in the kitchen, lifting her hand in a wave. Returning the good-bye, he waved and put his hand over the horn to give a little beep . . . but then stopped, figuring she wouldn't appreciate any attention being drawn to her.

He headed off with a frown cranking his eyebrows together, her situation chillingly obvious. She was still running from that ex-husband of hers . . . running not just scared, but terrified, and expecting at some point to be found. For God's sake, she wasn't even chancing it by opening her car door until she was locked in the garage.

His first thought was that he wanted to build her a fortress and arm the fucking place with a platoon of soldiers like Jim.

His next was of the way she'd answered his question before she'd left his car:

Can I see you again?

I hope so.

She was going to bolt. Whether or not those two deaths last night had anything to do with her, she was going to pull a runner. And the idea of never seeing her again, of not knowing what happened to her, of not doing anything to help, panicked the shit out of him.

About fifteen minutes later, he pulled into the Commodore's garage and parked next to his black Range Rover. For some reason, as he got into the elevator, echoes of the nightmare he'd had about Devina came back and he heard that voice again:

You're mine, Vin. And I always take what is mine.

On the twenty-eighth floor, he stepped out into the corridor—

Vin stopped. The door to his duplex was open and voices were coming out of his place. A number of them.

It was hard to believe Devina had gotten movers to come over this late—it was past midnight, for fuck's sake. So what the hell was going on?

Striding over, ready to give whoever was in his digs a hard time and then some, Vin burst inside with all proverbial guns blazing.

Cops.

There were four cops standing in his front hall, and they all looked over at him at the same time.

Holy shit, it had finally happened. All those bribes to city officials, all the misrepresentations, all the tax evasions . . . it had finally caught up with him.

"Can I help you, Officers?" he said, going total poker face.

"He's here," one of them called out.

As he wondered how many were in his study, his eyes shifted to the living room—

With a whispered curse, he took halting steps forward and gripped the carved jamb of the archway. The place looked like it had been hit with gale-force winds, furniture tipped out of place, paintings hanging cockeyed, liquor bottles smashed.

"Where's Devina?" he asked.

"In the hospital," someone answered.

"She's *what*?"

"Hospital."

He turned to the cop who had spoken. The guy was built like a bulldog, and with the hard expression he had on his face, he looked like one, too.

"Is she okay? What happened?" Vin eyed the handcuffs that were being unclipped from the man's belt. "What do you need those for?"

"You're under arrest for assault and battery. Please show me your hands."

"Excuse me?"

"You are under arrest for assault and battery." The cop didn't wait for compliance, but grabbed Vin's right wrist and slapped the cuff over it. A quick wrench and Vin was locked in. "You have the right to remain silent. Anything you say can and will be used against you in a court of law. You have the right to have an attorney present during questioning. If you cannot afford an attorney"—now the guy's voice grew wry—"one will be appointed to you. Do you understand these rights as I've stated them?"

"I haven't been here since this afternoon! And the last time I saw Devina, she was leaving—"

"Do you understand your rights?"

"I didn't do any of this!"

"Do you understand your rights?"

Vin hadn't been arrested for years, but it was like riding a fucking bicycle; it all came back to him. Except for one salient part—back then, he'd known precisely why he was being taken into custody because he'd actually commited the crime.

"Answer me something," he demanded as he wheeled

around to confront the badge. "Why do you think I hurt her?"

"Because she said you did, and going by the busted knuckles on your right hand, I'd say you were in an altercation very recently."

Devina . . . had lied. Big time.

"I didn't hit her. Ever. I had no reason to."

"Oh, really? You mean when she told you she'd been with your buddy, that didn't tick you off? Hard to believe."

"*My buddy?*"

"Let's get you booked. And then you can call your lawyer." The cop glanced around the ruined living room—which still managed to look expensive, even as trashed as it was. "Something tells me you won't be needing a public defender."

CHAPTER
25

Jim woke up on Sunday lying on his side, with Dog tucked into his chest, and the television on mute in the background.

The on-the-side part and the soundless TV were standard operating procedure. Dog, however, was a nice addition: Warm, friendly, and he smelled like summer air for some reason. The only time it got a little disorientating was when Dog dreamed, his paws twitching, his jaw working, muffled growls or woofs coming every once in a while.

You had to wonder what he dreamed about. Clearly, there was running involved, given all that footwork, but hopefully it was because he was doing the chasing.

Jim arched his neck and checked out what was on the television. The local news was featuring that almost beautiful but very blond newscaster, who evidently covered weekend mornings. As she ran through her reports, images appeared to the left of her head and taped footage replaced her every now and again. School board vote. Pothole problem. At-risk youth program.

And then a familiar picture flashed: Vin's face.

Jim shot up, grabbed the remote, and hit the volume . . . and could not believe what he heard:

Vin arrested for beating his girlfriend. Bail to be set shortly. Devina in the hospital for overnight observation.

"And in other news," the anchorwoman continued, "there has been a second brutal attack downtown. Robert Belthower, thirty-six, was found after midnight in an alley not far from where Friday night's two victims were shot. He is now at St. Francis Hospital in critical condition. No suspects have been identified yet in the crime, and Police Chief Sal Funuccio issued a statement urging caution...."

Jim stroked Dog's back. Holy shit ... Vin diPietro was a lot of things, but a woman beater? Hard to believe that, given the way he'd gone after those two college kids for harassing Marie-Terese.

And another guy found in an alley? Although maybe that wasn't related to the—

As if on cue, because this shit storm clearly needed another tornado in the mix, his cell phone went off.

Jim picked the thing up from the bedside table without looking where it was—a little trick he'd taught himself thanks to having worked in the pitch-black a lot. Amazing how sound made up for sight.

"Good morning, sunshine," he said without looking to see who it was.

His old boss's voice was about as cheerful as he felt. "She doesn't exist."

Jim's hand tightened its hold, even though this was not a surprise. "You couldn't find anything?"

"Didn't say that. But your Marie-Terese Boudreau is an identity cooked up by a guy in Las Vegas. As far as I can tell, it was created about five years ago and first used by some lady who ended up in Venezuela. Then your girl bought the documents the year before last, traveled east and settled in Caldwell, New York. Address is One Eighty-nine Fern Avenue. Has a cell phone." The digits rolled off his boss's tongue and went right into Jim's razor-sharp memory. "On her income taxes, her W-twos are from a place called ZeroSum, and then at the end of last year, for about a month, the Iron Mask. Occupation listed as dancer in both places. Dependent is one."

"Who is she really?"

There was a pause. "Well, now, isn't that the question."

The satisfaction in that deep voice was not the kind of thing you ever wanted to hear: It meant your balls were in a vise grip and someone with a sadistic stretch a mile long had his hand on the crank.

Jim closed his eyes. "I'm not coming back. I told you when I left, I'm out."

"Come on, Zacharias, you know the drill. A toe tag is the only way you're truly done with us. The only reason I let you have a little vacation was because you were too close to the edge. But what do you know, you sound soooo much better now."

Jim fought the urge to punch his fist through the wall. "For once in your miserable, godforsaken life, can you do something without expecting anything back? Try it. Maybe you'll like it. You could start now."

"Sorry. Everything is a negotiation."

"Did your father beat the morality out of you? Or were you just born a shit?"

"You could ask him, but he's been dead for years. Poor guy got in the way of my bullet. Damn shame, really."

Jim bit his frickin' lip and clenched every muscle in his jaw and neck. "Please . . . I need to know about her. Just tell me. It's important."

Naturally, Matthias the fucker didn't fall for the mother-may-I shit. "The 'favor' I supposedly owe you only gets you so far. Then if you want more, you have to give me something to earn it. Up to you. And before you ask, the assignment I have in mind is right up your alley."

"I don't kill people anymore."

"Hmm."

"Matthias, I need to know who she is."

"I'm sure you do. And you know where to find me."

The line went dead, and for a moment, Jim seriously considered firing the phone across the room. The only thing that stopped him was Dog, who lifted his sleepy head and somehow managed to drain the urge right out of Jim's arm.

He dropped the phone on the bedspread.

As his mind raced and his temper seethed, he didn't know what the fuck to do with himself . . . so he just reached out to the animal and tried to pat down the fur that was sticking straight up between his ears.

"Get a load of this 'do, man. You look like Einstein when you wake up . . . you really do."

Eye contact was everything when you were in jail.

Vin had learned this during his forays through the juvie system: Behind bars, how you met the stares of the guys you were in with was your *Hello, My Name Is* . . . and there were five main categories.

Junkies had unfocused peepers, usually because they couldn't control their optic nerves any better than they could their sweat glands, bowels, or nervous systems. As the prison equivalent of lawn sculpture, they tended to pick a place and stay there, and for the most part, they kept out of the drama because they didn't instigate and easy targets were a bore.

Dime-sizers, on the other hand, who were usually on their first trip through the penal system and more than a little freaked out, had stares like Ping-Pong balls, all willy-nilly, not-for-longs, their eyes bouncing around. This made them perfect candidates for ridicule and verbal harassment, but generally not fists—because they'd be the ones who'd yell for the guards at the drop of a hat.

Motherfuckers, in contrast, had seeker stares, always probing for weakness and ready to pounce. They were the ones who picked at everyone and loved playing the ha-rasser, but they were not the dangerous ones. They insti-gated, but let the hotheads follow through—they were kids in the sandbox who broke toys and blamed it on others.

Hotheads had crazy eyes and loved to fight. All it took was the slimmest of openings and they were ready to go to town. 'Nuff said.

And finally, you had your bona fide sociopaths, the ones who didn't give a fuck and could kill you and eat your liver. Or not. Didn't matter either way. Their eyes drifted around, ocular sharks that swam in the middle distance of the room for the most part—until they ID'd a victim.

As Vin sat among a representative sample of the above, he was part of none of these groups, falling into a category that was fairly atypical: He stayed out of people's biz and expected others to extend the same courtesy. And if they didn't?

"Nice suit you got there."

With Vin's back against the concrete wall, and his eyes on the floor, he didn't have to glance up to know that out of the eleven other guys in the holding bin, he was the only one with a pair of lapels.

Ah, yes, a motherfucker stepping up to the plate.

Vin deliberately shifted forward and put his elbows on his knees. Bringing his fist into his palm, he slowly swiveled his head toward the guy who'd spoken.

Wiry. Tattooed up the neck. Earrings. Hair cut so short that his skull showed. And as the SOB smiled like he was looking forward to a meal he intended to enjoy, he flashed a chipped front tooth.

Clearly he thought he had a dime-sized newbie by the tail.

Vin flashed his own teeth and one by one cracked the knuckles on his striking hand. "You like my threads, asshole?"

As the reply came back at him, Mr. Personality was instantly cured of his this-is-gonna-be-funsies. His brown eyes did a quick measure of the size of Vin's fist and then returned to the steady stare that was locked on him.

"I asked you," Vin said loud and slow, "do you like my threads, *asshole*."

While the guy considered his answer, Vin hoped the response was obnoxious, and something about that must have come through: As the rest of the men made like spectators at a tennis match, going back and forth, back and forth, the tension eased out of the motherfucker's shoulders.

"Yeah, it's real nice. Real nice suit. Yeah."

Vin stayed right where he was as the other guy settled back on the bench. And then one by one he met the stares of the peanut gallery ... and one by one the men looked down at the floor. Only then did Vin relax a little.

As half of his brain stayed plugged into office politics, such as they were, the other part went back to churning over how the hell he'd ended up where he was. Devina had lied through her teeth to the police, and so help him God, he was going to find out what the fuck had really happened. And "buddy"? What the hell was she talking about?

He thought back to the blue dress that had smelled like men's cologne. The idea that she'd been fucking around on him made him dangerously psychotic, so he forced his brain to consider the more important stuff. Like, oh, the fact that she had been beaten by someone other than him, but it was his cock and balls in the clink.

Christ, if only his security system at home had the same kind of monitoring shit his office did. Then he'd have a video of every room, twenty-four/seven.

The chiming of keys announced the arrival of a guard. "DiPietro, your lawyer is here."

Vin got up off the bench, and as the door slid open with a clang, he stepped out and put his hands behind his back, presenting himself to the guard for cuffing.

Which seemed to surprise the guy with the keys, but not the ones who'd just witnessed Vin be all ready to Rocky it with the motherfucker.

There was a *click*, *click* and then he and the badge walked down a hall to another bank of iron bars that had to be released by someone on the far side. After that they hung another right and a left and stopped in front of a door that was something out of a high school, the thing painted blech beige, its window marked with chicken wire embedded in the glass.

Inside the interrogation room, Mick Rhodes was leaning back against the far wall, his wingtips crossed, his double-breasted suit the kind that Mr. Personality would also have approved of.

Mick stayed quiet as the guard released the cuffs and ducked out of the room. After the door shut, the lawyer shook his head. "Never expected this one."

"That makes two of us."

"What the hell happened, Vin?" Mick then nodded up at a security camera, indicating that attorney-client privilege was probably more of a theory than an actuality here in the station house.

Vin sat down at the little table, taking one of the two chairs. "No fucking clue. I came home around midnight and the cops were in my place—which had been trashed. They told me Devina was in the hospital and she said I was the one who'd put her there. My alibi is airtight, though. I was at my office for the whole afternoon and into the evening. I can get them videos of me sitting at my desk for hours."

"I've seen the police report. She said she was attacked at ten o'clock."

Shit. He'd assumed it had happened earlier.

"Right, we're going to talk about all that where-were-you stuff a little later," Mick murmured, as if he knew the answer to that one was complicated. "I've pulled some strings. Your bail's going to be set within the hour. It'll be a hundred thousand or so."

"If they give me my wallet, I can do that right now."

"Good. I'll take you home—"

"Only to get clothes." He never wanted to see the duplex again, much less stay there. "I'm going to a hotel."

"Don't blame you. And if you find you need some privacy from the media, you can stay with me in Greenwich."

"I just need to talk to Devina." He needed to find out not only who had busted her up, but who the hell she'd been sleeping with. He had a lot of friends . . . a man like him with money like his? He had friends all over the fucking place.

"Let's get you out of here first, okay? And then we'll talk about next steps."

"I didn't do it, Mick."

"Do you think I would be dressed up like this on Sunday morning if I thought otherwise? For God's sake, man, I could be cozied up with the *Times* right now."

"At least that's a priority I can respect."

And Mick was true to his word: Thanks to a quick hundred grand taken off his debit card, Vin was out of the police station and getting into his buddy's Mercedes by ten thirty a.m.

Getting released was hardly cause for celebration, though. As they went over to the Commodore, Vin's head was an utter mess, spinning out of control as he tried to find some kind of inner logic to the whole thing.

"Vin, buddy, you're going to listen to me because I'm not only your frat brother, so you can trust me, but I'm also your lawyer. Do not go to the hospital. Do not talk to Devina. If she calls or reaches out to you, do not interact with her." The Mercedes eased to a halt in front of the Commodore. "Do you have an alibi for where you were between ten and twelve last night?"

Staring out the windshield, Vin remembered exactly where he had been . . . and what he'd been doing. The decision was clear. "Not that I can give the police. No."

"But you were with someone?"

"Yes." Vin opened the door. "I won't be involving her—"

"Her?"

"You can reach me on my cell phone."

"Wait, who is this 'her'?"

"None of your business."

Mick braced his forearm on the steering wheel and leaned across the seat. "If you want to save your ass, you may have to reconsider that."

"I didn't hurt Devina. And I have no idea why she would want to frame me for this shit."

"You don't? She know about this 'her' of yours?"

Vin shook his head. "No, she doesn't. Call me."

"Don't go to that hospital, Vin. Promise me."

"Not where I'm headed next." He shut the door and strode over to the Commodore's entrance. "Trust me."

CHAPTER
26

The St. Francis Hospital complex was laid out with all the logic of an ant farm. Reflecting an iterative architectural philosophy, like so many medical centers of its kind, the buildings that covered its acreage were a hodgepodge of styles, and they were positioned where they could be squeezed in, like round pegs shoved into square holes. On the campus, you had a little bit of everything from Gothic brick, to institutional steel and glass, to sprawling be-columned stone, with the only commonality being that everything was cramped.

Jim parked his truck in a lot next to a fifteen-floor high-rise, and figured this big daddy was a good bet to start with, as it was where he'd been admitted as an inpatient from the emergency room. Cutting through the rows of cars, he crossed the lane and went under the porte cochere, entering the building through a set of retracting glass doors.

At the information desk, he said, "I'm looking for Devina Avale."

The hundred-and-twelve-year-old blue-hair manning the station smiled up at him so warmly, he felt like an asshole for reducing her to nothing but her age.

"Let me find her room for you."

As her twiglike fingers did a hunt and a peck over the keyboard, he thought of how much faster his own had been back at his apartment. He'd figured the name Devina was unusual enough in the modeling trade that if he Googled it on his laptop, he'd find Vin's girlfriend—and what do you know, it wasn't tough. Although she went by her first name in her professional trade, she and Vin had been photographed together at a fund-raiser for the *Caldwell Courier Journal* about six months ago, and there it was, Avale.

"She's in twelve fifty-three."

"Thank you, ma'am," he said with a little bow.

"You are so welcome. Just go up on those elevators by the gift shop."

He nodded and strode over to the lifts. There were a bunch of people waiting in a group, all of whom were tracking the little number displays over the three doors, and he joined the fray.

Seemed to be a race between the one all the way on the right and the one in the middle.

The center elevator won, and he piled in with the rest of the people, joining the scramble of reach arounds as he punched in his floor and then oriented himself facing the digital number readout above. *Bing. Bing. Bing.* Doors opened. People shuffled. *Bing.* Doors opened. More shuffling.

He got out on twelve and did not say anything to anyone at the nurses' station. It had been easy to get this far, maybe too easy, and he wasn't volunteering for any bottlenecks. Hell, it wouldn't surprise him to find a CPD uni outside 1253 ... but there wasn't. There also weren't any family or friends milling around the closed door.

He knocked softly and leaned in. "Devina?"

"Jim?" came the quiet voice. "Hold on a minute."

As he waited, he glanced up and down the corridor. A cleaning cart was parked in between Devina's and the room next door, and an upright cupboard on wheels was coming down toward him—which given the smell of wax beans and hamburgers as it passed, meant it was lunch. Nurses were walking here, there, and everywhere, and down at the far end, a patient was taking baby steps in his johnny, his hand on his IV pole.

Looked like he was taking the thing out for a walk so it could pee on the doorjambs.

"Okay, come in."

He stepped into a dim room that was exactly as his had been: beige, stark, and dominated by the hospital bed in the middle. Across the way, the curtain that was drawn against the daylight was moving ever so slightly, as if she had closed it—maybe so he couldn't get a clearer picture of her face.

Which was a mess.

So much so, he paused for a moment. Her beautiful features were distorted by swelling on the cheeks, chin, and eyes; her lip was split open; and the purple bruising on her pale skin was like a stain on a wedding gown—ugly and tragic.

"It's that bad, isn't it," she said, raising a shaking hand to shield herself.

"Jesus . . . Christ. Are you okay?"

"I will be, I think. They held me over because I have a concussion." As she tugged up the thin blanket that covered her, Jim eagle-eyed her hands. No bruising on the knuckles.

Which meant she didn't do this to herself and didn't—or more likely couldn't—fight back.

Staring at her, Jim felt his resolve shift around like it was trying to find level ground. What if . . . no, Vin couldn't have done this.

Could he?

"I'm so sorry," Jim murmured, sinking down onto the corner of the bed.

"I shouldn't have told him about you and me. . . ." She snapped a Kleenex out of a box and carefully dabbed under her eyes. "But my conscience was killing me and I . . . didn't expect this. He broke off the engagement, too."

Jim frowned, thinking last he'd heard, the plan had been

for the guy to break up with her. "He asked you to marry him?"

"That's why I had to tell him. He got down on one knee and asked me ... and I said yes, but then I had to tell him what had happened." Devina sat forward and gripped his forearm. "I'd stay away from him. For your sake. He's furious."

Thinking back on the guy's expression when he'd been talking about Devina's blue dress smelling like another man's cologne, it wasn't hard to imagine that was true. But there were parts of this situation that just didn't compute—although it was hard to think like that, looking at Devina's face ... and her arm.

Which had a series of bruises that formed the shape of a man's hand.

"When are they letting you out of here?" he asked.

"Probably this afternoon. God, I hate that you're seeing me like this."

"I'm the last person you should worry about."

There was a silence. "Can you believe where we ended up?" she said softly.

No. On so many levels. "You got family coming to pick you up?"

"They're due here around one when I'm supposed to be discharged. They're really concerned."

"I can understand why."

"The thing is, part of me wants to see him. I want to ... talk this through. I just don't know. ... And before you judge, I'm aware of how bad that sounds. I should just walk away, put as much distance as I can between us. But I can't let go that easily. I love him."

The defeat in her was as hard to bear as the condition she was in, and Jim took her hand.

"I'm sorry," he whispered. "I'm so damned sorry."

She squeezed his palm. "You are such a good friend."

There was a sharp knock and then a nurse came in. "How're we doing?"

"I'd better go," Jim said. As he got to his feet, he nodded

to the nurse and refocused on Devina. "Is there anything I can do for you?"

"Can I have your number? Just in case ... I don't know ..."

He gave her the digits, said another good-bye, and took off.

As he left the ward, he felt the way he had on many of his military missions: Conflicting information, incomprehensible actions, unpredictable choices ... he'd seen it all before, with only the vocabulary of names and locations changing.

Sifting through what he knew to be true, there were a lot of blanks to be filled, and more questions were raised than solid answers found.

As he got on the elevator and watched the numbers decrease until the readout showed an L, he fell back on training and experience: When you didn't know what was doing, you gathered information.

Back at the help desk, he approached the little old lady and pointed to the double doors he'd come into the building through. "Is this the only way out for patients?"

She smiled in that warm way—which gave him the impression she might make really good Christmas cookies. "Most of them leave from here, yes. Especially if they're getting picked up."

"Thanks."

"You're welcome."

Jim went out and scoped the front of the building. There were a number of places to sit down and watch the exit, but the little benches between the bald trees that ran along the sidewalk didn't have enough cover. And there were no corners to duck behind.

He looked past the overhang of the porte cochere to the parking lot, wishing like hell he could find a spot—

At that very moment, an SUV backed out of a space that was two down from the ones marked with blue-and-white handicapped signs.

Three minutes later, Jim pulled his truck into the empty

slot, killed the engine, and trained his eyes on the inpatient center. The fact that he had to look through the window of the minivan next door was the perfect camouflage.

He'd learned long ago that the information you got when you gathered in secret was likely to be the most helpful.

"Are you ready?" Marie-Terese called up from the kitchen.

"Almost," Robbie shouted down.

Checking her watch, she decided a more hands-on approach was needed to get them out of the house on time. Mounting the carpeted stairs one by one, her flats were quiet on the blue-and-maroon zigzag pattern. Like the rest of the decor, the runner was nothing she would have picked, but understandable for a high-traffic area in a rental house.

She found her son in front of his mirror, trying to get his mini–man tie to hang straight.

For a moment, she was overcome by maternal extrapolation: In a flash, she saw him standing gangly but strong on his way to his senior prom. And then proud and tall at his college graduation. And even later, in a tuxedo at his wedding.

"What are you looking at?" he said, fidgeting.

The future, she prayed. A nice, normal future that was as far away as possible from what the last couple years had been like for them.

"Do you need help?' she asked.

"I can't do this." His hands flopped to his sides and he pivoted to her in capitulation.

Coming forward, she knelt down before him and loosened the off-kilter knot. While she worked, he stood with such patience and trust, it was hard not to think of herself as at least a halfway decent mother.

"I think we're going to have to get you a bigger blazer."

"Yeah ... it's getting tight in the top part. And look ... see?" Putting out his arms, he frowned at the way the sleeves rode up halfway to his elbows. "I hate it."

She made quick work of the short strip of navy blue and red, not at all surprised he approved of the jacket's fit. Her son always liked dressing up in suits, and he preferred his shoes, even his sneakers, to be scuff-free. The same was true about everything he had: Open his drawers or his closet and the clothes were all arranged and hanging neatly; his books were lined up on the shelves; and his bed was never unmade unless he was between the sheets.

His father had been the same, always particular about how his clothes and his things were.

Her son also had Mark's dark hair and dark eyes.

God . . . she wished there were no part of that man in him, but biology was biology. And the stuff she really worried about, her ex's temper and meanness, had never been apparent.

"There, you're good to go." As he turned around to inspect, she fought the urge to hug him hard. "Look okay?"

"It's much gooderer than I did." She glanced over at him. "Sorry, *better* than I did."

"Thank you."

Staring at his reflection, she thought about the cost of new blazers . . . and shoes . . . and winter coats and summer shorts and tried not to panic. She could always waitress, after all. It wouldn't bring in nearly as much as she had been making . . . but it would be enough. It would have to be enough.

Especially when she moved them to a smaller city where rents were less.

God . . . she didn't want to leave Caldwell, though—she truly didn't. Not after last night with Vin.

"We're going to be late, come on," she said.

Downstairs, they coated and gloved up together and then got in the Camry. The morning was chilly, which meant the garage was an icebox, and the engine wheezed and sputtered.

"We need a new car," Robbie said as she cranked the key again.

"I know."

She hit the garage door and waited as it revealed the drive and the world beyond. Backing out, she K-turned, punched the remote again, and took off for St. Patrick's.

By the time they got to the cathedral, there were cars parked all along the street, stretching for blocks. She drove around, checking out the illegal options, and settled on a corner slot that put the butt of her car in the breeze. Getting out, she walked around and measured how far her bumper was over the yellow-curbed no-parking zone.

'Bout two feet. "Damn it."

As the cathedral's bells started to ring, she decided she was going to hope that if a policeman drove by he or she was either a good Christian or color-blind.

"Let's go," she said, holding out her hand to Robbie, who'd come over. As his palm slid into hers, she started walking fast and he clipped right along next to her, his little loafers having to go twice as fast over the bare sidewalk.

"I think we're late, Mom," he said breathlessly. "And it's my fault. I just wanted my tie to be right."

She glanced down at him. As they rushed along, the top of his hair flopped to the same beat as his navy blue peacoat did, but his eyes were unmoving: They were locked on the pavement and he was blinking too fast.

Marie-Terese stopped, tugged him to a halt, and sank down on her haunches. Putting her hands on both his arms, she gave him a little shake. "There's nothing wrong with being late. People are late all the time. We do our best to be on time for everything and that's all we can do, okay? Okay? Robbie?"

The cathedral's bells went silent. And a moment later a car eased by them. Then off in the distance a dog barked.

This had nothing to do with being late, she realized.

"Talk to me," she whispered, putting her face in the line of his vision, even though she practically had to lie down to do it. "Please, Robbie."

His words exploded out of his mouth: "I liked my own name better. And I don't want to move again. I like my babysitters and my room. I like the Y. I like ... here and now."

Marie-Terese sat back on her heels ... and wanted to kill her ex-husband. "I'm really sorry. I know this has been so hard on you."

"We're leaving, aren't we. You came home early last night and I heard you talking to Quinesha. You told her you might have to make other arrangements." The word *arrangements* came out *mermangements.* "I like Quinesha. I don't want other arrangements."

Again with the *mermangements.*

Looking at her son, she wondered just exactly how she could tell him that they had to move because she had the unshakable conviction that "the bad times," as he'd called them, were definitely back.

The car that had passed them before came around again, having evidently failed to find a place to park.

"I quit my job last night," she said, getting as close to the truth as she could. "I stopped waitressing where I had been because I wasn't happy there. So I'm going to need to get another job somewhere."

Robbie's eyes lifted to hers and he measured her face. "There are a lot of restaurants in Caldwell."

"True, but they might not need help right now and I have to make us money to live off of."

"Oh." He seemed to be thinking the whole thing over. "Okay. That's different."

Abruptly, he relaxed, as if what had been bothering him were a helium balloon that he'd just released into the wind.

"I love you," she said, hating that precisely what he'd been worried about was in fact happening. They were leaving for reasons other than her "job." But she didn't want him having to carry that burden.

"Me, too, Mom." He gave her a quick hug, his little arms not reaching even halfway around her. Still, she felt the embrace through her whole body.

"You ready?" she said roughly.

"Yup."

They fell back into hustle mode, jangling their way over to the cathedral and up its broad stone steps; then sneaking in through its massive door. Inside the vestibule, they removed their coats and she took a program from the greeter who was positioned in the narthex. At the man's urging, she and Robbie headed for one of the side doors and ghosted down to a pew that was fairly empty.

Just as they sat, the call for children to come forward for Sunday school went out. Robbie stayed right with her, though. He never went off with the other kids—had never asked to and she'd certainly never suggested it.

As the priests and the choir got the service rolling, she took a deep breath and let the balmy warmth of the church seep into her. And for a split second, she imagined what it would be like to have Vin sitting with her and Robbie, maybe on the far side of her son. It would be nice to look over Robbie's head and see a man she loved. Maybe they would share a secret smile as couples did from time to time. Maybe Vin would have been the one to help with Robbie's tie.

Maybe there would be a daughter between the bookends.

With a frown, Marie-Terese realized that for the first time in nearly forever, she was daydreaming. Actually fantasizing about a pleasant, happy future. God . . . how long it had been?

In the beginning with Mark . . . that was how long.

She'd met him at the Mandalay Bay casino. She and her girlfriends, who'd all turned twenty-one the same year, had flown to Las Vegas for their first girls' weekend out of town, and she could remember how ready they'd all been for their taste of truly grown-up freedom.

As she and her friends had futzed around with one-dollar bets on the cheap side of the velvet rope, Mark had been at a high rollers' table in the VIP section. After he'd caught sight of her, he'd sent a waitress to invite them into the deluxe section—where the drinks were free and the lowest you could wager was twenty dollars.

At first, she'd assumed it was all about Sarah. Sarah had been, and no doubt still was, a six-foot-tall blonde who somehow came across as naked even while fully clothed. That girl had been a man magnet, and given how many candidates she had to choose from, she'd had very high standards. And what do you know, someone who could afford high stakes was definitely up her alley.

But no, Mark had had eyes only for Marie-Terese. And he'd made that clear when she had been seated at his elbow and Sarah had been left to fend for herself.

Mark and his two associates, as he had referred to the pair of suits who were with him, had been nothing but gentlemen that night, buying drinks, talking, being attentive. There had been a lot of kissing dice and shiny chatter, the kind of thing that made you, when you were young enough to believe in glamour, feel like a celebrity.

It had been the perfect start to the weekend: To be twenty-one and in the exclusive part of the casino, surrounded by men in expensive suits, was everything that she and her friends had hoped for, and after three or four hours, they'd gone up to the suite Mark owned. Not the brightest move, maybe, but there had been four girls and three men, and after they'd all spent time together on a collective winning streak, the illusion of friendship and trust had been created.

But nothing bad had happened. Just more drinks and chatter and flirtation. And Sarah ending up in a bedroom alone with the taller of the two "associates."

At the end of the night, Marie-Terese had gone out onto the balcony with Mark.

She could still remember the feel of the dry, hot air blowing over the sparkling view of the Las Vegas strip.

It had been ten years ago, but that night was still as clear to her as the moment it had become memory: the two of them out on that terrace, high above the man-made city, standing side by side. She had been looking at the view. He had been staring at her.

Mark had swept her hair aside and kissed her on the nape of her neck ... and in that soft contact given her the best sexual experience of her life.

That was as far as it went.

The next evening had been much of the same, except Mark had taken them all to see a Celine Dion concert and then they had gone back to the tables. Glittering. Fancy. Exciting. Marie-Terese had soared on the heated gusts of promise and romance and fairy tale, and at the end of the second night, she had gone back to that suite and kissed Mark on that terrace again.

And that was it.

She'd been disappointed he hadn't wanted more, although she wouldn't have been able to sleep with him. She wasn't hard-wired like Sarah, capable of meeting a man and going to bed with him hours later.

How ironic she'd ended up where she had.

The next morning, they'd had to leave and Mark had had his limo take them all to the airport. She'd been crushed, assuming that was the end of it: a fun forty-eight hours—just what the travel agent had promised and exactly what they had paid for.

As she and her friends had been driven away from the hotel, she'd hoped Mark would come running out and wave them to a stop, but he didn't, and she'd guessed that the last she'd ever see of him was him kissing her hand at the hotel room she and her friends had all stayed in together.

The crushing weight of back-to-normal had brought tears to her eyes. Compared to Las Vegas, her life at home, with her job as a secretary and her night school for college, had seemed like a kind of death.

When the limo had pulled up to the terminal, the driver had gotten out and opened the car door as a redcap had come along and started unloading their nothing-special luggage. Marie-Terese had stepped out onto the curb and turned her face away from the others because she didn't want to be razzed about being sad.

The chauffeur had stopped her. "Mr. Capricio asked me to give this to you."

The box had been about the size of a coffee mug and done up in red tissue with a white bow—and she'd opened the thing right then and there, litter-bugging the wrapping paper and the length of satin. Inside had been a delicate gold chain with a gold pendant in the shape of an M. There had also been a slip of paper, the kind you'd find in a fortune cookie. The message had read: *Please call me as soon as you get home safe.*

The number had been instantly memorized and she'd beamed all the way back to home.

Such a perfect start. There had been no signs in the beginning of the way things would go—although looking back on it, she saw that the M pendant had been a mark of ownership, a kind of human dog tag.

God, she'd worn that necklace with such pride—because she'd wanted to be claimed back then. As a woman who had grown up with a harried mother and a father who wasn't around, the idea that a man had wanted her had been magical. And Mark hadn't been some middle-of-the-road, middle-class type—which would have been a step up for her anyway. No, he was the VIP section, whereas she was more like the janitor's closet.

And over the next couple of months, he'd played her perfectly, seducing her carefully and with calculation. He'd even told her he didn't want to have sex before they were married—so he could introduce her to his Catholic grandmother and mother with a clean conscience.

They were married five months later, and things had turned on a dime after the ceremony. As soon as she'd moved into that hotel suite with him, Mark had controlled her as tightly as a fist. Hell, when her mother had died, he'd insisted his chauffeur accompany her back to California and be at her side from the second she stepped off the plane to the moment she put her foot back in the suite.

And the sex-before-marriage thing? Turned out that hadn't been a big sacrifice for him because he'd been sleeping with his various mistresses—and she'd learned this when one had turned up with a belly the size of a basketball about a month after the ink was dry on the marriage license.

Coming back to the present, she got to her feet with the rest of the congregation and sang words from the hymnal that Robbie held in his hands.

Considering what the past had taught her, she worried about the fairy tale she'd spun in her head about Vin.

Optimism wasn't for the faint of heart. And daydreams could get you in troubnle.

He sat behind her and she never knew it. Which was the beauty of disguises.

Today he was wearing his churchgoer one, which meant blue contact lenses and wire-framed glasses.

He'd waited in the back of the church for her to come in with the son, and when the two didn't show up, he'd figured they were missing the service for once and still back home. He'd left and gone to his car, but as he'd been driving away, he'd seen the two of them on the sidewalk, talking intently. Circling the block, he'd watched them talk together until they had run into the cathedral and disappeared through the big doors.

By the time he'd reparked his car, he'd missed half the service, but he'd managed to sit right behind her and the son, slipping from the shadows and lowering himself into the pew.

She spent most of the service staring up at the frescoes that were being cleaned, her head tilted to the side so that the angle of her cheek was especially lovely. As usual, she was dressed in a long skirt and a sweater—today they were a deep maroon—and she had a pair of pearl earrings on. Her dark hair was coiled up in a loose bun and she was wearing light perfume . . . or maybe it was just that laundry detergent or those dryer sheets she used?

He'd have to go to the supermarket and sniff the Tides and Cheerses and Gains and Bounces, to see which one it was.

Sitting in the pew, she looked like such the Good Mother, helping her son find the right pages in the hymnal, bending down from time to time when he had a question to ask her. No one would even have used the word *slut* within hearing distance of her . . . much less apply it to her: She seemed to be one of those women who had immaculately conceived her child.

It made him think about the guy he'd beaten with the tire iron. Not the part about killing him, although evidently that hadn't gone as planned, as the fool was just in a coma—another reason disguises were so very necessary. No, he thought about the expression on the man's unbusted face as he'd come out of that dirty, filthy bathroom at that dirty, filthy club.

What a lie her illusion was.

Rage boiled in him, but it was so not the right time for that, and to distract himself, he stared at the delicate muscles that ran up the nape of her neck. Soft curls formed around the gentle curve, and more than once he found himself leaning forward as if he would touch them . . .

Or maybe wrap his hands around her throat.

And squeeze until she was his and his alone.

He could just imagine what it would be like to subdue her struggles and claim her as his . . . could picture the rapture in her eyes as she died.

As he got wrapped up in the future, he nearly acted on his impulse, but fortunately, the singing parts of the service helped to break his furious concentration and occupy his hands. He also looked over at the son from time to time to keep his obsession from locking on her in a place that, if things got away from him, he'd lose everything.

The son was so well behaved. So grown-up. A little man of the house, no doubt.

She never released him to go with the other children

to Sunday school, keeping him instead right by her. Which was a little frustrating, although she was wise not to let him out of her sight. Very wise.

But she shouldn't worry. The little boy was going to be with his Father very soon . . . and she was going to be with her forever husband.

The perfect future was mapped out for them all.

CHAPTER
27

Vin walked through the door to the duplex, closed himself in, and felt like someone had kneed him in the gut. From the hall, he stared at the ruined living room, and could not believe what he was looking at.

As he walked into the space, all he could do was shake his head. The couches were overturned and the silk pillows were trampled and a number of statues had been knocked off their stands. The rug was ruined over by the bar, stained by liquor that had bled from broken bottles, and the walls were going to have to be repainted and repapered because it looked as if a couple of Bordeaux wines had been thrown at them.

Taking off his coat and tossing it on a ransacked sofa, he wandered around the once perfect space. It was amazing how all those priceless things had been turned into trash so quickly. Shit, add a layer of grime and some food garbage and you had a Dumpster.

Bending down, he picked up some shards that had broken loose from a Venetian mirror. The thing had been struck with something that vaguely resembled a human back, the center of the piece smashed in a long, torso-like column.

The fine spray of white powder all over it seemed to suggest that the police had gotten busy dusting for fingerprints.

Man, someone sure as hell had been thrown around the room.

Vin went over to the bar and put the jagged pieces of mirror next to some of the busted bottles. Then he resumed the search for exactly what the cops had no doubt been after.

No blood that he could see. But maybe they had already removed the things that had been marked by it.

Besides, bruises bled under the skin, so it wasn't as if a lack of the stuff here was necessarily going to help him.

While the CPD had been in the building, undoubtedly they'd questioned the lobby guard—except it wasn't like the guy could testify to Vin's not being in the apartment. After all, residents could take the elevators up from the parking . . . garage.

Vin went over to the phone and called down to the front desk. When a male voice answered, he didn't fuck around. "Gary, it's Vin—did you give the police access to the security tapes of the elevators and the stairwells in the building?"

There was absolutely no pause whatsoever. "Jesus, Mr. diPietro, why'd you do it—"

"I didn't. I swear. Did the CPD get those tapes?"

"Yeah, they got everything."

Vin exhaled in relief. There was no way he could have gotten to the duplex without showing up in one of those recordings. In fact, what they were going to prove was that he'd left the building that morning and not returned until after midnight.

"And you were on camera," the guard said.

Vin blinked. "What?"

"You came up in the garage elevator at ten o'clock. It's on the tape."

"What?" That would have been impossible—at the time

he'd been in the car, driving to the Woods with Marie-Terese. "Wait, you saw my face. You actually *saw* my face."

"Yeah, clear as day. She came through the front doors and went up to the duplex, and then twenty minutes later you came in through the garage. You had on your black trench coat and you left like a half hour later, with your Boston Sox cap pulled low."

"It wasn't me. It—"

"It was."

"But . . . I didn't park my BMW in my spot—it was gone, and my other car was there. I didn't use my pass card to get through the gate. Explain—"

"You got a ride, then, and came in through the pedestrian door. I don't know. Look, I got to go. We're running a test of the fire alarm."

The line went dead.

Vin hung up the receiver and stared at the phone, feeling like the whole fucking world had lost its damn mind. Then after a moment, he went over to the couch, arranged the cushions into some semblance of order, and all but fell on his ass.

As the alarm system in the building started to go off and strobe lights flashed from the fixtures out in the front hall, he felt like he was in the dream he'd had, the one where Devina fell upon him like something out of *Night of the Living Dead*.

Chess pieces were being arranged around him, blocking his moves, boxing him in.

You're mine, Vin. And I always take what is mine.

As he heard those words in his head again, the sound of the alarm was the perfect accompaniment to the panic burning through his veins. Shit. What the hell did he do now?

From out of nowhere, Jim Heron's voice cut through Devina's: *I'm here to save your soul.*

Ignoring that summarily unhelpful cue, Vin got up and went to his study in search of something far more likely to chill him out. Over at the intact liquor bottles, he poured himself a bourbon, drank it, and then refilled the squat glass. The television had been left on, but was muted, and as he parked it behind his desk, his eyes latched onto the local news.

When a photograph appeared next to the anchor's blond head shortly thereafter, he could not say he was surprised. With the way things were going, it would take a dirty bomb set off in downtown Caldwell to get a rise out of him.

He reached for the remote.

" . . . Robert Belthower, thirty-six, was found early this evening in an alley not far from where Friday night's two victims were shot. He is now at St. Francis Hospital in critical condition. No suspects have been identified yet in the crime. . . ."

It was the guy from the Iron Mask. The one who had come out of the bathroom with Marie-Terese.

Vin picked up the phone and dialed.

The call wasn't accepted until the fourth ring, and Jim's voice was tight, like he didn't want to answer: "Hey, my man."

Still feel like saving my soul now? Vin wanted to taunt. "Have you seen the news?"

Long hesitation. "You mean about Devina?"

"Yeah. I didn't do that, though, I swear—last I saw her was when I broke up with her that afternoon and let her walk out of my place with the ring I bought her—you're welcome. But I'm more calling about the guy they found beaten in an alley downtown. He was with Marie-Terese last night. I saw him with her. Which would make it three men in twenty-four hours who've . . . Hello? Jim?" When there was an *uh-huh*, it was clear what the problem was. "Look, I didn't do that shit to Devina, although I know you won't believe me." Another long silence. "Hello? Oh, for fuck's sake, do you honestly think I could hurt a woman?"

"I thought you were calling because of me."

Now it was his turn to pause. "Why?"

Another long silence. "She said she told you. About us."

"Us? What 'us'?"

"She said that was why you lost it and hit her."

Vin tightened his hand on his glass. "Exactly what is there to tell about the two of you."

The soft curse coming across the line was in the universal language for sex-that-shouldn't-have-happened.

Vin's muscles around his shoulders and down into his arms went rigid. "Are you kidding me. Are you fucking kidding me."

"I'm sorry—"

The glass shattered in Vin's palm, bourbon going everywhere, soaking his sleeve and cuff, splashing on the front of his shirt and his pants.

He ended the call by hurling the cell phone across the room.

While Jim hit the *end* key, he was willing to bet that wasn't the way Vin had terminated the call.

No, he had a feeling that whatever phone had been up at Vin's ear was now fodder for a dustpan.

Great. Just fucking wonderful.

After he rubbed his eyes, he refocused on the entrance of the inpatient building and let the first part of the conversation register: another beaten guy tied to Marie-Terese. And when Vin called, that had been the number one thing on his mind, even above the fact that, oh, yeah, he was up on felony assault for buzz-sawing his girlfriend with his knuckles.

That shit with Marie-Terese was as strong as ever for him. Which somehow didn't feel like such a great thing.

Man, this particular mission was going to hell faster than a free fall.

Jim glanced down at his watch and then resumed staring at each person who went in and out of the doors. It was close to one, so Devina's people would supposedly be coming any second, and then she would be leaving with them.

God, Devina was such a liar.

It felt like sacrilege to come to that conclusion, given

how that woman's face looked, but the truth was what it was: Vin hadn't known a thing about Thursday night and what had happened in Jim's truck. Not one thing. The totally-in-the-dark had resonated through his shocked voice.

Why had she lied about telling the guy? And what else had she lied about?

Sure as shit it made Vin's denial more credible.

One o'clock came and went and so did one thirty. Then two. Devina had to be coming out soon, assuming it took about an hour to process her paperwork and her folks were on time—and assuming she didn't go out another way.

And assuming anyone was coming to pick her up.

Wishing he had a cigarette, he held on to his phone and rubbed the flat surface of the screen until it grew warm. Truth. He needed a truth injection into this situation. He needed to know who Marie-Terese was and who Devina was and what the fuck was going on.

Unfortunately, that was going to cost him—

Devina abruptly stepped out of the double doors, a pair of big sunglasses taking up most of her face. She was dressed in a black yoga suit, and her oversize crocodile shoulder bag made her seem thin as a ruler in comparison. As she came out to porte cochere's curb, people stared at her as they passed, like they were trying to place her in the celebri-verse.

There was no one with her.

And . . . the bruising that had been on her face was now gone. All of it. She was photo-op ready, as lovely and perfect as she'd been over dinner Friday night.

Ice-cold warning splashed through Jim's veins, the kind that had come only a couple of times in his life.

This was wrong. Way wrong.

Straightening in the truck's seat, he braced himself as he looked at the pavement down at her feet.

In the light that was pouring out of the sky and creating echoes of objects large and small on the ground, she did not throw a shadow. She was form, but not substance, shape but not flesh.

This was the enemy.

He was looking at the enemy.

He'd *fucked* the enemy.

As if she heard his thoughts, Devina looked right where he was parked. And then her brows tightened and her face slowly panned from side to side—which he took to mean she couldn't see exactly where he was, but she knew someone was staring at her . . .

Her expression was stone cold. Nothing like the warmth she'd radiated in front of Vin or what she'd thrown around at Jim in the truck or in the car or in that hospital bed.

Stone. Cold.

Serial-killer cold.

Talk about a truth: She was a seducer and a liar and a manipulator . . . and she was after Vin. And not as in marriage, but as in owning the man's very soul.

In the center of his chest, Jim also had the sure feeling that she knew who he was and what he was. Had known from that first night when they'd had sex—because she'd seduced his ass on purpose. Hell, the logic was unassailable. His new bosses, the Four Lads, had put him on the field, and it looked like the other side had likewise sent an operative into the situation—who knew more than Jim did.

As that old refrain of "Devil with a Blue Dress" rolled through his head, he started to wonder about guys on Harleys who didn't cast shadows either. And probably were liars, too.

Goddamn it.

Devina scanned the parking lot again, snapped at some poor guy who backed into her by mistake, and then lifted her hand to call up one of the cabs from the line to the right. When a taxi came forward, she stepped inside and off they went.

Time to roll, Jim thought as he started his truck and

backed out of his space. As she knew his ride but only in the dark, he had a veil, not a cover, so he had to settle in two cars behind her and pray that her cabbie wasn't in the habit of blowing through orange lights.

While he trailed her, he tuned up his cell phone for a call, and as he pressed *send*, nothing else mattered other than getting what he needed. Nothing he had to do was too much. No sacrifice was too great or too demeaning. He was back in the land of single-minded focus, as determined and unswerving as a bullet in midair.

"Zacharias," he said as the line was picked up.

Matthias the fucker laughed low. "I swear I'm talking to you more than my own mother."

"Didn't know you had one. I thought you'd been spawned."

"You call me to discuss family trees or is there a purpose to this?"

"I need the information."

"Ah. Now why did I have the sense you'd come around."

"But I want the info on two names. Not just one. And I can't do a job for you until I finish what I'm working on in Caldwell."

"What exactly are you working on?"

"None of your business." Although Matthias was going to get a pretty good picture of the whos involved.

"How long are you tied up for."

"I don't know. Not six months. Maybe not even one month."

There was a pause. "I'll give you forty-eight hours. And then you're mine."

"I'm not anybody's, asshole."

"Right. Sure. Expect an e-mail from me explaining everything."

"Look, I'm not blowing out of Caldwell until I'm good and frickin' ready. So send whatever you like, but if you think you're shipping me overseas the day after tomorrow to off someone, you've got your head up your ass."

"How do you know what I'm going to ask you to do?"

"Because you and all my bosses before you have wanted only one thing from me," Jim said hoarsely.

"Well, maybe we'd mix it up a little if you weren't so fucking brilliant at what you do."

Jim cranked his hold down on the cell phone, and decided that if there was any more of this bullshit banter, he was going to take up Vin's method of terminating connections.

He cleared his throat. "E-mail won't work. I don't have an account anymore."

"I was going to send you a package anyway. You don't honestly think I trust Hotmail or Yahoo!, do you?"

"Fine. My address is—"

"As if I don't already know." More of that laugh. "So I'm guessing you want Marie-Terese Boudreau's rundown?"

"Yes, and—"

"Vincent diPietro?"

So not a surprise. "Nope. Devina Avale."

"Interesting. She wouldn't happen to be the woman who said good ol' Vincent put her in the hospital last night, would she? Why . . . yes, she is. It's right here on my computer screen. Terrible set of people you're hanging around with. So violent."

"And to think it's a step up from the likes of you."

Now there was a little less of that amusement: "How does that saying go? It's not wise to bite the hand that feeds you. . . . Yup, I think that's right."

"I'm more likely to shoot than use my teeth. FYI."

"I'm well aware of how much you like guns, thank you very much. And in spite of your piss-poor opinion about me, I have all the intel on Marie-Terese right here." Matthias, to his credit, got to the point. "Born Gretchen Moore in Las Vidas, California. Age thirty-one. Graduated from UC San Diego. Mother and father deceased." There was a shuffling sound and a grunt, as if Matthias were switching position—and the idea that the guy had to deal with chronic pain was satisfying as hell. "Now for the interesting part. Married Mark Capricio in Las Vegas, nine years ago. Capricio is a bona fide card-carrying member of the mob, a real sick shit who has a personality disorder and a half, given his rap sheet. Total skull cracker. She evidently tried to leave him about three years ago and he beat her up, grabbed the kid, and split. Took her a couple months and a PI to find him. When she got the son back, she divorced the asshole, bought herself the Marie-Terese ID, and disappeared, eventually ending up in Caldwell, NY. Since then, she's kept her profile ultra-low, and with good reason. Men like Capricio don't let their wives go."

Holy. Shit. So . . . chances were good that those two dead boys and that beaten man in the alley last night meant Capricio had found her. Had to be. Vin had said the second attack had been on a guy seen with her—

"But when it comes to her ex-husband, she has nothing to worry about in the short term."

"Excuse me?" Jim said.

"Capricio's been doing twenty in federal prison for a salad bar of felonies including embezzlement, money laundering, witness intimidation, and perjury—and after that he's got a bunch of state felonies to serve out, including accessory to murder, assault, battery. Guy could be an exam question in law school, for fuck's sake." Another shift around was marked with a soft curse. "Apparently, it was all crashing down on him right about the time Gretchen/Marie-Terese was going to leave him. Which is logical. He was probably getting more and more violent on the home front as the feds and the Nevada staties closed in on him. When he snatched the son, he was running from the law, not just his wife—which made the fact that he managed to disappear for three months a testament to the depth of his connections. Clearly, someone ratted on him, though—maybe her PI applied the right pressure at the right time by threatening to turn one of his protectors in. Who knows."

"But I wonder if his family's coming after her now."

"Yeah, I read about those two gunshot murders in that alley. Doubtful it's his family. They'd just kill her and take the son. There'd be no reason to expose themselves to any added risk by wiping out innocents."

"Yeah, and besides, you kill someone just because she's been with him, that's personal. So the question is, who's after her—assuming she is the common thread between Friday and Saturday night's attacks."

"Wait, someone else got blown, and not in a good way?"

"And here I thought you knew everything."

There was a long pause and then Matthias's voice came back—this time without its usual swinging-dick tone. "I don't know everything. Took me a while to realize that, though. Anyway, I'll do the Devina thing for you. Stay by your phone for my call."

"Roger that."

As Jim hung up, he felt as if he were dressed in a familiar set of clothes: The back-and-forth with Matthias was just as it had always been. Quick, to the point, smart, and logical. That was the problem. They'd always worked well together. ·

Maybe a little too well.

Jim refocused on his pursuit, tracking Devina's taxi as it headed across downtown to the old warehouse district. When they got into the maze of industrial buildings that had been converted into lofts, he let the taxi turn off onto Canal Street by itself and proceeded to the next left-hand turn. Going around the block, his timing was perfect: As he came back to Canal, he got to see Devina get out of the cab and stride up to a door. When she entered using a key, he took that as an indication she had a place there.

Jim kept going, and as he headed out of the district, he made another call.

Chuck, the diPietro Group's crew foreman, answered in his usual gruff way. "Yeah."

"Chuck, it's Jim Heron."

"Hey." There was an exhale, like the guy was in mid-cigar. "How you doing?"

"Good. Wanted you to know I'm coming to work tomorrow."

Guy's voice actually warmed a little. "You're a good man, Heron. But don't be pushin' it."

"Nah. I'm fine."

"Well, I 'preciate it."

"Listen, I'm trying to get in touch with two of the guys I usually work with and I wondered if you have their numbers."

"I got everyone's number but yours. Who you need?"

"Adrian Vogel and Eddie Blackhawk."

There was a pause, and the image of the guy chewing on the stub of a fattie was irresistible. "Who?" Jim repeated the names. "Don't know who you talking about. Nobody by those names on the bluff job." There was a hesitation, like the guy was wondering whether Jim was all there. "You sure you don't need a couple days off?"

"Maybe I got the names wrong. They ride Harleys. One's got short hair and piercings. The other's huge and has a braid down his back?"

Another exhale. "Look, Jim, you're gonna take tomorrow off. I'll see you Tuesday at the earliest."

"No one like that on the crew?"

"Nope, Jim, there ain't."

"Guess I'm confused, then. Thanks."

Jim tossed his cell phone on the seat next to him and all but strangled the steering wheel. Not part of the crew. Big surprise.

Because that pair of bastards didn't really exist any more than Devina did.

Christ, it appeared as if he were surrounded by liars in this new job. Which really put him back in familiar territory, didn't it.

His phone rang and he picked it up. "You can't find her, can you. Devina Avale is nothing but air."

Matthias wasn't laughing this time. "Nothing. Not a damn thing. It's like she dropped onto the earth out of nowhere. The thing is, she has all the right surface credentials—but only to a point. No birth certificate. No parents. Established credit only seven months ago, and the social security number is actually that of a dead woman. So it's not a great facade, which means I should have been able to find something, anything on the real her. But she's a mirage."

"Thanks, Matthias."

"You don't sound shocked in the slightest."

"I'm not."

"What the hell have you gotten yourself into?"

Jim shook his head. "Same shit, different day. That's about it."

There was a short silence. "Expect a package from me."

"Roger that."

Jim hung up, put the phone in the front pocket of his jacket, and decided it was time to go face the music over at the Commodore. Vin diPietro had a right to know who and what his ex was, and here was hoping that the guy would be open to the truth—even though it sounded a lot like fiction.

Abruptly, the memory of Vin looking up from the stool in the locker room at the Iron Mask came back.

Do you believe in demons?

Jim could only hope that question had been a rhetorical one.

CHAPTER
28

Funny thing about glass. When you broke the shit up, it got pissed and bit back.

Upstairs in the duplex's master bath, Vin was surrounded by gauze and white surgical tape. What he'd done to his palm squeezing that bourbon to shreds was way out of Band-Aid land, so he'd had to call in reinforcements of the Red Cross variety and things were not going well. With the injury being on his right hand, he was a floundering, cursing nurse, fumbling with all the wrapping and the scissors and the tape.

Damn good thing he was his own patient. The vocabularly alone, much less the incompetence, would have gotten him disbarred—or whatever the hell the candy-striper equivalent to that was.

He was just coming to the end of the ordeal when the phone by the sinks rang, and wasn't that just loads of fun. With a tiny pair of nail scissors locked in his leftie, a strip of gauze in his teeth, and his right hand all but a paw, it took every bit of coordination he had to answer the call.

"Let him up," he told the lobby guard.

After putting the receiver back, he did a half-assed taping job and left the mess on the counter as is, heading for the stairs and going down to the front hall door. When the elevator *bing*ed and opened, he was in the corridor, waiting.

Jim Heron stepped out and didn't hang around for a hello or an invitation to speak. Which you had to respect.

"Thursday night," the guy said. "I didn't know you. I didn't know her. I should have told you, but to be honest, when I saw the pair of you together, I didn't want to fuck things up. It was a mistake and I'm goddamn sorry—mostly that you found out from someone other than me."

The whole time he was talking, Heron's arms hung loosely by his sides, like he was ready for a fight if things went that way, and his voice was as steady and even as his eyes were. No prevaricating. No artifice. No bullshit.

And as Vin faced off at him, instead of rage, which was what he'd have expected himself to have toward the guy, he just felt exhaustion. Exhaustion and the thumping pain of his hand.

Abruptly, he realized he was getting tired of channeling his fucking father when it came to women. Thanks to that legacy, over the past twenty years, Vin's suspicious nature had found so many shadows where none had existed—and yet essentially missed the actual time when someone he was sleeping with cheated on him.

So much energy wasted, all in the wrong place.

God, he just didn't care about Devina. At this moment, he really didn't care what she'd done while they were together.

"She lied about what happened here last night," Vin said roughly. "Devina lied."

There was absolutely no hesitation in the reply: "I know."

"Oh, really."

"I don't believe a word she's said about anything."

"And why's that."

"I went to the hospital to see her because I was having a hard time believing any of this shit. And she gave me this hearts-and-flowers routine about telling you what had happened Thursday night, how that was the reason you went after her. But you didn't know, did you. She never said a thing to you, did she."

"Not a peep." Vin turned away and headed into the duplex. When Jim didn't follow, he said over his shoulder, "You just going to stand there like a statue or do you want lunch."

Food was evidently preferable to playing marble, and after they were both through the front door, Vin locked it and put the chain in place. With the way things were going lately, he wasn't taking any chances with anything.

"Holy fuck," Jim said, "your living room . . ."

"Yeah, it's been redecorated by Vince McMahon."

In the kitchen, Vin got out some cold cuts and the jar of Hellman's using his left hand. "You got a choice between rye or sourdough."

"Sourdough."

As Vin grabbed some lettuce and a tomato from the crisper, he braced himself. "I need to know how it went down. With Devina. Tell me everything— Shit . . . not *everything*. But how did she come on to you?"

"You sure you want to go there?"

He took out a knife from the drawer. "I have to, man. Need to. I'm feeling like . . . I'm feeling I was with someone I didn't know at all."

Jim cursed and then parked it on one of the bar stools at the counter. "Not so much mayo for me."

"Cool. Now talk."

"I don't believe she is who she says, by the way."

"Funny, me neither."

"I mean, I did a background check on her."

Vin glanced up in the process of getting the blue lid off the plastic jar. "You gonna tell me how you managed that?"

"Not on your life."

"And the result was . . . ?"

"She doesn't exist, literally. And trust me, if the people I use can't find her true identity, nobody can."

Vin went light with the Hellman's on Jim's sourdough, heavier on his own rye, but it was a messy, imprecise job. Ambidextrous he was not.

God, it was so not a surprise about Devina. . . .

"Still waiting for Thursday-night deets over here," he said. "And do us both a favor and just talk. I don't have the energy to be polite right now."

"Fuck . . ." Jim rubbed his face. "Okay . . . she was at the Iron Mask. I was with . . . friends, I guess you could call them, although 'sonsabitches' would also cover it. Anyway, she followed me out into the parking lot when I left. It was cold. She seemed lost. She was . . . You sure about this?"

"Yup." Vin picked up a tomato, put it on a cutting board, and started slicing with the grace of a five-year-old. Hacking was more like it. "Keep going."

Jim shook his head. "She was upset about you. And she appeared to be really unsure of herself."

Vin frowned. "How was she upset?"

"How . . . you mean what for? She didn't go into specifics. I didn't ask. I was just . . . like, I wanted her to be okay with herself."

Now Vin was doing the head shaking. "Devina is always okay. That's the thing. No matter her mood, down deep she's tight. It was one of the things that attracted me to her . . . well, that and the fact that she's one of the most physically confident women I've ever met. But that's what you get when you're built perfectly."

"She said you wanted her to get breast implants."

Vin's eyes flicked up. "Are you kidding me? I've told her she was perfect since the night I met her, and I meant it. I never wanted her to change a thing."

Abruptly, Jim's brows drew in tight, a hard look coming onto his face.

"Looks like you were played, buddy." Vin cracked apart the lettuce and went over to the sink with a couple of leaves to wash. "Let me guess, she poured her heart out to you, you saw a vulnerable woman tangled up with a mofo, you kissed her . . . maybe you didn't even think you would take things that far."

"I couldn't believe where it ended up."

"You felt bad for her, but you were also attracted." Vin turned off the water and shook the romaine. "You wanted to give her something to make her feel good."

Jim's voice grew low. "That's exactly how it was."

"You want to know the way she got me?"

"Yeah. I do."

Back at the counter, Vin laid out slices of roast beef that were thin as paper. "I went to a gallery opening. She was there by herself, wearing a dress that was cut down to the small of her back. They had these lights in the ceiling that were directed at the paintings that were for sale, and when I walked in, I saw her standing in front of the Chagall I had come to buy, that light hitting the skin of her back. Extraordinary." He added on a layer of ragged tomato and a fluffy blanket of lettuce, then top-hatted the sandwiches. "Sliced or whole?"

"Whole."

He handed the sourdough over to Jim and cut his rye in half. "She sat in front of me at the auction and I smelled her perfume the entire time. I paid a fuckload for the Chagall, and I'll never forget the way she looked back at me over her shoulder as the gavel went down. Her smile was what I liked to see in a woman's face at that point." Vin took a bite and remembered vividly as he chewed. "I used to like it dirty, you know, porn-style. And her eyes told me she had no problem with that kind of shit. She came home with me that night and I fucked her right here on the floor. Then on the stairs. Finally on the bed. Twice. She let me do anything to her and she liked it."

Jim blinked and stopped chewing, like he was trying to match up the *Leave It to Beaver* lines he'd been fed with the Vivid Video routine Vin had gotten.

"She was"—Vin leaned to the side and snapped free two paper towels—"exactly who I wanted her to be." He handed one to Jim. "She gave me free rein to do whatever

I wanted business-wise, didn't care if I was gone for a week on no notice. She'd come with me when I wanted her to, stayed home when I didn't. She was like . . . a reflection of what I wanted."

Jim wiped his mouth. "Or in my case, what would get to me."

"Exactly."

They finished their sandwiches and Vin made two more, and while they ate the second round, they were mostly quiet, as if they were both recalling their time with Devina . . . and wondering how they'd been played so easily.

Vin eventually broke the silence. "So they say they have me on a surveillance tape from last night. Coming up in the elevator. Security guard tells me he saw my face, but that's impossible. I wasn't here. Whoever that was, it wasn't me."

"I believe you."

"You're going to be the only one."

The other man paused with the sourdough halfway to his mouth. "I'm not sure how to say this."

"Well, considering you just told me you fucked my ex-girlfriend, hard to imagine anything's trickier than that."

"This is."

Vin paused in midbite himself, not liking the look on the guy's face. "What."

Jim took his own damned time about it, even finishing his frickin' lunch. Finally, he laughed short and tight. "I don't even know how to talk about this."

"Hello? The aforementioned ex-girlfriend sex thing? Come on, grow a set."

"Fine. Fuck it. Your ex doesn't cast a shadow."

Now it was Vin's turn to laugh. "Is that some kind of military lingo?"

"You want to know why I believe that wasn't you in the elevator last night? It's because you called it. She's a reflection, a mirage . . . she doesn't exist and she's totally dangerous, and yeah, I know this doesn't make sense, but it's reality."

Vin slowly lowered what was left of his roast beef. The guy was serious. Dead serious.

Was it possible, Vin wondered, that he could talk for once about the other side of his life? That part that involved things that couldn't be touched or seen, but that had shaped him sure as his parents' DNA had?

"You said . . . you'd come to save my soul," Vin murmured.

Jim braced his hands on the granite counter and leaned in. Under the short sleeves of his plain white T-shirt, his arm muscles thickened under the weight. "And I mean it. I have a happy new job of pulling people back from the brink."

"Of what?"

"Eternal damnation. As I said before . . . in your case, I used to think it was making sure you ended up with Devina, but now I'm damn clear that's the wrong outcome. Now . . . it means something else. I just don't know what."

Vin wiped his mouth and stared down at the man's big, capable hands. "Would you believe me . . . if I told you I had a dream about Devina—one where she was like something out of *28 Days*, all rotted and fucked-up? She maintained that I'd asked for her to come to me, that we'd entered into some kind of bargain that there was no getting out of. And the most ridiculous thing about it? It didn't feel like a dream."

"And I believe it wasn't. Before I had Friday's little lights-out session with the extension cord? I'd have said you were nuts. Now? You bet your ass I believe every single word of that."

Finally, at least something was working for instead of against him, Vin thought as he decided to pull a bare-all.

"When I was seventeen, I went to this . . ." God, even with how well Jim was taking things, he still felt like a complete ass. "I went to this palm reader, fortune-teller . . . this woman in town. Remember that 'spell' I had back at the diner?" When Jim nodded, he continued. "I used to get them a lot, and I needed . . . shit, I needed some way to get them to stop. They were ruining my life, making me feel like a freak."

"Because you saw the future?"

"Yeah, and that shit just ain't right, you know? I never volunteered for it and I would have done anything to get it to stop." Images from the past, of him collapsing at malls and at schools and in libraries and movies, flooded his brain. "It was torture. I never knew when the trances were coming and I didn't know what I said in them and the people I didn't scare the shit out of thought I was crazy." He laughed in a hard burst. "Might have been different if I'd been able to predict the lottery, but I've only ever had bad news to share. Anyway, so there I was, seventeen, clueless, at the end of my rope, with nothing but a pair of violent, alkie parents at home who couldn't offer me any help or advice ... I didn't know what else to do, where to go, who to talk to. I mean, my mom and dad? Fuckin' A, I wouldn't have asked them what to make for lunch, much less anything about that stuff. So one day close to Halloween, which is my birthday, by the way, I see in the back of the *Courier Journal* a bunch of ads for these psychics, healers, whatever, and I decided to give one of them a try. I went downtown, knocked on some doors and finally one of them opened. The woman seemed to understand the situation. She told me what to do and I went home and I did it ... and everything changed."

"Like how?"

"The trances stopped, for one thing, and then I just had luck on my side. My parents finally imploded—I'll spare you the details, but let's just say the end was simply an evolution of the alcoholism. After they were gone, I was relieved and free and ... different. I turned eighteen, inherited the house and my father's plumbing jobs ... and that's how it all started."

"Wait, you say you were different—how?"

Vin shrugged. "When I was growing up, I was laid-back. You know, never much interested in school, content to kind of flake along. But after my parents died ... yeah, nothing about me was chill. I had this hunger." He put his hand on his gut. "Always with the hunger. Nothing was ... or has been ever enough. It's like I'm obese when it comes to money—starved no matter what's in my accounts or how much I have. I used to think it was just because I went from teenager to adult the second my parents were gone— I mean, I had to support myself because no one else was going to. But I'm not sure that completely explains it. The thing was, while I was working full-time for those plumbers, I got into drug dealing. The cash was crazy and as it began to stockpile, I just wanted more and more. I got into doing houses because I could be legit that way—and that mattered not because I was afraid of jail, but because I couldn't make as much paper behind bars as I could out. I was relentless and uncurtailed by ethics and laws and anything but self-preservation. Nothing eased me ... until two nights ago."

"What changed then?"

"I stared into the eyes of a woman and felt ... something else."

Vin reached into his back pocket and took out the card of the Madonna. After taking a good long look at it, he put it down on the counter and turned it around so Jim could see it.

"When I looked into her eyes ... I felt satisfied for the first time."

Jim leaned in and stared at the icon. Holy shit ... it was Marie-Terese. The dark hair, the blue eyes, the soft, kind face. "Okay, that's eerie as fuck."

Vin cleared his throat. "She's not the Virgin Mary. I know. And this picture is not of her. But when I saw Marie-Terese, that burning pit in my stomach eased off. Devina? She just fed the drive. Whether it was the sex we had and the boundaries we pushed there, or the things she wanted or the places we went. She was a constant ramp-up of the hunger. Marie-Terese on the other hand ... she's like a warm pool. When I'm with her, I don't need to be anywhere else. Ever."

The guy abruptly took back the card and rolled his eyes.

"Jesus Christ, listen to me. I sound like a Lifetime movie or some shit."

Jim cracked a smile. "Yeah, well, things don't work out, you could always go into the greeting-card biz from prison."

"Just the kind of career change I was looking to make."

"Better than license plates."

"Wittier, certainly."

Jim thought about Devina and the so-called dream Vin had had. Chances were very good that hadn't been a nightmare. For God's sake, if she didn't cast a shadow in broad daylight, what other tricks did she have up her sleeve?

"What exactly did you do?" Jim asked. "When you were seventeen."

Vin crossed his arms over his chest and you could practically hear the sucking sound as he was drawn back into the past. "I did what the woman told me to do."

"Which was . . . ?" When Vin just shook his head, Jim guessed it was some hard-core creepy. "This woman still around?"

"Dunno."

"What's her name?"

"Why does it matter? That's in the past."

"But Devina is not, and you're up on charges for something you didn't do, thanks to her." As a whole lot of cursing rolled out, Jim nodded. "You open a door, not a bad idea to go back and get the key to lock it back up."

"That's the problem. I thought I was locking it. As for that woman, it was like twenty years ago. I doubt we can find her."

As Vin started to clean things up, Jim watched his awkward bandaged hand. "How'd you hurt yourself?"

"I crushed a glass as I was talking to you."

"That'll do it."

Vin stopped in the middle of twisting shut the sourdough bread. "I'm worried about Marie-Terese. If Devina can do this to me, what isn't she capable of, you know?"

"I hear you on that. Does she have a clue about—"

"No, and I'm going to keep it that way. I don't want Marie-Terese involved in this shit."

More evidence Vin wasn't an idiot. "Listen . . . about her." Jim wanted to be careful how he packaged this one. "I took a look around her background after you told me that other guy who was killed downtown had been with her."

"Oh, Jesus . . ." Vin wheeled around from the cupboard he'd opened. "That ex-husband of hers. He's found her. It's—"

"Not him. He's in jail." Jim did a download on what Matthias the fucker had found and what do you know . . . the more the story came out, the bigger the frown on Vin's face got. "Bottom line is," Jim concluded, "although it's possible an associate of Capricio's would come after her, it's not likely given those other deaths because they'd really just be concerned with Marie-Terese."

Vin cursed—which meant he got the picture and all the implications. "So, who is it? Assuming she's the tie between the two attacks."

"That's the question."

Vin settled back against the counter, crossing his arms and looking as if he'd like to fight someone.

"She's quit, by the way," he said after a moment. "You know, doing that shit at the Iron Mask. And I think she's going to leave Caldwell."

"Really."

"I don't want her to, but maybe it's for the best. It could be that one of those . . . men, you know, from the club, that she . . . yeah."

As the guy's lips flattened out like his gut had frozen up on him, Jim realized things had progressed between the two of them. Fast. Although he wasn't willing to bet Dog on it, he'd wager his truck and his Harley that Vin and Marie-Terese had become lovers—because that expression on the guy's face was kind of heartbreaking.

"I don't want to lose her," Vin muttered. "And I hate to have her running for her life."

"Well," Jim said, "then I think you and I need to make it safe for her to stay here."

Safe from Devina ... and from whatever psycho was after her.

At least Jim knew what the hell to do to some creep who had a case of the obsessions with the woman. As for Devina? Well, he was going to have to pull that one out of his ass.

Across the way, Vin looked over, and as they locked eyes, the guy nodded once, like he knew that things were going to get freaky and he was good with that. Extending his bandaged hand, he said, "Excellent plan, my friend."

Jim carefully clasped the paw that was offered. "I have a feeling it's going to be a pleasure working with you."

"Likewise. Guess that bar fight was just a warm-up."

"Clearly."

CHAPTER
29

As Marie-Terese sat down after the last hymn of the service, she felt her phone vibrating in her purse and put her hand in to stop its rattle-and-shake routine.

Robbie looked over, but she just settled back in the pew, and gave him a little smile. The way she saw it, there were three possibilities for the call: wrong number, baby-sitters . . . or Trez. And as much as liked her old boss, she hoped it wasn't him.

Abruptly, she thought of something she'd learned in college about veteran parachuters. It had been in psychology class and part of a study on perceived danger and anxiety. Asked when or if they had ever been afraid, the parachuters, who fit the profile of risk takers, overwhelmingly replied that the only time they'd been nervous was on their last jump—as if they might have used up all their luck over time and the odds they had beaten until that point could suddenly reach out and grab them just as they were getting out.

Funny, when she'd been eighteen and sitting in a lecture hall, it had seemed so ridiculous. After all the jumps those highfliers had taken, why would they have lost their iron nerve on the last one?

Now she so got that.

She might have quit the night before ... but what if that was Trez calling her back to meet with the CPD again? And what if this time, it wasn't about those shootings, but what she had done for money?

As she sat next to her son in church, the risk she had assumed seemed real for the first time. The thing was, the evolution from sexy waitress to something more had been done in an environment where that was a "career choice" a lot of people around her had made safely. Abruptly, though, she realized she must have been crazy. If she got jailed, Robbie would end up in foster care—with both of his parents behind bars.

Sure, neither Trez, nor her first boss, had ever had any problems with the police, but how could she have put so much faith in that track record considering what was at stake?

God ... in cutting herself loose from that whole seedy underside of life, she was able to view her choice to do what she'd done for the money with very different eyes. ...

Glancing around at all the people in the pews, she was shocked to realize that these were normal eyes she was re-garding her actions with. And as a result she was horrified with herself.

Be careful what you wish for, she thought. She'd wanted to be among the worried well, because that had seemed so much easier than where she'd been. Now that she was dipping her foot in that pool, though, it just made what she'd done seem all the more terrible and irresponsible and dangerous.

And actually, that had been the way she'd lived for the last ten years, hadn't it. Her marriage to Mark had been the first step into a kind of lawless life she'd seen only on TV. Going rogue to keep her son safe had been the second. Turning to prostitution to make money in order to survive had been the third.

As she looked down the long aisle to the altar, she got angry with herself and her choices. She was the only person

Robbie had in his life, and though she'd thought she was putting him first, she really hadn't done that, had she.

And the fact that she hadn't had many other options considering what kind of money she owed was a very cold comfort.

When the service was over, she and Robbie stood up and joined the crush of people who pooled in the vestibule around Father Neely. For the most part, she focused on ushering Robbie forward, but every now and again, because she couldn't avoid it without being rude, she nodded to people she knew from the prayer group or from previous Sundays.

Robbie held on to her hand, but made like the man, squiring her instead of being led—at least as far as he knew. When they came up to the priest, he let go and was the first to shake the man's hand.

"Lovely service," Marie-Terese, said laying her palms lightly on her son's shoulders. "And the cathedral renovations are coming along beautifully."

"They are, they are." Father Neely looked around with a smile, his white hair and tall, thin bearing perfect for a man of the cloth. In fact, he kind of looked like the cathedral, pale and ethereal. "Quite a lift on her, and about time."

"I'm glad you're cleaning up the statuary as well." She nodded over to the blank spot where the Mary Magdalene figure had been. "When is she coming back?"

"Oh, dear, you don't know? She was stolen." People pressed in, and Father Neely started meeting the stares of other churchgoers and smiling. "The police are looking for the vandal. We're lucky, though, considering what else could have been taken as well."

"That is terrible." Marie-Terese tapped Robbie and he took the hint, clasping her hand and starting to lead again. "I hope they get her back."

"Myself as well." The priest leaned forward and squeezed her forearm, his eyes kind under his cotton-ball eyebrows. "Be well, my child."

He was always nice to her. Even though he knew.

"You, too, Father," she said roughly.

She and Robbie walked out into the chilly April afternoon, and as she looked up at the milky white sky, she smelled a change in the air. "Wow, I think we may be getting a snow."

"Really? That would be so cool."

As they went along the sidewalk, car engines were starting up far and wide as the Sunday *Times* 500 lit off and the congregation raced back home to collapse on sofas and easy chairs with the newspaper. At least, that was what she assumed they did, given the number of people she saw coming out of the Rite Aid down the street with their arms full of the *New York Times* and the Sunday edition of the *Caldwell Courier Journal.*

Without being asked, Robbie took her hand again as they came to the curb at the end of the block and they waited together for a break in the bumper-to-bumper. Standing by him, she worried about what was waiting for her on her phone—except she knew better than to check with him around. Her poker face was good, but not that good.

It turned out her gamble with the parking laws had worked in her favor and the Camry hadn't been towed, but its engine was not happy about the cold weather that had rolled in. She finally got the thing started, though, and pulled out into traffic—

From the backseat, her purse let out a little purring sound: Her phone was vibrating again, this time against her wallet, which accounted for the sound.

Craning her arm around, she tried reach the thing, but Robbie's nimble little hands got there first.

"It says 'Trez,'" he announced as he handed the cell over.

She hit *send* with dread. "Hello?"

"You need to come down to the club right away," Trez said. "The police are here about the assault and they want to ask you some questions."

"What assau—" She glanced at Robbie. "I'm sorry, what are you talking about?"

"There was another man found in an alley last night. He had been badly beaten and he's in critical condition in the hospital. Listen, he's someone I saw you with—and others did, too. You need to—"

"Mom!"

Marie-Terese slammed on the brakes and the Camry went into a pig-squeal skid, narrowly missing the quarter panel of an SUV that had the right of way. As the other car's horn blared, the cell phone flipped out of her hand and bounced across the dashboard, ping-ponging all the way over to Robbie's window before disappearing onto the floor at his feet.

The Camry came to a stop with the lurching grace of a bull and she wheeled around at her son. "Are you okay?"

As she patted her hands over his chest, he nodded and slowly released his death grip on his seat belt. "I think . . . that light . . . was red."

"It sure was." She pushed her hair out of her face and looked through the front windshield.

The SUV's furious driver made eye contact, but as soon as the guy saw her face, the anger in him eased—which gave her an idea of how terrified she must appear. As he mouthed, *Are you okay?*, she nodded, and he lifted his hand in a wave before driving off.

Marie-Terese needed a minute, however—so thank God the Camry had essentially parallel parked itself at the curb.

Well, on the curb.

In the rearview mirror, she saw a man getting out of a blue Subaru that had pulled over behind her. As he walked up, he pushed his glasses a little higher on his nose and tried to smooth his thinning blond hair in the brisk wind. She knew him, she realized . . . from prayer group meetings and from the previous evening at the confessionals.

She hit the window button, thinking she was surprised he approached. He seemed shy and almost never spoke at the meetings. Which she supposed put him in the same quiet tribe as her.

"Everyone all right?" he asked, bending down and putting his forearm on the roof.

"We are, but that was a close one." She smiled up at him. "Nice of you to stop."

"I was behind you, and I should have honked or something when I didn't see any brake lights as you came up to the intersection. Guess you were distracted. You okay, too, son?"

Robbie kept silent, his eyes locked downward and his hands in his lap. He was not one for making eye contact with men, and Marie-Terese had no interest in forcing him to.

"He's fine," she said, resisting the urge to check him for injury again.

There was a long moment and then the man stepped back. "Guess you'll be on your way home then. Take care."

"You, too, and thanks again for checking on us."

"My pleasure. See you soon."

As she put up her window, a squawking came from the floor at Robbie's feet. "The phone!" she said. "Oh, no, Trez ... Robbie, could you get that?"

Robbie bent down and picked the thing up. Before he gave it to her, he asked grimly, "Would you like me to drive home?"

Marie-Terese nearly laughed, but what stopped her was the seriousness in his face. "I'll watch out better. Promise."

"Okay, Mom."

She patted his knee as she put the phone back to her ear. "Trez?"

"What the fuck was that!"

With a wince, she held the receiver away from her ear. "Ah ... it was a red light that I didn't handle very well." She checked every mirror on the car and all the windows before putting her blinker on. "But no one's hurt."

As the blue Subaru went by, she waved at the driver. Paul ... Peter ... what was his name?

"Jesus Christ ... I nearly had a heart attack," Trez muttered.

"What were you saying?" As if the near miss in traffic wasn't enough of a shocker.

"Why don't you call me back when you get home. I don't know how many stoplights there are between you and—"

"I'm paying attention now." She pulled out slowly. "I swear."

There was some male-oriented grumbling over the connection. Then: "Fine . . . here's the deal. The cops showed up here about a half hour ago, looking to talk to staff again, and you in particular. I guess they'd gone to your house and then tried to call you, and when they couldn't reach you, they headed over here. I don't know a lot, only that there's a footprint at both scenes that seems to suggest a link between the two attacks. The tread of a running shoe, I guess? I don't think I'm supposed to know this, by the way—it was just that two of the cops went outside for a smoke and they were passing some pics back and forth, and gee whiz, I picked up on the convo. Go. Fig."

Marie-Terese's first thought was that Vin didn't wear sneakers—or at least he'd had on flat-soled loafers both nights.

Odd, wasn't it: Her main concern was whether or not Vin was involved, not that Mark was sending people after her from jail. The thing was, though, she'd run from her ex once before—and she could do it again. But the idea that she was falling for another violent man wasn't the kind of thing she could get away from so easily.

"Trez, do you have any idea when the . . ." She glanced over at Robbie, who was drawing shapes on his window with his fingertip. "Do you know when it happened? Last night?"

"After you left."

So it couldn't have been Vin. . . .

"Your man's in trouble, by the way."

"Excuse me?"

"Vin diPietro. His face is all over the news. Guess his girlfriend ended up in the hospital, and she's saying he was the one who put her there."

As the second round of drama hit, Marie-Terese took her foot off the gas and deliberately looked up as she came to an intersection. Green. Green means go, she told herself. Go means gas. She carefully eased her foot down and the Camry responded with all of the gusto of a ventilator patient.

"By any chance," Trez murmured, "were the two of you together late last night around ten?"

"Yes."

"Then take a deep breath. Because according to the news, that's when she said it all went down."

Marie-Terese exhaled—but only briefly. "Oh, my God . . . what's he going to do?"

"He's out on bail already."

"I can help him." Although as soon as the words left her mouth, she wondered whether that was true. The last thing she needed was her face on the news: There was no way of knowing whether she'd been "safe" from Mark thus far because he was leaving her alone . . . or because people he'd sent after her just hadn't found her yet.

"Yeah, maybe you should try to stay out of it, though," Trez said. "He's got cash and connections, and lies are always revealed in the end. In any event, can I tell the police you'll talk to them now?"

"Yes—but have them wait with you." The last thing she wanted was the cops in front of Robbie again, so the club was the place for her to meet them. "I'll call the babysitter right away."

"One last thing."

"Yes?"

"Even though you're out of the business now, a past like ours has a long reach, feel me? Please be careful of everyone around you, and when in doubt, call me. I don't want to alarm you, but I don't like these attacks happening to people who've been tied to you."

Neither did she. "I will."

"And if you need to leave Caldwell, I can help."

"Thanks, Trez." She hung up and looked at her son. "I'm going to have to go out for a little bit this afternoon."

"Okay. Can Quinesha come?"

"I'll try to get her." When they came to a stop at a light, Marie-Terese quickly punched in the babysitting service's number and hit *send*.

"Mom, who's 'him' who you wanna help?"

As the phone rang, she met her son's eyes. And didn't know what to say.

"Is he the reason you were smiling in church?"

She ended the call before it was picked up. "He's a friend of mine."

"Oh." Robbie picked at the crease in his khakis.

"He's just a friend."

Robbie's brows pulled together. "I get scared sometimes."

"About what."

"People."

Funny, so did she. "Not everyone is like your ..." She didn't want to finish the sentence. "I don't want you to feel like everyone is bad and will hurt you. Most people are okay."

Robbie seemed to mull this over. After a moment, he looked up at her. "But how do you tell the difference, Mom?"

Marie-Terese's heart stopped. God, there were times as a parent that words escaped you and your chest went hollow. "I don't have a good answer for that."

As the light overhead turned green and they headed forward, Robbie focused on the road ahead and she left a message for the babysitters. After she hung up, she hoped that he was staring out with such fixation because he was watching for traffic lights with her. But she didn't think it was that simple.

They were halfway home when she thought, *Saul.* That man from the prayer group's name was Saul.

When Jim got back from the Commodore, he pulled in front of his garage and got out. As he went up the stairs, Dog parted the drapes in the bay window with his head, and going by the way his ears were pricked and his face was doing a shimmy, it was clear that stubby tail was going fast as an airplane prop.

"Yup, I'm back, big guy." Jim got his key ready as he came up to the door, but he paused before he put it into the shiny, spanking-new Schlage he'd installed after he'd moved in.

Looking over his shoulder, he focused on the dirt drive. A fresh set of tire tracks had marked up the partially frozen ground.

Someone had come and gone while he'd been out.

As Dog tap-danced with excitement on the other side of the door, Jim did a visual sweep around the landscape, and then looked down at the wooden stairs. Lot of muddy-ish footprints, all of which were dry and with a telltale Timberland tread—indicating they'd been made by him alone.

Which meant whoever it was had either wiped their feet off on the grass first or had hovered their asses up to his crib: He had a feeling they hadn't just pulled into his driveway, done a K-turn, and headed right back out.

Putting his palm to the small of his back, he unsheathed his knife and used his left hand to put the key to work.

Cracking the door amped up the *tic-tic-tic*'ing of Dog's paws on the bare floor . . . and also sent up a soft scraping noise.

Jim waited, sifting through the sounds of Dog's hello, searching for anything else. When there was nothing, he opened the door as sharply as he could without hurting Dog, and his eyes went around in a sweep.

No one was there, but as he stepped inside, he saw the cause of the tire tracks down below.

While Dog scampered around, Jim bent down and picked up a stiff manila envelope that was on the linoleum right under the mail slot. No name on the front. No return address. The thing weighed about as much as a book, and whatever was inside had a book feel to it, rectangular with clean edges.

"How'd you like to go out, big man?" he said to Dog while pointing to the great outdoors.

Dog trotted out with his telltale limp, and Jim waited at the door with the package in his hand as business was conducted on the fringe of bushes by the drive.

As he held on to Matthias the fucker's version of fruit-cake, he had to convince his stomach not to issue evac orders to those two roast beef sandwiches Vin had made him.

See, this was the problem: Your head could decide all kinds of things, but that didn't mean your body was all jolly-jolly with the plan of the hour.

After Dog came up the stairs and through the door, he headed right for his bowl of water.

With a lightning lunge, Jim ditched the delivery and got there first, picking up the bowl, dumping it out, and washing the thing with soap. As he refilled it, his heart was beating in a grim, steady rhythm.

The thing was, the package was just slightly larger than the mail slot. So they had been in here. And although it was unlikely that they had poisoned Dog's water, the animal had somehow become family in the last three days, and that meant any margin of risk was unacceptable.

As Dog had his drink, Jim went over to the bed, sat down and grabbed the envelope. The minute Dog was finished, he limped over and hopped up as if he wanted to know what was in the package.

"You can't eat it," Jim said. "But you could piss on it if you wanted to. I would definitely excuse the mess. Totally."

Using his knife, he pierced the stiff, thick paper and opened a slit that stretched wide, pouching out and revealing . . .

A laptop the size of an old-school VHS tape.

He took the thing out and let Dog have a sniff-spection of it. Evidently, there was an approval, because Dog gave it a nudge and curled up with a yawn.

Jim opened up the screen and hit the power button. Windows Vista loaded, and what do you know, when he went into the start menu and called up the Outlook that had been installed, he had an account. And his password was the same as his old one.

In the in-box, he found a welcome e-mail from Outlook Express, which he ignored, and two from a blank sender.

"God, Dog, every time I try to get out, they keep pulling me back in," he said, not even attempting an impersonation of Al Pacino.

Jim opened the first e-mail and went right to its attachment—which turned out to be an Adobe file of . . . a personnel report that was a good fifteen pages long.

The picture in the upper left-hand corner was of a hard-ass Jim knew, and the details included the guy's last-known address, his vital stats, his clearances, his honors, and his deficiencies. As Jim scanned and absorbed the intel, he was mindful of the time clock in the lower portion of the screen. It had started at five minutes, and quickly was down to two, and when the three digits separated by a colon read 0:00, the attachment was cyberdust, as if it had never existed. The same outcome occurred, only immediately, if he tried to forward, print out, or save the file.

Matthias was sharp like that.

So thank fuck for photographic memory.

As for the report itself? On the surface, it appeared as if there were nothing out of the ordinary; it was just your garden-variety rundown on a black-ops guy who was like the e-file—nothing but ether until he disappeared entirely. Except then there were the telltale three letters at the end next to the word STATUS.

MIA.

Ah, so that was the assignment. In the military branch Jim had been in, there was no such thing as MIA. There was AD, OR, or PB: active duty, on reserve, or pine box—the last being a term of art used unofficially, of course. Jim was OR—which meant that technically he was liable to be called back in at any moment and had to go or the letters DEAD were going to appear next to his status. And the truth was, he'd had to blackmail Matthias the fucker to even get into the reserves—although given what he had on the guy, he should have been able to stay there. If he hadn't had to resell his soul.

Well . . . the assignment was clear-cut: Matthias wanted this man killed.

Jim quickly rescanned the report until he was certain he could close his eyes and read the text and see the picture on the backs of his eyelids. Then he watched the clock zero out and the thing disappear.

He opened the second e-mail. Another e-file to crack and another ticker in the bottom corner that was triggered when he did. This time he just had a picture of the guy, only now the face was battered, with a split in the forehead that had let loose a tidal wave of blood. He wasn't a victim, though. His knuckles were wrapped for fighting and there was red chicken wire behind his head and shoulders.

The image the solider was a scan of a flyer for an underground mixed-martial-arts fighting group. Area code was 617. Boston.

The name the soldier was going by was both cheesy as fuck and pretty goddamn accurate, assuming he hadn't changed: Fist. His real one was Isaac Rothe.

This file lasted only a hundred and eighty seconds, and Jim hung out, staring at that face. He'd seen it a number of times, on some occasions right beside him while they worked together.

Dog nuzzled his way into Jim's lap and curled up, putting his face on the keyboard.

Yup, Matthias wanted the guy dead because Isaac had bolted from the fold—so it was a standard job and standard rules applied. Which meant if Jim didn't do it, someone else would—and the chaser would be that Jim woke up dead in the morning, too.

Pretty damned simple.

Jim ran his hand down Dog's flank and worried about who would feed and care for the little guy if something bad happened. Shit, it was weird to have something to live for . . . but Jim just couldn't deal with the idea of the animal lost and alone, hungry and scared again.

Lotta cruel motherfuckers in the world who couldn't care less about a scruffy ugly-ass dog with a limp.

And yet the idea of killing Isaac was repugnant. God knew Jim had wanted out of the service bad, so he couldn't blame the guy for leaving: A life that was led in the gray borderlands between right and wrong, legal and illegal, was a hard one.

If only the idiot had had the sense not to do anything with a public presence, even an underground one.

Then again, they would have found him eventually. They always did—

The twin sounds of Harley engines pulling up to the garage brought both his and Dog's heads around, and Dog immediately started wagging his tail as those growls silenced down below.

As boots came up the stairs, the animal leaped off the bed and headed for the door.

The knock was loud and it struck only once.

Dog paddled at the door, his excitement making him appear even scruffier than usual, and before the poor thing expired from ecstasy, Jim got up and walked over.

As he opened the door, he met Adrian's cool eyes. "What do you want?"

"We need to talk."

Jim crossed his arms over his chest as Eddie knelt down and showed love to Dog. Given the way the animal reacted, it was hard to believe the bikers were playing on Devina's team, but just because they weren't pally-pally with her didn't mean they were legit: All Jim had to do was think of the shadows he hadn't seen and the confusion in Chuck the foreman's voice when he'd been asked about the pair.

Made a guy wonder just what the fuck was standing on his doorstep.

"You two are liars," Jim said. "So that makes talking kind of pointless, doesn't it."

As Dog rolled over onto his back so Eddie could do

some serious belly rubbing, Adrian shrugged. "We're angels, not saints. What do you want from us."

"So you do know those four English whack jobs?"

"Yeah, we do." Adrian glanced pointedly at the refrigerator. "Listen, this is going to be a long conversation. You mind beering us?"

"Do you exist?"

"Beer. Then talk."

As Eddie got to his feet with Dog in his heavy arms, Jim held up his palm. "Why did you lie."

Adrian glanced over at his roommate; then looked back. "I didn't know whether you could handle shit."

"And what's changed your mind."

"The fact that you figured out what Devina is and you didn't bolt. You believed what you saw on that pavement on the hospital."

"Or didn't see, as was the case."

Jim stared at the two of them, thinking that clearly they'd been following him—and maybe Devina had sensed them instead of him in the parking lot of the hospital.

"No," Adrian said, "we masked you so she didn't see you. That's what she was picking up on when she looked around. There are advantages to her thinking you're on your own and you're clueless."

"You guys read minds, too?"

"And I'm full aware of how much you don't like me at this moment."

"Can't be a new thing for you," Jim said, wondering if he was ever going to work with people who weren't assholes. "So . . . you two are here to help me."

"Yup. Just like Devina's going to have people helping her."

"I don't like liars. I have too much experience with them."

"Won't happen again." Adrian ran a hand through his ridiculously gorgeous hair. "Look, this isn't easy on us. . . . To be honest, I had my doubts from the beginning that bringing you on was a good idea, but that's my damage. Bottom line is, you're here and that's that, so either we work together or she has a serious advantage."

Well, hell . . . that logic was pretty damn unassailable.

"I kicked all the Corona the other night so I only got Bud," Jim said after a moment. "In cans."

"And that's just what an angel has a craving for," Adrian shot back.

Eddie nodded. "Sounds good to me."

Jim stepped to the side and opened the door farther. "Are you alive?"

Adrian shrugged as they came inside. "Hard to answer that. But I know I like beer and sex, how 'bout that."

"What is Dog?"

Eddie answered that one: "Consider him a friend. A very good friend."

The animal . . . or whatever he was . . . gave a shy wag like he understood every word, and was worried he'd offended, and Jim felt compelled to lean in and give his chin a little scratch. "Guess I don't need to get him vaccinated, do I?"

"Nope."

"What's with the limp?"

"It's the way he is." Eddie's big palm smoothed over the dog's rough fur. "It just is."

As he and Dog sat on the bed and Adrian wandered around, Jim took his headfuck over to the refrigerator, grabbed three Buds, and dealt the cans out like cards. A trio of cracks and hisses cut through the room and then there was a collective *ahhhh*.

"How much do you know about me?" Jim asked.

"Everything." Adrian looked around and focused on Jim's twin piles of clean and dirty. "Guess you don't believe in dresser drawers, do you."

Jim glanced down at his clothes. "Nope."

"Ironic, really."

"Why?"

"You'll see." Adrian went over and sat down at the

table. Tipping the shoe box full of chess pieces toward him, he glanced inside. "So what do you want to know. About her, us, anything."

Jim took another drag on his Bud and thought it all over.

"Only one thing matters to me," he said. "Can she be killed?"

Both of the angels went still. And slowly shook their heads.

CHAPTER
30

Considering what he'd been arrested for and the way things were going, Vin couldn't believe what was showing on the screen of his cell phone as the ringer went off.

As he accepted the call, he muted the local news and held on hard. "Marie-Terese?"

There was a pause. "Hi."

Swiveling around in his desk chair, he looked out over Caldwell and found it hard to comprehend that mere nights ago, he'd stared at the view with such a sense of domination. Now he felt like his life was totally out of control and he was fighting to stay where he was instead of being king of the mountain.

Never one to beat around the bush, he said, "Have you heard the news? About me?"

"Yes. But you were with me late last night, when it happened. I know you didn't do it."

Relief rolled through him—although only about that particular part of the shit storm. "And the other attack, in the alley?"

"I'm on the way to the Iron Mask now. The police want to talk to me."

"Can I see you," he blurted with a desperation that would have shocked him under normal circumstances.

"Yes."

Vin was surprised by the quick answer, but sure as shit not going to argue with it. "I'm at home over in the Commodore, so I can meet you anywhere, anytime."

"I'll come to you as soon as I'm done with the CPD."

"I'm on the twenty-eighth floor. I'll tell the doorman to expect you."

"I'm not sure how long I'm going to be, but I can text you when I'm on my way."

Vin shifted his eyes over to the left, imagining her however many blocks west and south of where he was. "Marie-Terese . . ."

"Yes?"

He thought of her and her son . . . thought of the kind of people she'd managed to get away from—thus far. Her ex could easily reach out from prison, maybe already had: even if those attacks weren't tied to her, or were being done by someone else, she still needed to keep the lowest profile she could.

"Don't try to protect me."

"Vin—"

"I'll explain more when you get here," he said gruffly. "But let's just say I know how much you have to lose if your face gets into the media channels."

Silence. Then: "How."

He could tell by the tightness in her voice that she didn't appreciate the look-see into her background. "Jim, my friend . . . he has connections. I didn't ask him to do it, by the way, but he told me what he found."

Long pause. The kind that made him wish to hell he'd waited to drop that little bomb until she was in front of him. But then she exhaled. "It's kind of a relief, actually. That you know."

"It goes without saying that I'll tell no one."

"I trust you."

"Good, because I would never do anything to hurt you." Now it was Vin's turn to get quiet. "God, Marie-Terese . . ."

There was the slight squeak of brakes. "I'm just at the club now. We'll talk in a little bit."

"Don't protect me. Please."

"See you soon—"

"Stay quiet. Don't get yourself involved with the shit that's on my tail. For your son's sake and yours. It's not worth the risk."

He stopped himself right there. No way he was going into the whole truth about Devina—partially because he didn't understand it fully himself, and mostly because he hated the idea of Marie-Terese thinking he was crazy.

"It's not right." Her voice broke. "What she's accusing you of. It's not—"

"I know. Just believe me when I say I'm going to take care of it. I'm going to handle this."

"Vin—"

"You know I'm right. See you in a bit." As they ended the call, he prayed she would go with the reasoning—and figured, given the conflict in her voice, that the math was adding up correctly in her mind.

This was good.

Instead of heading downtown to try to find that psychic he'd gone to for help when he was seventeen—which was what he'd intended to do—Vin spent the next hour in the living room, cleaning up pieces of glass and busted leather books and putting the couches and chairs back together. He even got out the vacuum and tried to resuscitate the carpet, making some inroads with the shards and absolutely none with the liquor stains. He had his phone with him the whole time, and when the text came through that Marie-Terese was on her way, he rolled the Dyson into the closet and jogged upstairs to change into a clean silk shirt.

He was almost on the way out of the bedroom when it dawned on him that he was still in the pants and boxers he'd had on in jail.

Right. Back to the well.

Second trip out into the hall and he had on a sharp-ass pair of black slacks and some black boxer briefs. Changed his socks, too. Shoes were the same Bally loafers he'd been wearing for the past week.

Her timing was perfect.

The home phone rang just as he hit the foyer, and he told the front-desk man to let her up. On the way to the door, Vin double-checked in the shattered mirror that he'd tucked his shirt in properly and his hair was looking okay—which was kind of girlie when he thought about it, but whatever.

Out in the corridor, the elevator arrived with a *bing* and he stood back a little to give Marie-Terese some space, even though he would have rather taken her right into his arms—

Oh, man. She was gorgeous. Just in jeans and that deep red fleece, with her hair down and no makeup on, she was total pinup material to him.

"Hi," he said, like an idiot.

"Hi." She moved her purse farther up on her shoulder and her eyes shifted around to the open door of the duplex. As she got a load of his golden front hall, her brows lifted slightly.

"You want to come in?" He stepped to the side and motioned with his hand. "Be warned though ... the place is a mess after ..."

As she moved past him, he breathed in deep. What do you know. The scent of clean laundry was still his favorite perfume.

Vin shut the door, engaged the dead bolt, and put the chain in place. Which didn't seem halfway to safe enough: He had a heebie paranoia about Devina that made him wonder whether that kind of conventional stuff would keep her out of any place she wanted to go.

"Can I get you something to drink?" Not liquor, of course. At least, not in the living room. God knew there was none of it left there.

Marie-Terese headed toward the banks of glass. "This is quite a . . ." She hesitated as she came across a stain in the carpet and then looked around at the room and less at the view.

"It was even worse before I tried to clean it up a little," he said. "Christ . . . I have no idea what happened here."

"Why would your girlfriend lie?"

"Ex-girlfriend," he reminded her.

Marie-Terese glanced into the broken mirror to meet his eyes, and the sight of her features all scrambled in the field of cracks freaked his shit out—to the point where he had to go over in hopes of getting her out of its torturous reflection.

As she turned to face him, her eyes were scared. "Vin . . . that man who was attacked. He was the one I helped in the bathroom—we went in together and talked about this girl he wanted to impress." She put her hand over her mouth and trembled. "Oh, God . . . he was with me and then he . . ."

Vin went over and wrapped his arms around her, holding her closely. As she took a deep breath, he felt it from his thighs to his ribs, and goddamn it if he didn't want to kill to protect her.

"It can't be Mark," she said into his shirt. "But what if he's sent someone to find me?"

"Come here." He took her hand and started for the couch. But then, did he really want to talk to her amid the remnants of whatever violence had occurred?

Pausing, he thought about the study . . . but had memories of being with Devina on that fucking rug. Upstairs . . . yeah, right, the bedroom was a total no-go, and not just because asking Marie-Terese up there had letch connotations he didn't intend: too much Devina there as well.

Vin settled for the dining room table, walking her over and angling two chairs so that he could face her.

"You know," she said as she put her purse down and they sat together, "I'm actually a tough cookie."

He had to smile. "I believe that."

"You just seem to have come along at a hard time."

Vin extended his hand and touched one of the curled locks of hair by her face. "I wish I could do something to help."

"I'm leaving Caldwell."

His heart stopped. It was on the tip of his tongue to argue with her, but he didn't have that right—not by a long shot. Besides, he was hard-pressed to deny the decision: It was probably for the best.

"Where will you go?" he asked.

"Anywhere. I don't know."

In her lap, her hands tangled and twisted as if they were paralleling the thoughts in her mind.

"Do you have enough money?" he asked, even though he knew what she was going to say.

"I'll be okay. Somehow . . . Robbie and I will be okay."

"Will you let me help you?"

She shook her head slowly. "I can't do that. I can't . . . owe anybody else. I'm having a hard enough time paying off the people I'm in debt to already."

"How much do you owe them?"

"I have another thirty thousand to go," she said, her hands stilling. "I started with about a hundred and twenty."

"What if I gave it to you and you paid it back eventually? I'm sure they're charging interest—"

"A debt is a debt." She smiled in a sad way. "There was a time when I hoped that some man would come in and rescue me from my life. And one did—except the rescue turned out to be a nightmare. Now I rescue myself—which means I pay my own way. Always."

But thirty thousand dollars? Christ, that was couch change to him.

And to think she'd been working off all that money doing . . .

Vin squeezed his eyes shut for a moment. Shit, he hated the pictures in his mind—even though they were mere hypotheticals for what she'd forced herself into, they lashed at him. And it would have been so easy for him to make it all go away for her—although he could see where she was coming from: Precisely that kind of savior routine had soured on her big-time, and the lesson had been too hard-learned to let go.

He cleared his throat. "What did the police say when you spoke to them just now?"

"They showed me a picture of the guy, and I told them I'd seen him at the club and talked with him. I was in a panic that some eyewitness had popped out of the bushes and said that they'd seen me going into the bathroom with him, but the cop didn't mention anything like that. And then . . ."

When there was a long pause, he had a feeling she was trying to choose her words.

He cursed softly. "Tell me you didn't say anything about being with me last night."

She reached for his hands, holding them tightly. "That's why I'm leaving."

As his heart seized up, he wondered if he shouldn't tell the thing to quit bothering to beat altogether. "You didn't. Oh, God . . . you should just stay out of—"

"When they asked me what happened after I talked with the guy, I told them that I left the club with one Vincent diPietro and that you and I were together all night long. From nine thirty to about four a.m." When he would have jerked his hands back, she held them in place. "Vin, I've done enough in my life to be ashamed of. I've let a man abuse me for years . . . even in front of my son." Her voice cracked, but then grew strong. "I've whored myself out. I've lied. I've done things I used to look down on other women for . . . and I'm done with it. No more."

"Fucking hell," he muttered. "Fuck-ing hell."

Without thinking, he leaned in and gave her a quick kiss, then took his hands away and stood up. Unable to contain himself, he paced the length of the living room, up and back. Then did it again. She watched him the whole time, one arm draped along the back of the ornate chair she was on.

"I gave the police my cell phone number," she said, "and I'll come back to testify if I have to. I figure Robbie and I'll pack up tonight and just go. If the press doesn't know how to find me, my face isn't going to show up anywhere."

Vin stopped in the archway to the living room and thought of that security tape with his so-called face on it. Marie-Terese had no idea what she'd dropped herself into, because there was a fuckload more going on than simply an assault case. So, yeah, it was best that she just get out of town. He had a feeling he and his freaky-ass buddy Jim were going to have to figure out a way to get rid of Devina, and it wasn't just going to be a case of telling her to go pound sand.

As for who might be on Marie-Terese's tail? It couldn't be Devina because the trouble had started . . . shit, the night he'd first seen Marie-Terese at the Iron Mask.

"What?" Marie-Terese said.

He replayed the details of that evening. Devina had left before he and Jim had thrown down with those two college kids. Which meant it was theoretically possible that she could have killed the pair in the alley . . . except it made no sense. Why would she go after men who had been with Marie-Terese? Like that ex-husband, she wouldn't make others a target, and besides, Vin hadn't had anything much to do with Marie-Terese at that point.

"What's going through your mind, Vin?"

Nothing he could tell her, unfortunately. Nothing at all.

He paced down and back one more time—and then it dawned on him. Courtesy of her stepping up to the plate for him, he had her over a barrel. And he was a man who always took advantage of those kinds of things.

"Stay here," he said. "I'll be right back."

He strode out of the room and headed for the study.

Five minutes later, he returned with his hands full, and the second Marie-Terese saw what he was carrying, she opened her mouth to no-way him.

Vin shook his head and cut her off. "You say you pay your debts." One by one he laid out five stacks of one-hundred-dollar bills. "Well, I'm sure you'll allow me to do the same."

"Vin—"

"Fifty thousand dollars." He crossed his arms over his chest. "Take it. Use it to pay off the debt and carry you for a couple of months."

Marie-Terese shot up from her chair. "I'm telling the truth, not doing you a favor—"

"Sorry. You're not going to win this. I owe you for protecting me, and I have determined the going rate for that obligation is fifty grand. You're just going to have to deal with it."

"The hell I will." She picked her purse up from the table and slung it onto her shoulder. "I'm not—"

"A hypocrite? I beg to differ. You think you're the only one with pride? You're saying I'm not allowed to feel indebted to you? Pretty damn closed-minded."

"You're twisting my words!"

"Am I." He nodded at the cash. "Don't think so. And I also don't think you're crazy enough to bolt out of town with no resources. You use your credit cards, there's a trail. You withdraw the funds from your bank account, there's a trail."

"Damn you to hell."

"I have a feeling I've done that to myself already, thank you very much." He leaned down and shoved the piles in her direction. "Take the money, Marie-Terese. Take it and know that there are no strings attached. You never, ever want to see me again, that's okay. Don't go with nothing, though. You can't do that to me. I wouldn't be able to live with it."

In the tense stretch of silence, he realized that this was the first time since he'd started making paper that he was giving any of it away. Or at least trying to give it away. Over the years, he'd never supported charities or causes of any kind—if money was going out of his pocket, he had to get something tangible in return, and always at an increase in value.

"You're going to take this," he murmured. "Because this isn't knight-in-shining-armor time. I'm not trying to save you. I'm repaying a debt and giving you one of the tools you're going to need to build your better future."

When she didn't reply, he tapped one of the bundles. "Think of it like this—I'm helping you buy your own white horse. . . . Gretchen, for God's sake, you need to take the money."

The bastard used her real name.

Damn him.

God . . . it had been so long since anyone had called her Gretchen. To Robbie she was "Mom." To everyone else, she was Marie-Terese. She'd always loved her real name, though, and hearing it now, she wanted it back.

Gretchen . . . Gretchen . . .

She stared at the money. Vin was right: She took that and she had serious breathing room. Except . . . how was this different from before? It was still a man bailing her out.

It just didn't feel right.

She stepped up to him and put her hands on either side of his face.

"You are a lovely, lovely man, Vincent diPietro." She pulled him down to her lips and he went willingly, his palms settling lightly on her shoulders as their mouths met. "And I want to thank you."

Happiness flared in the hard lines of his face. But only for a moment.

"I'll always remember your gesture," she murmured.

"You don't have to take the hard route," he said, his brows drawing together. "You—"

"But see, that's what I learned. Things are hard for me now because I tried to take the easy way out first." She smiled up at him, thinking that she was going to remember how he was looking at her now for the rest of her life. "That's the problem with white horses. You have to pay for them yourself or you'll always be using someone else's reins."

He stared down at her for the longest time. "You're breaking my fucking heart in half right now, you really are." His hands tightened on her arms and then released as he stepped back. "It's like . . . I can reach out and touch you, but you're already gone."

"I'm sorry."

He looked over at the cash. "You know . . . I've never realized this before. But money is really just paper when you come down to it."

"I'm going to be okay."

"Are you." He shook his head. "Sorry, that came out wrong."

Except he was right to be worried. Hell, she was, too. "I'll stay in touch."

"I'd like that. . . . Any idea where you're headed?"

"I don't know. Haven't given it a lot of thought."

"Well . . . what if I told you I had an empty house I could lend you. It's out of state—" He held up his hand as she went to interject. "Just wait a minute. It's in Connecticut, in horse country there. It's a farmhouse, but it's close to the town, so you wouldn't be isolated. You could crash there for a couple of nights, get your feet under you, figure out where to go next. And it's better than a hotel, because you won't have to use a credit card. You could leave your house tonight after dark and get there in less than two hours."

Marie-Terese frowned as she thought it over.

"Not a handout, not cash, no strings," he said. "Just a place for you and your son to lay your heads. And when you're ready to leave it, just lock the place up and mail the keys back to me."

Marie-Terese walked around to the windows in the dining room and looked out at the stunning view as she tried to think through what the next day and week and month would be like. . . .

She got nothing back. Not a clue.

Which was a pretty clear signal she needed somewhere safe to figure it all out.

"Okay," she said quietly. "This I will take you up on."

She heard Vin approach from behind, and as his arms went around her, she turned and embraced him as well.

They held each other for a long, long time.

It was hard to say when things changed for her . . . when she started to notice not just the comfort of his broad chest against her, but the warmth of his body and the strength in his muscles and the spice of his expensive cologne.

He was warm, though.

And so very strong.

And so . . .

Marie-Terese ran her hands up his back, feeling the softness of the silk shirt he had on, but concentrating on the hard man beneath the fabric. In a flash, she saw him in the mirror in his old bedroom, naked and rearing up before her, his muscles flexing along his spine.

Vin moved his hips back. "I think . . . I think we should probably—"

She arched into him and felt the erection he was trying to hide. "Be with me. Before I go . . . be with me?"

Vin's entire body shuddered. "God, yes."

He took her hand and the two of them hit the stairs fast. On instinct, she headed left toward a black-and-gold room with a massive bed, but he tugged her in the opposite direction.

"Not there."

He took her into another bedroom, one that was smaller and done in warm reds and tans. As they landed on the satin-covered mattress, they melded hip to hip, mouths fusing, tongues meeting, hands going to zippers and buttons and belt buckles.

She all but ripped off his shirt, and when his chest was

bared, her palms rubbed over his smooth skin and his tight muscles. Shifting back, she helped with the shucking of her jeans and tops and then focused on getting his pants off.

"Holy *Christ*," he grunted as she pushed his slacks down to the middle of his thighs and gripped his erection through his briefs.

Fusing their mouths and sucking on his tongue, she stroked him through the thin, flexible cotton of his boxer briefs until the head of him burst out past the waistband. The instant she went skin-on-skin with him, he broke the contact of their lips and hissed in a breath through clenched teeth.

His Armanis went the way of his pants, getting shoved roughly down his legs, and she eased her way over his chest, kissing, nipping, allowing her hair to fall all around and tickle him as she went lower.

Just as she stood his arousal up and was ready to take him between her lips, his hands tightened on her arms. "Wait. . . ."

A single, glistening tear formed at his tip and wept down his head and onto her hand.

"Your sex doesn't want to wait, Vin," she said huskily.

Another tear followed the first, as if her words were just as erotic as anything she could have done to him physically.

"I need you to know . . . something."

Marie-Terese frowned. "What?"

"I . . ." He put both hands to his face and rubbed so hard it was like he wanted to sand his features down. "When I'm with you, it's not like how I've been. You know, with anyone else lately."

"Is . . . that a good thing?"

"I definitely think so." He dropped his arms. "But I've done some out-there shit, to be honest. With strangers."

Marie-Terese felt her brows pop, as if they were doing so of their own volition. "Like what?"

He shook his head like he didn't want to remember. "Nothing with men. But that's really about the only line I've drawn. I just ... I haven't been tested and I haven't always been careful. I feel like you deserve to know that before we do anything riskier than kissing and sex with a condom."

"Weren't you monogamous with Devina?" Although even as she asked, she realized the question was pointless because the woman hadn't been monogamous with him.

"There were other women along with her sometimes. If you know what I mean."

An unwelcome picture of Vin covered in female flesh barreled in. "Wow."

She was about to make a crack about it taking a special man to get a prostitute to blush, but given how he'd reacted before to her bringing up her "profession," she stopped herself.

"But it's not going to be like that with you." His eyes drifted around her hair and her face and her bare breasts. "To me ... you're everything I need, all that I want. I can't describe it. Just when you kiss me, that's all I'm after— What?"

She smiled as she stroked him slowly. "You make me feel precious."

"Come up here and let me show you exactly how precious."

He pulled gently on her arms, but she resisted, not wanting to be diverted. Funny, it felt odd and wonderfully unfamiliar to want to do what she had been on her way to doing.

"Vin, please let me give you this ..." Moving her palm up and down, she watched his head fall back and his mouth open and his chest heave. "And I'll just make sure you don't finish. How about that."

Before he could argue, she bent down and used the head of him to part her lips—in a rush, he groaned and his hips shot up, the movement pushing his erection deeper into her mouth. As she sucked him in, his fists balled up the duvet, his arm muscles straining, his pecs and his six-pack going rigid.

He was gorgeous like this, stretched out on the red satin, his big body sexed up to the point of no return. . . .

In this hot, erotic moment, Marie-Terese had him exactly where she wanted him to be.

CHAPTER
31

"Wait ... say what? Vin gave her exactly what?"

Jim glanced across his studio at Adrian and didn't like the expression on the guy's face. Fucker seemed a little pale. "A ring," Jim said. "He gave her an engagement ring. Or at least, he said she left with it when he broke up with her."

The angel's puss tightened even more. "What was it made of."

"It was a diamond."

"Not the stone. What was the setting made of."

"I don't know. Platinum, I'd guess. Vin's the kind of guy who always goes top-drawer." As Eddie shook his head and cursed, Jim said, "Right, now is the happy moment when you tell me why the hell you both look like someone pissed in your gas tanks."

Adrian knocked off the rest of his beer and put the can down on the crappy kitchen table. "You know anything about black magic, my friend?"

Jim shook his head slowly, not at all surprised at the way the conversation was heading. "Why don't you enlighten me."

Adrian fished around the shoe box full of chess pieces

and one by one took out all the pawns, lining them up. "Black magic is real. It exists and it's more prevalent than you think—and I'm not talking about singers biting off the heads of bats onstage, or a bunch of sixteen-year-olds getting stoned and playing games with an Ouija board, or so-called paranormal investigators jacking off their adrenal glands in some creepy old house. I'm talking about the real shit that will bite you on the ass hard. I'm talking about the way demons get to owning souls. . . . I'm talking about spells and curses that not only work in this world, but the hereafter."

There was a heavy, dark pause of vast significance.

Which Jim broke by flashing his hands and belting out, *"Booga-wooga!"*

At least Eddie laughed. Adrian flipped Jim the bird and headed to the fridge for another beer. "Don't be an ass-hole," the guy snapped as he cracked a freshie.

"Oh, right, because two in this group would be overkill." Jim eased back on the bed so that he was leaning against the wall. "Look, I just felt the need to break the tension. Keep going."

"This is *not* a joke." When Jim nodded, Adrian took a deep one from the Bud can, parked it in his seat again, and seemed to be filing through the catalog of his mind. "There's a lot you're going to learn over time. So let's just call this lesson one. Demons collect shit from the people they're targeting. The more they get the better, and they keep it with them unless someone takes it back. Within this practice, there's like . . . think of it as a rating system. Gifts are worth more than shit they steal, and one of the strongest is a gift of true metal. Platinum will do it. Gold. Silver to a lesser extent. It's like a binding agent. And the more they get from a person, the stronger those bonds are."

Jim frowned. "To what end, though? I mean, what does it get Devina other than an account with PODS?"

"When she kills him, she can keep him with her for eternity—those binds translate into a kind of ownership, in effect. Demons are like parasites. They latch on and it can take them years to overcome someone's soul—but that's what they do. They get into the person's head and affect their choices, and with each passing day, week, month, they slowly invade the life that is led, corrupting, fouling, destroying. The soul dims from the infection, and when it gets to the right point, the demon steps in and a mortal event occurs. Your boy Vin's right at that critical point now. She's setting the events in motion, with the first being his arrest. It's a domino thing, and it's going to get worse fast. I've seen it too often for words."

"Jesus . . . Christ."

"Or very much not Him, as is the case."

As questions spun in Jim's head, he said, "But why Vin? Why was he chosen by her in the first place?"

"There has to be a place of entry. Think of it like getting tetanus from a rusty nail. There's an injury to the soul and the demon enters through the 'wound.' "

"What makes a wound?"

"Lots of shit. Every case is different." Adrian moved the pawns around to form the shape of an "X." "But once the demon's in there, it has to be removed."

"You said Devina can't be killed."

"We can give her one fuck of an eviction notice, however." At this Eddie let out a low growl of approval. "And that's what we're going to teach you how to do."

Well, wasn't that a lesson he was goddamn aching to learn.

Jim ran a hand through his hair and got up from the bed. "You know what? Vin said something about . . . Vin said when he was seventeen he went to, like, a fortune-teller/ psychic kind of thing. He was getting these seizures where he was seeing the future and he was blind desperate for them to stop."

"What did she tell him to do?"

"He didn't go into it, but the seizures stopped until recently. He mentioned, though, that after he followed orders, so to speak, his luck changed altogether."

Adrian frowned. "We've got to find out what he did."

Eddie spoke up, "And we need to get the ring back. She's trying to lock him in even harder before she kills him and that is one hell of a strong bind."

"I know where she lives," Jim said. "Or I saw her go into a warehouse downtown."

Adrian got to his feet and so did Eddie. "Then let's do a little breaking and entering, shall we?" Ad said, scooping up the pawns and putting them back in the box. After he finished his beer, he cracked his knuckles. "Last fight I had with the bitch ended way too soon."

Eddie rolled his eyes and glanced at Jim. "It was back in the Middle Ages and he still hasn't gotten over it."

"Why so long ago?"

"We got put on ice," Eddie said. "We were a little more fallen than the bosses were comfortable with."

Adrian grinned like a motherfucker. "As I mentioned, I like the ladies."

"Usually in pairs." Eddie put Dog down and stroked his ears. "We'll be back, Dog."

Dog didn't seem happy with the parting and began circling all of the feet in the room, including the couch's—which seemed to suggest he thought the piece of furniture was on backup.

Not exactly what Jim had in mind.

Nope, he was going in with something a little more powerful.

Going over to the empty bookshelves in the far corner, he pulled out a black duffel bag and unzipped the thing, revealing a stainless-steel case that was about four feet by three feet. Running his forefinger over its keypad, he released the lock and opened the top. Inside, the three guns that were packed in egg padding caught no light whatsoever on their matte gray finishes and he left the assault rifle where it was. Of the pair of SIGs, the grips of which had been custom-designed for him, he took the one that fit his right palm.

Adrian shook his head, as if the auto-loader was nothing more than a squirt gun. "Just what do you think you're going to do with that piece of metal there, Dirty Harry?"

"It's my safety blanket, how 'bout that."

Jim put the gun through a quick check, locked up the briefcase, and stashed the duffel. The ammo was behind the cans in the cabinets over the sink, and he took enough to fill the clip.

"You can't shoot her with that," Eddie said softly.

"No offense—but until I see it, I'm not going to believe it."

"And that is why you will fail."

Adrian cursed and hit the door. "Great, you've got him channeling Yoda again. Can we get moving before he levitates my fucking bike?"

As Jim locked things up and they all went down the stairs, Dog took up res on the back of the couch, and watched them out the window. He pawed at the glass a little, like he was protesting the fact that he'd been left out of the action.

"Let's take my truck," Jim said as he hit the gravel. "Less noise."

"And it has a radio, right?" With tragic concentration, Adrian started warming up his voice, sounding like a moose being backstroked by a cheese grater.

Jim shook his head at Eddie as doors were opened. "How do you stand the racket?"

"Selective deafness."

"Teach me, master."

The trip into town lasted about four hundred years—largely due to the fact that Adrian found the classic rock station: Van Halen's "Panama" had never sounded so bad, but that was nothing compared to what happened to Meat Loaf's "I Would Do Anything for Love (But I Won't Do That)."

Which evidently referred to Adrian's shutting his piehole.

When they got to the warehouse district, Jim put the kibosh on Ad's crap-aoke, and he'd never been so glad to work a volume button. "The building is two streets over."

"There's a parking space," Eddie said, pointing to the left.

After they ditched the F-150, they walked down a block, hung a rightie, and what do you know—once again, timing was everything. Just as they rounded the corner, a taxi rolled to a stop in front of the door Devina had disappeared into before.

The three ducked for cover and a moment later the taxi rolled past with Devina in the backseat putting lipstick on with a compact mirror in her hand.

"She never does anything without a reason," Adrian said softly. "That's one thing you can take to the bank. Anything that comes out of her mouth is almost always a lie, but her actions . . . always a reason. We need to get in, find that ring and get out fast."

Moving quickly, they went over to the double doors, pulled them open, and entered a vestibule that had as much architectural nuance as a meat locker: Floor was concrete, walls were whitewashed, and the space was colder than the outside air. The only fixture it had, aside from an industrial-style ceiling light, was a row of five stainless-steel mailboxes and an intercom with a list of five names.

Devina Avale was number five.

Unfortunately, the inside set of doors was secured by a dead bolt, but Jim gave it a yank anyway. "We could always wait until someone—"

Adrian walked over, grabbed the handle, and pulled one half wide without missing a beat.

"Or you could just open the fucker," Jim said wryly.

Ad flashed his glowing palm and grinned. "I'm good with my hands."

"Better than with your vocal cords, clearly."

He hated working.

Hated spending his days taking ungrateful people around Caldwell in a taxi that smelled like whatever the last driver had had to eat. But the practicalities of life had to be met, and besides, at least the object of his affection tended to stay home during daylight hours.

There was also his ignore policy. He didn't look at his

customers, refused to help with luggage, and never talked more than was absolutely necessary. It was a good way to go—especially given what his nightly pursuits had been like lately: No reason to risk triggering someone's dim memory. You never knew what people were likely to recall from a crime scene.

Another lesson he'd learned the hard way.

"How's my lipstick."

At the sound of the female voice, his hands tightened on the wheel. He didn't give a shit about what some stupid woman's mouth looked like.

"I asked you . . . how is my lipstick." The tone was sharper now and made his palms squeeze down even harder on the wheel.

Before she repeated the demand and he got nasty, he glared into the rearview mirror. If whatever bitch was in the back expected him to—

Black eyes grabbed him and held him as sure as if she'd leaned forward and put him in a headlock. And then he sensed her reaching into him and . . .

"My lipstick," she said, with deliberate, flaring pronunciation.

He did a quick check on the street ahead, which was clear to the traffic light two blocks ahead, and went right back to the rearview. "Ah . . . it looks good."

With a deliberate stroke of her manicured forefinger, she wiped the line of her lower lip, then pursed her mouth and released.

"You're a religious man, I see," she murmured, closing her compact.

He glanced at the cross that was glued to the dashboard. "Not my cab."

"Oh." She brushed her hair back and kept staring at him.

It didn't take long before he felt like the heater had been turned on high, and he even double-checked to see if the blower was working overtime. No. She was just a beautiful woman who was looking at him like he was something. Which happened about as often as—

"What's your name," she whispered.

Tongue-tied, and abruptly unsure of the answer, he pointed to the cabbie license that had his picture on it. Reading what was written, he said, "Saul. Saul Weaver."

"Nice name."

As they came up to the red light at the intersection, he braked, and the instant the taxi was at a full stop, he was back looking into the rear . . . view . . . mirror. . . .

The irises of her eyes expanded until there was no white part to contrast with the dense black—and though that should have been the kind of thing to leave him screaming, he felt like liquid orgasm had taken the place of the blood in his veins.

Pleasure soared through him, lifting him up even as he remained on the seat of the taxi, invading him even as his skin remained intact, owning him though there was no tangible leash between them.

"Saul," the woman said, her voice morphing into something that was both deep as a man's and breathy as a woman's. "I know what you want."

Saul swallowed hard and heard his voice come from a long distance. "You do?"

"And I know how you can get it."

"You . . . do?"

"Pull over into that alley, Saul." With that, she opened her coat, flashing a skintight white blouse that showed her nipples clear as if nothing covered them. "Pull over, Saul, and let me tell you what you need to do."

With a wrench of the wheel, he shot into the shadows between two high buildings and threw the taxi in park. As he turned around to look at her, he was utterly captivated: However arresting her eyes were in the mirror, the rest of her more than lived up to the hype. She was . . . unreal, and not just because of how beautiful she was. Staring into those black pits, he was fully accepted, fully understood, and he knew without a doubt that he would find what he was seeking with her. She had his answers.

"Please . . . tell me."

"Come back here, Saul." The woman trolled her manicured fingers down her long neck to her cleavage. "And let me in."

CHAPTER
32

Not finishing was not going to be easy.

As Marie-Terese worked magic on his arousal, Vin felt like his skin was on fire and his blood was boiling and his bone marrow had turned into lightning. With every sucking draw and grabbing slide, she was sending him right to the edge, his body dangling off a precipice he was dying to fall from—and was completely unwilling to let go of. God . . . his self-control was killing him in the best way; his head jacked back against the pillow, his thighs rigid, his chest pumping. She was taking him to Heaven and putting him through Hell in equal measures, and he wanted it to go on forever.

But he really wasn't going to last much longer.

Lifting his head took all his strength, and when he looked down his body, he positively spasmed. Marie-Terese's mouth was stretched wide, her beautiful breasts hanging lush and full, her nipples brushing against his thighs—

"Oh, *fuck*." He lunged up and pulled her from his erection, his fingers biting into her upper arms as he struggled not to come.

"Are you—"

Vin cut her off by kissing her hard and rolling her over.

Before he could stop himself, he linked his arm under one of her knees and stretched her up. He was growling, he was wild, he was—

"I need you now, Vin!" Her nails sank into his ass as she went boneless beneath him.

"Shit . . . *yes*—"

Except both of them froze at the same time.

Together, they said, "*Condom.*"

Vin grunted and stretched out for the bedside table, the movement driving him even harder into her curves—and she didn't help things in the slightest by moving herself against him in a wave.

As the erotic sensation of flesh on flesh reverberated through his body, Vin lost contact with the Trojan he'd palmed, the little square flipping out of his grip like it had been taking flying lessons. "Goddamn it!"

Leaning down to the floor, his hips shifted and his cock went along for the ride, brushing right over her hot, sweet core. With a quick jerk, he moved back, because he didn't want to lose control, and . . .

Man, things didn't go well on the lower level as the square played keep-away from his sloppy hand.

"Let me help," Marie-Terese said, joining the hunt.

She was the one who finally caught the pale blue prize, pushing herself up and laughing as she held it over her head. "Got it!"

Vin started laughing along with her, and in a flash, he pulled her in close, hugging her. He was still fully erect and panting to come, but he was also light and free as he grinned and she giggled and they rolled around together, messing up the duvet. The condom got lost in the process, resurfacing and disappearing by turns like a fish in the water.

The thing ended up stuck to his side, like it had finally decided to be claimed. Or had decided to claim him.

Vin peeled it off, broke the foil open, and sheathed himself. Rolling her over onto her back again, he nudged his way between her thighs and swept her hair back from her eyes.

The collision was impending and electric, but the moment was soft and sweet: She positively glowed as she looked up at him.

"What," she whispered, palming his face.

Vin took a moment to memorize her features and the way she felt beneath him, seeing her not just through his eyes, but feeling her with his skin and his heart. "Hello, lovely lady . . . hello."

As she blushed beautifully, he kissed her deep, his tongue stroking against hers, their bodies settling in. One shift of his hips and his erection moved into position, and then he was driving forward slowly, easing into her. As her core took him inside and that spectacular constriction resonated, he dropped his head into her gorgeous hair and let go.

Long, deep, pounding . . . no more laughter now—only delicious desperation that choked him and revived him by turns. It was the same as it had been when she'd had her mouth on him: the kind of thing he never wanted to end, although that just wasn't possible.

Overcome, Vin roared as he contracted from his head to his calves, and from a distance he heard her say his name, felt her nails rake down his spine, absorbed the waves of her release.

When they'd caught their breath, he was still hard as he held on to the base of the condom and withdrew. "I'll be right back."

After he was finished in the bath, he returned and stretched out next to her. "You know what I have in there?" He pointed with his thumb toward the marble expanse he'd used to clean up.

"What?" She ran her hands over his arms and onto his shoulders.

"Six. Shower. Heads."

"Reeeeeally."

"Yup. Larry, Curly, Moe, Joe, and Frankie."

"Wait, only five have names?"

"Well, there's Freaky, but I'm not sure whether he's fit for mixed company."

Her laugher was another kind of orgasm for him, the sort of thing that warmed him from the inside out.

"Will you let me visit you?" he whispered. "After you leave."

Wrong thing to say. Drained the happy right out of her face. "I'm sorry," he said quickly. "I shouldn't have asked. Shit, I shouldn't—"

"I would like that."

Her answer was as quiet as his question had been, and the unspoken *but* hung between them like a draft of acrid smoke.

"Come with me," he said, prepared to drop it. If they didn't have a lot of time left together, he wasn't about to ruin what they had. "Let me wash my sweat off your skin."

She held on to his arms, her hands tightening to stop him.

Shaking his head, he brushed her mouth with his. "There are no promises and I understand that."

"I wish I could make them."

"I know." He slid his legs off the bed and scooped her up in his arms. "But I have you now, don't I."

He held her aloft as he walked into the bath . . . held her up off the marble floor as he turned on the shower . . . held her in his arms as he put his hand under the spray and waited until it got warm enough.

"You don't have to carry me," she said into his neck.

"I know. I just don't want to let you go while you're still here."

"Did you ever see *Fatal Attraction*?" Adrian said.

As the cargo elevator in Devina's warehouse closed its doors, Jim looked across what was essentially an entire room's worth of space. Hell, you could take a grand piano upstairs in the damn thing.

"Excuse me?" he asked.

"*Fatal Attraction*. The movie." Adrian ran his hands up and down the metal walls. "Great scene in an elevator just like this one. In my top ten."

"Let me guess, the other nine are on the Internet."

Eddie pushed the button marked FIVE and the thing lurched like a bronco. "Glenn Close was a psycho in that movie."

Adrian shrugged and the sly smile on his face seemed to suggest that he was putting himself in the picture, so to speak. "How much does that *really* matter, though?"

Eddie and Jim glanced at each other and the rolled eyes went unexpressed, because what was the point? You picked that habit up around Adrian and you'd spend your life staring at the ceiling.

On the fifth floor, the elevator bumped to a halt and the doors rattled as Eddie worked the release lever and threw them open.

The hall was clean, but dark as a shed, with brick walls held together by ancient, sloppy mortar and a wooden plank floor finished in old-age wear and tear. Down to the left, there was a metal door on the scale of the elevator with an EXIT sign over it. All the way to the right, there was another door—this one made of nickel-plated steel panels.

Jim unholstered his gun and took the safety off. "She likely to live with anyone?"

"Solo operator, generally speaking. Although she has been known to take pets from time to time."

"Rottweilers?"

"Spitting cobras. Copperheads. She likes snakes—but then maybe it's a recycle, reuse thing for her shoes and handbags. Who the fuck knows."

As they walked over to the nickel-plated door, Jim whistled softly. Stacked up one on top of another, the seven dead bolts gleamed like honor medals on the chest of a soldier. "Jesus, check out the locks on this thing."

"Even the paranoid have enemies, son," Adrian murmured.

"Yeah, you can lose the 'son' shit."

"How old are you? Forty? I'm four hundred if I'm a day."

"Okay, fine." Jim glared over his shoulder. "Can you work your magic on this, *Gramps*?"

Adrian flipped his middle finger, put his hand on the knob, and . . . got nowhere. "Fuck. She's blocked this."

"What do you mean?"

"The worst kind of spell." Adrian nodded grimly at Eddie. "You're up."

As the silent man stepped forward, Adrian grabbed onto Jim's arm and pulled back. "You're going to want to give him some space."

Eddie lifted his palm and closed his eyes and went statue still. His strong face with its prominent lips and square jaw assumed a calm determination, and after a moment, soft chanting emanated from him—except as far as Jim knew, the man's . . . angel's . . . whatever . . . lips were not moving.

Oh, wait . . . it wasn't singing.

Waves of energy pulsed out of the angel's palm, like heat rising on asphalt in the summer, and making a rythmic sound as they rippled through the air.

One by one there were a series of shifts as the dead bolts released, and then there was a final click and the door wafted open as if the space beyond had let out a breath.

"Nice," Jim murmured as Eddie's hooded lids lifted.

The guy took a deep breath and moved his shoulders around as if they were stiff. "Let's be quick about this. We don't know how long she's going to be out for."

Adrian went in first, a vicious kind of hatred burning in his expression, and Eddie was right on his tail.

"What . . . the . . . fuck . . ." Jim said as he entered.

"Always with the collecting," Adrian spat. "The bitch."

Jim's first thought was that the vast, open place was like some kind of fucked-up furniture liquidator's store. There were hundreds and hundreds and hundreds of clocks, all grouped by type, but otherwise unorganized: Grandfathers stood in a messy circle in the far corner, like they had been milling around and had frozen in place as soon as the door opened. Circular wall hangers were nailed to the thick wooden support beams that ran vertically from floor to ceiling. Mantel showpieces sat scattered on shelves and so did alarm clocks and metronomes.

But the pocket watches were the freakiest.

Suspended from the lofty I-beamed ceiling, like spiders on tendrils, pocket watches of all ages and makes dangled from black strings.

"Time keeps on ... slippin' ... slippin' ... slippin' into the future," Adrian drawled as he walked around.

Except actually, it didn't. Every one of the clocks and watches was stopped. Hell, more than stopped—the pendulums in those grandfathers were frozen in space, at the top of their arcs.

Jim shifted his eyes away from the time-keeping mélange and found another collection.

Devina had one and only one kind of furniture: bureaus. There must have been twenty to thirty of them, and they were crowded in a disorganized huddle, like the one in the middle had called a quick meeting and they had just rushed over. As with the clocks, there were all different kinds— antique ones that looked like they belonged in museums, new ones with sleek lines, cheapos that had to have been made in China and sold at Target.

"Shit, I'll bet she put it in one of these," Adrian said as he and Eddie went up to the jumbled assembly.

"What is that smell?" Jim asked, rubbing his nose.

"You don't want to know."

The fuck he didn't. Something was very wrong, and not just because she had some serious OCD issues when it came to decorating: The air was tainted with a scent that made Jim's flesh crawl. Sweet ... way too sweet.

Leaving Eddie and Adrian to their needle-in-a-haystack routine, Jim went exploring. Like all lofts, there were no divisions of the space except for the one in the corner that had to demarcate the bathroom.

Which meant the knives in the kitchen were on full display.

On the granite counter, there were all sorts of blades: hunting ones and Swiss armies and steaks and butchers

and prison-made roughies and cooks' delights and box cut-
ters. The business ends were long and short, smooth and
serrated, rusted and shiny. And like the bureaus and the
clocks, they were in a hodgepodge of disorder, the handles
and the tips facing all which ways.

For a man who had found himself in a lot of nasty-ass
situations, this was a new one.

Jim felt as if he'd walked into All-wrong Land.

Inhaling deep he tried to clear his head, but just ended
up clogging his nose. That smell . . . what was it? And where
was it coming from?

The bathroom, he realized.

"Don't go in there, Jim," Eddie called out as he started
in that direction. "Jim! No—"

Yeah, fuck that. The smell was the nostril equivalent of
new pennies in your mouth, and there was only one thing
that made that—

From out of nowhere, Eddie appeared in front of him,
blocking the way. "No, Jim. You can't go in there."

"Blood. That smell is blood."

"I know."

Jim spoke slowly, as if Eddie had lost his damn mind.
"So someone's bleeding in there."

"If you breach the seal on that door, you might as well
trigger a security alarm." Eddie pointed to the floor. "You
see that."

Jim frowned and looked down. Right in front of his
boots, there was a faint line of dirt, as if it had been lightly
sprinkled there by a careful hand.

"If you open this," Eddie said, "it's going to pass over
that barrier and our cover will be blown."

"Why?"

"Before she left, she treated the edge of the door with a
specific kind of blood and that dirt's from a graveyard. One
passes over the other and it releases energy she's going to
sense clear as an atomic bomb going off."

"What kind of blood is it?" Jim asked, even though he

knew he wasn't going to like the answer. "And why didn't she do it to where we entered through?"

"She needs a controlled environment to pull the protection spell off. The hall outside? She can't be sure the cleaning staff wouldn't disturb the dirt or that someone wouldn't mess it up. And all this stuff"—Eddie swept his hand around—"is not as important as what's inside here."

Jim stared at the closed door as if at any second he might pull a Superman and be able to see through the thing.

"Jim. Jim . . . you can't go in there. We need to find the ring and take off."

There was more to this, Jim thought. As much as Adrain had revealed back at his studio, the angels had a pattern of telling him what he needed to know for the moment and not one byte of information more than that. So there was definitely shit going on here that he was unaware of . . .

"Jim."

Jim focused on the doorknob that was within grabbing distance. He was kind of through with being out of the loop, and if it took a showdown with Devina to bring him up to speed, it was hard to think that was a bad thing.

"Jim."

CHAPTER
33

W arm water over her breasts and thighs ... warm lips on
her mouth ... warm steam billowing out around her.

Marie-Terese ran her soapy hands up the massive shoulders of her lover, marveling at the difference between their
bodies. He was so hard, his muscles flexing and releasing
as the two of them moved against each other, shifting, rubbing, seeking, and finding. His hot erection stroked against
her upper stomach, and between her legs she was just as
ready for more as he was.

Vin's lips broke off from her own and nuzzled into her
neck, then down to her collarbone ... and he went even
lower, bending to suck on her nipples before licking at the
tight tips. As she sank her fingers into his slick wet hair,
he knelt on the marble before her, gripping her hips and
staring up at her with hot eyes. With their stares locked, his
mouth went to her belly button, brushing soft as the water
did before being replaced by his pink tongue.

Falling back against the marble wall between two of
the showerheads, Marie-Terese widened her stance as he
kissed his way over to her hip. White teeth made a brief appearance on the bone, and then he was raking them gently

across the skin of her lower belly before retracing the path with sucking lips.

Lower.

To make even more way for him, she put her foot up on the marble bench that was built into the corner, and his mouth went immediately to her inner thigh. He was urgent and he was gentle at the same time as he got closer and closer to the core that throbbed between her legs. She was dying for him to go exactly where he was headed, and as he paused at the very top of her inner thigh, she could barely breathe.

"Please . . ." she said roughly.

Vin nuzzled over and licked into her with one sure stroke. As her voice keened above the sound of the falling water, his fingers sank into her thighs and he groaned against her sex. Drugging laps mixed with tugging sucks until she found herself falling down onto the bench and bracing one foot against the soap shelf on the wall and throwing the other down the far side of his back.

And then he got serious. Lifting his head from her and meeting her eyes, he brought up two of his fingers and drew them inside his mouth. As they came out all glossy from being between his lips, he leaned back down to her sex, leading with his pink tongue.

The thick penetration was compounded by a flicking tickle at the top of her sex.

Marie-Terese came hard and loud and long, and when she was finally spent, she collapsed against the hard stone, boneless as the water itself. After he slid out of her, he licked his fingers, tongue tracing in and around while he looked at her from under his brows.

He was hard. Maybe even brutally so, given the straining length at his hips.

"Vin . . ."

"Yeah." His voice was nothing but gravel.

"It's really far to the bedroom, where the condoms are."

"It is."

She looked down at his erection. "I wouldn't want you to wait that long."

His smile was fierce. "What did you have in mind?"

"I want to watch."

His laugh was deep and low, and he settled back against the glass wall, his thighs opening, his massive arousal running up his ribbed stomach. God, he looked spectacular against the creamy marble.

"What exactly do you want to watch?"

She blushed. God help her, she actually blushed. But then, he was sprawled out on the floor of the shower, glistening from head to toe, ready for sex . . . and looking for direction.

"What do you want me to show you," he drawled.

"I want you . . . to put your hand—"

"Here?" he said, laying one over his pec.

"Lower," she whispered.

"Hmm . . ." His broad palm drifted down across his ribs to the top of his six-pack. "Here?"

"Lower . . ."

He bypassed the head of his erection and went over to his hip. "Lower still?"

"To your left. And higher."

"Oh, you mean"—as his palm found his arousal, he arched and his eyes squeezed shut—"*here?*"

"God, yes . . ."

Rolling his hips, he kept his hand still and she got exactly what she wanted: a stunning view of his blunt head piercing through his grip and disappearing, piercing through, disappearing. His heavy chest rose and fell, his lips parting as he pleasured himself.

"Vin . . . you're so beautiful."

His lids lifted slowly and he stared up at her, his gleaming eyes pulling her into him. "I love that you're watching me. . . ."

With that his other hand went between his thighs and captured his potent sac. As he squeezed himself, he worked his arousal in long strokes and moaned.

"I don't know how long I'm going to last. . . ."

Good ... Lord. The entire building could have been on fire and she would not have been able to move as he squeezed his sac again and then focused on the head of his erection. After he pinched himself with his thumb, he went two-handed, his breath coming in punches.

He stayed locked on her eyes as he worked himself.

He was so sensual, so ... unfurled in front of her, hiding nothing, both vulnerable and powerful.

"Are you going ... to make ... me hold it ... ?" he groaned between gulping inhales.

Her greedy stare roamed over him, and she committed the erotic sight of him to permanent memory as surely as if she had carved the images out of stone.

"I have ... to ..."

"Come for me," she said. She wanted it to last forever, but she knew it was going to start to hurt in earnest soon.

Now his chest really got to pumping and so did his hands—faster and hard enough so that the muscles in his arms strained.

When he orgasmed, he came all over his stomach and his thigh because he couldn't seem to stop. And his eyes never left hers even as his palms finally came to rest and then released and flopped to the side.

As his breathing eased, she smiled and went to him, capturing his face, kissing him softly. "Thank you."

"Anytime you have a hankering for that kind of show, just let me know?"

"You can bet on it."

When they finally rinsed off and stepped out of the shower, they had identical ahhh-lovely smiles on their faces, and Vin got her a monogrammed towel from one of the warming racks. The white terry-cloth expanse was so big it covered her from breast to ankle, and by the time she'd turbaned her hair with a second one, she felt as if she'd been slip-covered in velvety softness.

Vin picked up a third, dried his hair until it sat straight in spikes, and covered his hips. "I like you in my towels."

"I like being in them."

He came over and kissed her, and in the pause that followed, her breath stopped in her throat.

She knew what he wanted to say. And agreed it was far, far, far too early for it.

"You want something to eat?" he asked.

"I . . . probably should head off." She had a lot of packing to do.

"Okay . . . all right."

Sadness thickened the steamy air as they slipped their arms around each other and left the bathroom—

"Am I intruding?"

Marie-Terese froze and so did Vin.

The woman he'd shown up with at the Iron Mask was standing just inside the bedroom, her hands hanging loosely at her sides, her long glossy hair down over her shoulders, her black coat belted tight around her tiny waist.

In her resonant stillness, she looked exactly as any model-chic female would on the surface, but there was something way off about her.

Way. Off.

First of all, if she'd been badly beaten the night before, her face wasn't showing any signs of it; her features and skin were as smooth and pristine as fresh-cut marble. Second, she looked perfectly capable of killing someone as she stared at the two of them.

Oh . . . God. Her eyes. There wasn't a white rim around her black iris, her glaring gaze nothing but a pair of pits that were as dark and bottomless as sinkholes.

Could that be right, though?

As the skin across the back of Marie-Terese's neck tightened, the woman focused on her and smiled like an axe murderer who was looking at his next victim. "I saw your purse down on the dining room table, darling. Given how much money was next to it, I'd say your prices have gone through the roof. Congratulations."

Vin's hard voice sliced through the air. "How did you get in. I locked everything—"

"Don't you get it, Vincent. Your door is always open to me."

Vin put his body in front, shielding Marie-Terese. "Leave. Now."

The laughter that sounded out was all nails-on-a-blackboard, high and cringe-worthy. "Ever since we first met, things have been on my terms, Vin, and that isn't going to change now. I've invested a lot in you, and I do believe it's time to call you home."

"Fuck you, Devina."

"You certainly did," the woman drawled. "And very well, I might add. But you weren't the only one. Your friend Jim also did right by me, and I think I liked him better than you. With him, I didn't need someone else."

"Yeah, I had to have more than you gave me as well," Vin snapped.

A wave of coldness rippled out from the woman, and her eyes, those awful black holes, shifted to Marie-Terese and locked on. "You've met Jim, haven't you. You ever been alone with him? Maybe . . . in a car? Maybe when you were taking him back home yesterday?"

How the hell did she know that? Marie-Terese wondered.

As Vin's body stiffened, the woman continued. "When you took him back to that shitty studio of his over the garage, you liked the taste of his cock, didn't you—but you would have blown him even if you hadn't. You need all the money you can get, and he was willing to pay for it."

Marie-Terese glared across the room. "That never happened. Never. I didn't go to his place."

"So you say."

"No, so *you* say. I know what I did and didn't do and with whom. You, on the other hand, are a desperate bitch who's trying to hold on to someone who doesn't want her."

The woman recoiled a little, and Marie-Terese had to admit there was some satisfaction to be had with that.

But then Vin stepped away, and one look in his pale face

made her realize that Trez had been tragically right. A past like hers had a long reach, and Vin and she hadn't known each other long enough for even rudimentary trust to have developed—much less the kind of faith required for a man to believe that a prostitute wouldn't be doing her "job" with his friend.

Thank God for all the towels she had on, she thought.

Because she suddenly felt as though she were out in the frigid wind.

"*Jim.*"

Standing in front of Devina's bathroom door, Jim measured the expression on Eddie's face: dead serious. More to the point, that big-ass body was going to be in the way if Jim made any move for the doorknob.

Releasing his tight muscles, Jim eased up his body and looked over his shoulder at the bureaus. Adrian was pulling open drawers in a methodical manner and rifling through whatever was in them—and there evidently was a lot given all the rattling.

"Fine," Jim murmured. "Guess we should join in the Easter-egg hunt?"

"I know it's hard," Eddie said. "But you have to trust me."

Eddie clapped him on the back and together they turned to head over to his buddy. Jim followed one footstep—

And wheeled around for the doorknob. As the fallen angel barked out a curse, Jim yanked open the slab of wood and jerked to a halt.

A young woman was hanging naked and upside down over the porcelain tub, her legs open in a V, her ankles bound with black rope to the circular rod that should have held a shower curtain. Her hands were tied together with the same black rope and pulled tautly up her body so that her fingers just barely touched the top of her sex. All around her belly there were deep cuts, arranged in a pattern of some kind, and red blood covered her white skin, running down her torso before splitting around the jut of her chin and jaw and flowing through her blond hair.

The tub was plugged and full.

Oh, Lord ... about two inches above the pool she hung. Her eyes were open and fixed straight ahead, but her mouth was working ever so slightly....

"She's alive!" Jim called out as he leaped forward.

Eddie caught him and yanked him back. "No, she's not. And we've got to get out of here now, thanks to you."

Jim thrashed free of the hold and rushed forward, raising his hands, ready to start on the complex series of knots—

A hard, heavy palm locked onto his shoulder. "She's fucking dead, man, and we've got a problem now." When Jim shook his head roughly and fought against the hold, Eddie's voice rose. "She's *dead*—those are autonomic spasms, not signs of life. See the cuts on either side of her throat?"

Jim's eyes careened around her body, desperately looking for a shallow draw of breath or recognition in her face that she was going to be saved ... something ... anything....

"No!" He pointed to her fingers as they twitched ever so slightly. "She's alive!"

As he strained until he roared, the scene changed before his eyes, flipping from current horror to remembered tragedy. He saw his mother surrounded by blood, her eyes blinking slowly, her mouth working to form the words necessary to get him to leave her.

Eddie's calm voice came right into his ear, as if the guy weren't so much speaking, but implanting the words: "Jim, we've got to get the fuck out of here."

"We can't leave her." Was that his voice? That reedy croak?

"She's gone. She's not here anymore."

"We can't leave her.... She's ..."

"She's not with us, Jim. And we have to go. To save Vin, we have to get you the fuck out of here."

Adrian's voice exploded from the doorway, "What the *fuck* is wrong with you—"

"Shut the hell up, Ad." Eddie's words cut through the interruption. "He doesn't need you busting his balls right now. Jim ... I want you to back out of the room."

Jim knew the guy was right. The girl was dead, bled out like nothing but an animal, and that wasn't the worst of it. Her frozen death mask was one of horror, as if her suffering had been great.

"Come on, Jim."

So help him God, he knew he had to listen to the angel and force himself to accept that there was no battle to be fought here: The time for conflict and the possibility of victory had come and gone without his even being aware it existed. And he believed Eddie about the taking off part. At this moment, risking an altercation with Devina would not have been good.

Right now one-third of the team was a total head case.

Jim went to turn around, but got slapped from behind, Eddie's huge hand catching his face and holding it where it had been.

"Keep your eyes straight ahead and back out with me. Do not move your head. Do you understand? I want you to step back with me and keep your head where it is. We're going to back away—"

"I don't want to leave her," he moaned. "Oh, shit . . ."

Such suffering, the terror etched into the soft, pale planes of her lovely face. Where were her parents? Who was she? As he stared at the young woman's corpse, he memorized everything about her, from the mole she had on her thigh, to the light blue of her lifeless eyes, to the pattern that had been cut into her stomach.

"She's gone," Eddie said softly. "Her body's just a leftover—her soul's not here anymore. You can't do anything for her, and we are in a dangerous situation right now. We need to get you out of here."

The more he looked at her though, the more his insides started screaming again and he couldn't—

All at once, he heard a rush of noise that sounded like the feet of rodents in a sewer. It wasn't hundreds of rats, however. The clocks had started up, every single one of them energized at precisely the same moment, the chaotic ticking of countless second hands rising up in the loft, filling the air.

Abruptly, Adrian's voice was grim instead of angry. "We have to leave—"

His words were cut off by a rumbling and then a vibration that emanated from the floor, one so great it rattled the smoky window over the toilet and created waves on top of the blood in the tub.

"Like exactly now."

"I don't want to leave her—"

Eddie's voice turned into a growl. "She's gone. And we need to—"

"Fuck you!" Jim lunged forward.

Eddie's massive arms were iron bars. Even as Jim fought the hold, and went animal on the guy, clawing and ripping to get free, he got nowhere.

Voices rang out—his and Adrian's. But Eddie was silent as he started to pull Jim from the room.

Then Eddie cut through the vocal chaos and the flapping of clothes: "Knock him the fuck out! I can't keep him from seeing the mirror!"

Adrian stepped in, rolled up a fist, and cocked his arm back. The strike was hard and fast, the crack cutting through everything . . . and stunning Jim into compliance.

He was dragged out in a daze, the heels of his Timberlands streaking across the hard floor, his head ringing like a bell. Once his boots were past the bathroom door, Adrian slammed the thing shut, and Eddie flipped Jim up off the floor and into a firemen's hold.

Dizzy and disoriented, Jim tried to place a new fleet of strange sounds that came from a vast distance. Glancing over at the counter in the kitchen, he saw that the knives were moving around, arranging themselves, making order out of the mess they'd been in. And it was the same with the dressers—which explained the reverberations: The chests of drawers were trembling on their feet, finding positions like soldiers called for a lineup.

He barely remembered leaving the loft and he didn't register much of the trip down the stairs . . . but the cold air outside did revive him enough so that he was able to push himself free of Eddie's hold and make it to the truck on his own two feet.

As Adrian drove them away from the warehouse, all Jim could see was the girl's face.

There was no singing as they went off this time.

No talking, either.

CHAPTER
34

Devina's taunt ricocheted around Vin's inner pinball machine, triggering all kinds of evil bells and anti-bonus points: Jim and Marie-Terese had been alone . . . in her car . . . going back to his studio . . .

"You know everyone you've been with?" Devina said to Marie-Terese. "You must have an incredible memory. But right now only one of those men matters—isn't that true, Vin?"

This was a crossroads, he thought, a place of choosing one or the other way to go.

And he had the crystal clear sense that if he let what Devina was saying sink in, he was lost forever—yet there was a side of him that found what she was saying inescapable: Marie-Terese had been alone with Jim, and she had been with men for money, and if those the pair of them had been together sexually, that was something he wouldn't be able to get over.

Devina's voice dropped low. "You were always afraid of turning into your father. And here you are, getting played by a whore."

Vin took a halting step toward her and away from Marie-Terese. *Played by a whore* . . .

Images of his father and mother were amplified by

Devina's words and the reality of what Marie-Terese had done for a living.

Played by a whore ...

He focused on Devina, really *seeing* her ...

"You're so right," he whispered, the truth revealed to him.

Abruptly, Devina's face and eyes changed, sympathy warming her features and draining out the anger. "I don't want this for you. Any of it. Just come back to me, Vin. Come back."

He walked forward, getting closer and closer, and she lifted her arms out to him. When he was in front of her, he reached up and brushed one of those dark waves back from her ear. Leaning in, he put his mouth close and tightened his hold on her hair.

"Vin ... yes, Vin." His name was spoken with relief and triumph. "This is the way it needs to be—"

"Fuck. You." When she started to yank back, he held her in place by the skull. "You're the whore."

Trez had called it. Back at the Iron Mask, the guy had said that a moment would come when he'd have to believe what he knew of Marie-Terese instead of what he had always feared would be true about a woman he cared about.

"You're not welcome here," he said, releasing Devina with a shove and going back to Marie-Terese. As he grabbed onto his woman's arms and held her behind him, he wished he were in the master bedroom, because his gun was there. "Get. Out."

All at once, the air around Devina warped, as if her fury were causing a molecular disturbance, and he braced himself for impact. Instead of lashing out, though, she seemed to gather herself.

With an eerie control, she walked over to the windows, and his first thought was sending Marie-Terese from the room. Unfortunately, the distance between the view and the open door was short enough so that Devina could close it easily—and the bitch was staring into the glass, effectively giving herself eyes in the back of her head.

"You can't rescind the pact, Vin. It doesn't work that way."

"The hell it doesn't."

Devina turned around and wandered over to the bed. Bending down, she picked up his boxers and looked over the rumpled duvet and the tossed-around pillows.

"Messy, messy. Do you want to tell me exactly what you did to her, Vin? Or should I use my imagination? She's had so much practice, I'm sure she satisfied you."

Devina deliberately rearranged a pillow, returning it to a spot against the headboard. With her attention briefly distracted, Vin moved fast, pushing Marie-Terese backward into the bathroom and slamming the door shut. When the lock was immediately turned, he took a deep breath even though it was clear that Devina had no problems getting through Schlage's best dead bolts.

Devina's black orbs flicked up. "You do realize if I wanted to get in there I could."

"You'd have to go through me first. And somehow I don't think you can do that, can you. If you were going to kill me or her right now, you'd have done so the second you walked in here."

"You just tell yourself that if it makes you feel better." Leaning down, she took something off of the twisted duvet. "Well, what do you know. I believe I have—"

Devina froze in midspeech and swiveled her head around so that she looked out the windows. Abruptly, her brows screwed down over the black holes of her eyes, and the features of her face morphed briefly, showing a flash of what he'd seen of her real side: For a split second, all that gorgeous beauty was replaced with rotted, gray sheets of flesh, and he could have sworn he caught a whiff of dead meat.

Shit, maybe it should have freaked him out more, but he knew from experience that the unexplained and unexplainable were no less real for their being crazy. More important, Marie-Terese was on the other side of a thin door, and he was going to fight to the death to protect his woman—no matter what the fuck it was coming at her.

Human . . . demon . . . combo of the two. Definitions didn't matter.

Devina looked back at him. Slipping something into the pocket of her coat, she said in an oddly echoing voice, "I'll be seeing you both very soon. I have business elsewhere."

"You're going to get a facial?" he said. "Good call."

With a hiss, like she wanted to claw his eyes out, she dissolved into a gray mist and ghosted out of the room, boiling across the carpet and down the stairs.

Vin jolted forward, slammed the bedroom door, and locked it, even though he had a feeling that in that form she could just gust right under the thing. Whatever, it was the best he could do.

He went right to the bathroom and knocked. "She's gone, but I don't know for how—"

Marie-Terese threw open the door. She was white faced and scared to death, but her first words were: "Are you okay?"

It was at that moment that he knew he loved her. Plain and simple.

There was no time to go into that shit now, though.

Vin kissed her quickly. "I want you out of this place. In case she comes back here."

And as soon as Marie-Terese was safe, he was going to call Jim. He needed one hell of a wingman, and he couldn't think of anyone better than a son of a bitch who'd already beaten death once and didn't seem freaked out by shit that would make most guys take a crap in their Calvins.

Abruptly, she wobbled. "I—I think I'm going to pass out—"

"Put your head down—come on, kneel for me. . . ." He laid his hand on her bare shoulder and gently eased her onto the floor. Then he bent her over so that her long hair touched the marble and her hands fell to her ankles. "Breathe nice and slow."

As she took a couple of inhales and her body shuddered, he wanted to peel his own skin from his bones. Goddamn him, he was worse than her ex-husband. Much more destructive.

Even though his heart was in the right place for the first time in his adult life, what he had exposed her to was more horrifying than anything the mob could pull out of their back pockets.

And it wasn't like that bunch of sleep-with-the-fishes types were nancies.

Marie-Terese glanced over at him. "Her eyes ... What the hell did I just see?"

"Vin! Yo, Vin?"

At the sound of the muffled holler, he leaned around the doorjamb and called out, "Jim?"

"Yeah," came the response. "I'm here with reinforcements, as they say."

"In that case, come up." This was perfect. There was a back exit on the second floor they could get Marie-Terese out of—and wouldn't it be great to do that with some cover.

"I'm going to run across and get some clothes on," he told her. "How about you get dressed, too?"

When she nodded, he kissed her, went and gathered up her clothes for her and then closed the bedroom door on his way out.

As heavy boots hit the stairs, Vin went to his room, pulled on a pair of sweatpants, and got his gun out of the bedside table—all the while hoping like hell that the "backup" was along the lines of Jim.

And what do you know, they were. The two big bastards were the ones who'd been at the hospital after Jim had been electrocuted—and in spite of the fact that the pair were dressed as civilians, they had the stares of fighters.

Jim, on the other hand, had the glassy, hollow eyes of someone who'd been in a bad car accident. Clearly, he'd had some bad news recently, and yet his voice was still strong and level as he nodded to the one on the left first.

"This is Adrian. And Eddie. They're our kind of friends, if you know what I mean."

Thank fuck, Vin thought.

"Your timing couldn't be better," he said, shaking the guys' hands. "You wouldn't believe who just left."

"Oh, I bet we would," Jim muttered.

"So I got some questions for you," the one with the piercings said. "We know your girlfriend. Very well, unfortunately."

"She's not my girlfriend."

"Well, she's not out of your life yet, unfortunately. But we're going to try to take care of that. Our boy Jim here says that when you were seventeen, you performed some kind of ritual. Can you describe it?"

"It was supposed to get rid of what's inside of me."

Naturally, Marie-Terese opened the guest room door at that moment. Dressed in her jeans and fleece, she had pulled back her hair and tucked her hands into the front pockets of her pullover.

"What's inside of you?" she asked.

Vin rubbed his face and glanced back at the men. Before he could figure out how to shade the truth appropriately, Marie-Terese cut off his mental gymnastics. "I want to know everything, Vin. The whole deal. And I deserve to know now that I've seen her up close—because frankly, I'm not sure what I saw just now."

Shit. As much as he wanted to keep her out of things, he was hard-pressed to deny her reasoning. But man, he wished like hell he didn't have to have this conversation.

"Gentlemen, will you give us a minute alone?" he said without looking away from her eyes.

"You got any beer around here?" Adrian asked.

"Fridge by the wet bar in the living room. Jim knows the way."

"Good call. Because he's the one who needs it. You two

come down when you're ready—and don't worry, we'll make sure Devina doesn't get back in here. I'm assuming you have salt in your kitchen?"

"Ah, yeah." He glanced over with a frown. "But why do you need—"

"Where do you keep it?"

After he shrugged and told the guy to go to the dry-goods cupboard, the men hit the stairs again, and Vin ushered Marie-Terese over to the bed. He couldn't stay put, though, and took up pacing around.

Going over to the view, he wondered why life had brought him to this point. Wondered why he'd started where he had. Wondered . . . how it was all going to end for him.

Looking down at the highway by the river and seeing the cars traveling in their prescribed lanes, he envied the people behind those steering wheels and in those passenger seats. It was a good bet the vast majority of them were doing normal shit, like going home or heading out for a movie or struggling with weighty decisions like what to have for dinner later.

"Vin? Talk to me. I promise I won't judge you."

He cleared his throat, and hoped like hell that was true. "Any chance you believe in . . ."

Well, now, just how was he finishing that one? By listing a bunch of crap like Ouija boards and tarot cards and black magic and voodoo and. . . demons . . . mostly the demons?

Great. Fabulous.

She broke the silence he couldn't bear to fill. "You mean about the episodes you get?"

He rubbed his face. "Listen, what I'm about to say isn't going to sound real—shit, it's not even going to sound plausible. But can you please not leave until I finish? No matter how weird it gets?"

He kept looking out at the view because he didn't want her to see the weakness he knew was in his face, and at least his voice sounded halfway normal.

The headboard of the bed creaked, indicating that she'd

sat back even farther on the mattress. "I'm not going any-where. Promise."

Another reason to love her. As if he needed one.

Vin took a deep breath and threw himself off the pro-verbial cliff: "When you're young, you think whatever is going on with you, around you . . . inside of you, is normal. Because you don't know any different. It wasn't until I was five and went to kindergarten that I learned the hard way other kids couldn't move forks without touching them or stop the rain in their backyards or know what was going to be for dinner without talking to their mothers. See, my parents couldn't do any of the things I could, but I felt to-tally different from them anyway, so I didn't think it was weird. I just thought they weren't the same because they were parents, not a kid."

He refused to go into the various ways he'd learned he wasn't like other kids—and what those little shits did to punish him because he was out of the ordinary: The details of getting pounded on a regular basis by groups of boys or sneered at and laughed at by girls were not going to change whether or not she understood or believed him. Besides, pity had always given him a case of the scratch.

"I figured out pretty damn quick to shut my mouth about what I could do, and it wasn't hard to hide. Basically, I just had parlor tricks at that point, nothing that got in the way of life, but that changed when I was eleven and I started to pull that on-my-ass babbling crap. That was a big problem. It happened whenever and wherever it wanted to. I had no control over it, and instead of growing out of it, like I did all that manipulation and small-scale clairvoyance stuff, it got worse and worse."

"You were gifted," she said, with no small amount of awe.

He looked over his shoulder. Most of the color had come back into her face, which was more than he would have hoped for, but he did not agree with her assessment.

"Cursed was the way I saw it." He went back to star-ing out at the lines of tiny cars far, far below. "As I grew up, I got bigger and tougher, so getting harassed was less of an issue, but the episodes didn't stop, and I was getting more and more frustrated by feeling like a freak. Finally, I decided I had to talk to someone, so I went to this psychic downtown. I felt like a total fucking fool, but I was desperate. She helped me, told me what to do, and even though I didn't believe in it, I went home and did what she said . . . and everything changed."

"You stopped getting the seizures?"

"Yeah."

"So why are they back now?"

"I don't know." And he didn't know why they'd started, either.

"Vin?" When he glanced back at her, she patted the bed. "Come and sit down. Please."

After he searched her face and saw nothing but warmth and empathy, he went over and lowered his ass on the mattress beside her. As he braced his fists on the duvet and leaned into his shoulders, her hand landed lightly on his back and she rubbed him in a slow circle.

He drew incredible reserves of strength from her touch.

"After the seizures stopped, everything was different. And in a totally unrelated weirdness, my parents died accidentally soon thereafter—which really was not a total surprise, because as violent as they were with each other, it was only a matter of time. As soon as they were gone, I dropped out of school and went to work for my dad's boss as a plumbing assistant. I'd turned eighteen by then, so I was legal to work in the trade and I made it my business to learn everything. Which was how I ended up on the contracting side of things. I never took a vacation. I never looked back, and ever since then, life has been . . ."

Funny, up until a couple of days ago he'd have said *great*. "Life has been really good-looking from the outside, since then."

But he was starting to think that all he'd done was slap a shiny, pretty coat of paint on a rotting barn. He'd never been happy, had taken no joy out of the money he'd made ... had deceived honest people and raped countless acres of land, and for what? All he'd done was feed the tapeworm in his gut that had driven him. None of it had nurtured him.

Marie-Terese took his hand. "So ... who is that woman? What is she?"

"She's ... I don't know how to answer either of those questions. Maybe those two guys who came with Jim can." He glanced at the doorway and then looked at Marie-Terese. "I don't want you to think I'm a freak. But I won't blame you if you do."

As he dropped his head, for the first time in a long, long while, he desperately wished he was someone else.

Words were better than nothing when it came to explaining things, but that didn't mean they went nearly far enough in some situations.

This was one of them, Marie-Terese thought.

In her life, things like what Vin was talking about happened in the movies or in books ... or they were whispered about when you were thirteen and on a sleepover with your friends ... or they were lies that were advertised in the back of cheap magazines. They were not part of the real world, and her mind was fighting the adjustment.

The trouble was, she'd seen what she had seen: a woman with black holes for eyes and an aura that seemed to taint the very air that surrounded her; Vin collapsing and speaking words he didn't seem to hear; and now ... a proud man, hanging his head in shame for something that was neither his fault nor his wish.

Marie-Terese kept stroking his shoulders, wishing there was more she could do to ease him. "I don't ..." She let the sentence drift.

His reserved gray eyes flicked over to her. "Have any idea what to make of me, right?"

Well, yes ... but she wasn't about to put that thought into words for fear it would come out wrong.

"It's okay," he said, reaching out and giving her hand a squeeze before rising from the bed. "Believe me, I don't blame you in the slightest."

"What can I do to help?" she asked as he walked around.

He looked at her from over by the window. "Get out of town. And maybe we shouldn't see each other. It may well be safer for you and that is the single most important thing to me right now. I'm not going to let her get you. No matter what I have to do. She is not going to get at you."

Staring up into his face, she felt a stirring down deep as she realized he was her real-life fairy tale: Standing before her, he was willing to do battle for her, on whatever killing field the war took place. . . . He was prepared to accept wounds and make sacrifices for her. . . . He was the dragon slayer she had looked for when she was younger and had lost faith in ever finding as she'd aged.

And just as important, when it would have been easier for him to believe the lies that woman had said, when he could have listened to Devina spinning that total fallacy about her having been with Jim, he had chosen to think more of her, instead of less. He had had faith in her, and had trusted in her, in spite of her past and his.

Tears stung her eyes.

"Look, I should go downstairs and talk to them," he said roughly. "You might want to leave."

But she shook her head and rose to her feet, thinking that two could play at the knight-in-shining-armor game. "I'll stay, if you don't mind. And I don't think you're a freak. I think you're . . ." She tried to choose the right words. "You're just fine exactly the way you are. More than just fine—you're a wonderful man and a great lover and I just . . . like you." She shook her head. "I wouldn't change anything about you and I'm not scared of you, either. The only thing I might wish were different . . . is that I met you years and years ago. But that's it."

There was a long stretch of silence. "Thank you," he said hoarsely.

She went to him, and as she wrapped her arms around him, she murmured, "You don't have to thank me. It's how I feel."

"No, it's a gift," he said into her hair. "You always should thank the person who gives you something irreplaceable, and to me ... acceptance is the most priceless thing you could ever offer me."

As she choked up against his chest, he spoke three little words: "I love you."

Marie-Terese's eyes popped, but he pulled back and held up his hand to keep her from stammering. "That's the way I feel. That's where I am. And I don't expect any kind of response. I just wanted you to know." He nodded to the door. "Let's go down and face the music."

When she hesitated, he tugged her gently. "Come on."

After he kissed her, she allowed herself to be led from the room. And considering the way her head was reeling, she was impressed that her sense of balance was good enough that she made it down the stairs and into the living room without falling over.

Even as they joined the others, she felt she should say something back to him, anything, but he honestly didn't seem to be waiting for reciprocation or even an acknowledgment.

Which made her feel honored in some strange way—probably because it meant that his gift to her was unconditional.

The men had obviously found the beer, as they all had bottles in their hands, and Jim introduced the two who'd come with him to her. For some reason, she trusted them all—which was very unusual given the way she usually felt around big, muscle-bound members of the opposite sex.

Before any of them could speak, she said loud and clear, "What the hell is she? And how worried do I need to be?"

The men all stared at her as if she'd grown two heads.

Eddie, if she heard the name correctly, was the first to recover. He leaned forward and put his elbows on his jeans-clad knees. After a moment of concentration, he just shrugged, like he'd tried to find a way to sugarcoat things and decided to give up on the lie.

"A demon. And very concerned barely covers it."

CHAPTER
35

Vin was totally impressed by his woman. Having just been through a hideous and frightening welcome-to-the-unreal-world, and then having gotten hit with an I-love-you bomb, she was holding her ground, staring at Eddie with steady, intelligent eyes as she absorbed his answer.

"A demon," she repeated.

As Eddie and Adrian nodded in unison, Jim just took a seat on the couch, put his cold beer bottle on his swollen face and leaned back into torn-up cushions. The rippling sigh that came out of his mouth seemed to suggest that new bruise he was sporting looked bad, hurt worse.

God only knew how he'd—oh wait, Adrian's knuckles were split.

"What does that mean?" she said.

Eddie's voice was level and reasonable. "Your common conception of one is largely accurate in her case. She's an evil entity who overtakes the lives and then the souls of people. She's hardwired for destruction and she's after Vin. Anything or anyone who gets in the way is in immediate danger."

"But why Vin?" She looked across the way. "Why you?"

Vin opened his mouth and nothing came out. "I . . . I really don't have a clue."

Eddie paced around, going from the bookshelves to the ruined mirror. "You said you went to a psychic who gave you a ritual to perform. What did you do to call her to you?"

"But that's the thing," Vin said. "I didn't call her at all. I was trying to get rid of the visions. That was it."

"You did something."

"It wasn't to volunteer for this shit, I assure you."

Eddie nodded and glanced over his shoulder. "I believe you. The trouble is, I'm pretty damn sure that you were set up. I don't know what you were told exactly, but I'm willing to bet it was not about dumping those trances. The thing is, for Devina to go to work, you have to give her a way to get in." Eddie refocused on Marie-Terese. "So in this case, I'm thinking what he was told to do opened him up wide and Devina took advantage of it."

"So she's not tied to his visions?"

"Nope. She can eclipse them as long as her hold on him is strong—but he's probably getting them again because the tie is weakening a little. As for, why him? Think of it like . . . the metaphysical equivalent of a car accident. Vin was in the wrong place at the wrong time, thanks to some very bad advice." Eddie met Vin's eyes again. "That psychic—how did you find you her? Did she have some kind of vendetta against you?"

So the visions were going to come back. Great.

"Ah, I didn't even know her." Vin shrugged. "She was just some woman downtown who I went to randomly."

Eddie seemed to shudder—as if Vin had just told the guy he'd had a plumber operate on his colon. "Yeah, okay . . . and what did she tell you do?"

Vin wandered around, hands on his hips. The night that he had gone upstairs and locked himself in his old room came back to him—and what he remembered doing was not exactly something he felt comfortable sharing in very mixed company.

Eddie seemed to get that. "All right, we'll come back to that. Where did you do it?"

"In my bedroom. At my family's house— Wait, wait, hold the fuck up here . . . am I responsible for all this?" Vin rubbed his chest, the crushing weight over his heart making it difficult to breathe. "If I hadn't gone to her, I wouldn't have . . . lived this life of mine at all?"

The silence was the answer, wasn't it. "Oh . . . fuck me." And then it dawned on him. Devina had said that she had given him everything . . . did that also mean she'd taken things away as well? "Oh, my God . . . even the deaths? You're saying . . . I'm the cause of the deaths, too?"

"Which deaths?"

"My parents'. They died a week or so later."

Eddie looked over at Adrian. "That depends."

"On whether I ever wished them dead?"

"Did you?"

Vin stared at Marie-Terese and hoped that as he answered, she saw the regret in his eyes as he spoke. Shit, his parents had been horrible to each other and worse to him, but that didn't mean he wanted to be the cause of their demise.

"There were two things I wanted when I was younger," he said harshly. "I wanted to be rich and I wanted to be out from under their reign of terror."

"How did they die?" Eddie asked quietly, like he knew this was tough stuff.

"After I . . . did what I did up there in my room, I just went about normal life, you know? School—well, kind of school, because I skipped out a lot. I never thought it worked, and then I didn't really think about it all. It wasn't until it dawned on me that I hadn't collapsed in a full week that I started to wonder if I might have fixed what was wrong with me." Vin went over to look out at the view, but instead ended up staring down at a stain on the carpet. It had been made by the broken bourbon bottle, and the dark round mark was the kind of thing no rug cleaner was going to get out. "I remember coming home from working my father's shift, which I used to do when he was too fucking drunk to stand. It was about midnight. I put my hand on the doorknob and I glanced up at the full moon and I was psyched as I counted all the days that had passed. I was like, Huh, you don't suppose I'm okay now? And then I walked into the house and found the two of them covered with blood at the bottom of the stairs. They were both gone—and it had probably happened because one of them had pushed the other and gotten pulled along."

"You are not the problem here," Eddie interjected.

Vin braced his palms on the window and dropped his head. "Fuck me."

For no good reason, and probably because it was the only thing that could make him feel worse than he did at the moment, he thought of a peanut-butter-and-jelly sandwich. A specific one. The only one that had been made for him by his father.

The two of them had come home from a job late and there had been no dinner on the table. Which made sense, because the only person who could have made it was passed out on the couch with a cigarette having burned to ash in her hand.

His father had headed for the beer in the fridge, but had broken with tradition by taking out the bread and the jam and the peanut butter on the way there. He'd lit a cigarette, laid out four slices, hit the strawberry and then the Jif. After grabbing a Miller, he'd tossed one of the sandwiches at Vin and walked out of the kitchen.

There had been black fingerprints on the white bread because his father hadn't washed his hands.

Vin had thrown the sandwich in the trash, used the sink and the soap, and made himself a clean one.

For some reason, he regretted now that he hadn't eaten the damn thing.

"What did you do?" Eddie asked. "What was the ritual?"

"The psychic told me . . ." Vin ricocheted back in time.

After having collapsed in front of the school at a fucking pep rally, he'd had it—and had gone to the newspaper looking for psychics because he figured if they saw into the future like he did, then maybe they'd know how the hell to *stop* seeing things before they happened.

Saturday morning he'd gotten on his bike and ridden all the way down to the riverfront, to a bunch of ratty little storefronts with cheap neon signs that said things like "Tarot Here!", "Astrology Readings!", and "100% Accurate! $15!" He'd walked into the first door that had a palm with a circle on it, but there had been a line. So he'd gone to the next one and found it locked. The third one was the charm.

Inside, the dark place had smelled like something he couldn't recognize. Dark. Spicy.

Later he learned it was no-holds-barred, grown-up sex.

The woman had come out from a beaded curtain and she'd been dressed in black, with black hair and black eyeliner—but instead of a caftan and a wig and wrinkled lids, she'd been in a catsuit and looked like something out of *Playboy*.

He'd wanted her. And she'd known it.

As the echo of meeting her rippled through him, he shook himself back to the present. "I told her what I wanted and she seemed to understand immediately. She gave me a black candle and told me to go home and melt it on the stove. When it was liquid, I was supposed to pulled out the wick and put it aside, then—" He glanced at Marie-Terese and wished like hell he had another story to tell. "Then I was supposed to cut some of my hair and put it in, along with some blood and . . . ah . . . something else. . . ."

Vin was so not the kind of guy who minced words or stuttered. But admitting to a peanut gallery and a woman he wanted in his life that whacking off had been part of the deal was not the kind of admission he was in a big hurry to make.

"Yeah, okay," Eddie said, saving his ass. "Then what."

"So I was supposed to cool the wax, re-form it with the wick, and go upstairs. Get naked. Draw a circle with salt. Ah . . ." He frowned. Weird, the first part was so clear; precisely what he'd done next was not. "It's fuzzy from then on . . . I think I cut myself again and dripped the blood into the center of the circle. I lay down, lit the candle. Said some words—I can't remember what they were exactly. Something like . . . I don't know, calling things to lift burdens or some shit."

"Which was actually bullshit," Eddie said with a hard tone. "But then what happened."

"I don't . . . I can't remember precisely. I think I just fell asleep or something, because I woke up like an hour later."

Eddie shook his head grimly. "Yeah, that's a possession ritual. The wax she gave you had parts of her in it, you added your half and that was how the door was opened."

"You're saying . . . that was Devina?"

"She comes in a lot of forms. Male, female. She can be an adult, a child."

Adrian piped in. "We don't think she jumps to animals or inanimate objects. But the bitch has tricks. Big-time. Is there any chance we can get access to that house? Or are we going to have to break in?"

"Actually, I own it still."

The two guys took a deep breath. "Good," Eddie said. "We're going to need to go there to try to get her out of you. We've got a better chance of success if we return to where the ritual was performed."

"We're also going to need to get your ring back," Adrian added.

"The diamond?" Vin asked. "Why?"

"That's part of the binding. Jim said he thought it was set in platinum?"

"Of course it was."

"Well, there you go. Noble metal, and a gift from you to her."

"But I didn't give it to her. She found it."

"You bought it for her, though. Your thoughts and feelings when you purchased it are embedded in the metal. The intent is transformative."

Vin eased off his hands and stood up properly. Both of his palms left prints on the slick, cool glass and he watched them fade. "You said she steals souls. Does that mean she's going to want to kill me?"

Eddie's voice was low. "But we can try to stop that."

Vin turned around and looked at Marie-Terese. She was subdued as she leaned against the archway into the room, and he went to her, taking her into his arms. As they embraced, he was amazed and grateful once again that she accepted him . . . even after another layer of the onion had just been peeled back.

"What can we do to keep Marie-Terese safe?" he asked. "Is there anything she can do to protect herself? Because Devina just left here after having seen us together."

As the guys considered his answer, her eyes flashed up and then slid over to Eddie. "I'm leaving town tonight—for reasons other than all this. Will that help? And are there any . . . ah, spells, or . . . ?"

The hesitation spoke volumes about both her disbelief and her resignation that all this freaky shit had just put the "real" in her reality.

Eddie met her stare head-on. "Devina can be everywhere and anywhere, so the answer for keeping you safe is freeing Vin—we get her out of him, then by definition you're off her radar, because you are not the one she wants or has claimed. She only has eyes for him—and anything that keeps him from her."

Adrian cursed. "Bitch only cares about people she's put her name on. It's one of her few virtues."

"Maybe the only one," Eddie seconded.

"So let's do it," Vin cut in. "Right now. Let's go to the house and take care of this, because Devina left in a hurry for God only knows what. I don't want her coming back here and—"

"She's going to be tied up for a while. Trust me." From across the way, Adrian smiled like a motherfucker. "She hates messes, and I'm really fucking good at making them in her drawers."

Vin frowned. "Watch your mouth."

"No, not those kind of . . . you know . . ." Adrian held up both his palms. "I mean dresser drawers—"

"Did Vin give you back your earring," Jim said abruptly to Marie-Terese. "The hoop that you lost outside the Iron Mask."

"How did you know that I . . ." Marie-Terese frowned. "Well, yes, he did."

"So where is it."

Her hands went up to her earlobes. "Oh . . . no. I lost that thing again."

And she'd had it on when she'd walked into the duplex, Vin remembered.

"The bed," he said, on a wave of dread. "Upstairs. The bed—Devina took something off the bed. Goddamn it."

As Vin rushed upstairs with Marie-Terese behind him, Jim supposed he should go help, but he felt like someone had Super Glued both of his ass cheeks to the couch.

Adrian put his beer down and headed out after them. "If Devina's got a gold earring of that woman's, we're further into the shitter."

Jim put his Dogfish back up to his face and let his head go lax on the pillow behind him again. Closing his eyes was dangerous because he was dizzy, so he kept his lids as low as possible while still being able to see a sliver of the once perfect, now trashed living room.

Man, wrecking things was so much easier than cleaning them up, wasn't it.

"She was a virgin, wasn't she," he said softly. "The girl over that tub."

"Yes."

"Part of a ritual."

There was a pause. "Yes."

God, and he'd thought what he'd seen in the military was ugly. What he'd found this afternoon, though, had been downright tragic: A young girl like that should have been out at the mall or something, but there were going to be no more high school notebooks or biology classes or boys at dances for her.

"What's going to happen to her body?" he asked.

"I'm assuming Devina will dispose of it. She'll have to fairly soon."

"So every time that bitch has to leave her place, she kills?"

"The seals last for a period of time or until someone other than her breaks them. That's the other reason I didn't want you going through that door."

Great. Now he had yet another death on his conscience—because sure as shit she was going to have to protect that space again.

Jim shifted the bottle to his mouth and took a long draw. After he swallowed, he said, "What's the big deal about that bathroom, though? There was nothing in it."

"Nothing you saw, thank fuck."

Eddie started pacing around. Most of the pictures and the books had been put back into some semblance of order, proof that Vin or his maid had been doing some cleanup. But nothing looked right, and Jim supposed it was kind of like some woman who'd had her salon hairdo busted apart by a stiff wind: No matter what she did to fix it, it wasn't going to go back to the way it had been.

Eddie evened out the spines of a collection of books, his big hands precise and gentle in their movements. "The bathroom is where she keeps her mirror, which is her way in and out of this world. It's also how she clothes herself and changes her appearance. It's the source of everything she is, the seat of her power."

"Why didn't we just break the mofo, then," Jim demanded, sitting upright. "Fuck that, you guys are so tough, why didn't you do that years ago?"

"You break it, it owns you." Eddie's voice got tight. "It can capture you if you look into it, but even if you were to walk up to it blindfolded with a hammer, the instant it shattered, the shards would splinter into a thousand portals and suck you in in pieces whether or not you can see the thing."

Abruptly, Eddie moved to a different section of the bookcase and went back to work lining more things up.

"She's going to be livid that we broke the seal and pissed off at Adrian for rifling through her shit. More than that, though, she's going to need a change of address. She won't want to leave that mirror in a compromised space."

"But why would she be worried about where it was? If we can't break the damn thing, why does it matter?"

"Well, we can bust it up—it's just that the one who does it sacrifices himself. Permanently. The afterlife he gets is not part of what you saw when you went over to meet the bosses. We axed Devina's predecessor that way—at considerable loss to the team."

Suicide mission. Fantasic. "So what power do we have?"

"We can trap her in there. It's hard to do, but it is possible."

Multiple footsteps came down the stairs and Adrian broke the news. "We couldn't find the earring, so we have to assume Devina's got it."

Eddie shook his head like another brick had been set in the load he was carrying on his back. "Damn it."

As Vin put a protective arm around Marie-Terese, Adrian went over and picked up his coat. "Here's the deal ... Marie-Terese, you need to be at the ritual now, and you can't go home beforehand. Not unless you want to run the risk that she'll follow you there and compromise your son."

The woman stiffened. "How ... how did you know I have a son? Oh, wait—you did the background check on me."

Adrian shrugged and lied, "Yeah. That's how. You got someone to sit with your little boy?"

Marie-Terese looked up at Vin and then nodded. "Yes, I do. And if she can't stay, my service will find me somebody to relieve her."

"Good, because we couldn't purify your house or set up a perimeter without giving Devina a heads-up where you live, and I do not want to fight her in front of your son."

"I just need to make a call."

"Wait a second," Vin cut in. "Why can't we just take care of the part of it that effects Marie-Terese here and now?"

"We don't have what we need to do it, and as Eddie said, there's a better chance of success if we go back to where you opened the door to Devina. First we get her out of you—then if I can't find the earring, we do the same for Marie-Terese. The good news is that the tie is not all that strong and she will be safest with us. I'm sure you agree—we take no chances."

Evidently, Vin was on board with that one because he nodded grimly. "Absolutely not."

"Call your babysitter now, 'kay?" As the woman got out her phone, Adrian nodded at Jim. "You and Eddie are going to oversee the ritual at the old house, but I'll help with the preparations before I leave."

Jim frowned, wondering about the hard line of the guy's jaw. "Where are you going to be?"

"I'm getting the fucking diamond and that earring back."

Eddie cursed under his breath. "I don't like you going in alone."

As he looked at his partner, Adrian's eyes became ancient. Positively ancient. "We gotta use every weapon we have. And let's face it, what I can do to her is one of the best we've got."

Yeah, and what do you want to bet that was not a case of giving her a mani-pedi, Jim thought.

As details were arranged for the night's battle, Jim knew he had to get back into game-head. This numbed-out, floaty-ass routine had to end, and not just because they were going to engage with the enemy. The thing was, up until now, he'd assumed that "fallen angel" meant perpetual life, but that was clearly not the case—and if he lost Eddie and Adrian before he learned more of the basics, he was fucked.

About ten minutes later, he and the boys headed back down in the building's elevator and out of the Commodore. The truck had been left no more than a block away, and the short walk through the cool air helped.

"First stop, Hannaford supermarket," Adrian said as he got behind the wheel again.

Jim and Eddie stuffed themselves into the cab and Jim shut the door. "I'll want to go let Dog out if we're going to be gone all night."

"And I left my bike at your place anyway." Adrian checked the side-view mirror and pulled out of the parking space.

As they went along, Jim thought about the two guys he was riding with and wondered about the kind of tricks they had up their sleeves—aside from evidently being able to choose when and by whom they were seen. And being able to get through locks and door chains—which he'd seen not only at Devina's warehouse, but Vin's duplex—

Something dawned on him.

Jim looked around Eddie's thick chest at Adrian. "That night the three of us went out together ... Thursday night. Why did you point Devina out to me like you wanted me to fuck her?"

Adrian stopped at a red light and glanced over ... only to resume looking out the front windshield in silence.

"Why, Adrian." Less question, more growl this time.

The guy's broad palm went around the steering wheel in a slow circle. "I told you. I didn't want to work with you."

Jim frowned. "You didn't goddamn know me."

"And I didn't want to work with you and I didn't like you and I'm an asshole." He held one finger up, the conversational signal for *hold your horses*. "But I did apologize. Remember?"

Jim leaned back against the seat. "You set me up. You practically gave me to her."

"I didn't follow her out into that parking lot. I didn't fuck her—"

"I wouldn't have seen her but for you!"

"What the hell are you talking about? There's no way in hell you would have missed the likes of—"

"Shut up. Both of you." Eddie uncrossed his arms like

he was prepared to break things up with force if he had to. "Water under the bridge. Let it go, Jim."

Jim ground his molars. Man, this was just like being in with Matthias's bunch of sharks. Even the people you worked with, who supposedly were on the same side as you, were capable of serving you up like dinner to the enemy.

"Tell me something, Eddie," he bit out.

"What."

"That binding scale you were talking about. Is sex one of the ways Devina binds herself to people." When there was only silence, he said, "Is it. *Is it*."

"Yes," the guy replied finally.

"Fuck you, Adrian," Jim said loud and hard. "Fuck you for real."

Adrian wrenched the wheel to the right, slammed on the brakes, and threw the truck into park. As the horns of other cars screamed and people cursed, the son of a bitch got out and marched around the hood wearing the expression of a guy who had a crowbar in his hand.

He yanked open Jim's door. "Get out and let's do this."

Jim's hair trigger went off, fueled by that dead innocent girl, the fear on Marie-Terese's face, the aggression that Adrian was throwing off . . . and the fact that he'd had a demon straddle his hips and ride him until they both came.

It was so on.

"Can you two steakheads not do this in public?" Eddie barked.

No chance of that. Jim's fists were up and ready to fly before the soles of his boots hit the shoulder of the road, and Adrian was likewise posed for punches.

"I said I was sorry," Adrian spat. "You think I like this job of mine? You think I was ready to come back and break in a fucking greenhorn?"

Jim didn't bother talking. He just hauled back and punched the bastard right in the jaw, knuckles snapping out and making contact in the blink of an eye. The impact was so hard, the fallen angel's skull kicked back and sent his great-looking hair into a full Farrah Fawcett, with locks blowing in the wind.

"That was payback for up in Devina's bathroom, motherfucker," Jim said. "Now I'll work off the other shit."

Adrian spat blood. "I knocked you out to save your ass, son."

"Fuck. Off. Gramps."

Last word anyone got in for a while.

Adrian bull-rushed, catching Jim around the middle and pile-driving him back against the side of the truck. As the impact stung him from ear to heel, Jim just shrugged off the pain in spite of the body-wide dent he was sure he'd left in the quarter panel. Without skipping a beat, he grabbed onto Adrian's hair and head-butted the guy's nose, and as the thing went geyser all over both of them, Ad's response was just as fast—he returned the insult by kneeing Jim in the groin so hard, he clutched his balls and gagged.

Fuuuuuuuuuuuck. Nothing made a man see stars like having his hey-nannies in a head-on collision with solid bone, and as his vision went wavy, his gut thought seriously about air-mailing the beer he'd just had at Vin's all over Ad's shirt. Willpower, and only willpower, had him overcoming cock agony and lunging forward, grabbing Ad around the calves, and forcing him off balance onto the grassy ground.

Rolling around. Lots of rolling around. Fists flying. Grunts traded. Mud everywhere.

The only thing separating them from a pair of animals was the fact that they were clothed.

And the only thing that stopped them was Eddie stepping in and picking Jim up by the back of the collar and the waistband of his jeans and lifting him out of range. After Jim was hauled free from the fight and tossed aside like a branch that had fallen off a tree, he landed facedown on brown sod, his entire body throbbing like something out of a commercial for HeadOn.

Or in his case, AlloverthefuckingbodyOn.

Breathing in cold air that smelled like fresh dirt and blood, he hurt all over and felt a lot better at the same time.

Easing onto his back, he let his hands fall to the sides as he looked up at the milky sky. In the clouds above, he thought he saw the face of the girl he had left behind in that bathroom: She seemed to be staring down at him, watching over him.

Lifting an arm, he tried to touch her face, but the swirling winds of spring shifted the cloud cover, disappearing her lovely, tragic features.

He was going to find out who she was.

And he was going to do right by her.

Just as he had done right by his mother.

Those fuckers in that Camaro had been the first three men he'd killed.

"Are we done, children?" Eddie snapped. "Or do I need to spank your asses until it'll be next winter before you can sit down again."

Jim tilted his head and glanced over at Adrian. The bastard looked no better than Jim felt.

"Truce?" the guy said through bloody lips.

Jim inhaled as deeply as he could—until pain stopped his ribs from expanding any more. Well, hell. He might not be able to trust either one of them, but he needed help—and he had a tragic expertise in working with people who were shits.

"Yeah," he replied roughly. "Truce."

CHAPTER
36

"Okay, I love you. And I'll be home later tonight. Be good for Quinesha. What?" As Vin drove them over to the residential part of town, Marie-Terese listened to her son speak and got choked up. His voice was so near and so far. "Yes. Yes, you may. I love you. Bye."

She hit the *end* button on her phone and stared down at the screen, waiting for Vin to ask how the conversation had gone. It was something her ex had always done. Anytime she got on a phone, whether it was a telemarketer or the housekeeper or someone for him, Mark had had to know everything.

Except Vin didn't ask and didn't seem to be expecting her to fill him in. And the space was . . . nice. She liked how it gave her the power to choose, and it spoke volumes about respect and trust and all those things she hadn't gotten the first time around.

Thank you, she wanted to say. Instead, she murmured, "He wanted ice cream. Guess I'm a horrible mother, huh. Probably going to spoil his dinner. He eats early. At five."

Vin's hand covered hers. "You are not a horrible mother. I can assure you."

As they went by a bus stop, she looked out of her window. The people standing in the Plexiglas box all stared at the M6 while Vin drove by, and when another group of pedestrians glanced over at the car a little later, she had a sense that everywhere Vin went, he drew eyes of envy and awe . . . and greed.

"Mark liked nice cars, too," she said for no particular reason. "He was a Bentley man."

God, she could remember riding in those cars of his. He'd gotten a new one every year as soon as the fresh models came out, and in the beginning, she had sat in the passenger seat beside him with her chin up and her hands stroking the leather. Back then, when people had stared, her chest had swelled with pride that the man who owned the car was hers, that she was a part of some exclusive club of luxury that barred everyone else, that she was a queen with her king.

Not anymore. Now she saw the ogling faces as nothing more than people caught up in a fantasy. Just because you could drive or sit in a fancy BMW didn't mean you had the winning lottery ticket in the life sweepstakes. Turned out she had been far, far happier when she'd been on the hard sidewalk rather than the soft bucket seat.

Far better off, too, considering where she'd ended up.

"But I am a bad mother," she murmured. "I lied to him. I had to."

"You did what you needed to in order to survive."

"I'm going to have to keep lying to him. I don't want him ever to know."

"And there's no reason for him to." Vin shook his head. "I think a parent's job is to protect their kids. Maybe it's old-school, but that's the way I feel. There's no reason he has to go through what you've been suffering with. That you've had to deal with it is plenty."

The thought that had been percolating in her brain on and off since she'd been with Vin the night before resurfaced. And she couldn't think of a reason not to say it out loud.

"I did something to survive, but sometimes I think . . ."

She cleared her throat. "I'm a college graduate. I have a degree in marketing. I could have gotten a job."

At least, theoretically she could have. One thing that had stopped her had been the fact that she hadn't been one hundred percent confident in her fake ID. If she'd actually put in for real work, she wasn't sure whether her social security number would have come up as someone else's.

But another driver of her choice had been something darker.

Vin shook his head. "You can't look back and cross-examine everything. You did the best you could with where you were—"

"I think I wanted to punish myself," she blurted. As he looked over, she met his eyes. "I blame myself for what my son was put through. I picked the wrong man to marry and that was my fault—and I feel like my son suffered. Being with those . . . men. I hated it. I cried every night it was over and sometimes I was physically sick. I stayed with it for the money, true . . . but I was hurting myself deliberately."

Vin took her hand, brought it to his lips and kissed it fiercely. "Listen to me. Your ex was the asshole in this—not you."

"I should have left him earlier."

"And you're free now. You're free of him and you're not doing that . . . other shit anymore. You're free."

She stared out the front window. Except if that was true, then why did she feel so trapped still?

"You've got to forgive yourself," Vin said roughly. "That's the only way you're going to get past this."

God, she was so self-involved, she thought. Assuming everything those men had said back at the duplex was true—and given what she'd seen in Devina's eyes she'd be an idiot to think otherwise—Vin had just found out tonight that he all but murdered his own parents.

"You, too." She squeezed his hand. "You need to do the same."

The grunt that he made was a stop sign and a half, and

just as he'd respected her privacy, she respected his: As much as she wanted to get him to talk about that what he'd been told, she wasn't going to push.

Leaning her head back against the rest, she stared at him as he drove them along. He was quick and comfortable behind the wheel, his brows low and his lips tighter than usual as he concentrated.

She was so glad that she'd met him. And grateful that he'd had faith in her when it had mattered so much.

"Thank you," she said.

He glanced over and smiled a little. "What for."

"You believed me. Instead of her."

"Of course I did."

His answer was just as steady as his hand on the wheel, and for some reason that made her tear up.

"Why are you crying?" He pushed a hand into his jacket and took out a pristine white handkerchief. "Here. Oh, love, don't cry."

"I'll be fine. And better to get the leaks now instead of later."

After wiping her cheeks with her fingertips, she took the super-soft, super-thin linen square and spread it flat on her lap. She had some mascara on still from how she'd made herself up for church, and she wasn't about to mar the delicate cloth by actually using it—and yet she liked having the thing. Liked running her finger back and forth over the raised stitching of his monogram, VSdP.

"Why are you crying?" he repeated gently.

"Because you're amazing." She touched the V that was done in block font. "And because when you say things like you love me I believe you, and it terrifies me." She touched the S. "And because I've hated myself for so much, but when you look at me, I don't feel like I'm so dirty." Finally, she touched the dP for his last name. "Mostly, though, it's because you make me look forward to the future, and I haven't done that in forever."

"You can trust me." His hand found hers again. "And as

for your past, it's not what you've done—it's who you are. To me, that's all that matters."

She wiped more tears away as she stared across the seats at him, and though his handsome face went blurry, she was getting to know his features by heart, so it didn't matter.

"You really should use my handkerchief."

"I don't want to mess it up."

"I have plenty of others."

She looked down at his initials again. "What does the S stand for?"

"Sean. My middle name is Sean. Mother was Irish."

"Really?" Marie-Terese's eyes watered even more. "That's my son's real name."

"You two assholes stay here."

Eddie slammed the driver's-side door so hard, the whole truck rocked, and as the guy stalked over to the Hannaford's entrance, people went out of their way to get out of his.

Jim's balls still hurt. Bad. Kinda felt like he'd rolled 'em in cut glass—all tingling and painful at the same time.

On the seat next to him, Adrian was rubbing his shoulder, his expression one of disgust. "Bastard telling us to stay here. What the hell—like he's grounding us? Fuck him."

Jim stared out his window and watched as a mother with a baby in her arms walked by the truck, got a look at his face, and shied away. "I don't think we're fit for visual consumption."

Adrian reached up and cranked the rearview mirror his way. "Whatever, I'm gorgeous—wow. I . . ."

"Look like shit," Jim finished. "But at least you could walk straight if you had to. Did you have to go for the jewels?"

Adrian prodded his nose. "I think you broke this."

"And now I'm probably shooting blanks for the rest of my life. At least your swelling's going to go away."

Adrian leaned back and crossed his arms over his chest. In concert, both of them took a deep breath.

"You *can* trust me, Jim."

"Trust isn't something you can cold lab. It has to be earned."

"Then that's what I'm going to do."

As Jim made a noncommittal noise, he shifted delicately in the seat and his 'nads didn't appreciate the repositioning. After he negotiated a comfortable arrangement, he went back to watching the people in the parking lot. There was a predictable rhythm of them getting out of their cars, going into the store, and returning with filled carts or a couple of bags hanging from their hands. Witnessing it all, he was struck by how great the divide was between him and the rest of the planet. And not just because he was now playing in a paranormal game most of these fine patrons of the supermarket wouldn't have believed was real.

He'd always been separate. Ever since he'd found his mother on that kitchen floor, it was as if his root system had been plucked out of the soil and carried across the road to another plot of earth. His job hadn't helped. His personality hadn't either. And now he was seated beside a fallen angel who might or might not actually exist . . . who fought dirty.

Shit, it didn't matter if he was sterile. He was never getting a shot at having kids now, and keeping his crappy DNA out of the gene pool was no doubt the nicest thing he'd ever do for the human race.

About ten minutes later, Eddie emerged with a cart full of plastic bags, and as he pulled up to the bed and started transferring the shit, Jim couldn't stand his own thoughts anymore and got out to help: All the mommies and dear little kiddies were just going to have to suck it up if they didn't like the way he looked.

Eddie didn't say one word as they worked together, which was a clear indication that whereas Jim and Adrian had kind of made up, Eddie was not on the "Kumbaya" train. Frankly, he looked like he'd had it with everything and everyone.

And no offense, the guy had one bizarre frickin' grocery list.

There were enough containers of Morton salt to deice a highway. Countless bottles of hydrogen peroxide and witch hazel. Vinegar by the gallon. Lemons. Fresh sage packed in see-through boxes.

And four huge cans of Dinty Moore beef stew?

"What the hell," Jim asked, "are we going to do with all this?"

"Plenty."

It took them about fifteen minutes to get back out to Jim's place, and the silence was a little less tense. As they pulled up to the garage, Dog's face parted the curtains at the big window.

"You need the stuff to come up?" Jim asked as everybody got out.

"Just one bag, and I'll get it."

Jim hit the stairs with his keys in his hand, and the second he unlocked the door, Dog was all about the OMG-you're-backs, running around in circles on the landing with his tail going propeller.

When Jim glanced down over his shoulder, he frowned and patted the dog absently. On the driveway below, Eddie and Adrian were standing close together and Eddie was shaking his head and talking as Adrian focused on a point by the guy's left ear—like he'd heard it all before and hadn't been interested the first time.

Eventually, Eddie grabbed the guy's neck and forced some eye contact. Adrian's lips moved briefly and Eddie squeezed his eyes shut.

After they embraced for a quick moment, Adrian roared off on his Harley.

With a curse, Eddie grabbed a bag from the truck bed and clomped up the stairs. "Your stove work?" the guy asked as he came inside and Dog circled and wagged at his feet.

"Yup."

Ten minutes later he and Eddie were sitting down to two huge bowls of stew—which explained the Dinty Moore.

"Haven't had this for years," Jim said as he spooned up.

"Got to feed yourself."

"What'd you say to Adrian?"

"None of your business."

Jim shook his head. "Sorry, wrong answer. I'm part of this team, and I think considering the amount of shit you two know about me, it's time to start returning the fucking favor."

Eddie smiled tightly. "It's a marvel the pair of you don't get along better."

"Maybe we would if you guys would talk to me."

The long quiet that followed went unbroken until Eddie put his bowl down so Dog could go to work with what had been left.

"There are three things I know about Adrian," the guy said. "One, he will always do exactly what he wants, when he wants to. There's no chance of reasoning with him or changing his mind. Two, he will fight until he cannot stand for something he believes in. And three, fallen angels don't last forever."

Jim eased back in his chair. "I wondered about that."

"Yeah, we're not infinite—just relatively so. And that can't be ignored when it comes to him."

"Why?"

"Death wish. One of these days . . . his luck's going to run out and we're going to lose him." Eddie slowly stroked Dog's back. "I've shared a lot with that bastard over the years. Known him better than anyone, and I'm probably the only person who can really work with him. When he goes up in flames, it's going to kill me. . . ."

Eddie didn't go on, but he didn't have to.

Jim had lost a partner once, too, and that shit sucked the will to live right out of you.

"What's he going to do with Devina tonight?"

There wasn't even a pause on that one: "You don't want to know."

CHAPTER
37

Before Vin had left the duplex, he'd packed a quick semi-picnic for him and Marie-Terese, and the remnants of it were scattered across the chipped table in his family's old kitchen: The tinfoil that had been around the sandwiches and the Cokes that were now mostly empty and the bag of Cape Cod potato chips they'd shared were going to be quick to clean up.

Dessert was the single Granny Smith apple he'd had at his place, and he'd been cutting off pieces of it and alternating one to her, one to himself. At this point, the thing was more core than apple, and as he cleaved the last viable slice from around the seeds, it was going to her.

For no apparent reason, he thought about what he'd said to Marie-Terese:

It's not what you've done—it's who you are.

He was very sure that was true about her . . . and also clear that it didn't apply to him in the slightest. The way he'd been living his life had been exactly who he was—a money-hungry bastard with absolutely no conscience.

But like her, he was leaving his old life behind. He still had the drive deep in his gut—except now he saw it as a problem, not something to act on. And the trouble was, he had no idea what form the future was going to take.

"Here, have the last piece." He took the slice from the blade of his knife and offered it across the table. "I cut it carefully."

She reached out her lovely hand and accepted what he wanted to give her. "Thank you."

As she ate the thing, he cleaned up, gathering the debris, stuffing it back into the Whole Foods bag he'd brought it in.

"When are they coming?" she asked.

"One hour after sunset, they said. This kind of stuff always seems to happen in the dark."

She smiled a little and wiped her mouth with a paper napkin. Leaning to the side, she looked out of the window, her hair swinging loose off her shoulder and bouncing. "Still pretty light."

"Yeah."

As he looked around, he imagined what the place could be like. Granite countertops. Stainless-steel appliances. Bust out the wall to the right and throw up an addition to make a family room. Rip out all the carpets. Paint. Wallpaper. Face-lift the shit out of the baths.

Young family would be happy here.

"Come with me," he said, holding out his hand.

Marie-Terese put her palm in his. "Where to?"

"Outside."

He took her through the garage and into the backyard—which was hardly a showpiece. The lawn was about as attractive as an old man's beard, and the oak in the back looked like the skeletal remains of a once gracious tree—but at least the temperature wasn't as cold as it had been.

Wrapping his arms around her, he hugged her close and gently closed her eyes with the tips of his fingers. "I want you to imagine we're on a beach."

"A beach." Her lips lifted.

"Florida. Mexico. South of France. California. Anywhere you like."

She put her head on his chest. "Okay."

"The color of the sky's changing to peach and gold and the sea is calm and blue." Vin focused on the setting sun as he spoke to her, trying to picture it going behind the horizon of the ocean instead of the asphalt roof of the ranch house next door.

Vin started to move, shifting his weight from side to side, and she followed his cue, swaying in his arms.

"The air is soft and warm." He put his chin on the top of her head. "And the waves are doing that thing on the sand, up and back, up and back. Palm trees are all around."

He rubbed her shoulders, hoping that she saw what he was describing, hoping she was lifted out of where they really were: the crappy-ass backyard of a shitty little house in chilly Caldwell, New York.

Closest shoreline they had was rocky and on a river.

He closed his own eyes and just felt the woman he held, and what do you know: she was what transformed his landscape, not his words. For him, she was the reason he was warm.

"You're a wonderful dancer," she said into his chest.

"Am I?" When she nodded, he felt it on his pec. "Well, that's because I have a good partner."

They moved together until light began to bleed out of the sky and the temperature dropped too far. As Vin stopped, Marie-Terese lifted her head and looked up at him.

When he put his hand on her face and just stared at her, she whispered, "Yes."

He led her back into the house and up to his bedroom. When he closed the door, he leaned against it and watched her as she took her fleece off over her head and then unbuttoned her simple white shirt. Her bra was next, which meant that as she bent down to shuck off her jeans, her breasts swayed.

Vin had been hard before she started to undress, but the sight of her so natural and beautiful made him strain against his slacks.

And yet this was not about sex.

When she stood before him naked, he came at her slowly and kissed her long and deep. Her body beneath his hands was warm and supple, so small and smooth compared to his own—and he loved the contrast and the cushion of her. Loved the way she smelled and tasted.

Capturing her breasts in his palms, he took one nipple between his lips to suck while he rubbed the other with his thumb, and as she arched against him, his name came out of her mouth in a rush.

Man, he loved the way that sounded.

With his free hand, he stroked her thigh and moved behind, sliding between her legs.

She was oh, so ready for him. Slick and hot.

Cursing under his breath, he carried her to his old bed and laid her out. A moment later, he was naked as the day he was born and he stretched himself beside her, tucking his cock up onto his stomach as he brought their hips together.

More kissing. Hands on his skin. Hers.

Hands between her legs. His.

Marie-Terese ended up on top, her thighs split over his hips, her sex parted for him. After he was covered by a condom, she covered him in a slow, devastating decent that robbed him of breath and sense. In response, he jacked into an arch, his back curling up off the bed, the shift pushing him even deeper.

Planting her palms on his shoulders, she braced herself and swung her hips up and back, falling into a shattering rhythm.

As Marie-Terese took him, he was more than willing to give her anything she wanted of him. He was panting and desperate underneath her as her body worked his to perfection.

With her lids down low as she watched him, her eyes were like blue fire.

But they consumed him without any pain.

"This is Vin's address."

As Eddie pointed to a Happy Meal–sized house on the

right, Jim pulled the truck over and put it in park. Out of habit, he scoped the area. Typical lower-middle-class residential neighborhood, with cars mostly in their driveways, street lamps every twenty yards, and lights coming on in small-scale family rooms and kitchens. No pedestrians because everyone was in for the night. Not a lot of cover because the bushes and the trees were leafless.

As he and Eddie got out and hit the bag stash in the back, the glooming light turned everything into a variation of gray, the landscape like a black-and-white photograph.

Vin's BMW was in the drive, and there were lights on inside, so as they came up to the front door, they knocked. The response was an immediate holler from upstairs, but it took a while before they were let in, and the reason why was pretty clear: Vin's hair obviously had had fingers running through it, and his cheeks were flushed.

Jim's first thought as he stepped in and looked around was that cheap furnishings really didn't age well. From what he could see, everything from the wilted wallpaper to the crappy couch in the living room to the dejected kitchen in the back had been done in twenty-year-old Sears Roebuck.

It was the same stuff he'd grown up with and the first time since he'd met the guy that he thought he had anything in common with Vin.

Eddie put one of his bags down and focused on an oddly newer stretch of rug in the hall. "They died here at the bottom of the stairs. Your parents."

"Yeah." Vin shifted uneasily. "How do you know that?"

"I can see their shadow." Eddie stepped to the side, glanced at Jim, and nodded downward.

Jim wondered what the big deal was, because when he looked at the floor all he could see . . . was . . .

He rubbed his eyes to make sure he was getting it right—but yeah, he was. At the base of the stairs where the fresher square of carpet was, he picked up on an odd disturbance, a visual echo of what had been two people intertwined in a heap. The woman had had frizzy, faded hair and a yellow housecoat. The man had been in green overalls, like the kind an electrician or a plumber would wear. The blood-stains beneath their heads covered yards of the carpet.

Jim cleared his throat. "Yeah, I see it, too."

Marie-Terese appeared at the top of the stairs. "Where do you want us?"

"I did it in my bedroom," Vin said.

Eddie left some of his load in the front hall and started for the second floor. "Then that's where we're going."

With all the bags he was holding, Jim had to turn side-ways to fit as he went up, and Vin was cool enough to take some of the load.

"What's all this stuff?" the guy asked.

"Lotta frickin' salt."

As the four of them crammed into a room that was deco-rated in faded navy blue wallpaper and seventies schoolboy furniture, Eddie reached down and pulled up the braided rug in the center.

"You did it here?"

Self-evident, given the faded circle that was left on the floorboards. "Do we need to clean that first?" Jim asked.

"Clean what?" Vin knelt down and ran his hands around the fake wood flooring. "There's nothing here."

"It's right—"

Eddie caught Jim's arm and shook his head, then started opening bags. He handed both Vin and Marie-Terese a con-tainer of Morton salt. "You guys are going to pour a line around the perimeter of the upstairs. It needs to be an un-broken barrier, except for that window." He nodded over to the right. "Leave that clear. If there is furniture in the way, it's okay—just go around it and then back against the wall. There's more in these bags if you need it."

When he seemed satisfied by how they were handling things, he took out a pair of stogies from inside his jacket and gave one of them along with some salt to Jim. "You and I are going to do the same and a little more downstairs."

"Roger that."

When they were back on the first floor, Eddie took out a black Bic lighter and fired his Cuban or whatever it was up. As he exhaled something that smelled like ... clean ocean air, he offered the flame and Jim bent at the waist and lit his own. One inhale and he was in Heaven. The tobacco tasted amazing, like nothing he'd ever had in his mouth before, and if this was going to be part of his ongoing duties, he was so on board.

Man, he'd liked smoking. And evidently all that cancer concern was off his list now.

Eddie pocketed his lighter and popped open his salt. "We're going to go from room to room and exhale while we make a barrier down here. We're purifying the environment and creating an obstacle for her. There's more Morton's in that bag."

Jim glanced down at his umbrella girl. "Is this really going to keep Devina out?"

"It'll make it harder for her to get in. Adrian's going to keep her busy for as long as he can, but even with his considerable talents, she's going to know something is up."

As Jim cracked the seal on his salt, he realized he liked the way he felt. For better or for worse—well, mostly worse—he was built to fight, and not just because he was a heavyweight motherfucker. Conflict was in his blood and his brain and his beating heart.

He'd missed being on missions.

Angling the Morton container downward, he happily smoked away as a thin white river poured out of the silver spout and onto the shitty carpet. Eddie was handling the back of the house, going down the hall and into the kitchen, so Jim headed for the living room. It was fast work, following along the baseboard while pushing dusty curtains out of the way, and it was satisfying: He felt as if he were pissing on his own territory, staking a claim.

Man, he almost hoped that bitch walked through that door just so he could kick her ass.

Talk about a sea change. In the past, he'd religiously

drawn a line between men and women. He wouldn't hesitate to kill a man. Same with maiming, trampling, or cold-
cocking one. Women, however, were totally different. A
female could come at him with a knife drawn and he would
disarm her. Period. Disabling would happen only if he absolutely had to, and in the least painful and permanent way.

But Devina wasn't a woman to him anymore. Hell, she
wasn't a woman, period.

The salt whispered as he made his wobbly little line, and
although it might have been hard to put a lot of confidence
in something that was used to spice up McDonald's french
fries, Eddie didn't strike him as a fool. Not by a long shot.

And the cigar rocked. Totally.

By the time they were finished, the downstairs of the
house smelled like Florida and needed a DustBuster, and
as they headed to the second floor, Eddie drew a white line
across each of the steps until the stairs looked like a landing pad.

Vin and Marie-Terese had been busy, and after Eddie
inspected their efforts, he told them to take a load off on
the little bed and asked Jim to join him in the bathroom
at the top of the landing. Using the sink as a mixing bowl,
the guy put in the hydrogen peroxide, the witch hazel and
the juice of the lemons along with the white vinegar, and
stirred with his own hands, weaving his fingers through the
solution.

Just as the pungent smell wafted up and drilled into
Jim's nostrils, Eddie started speaking softly as he continued
to make circles in the sink. The words were barely more
than breath, and in a language Jim didn't understand, but
the phrase was repeated over and over again.

Abruptly, the scent rising up changed. No longer nasty
in the nose, it became springtime-meadow fresh.

Eddie took his hands out and wiped them on his jeans,
then reached into his coat and produced two crystal ...

"Are those guns?" Jim asked.

"Sure are." The guy popped the stopper on one and submerged the thing, bubbles floating up to the surface until

the belly was full. He handed it to Jim. "Put this in your holster. As opposed to your auto-loader, this shit will actually work against her."

As Eddie filled up his own, Jim turned the wet crystal over in his hands. The weapon was a goddamn piece of art, carved from clear quartz, he was guessing, and engineered with precision. Palming it, he took aim at the bathroom wall and pulled the trigger. A fine, strong line of the solution licked out exactly where he'd wanted it to go.

"Nice," he murmured, ditching his SIG.

"I'll show you how to make them." Eddie sealed up his gun's belly and holstered it at the small of his back. "The fact that you can carve wood's going to help."

When they went back to the others, Vin was pacing around and Marie-Terese was sitting on the bed. Eddie ditched his coat, and rifled around in the Hannaford bags that were now mostly empty.

Taking out the fresh sage, he popped open its plastic container and gave the bundle of leaves to Marie-Terese. "You hold on to this and stay out of the way. No matter what you see or what happens, you do not drop this and you keep this against both of your palms. It's going to offer you some protection."

"What do I do?" Vin demanded.

Eddie glanced over his shoulder. "Take off your clothes."

CHAPTER
38

Last time Vin got naked for a crowd the context had been way different.

As he tossed his shirt and pants and boxers onto the dresser, he made sure his gun was front and center on the pile, and when he turned around, he was ready to get whatever this was over with. Funny, he'd been operated on only once in his life, back about a decade ago. He'd had to get his knee rebuilt after years of playing basketball and tennis and running on the damn thing—and he was exactly the same way now as he had been then: Ready to get back to normal. Hoping that the outcome after the pain faded was the right one.

He glanced over at Marie-Terese. She was sitting absolutely still on the bed, holding the sprigs of fresh sage between her hands so that the fluffy leaves peeked out by her thumbs and the little stems hung free on the far side. As her eyes met his, he had to go over and give her a quick kiss on the mouth. She was scared but she was strong—and however much he wished she weren't a part of this, he agreed with Adrian: No chances with her. There could be no chances with her, ever, so they had to assume Devina had taken that earring.

Eddie took out a compass and four white candles, and

after doing some Boy Scouting with his gadget, he and Jim did a north, south, east, and west, marking each of the points on the bare floor with the waxers. Then it was more salt running in a circle around the setup. As Vin watched them, he had to admit the ring-around they did was tidier than the one he'd pulled off over twenty years before, but he'd had to hurry back then. There had been no telling how long his parents would remain passed out.

"As I said, what you did was a possession ritual." Eddie went around and lit each of the four wicks. "You took the three elements of yourself as a man—hair, blood, and . . . you know—and offered them to her. She accepted the gifts and took up res in your spiritual skin, so to speak. We're going to clean her out of you."

"Yeah, listen," Vin cut in. "You sure we can't take care of Marie-Terese first, then worry about me?"

"No. You're the focal point. You called Devina to you. Besides, Marie-Terese has an easier tie to break, assuming that earring is in Devina's possession." The guy disappeared into the hall bath and returned with dripping hands that were held up like a surgeon's. "Jim, go into my coat and take out the leather roll that's in the right pocket."

Jim fished around and pulled free a ten-inch-long, two-inch-wide bundle that was secured with a white satin ribbon.

"Open it."

Jim's hands were quick to pull the bow free and then he unrolled the leather, revealing a dagger.

Made of glass.

"Don't touch the knife," Eddie said.

"What the hell are you going to do with that?" Vin demanded.

"We're going to open you up." The man pointed to the circle of burning candles. "This is spiritual surgery, and before you ask, yup. Gonna hurt like a bitch. But when we're through, you're not going to be scarred or anything. Now lie down, head here at the north."

Vin looked at the men's faces as the pair of them stared over at him. Grim. Serious. Especially Eddie.

"I've never seen a knife like that before," Vin murmured as he looked at the thing.

"It's crystal," Eddie said, as if he knew Vin needed a second before he turned himself over to the ritual. "And yeah, take a deep breath, but we do need to get started." He glanced at his buddy. "Jim? You stay next to Marie-Terese. Eventually you'll be doing these, but right now you're just on the watch team, and if the shit gets critical, you're in charge of her."

"Do you read minds?" Vin asked the guy.

"Sometimes. Now can we get down to business? I don't know how long Adrian's going to be able to hold her."

Vin stared into Marie-Terese's eyes and hoped she read all that he wished he could speak. When she nodded as if she understood perfectly, he stepped over the salt circle and stretched out in the center. Eddie had gauged the size perfectly: The soles of Vin's feet just touched the far edge when his head was right at the northern candle.

"Close your eyes, Vin."

Vin took one last look at Marie-Terese and then he lowered his lids and tried to relax his body. The floor was hard against his shoulder blades, his ass, and his heels; and his heart was going at a clip in his rib cage. The real shitter was not being able to see, however—not only did he feel isolated, but the sound of everything got cranked up too high. From his own breathing to the footfalls of Eddie walking around him to the whispering of strange words over his naked body, it was all in nerve-racking HD.

And it didn't take long for him to lose his patience. Here he was, laid out like some kind of meal to be consumed, in front of Marie-Terese, who was no doubt—

A subtle vibration came up through the floor.

Vin felt the tuning-fork reverberation first in his palms and feet and then it continued inward, the concentric circles drawing toward the center of him. As he absorbed the rhythmic waves, a subtle breeze tickled across the hair on his arms and his thighs and his chest, and he wondered whether someone had opened a window.

No ... things had begun to turn.

Whether he started to spin or the room did, he wasn't sure, but abruptly the waves and the breeze coalesced and became indistinguishable as they swirled around him ... or he swirled around. Like water rushing through a drain, speed gathered and his stomach revolted, nausea making that sandwich he'd eaten with Marie-Terese go green and spoiled in his gut.

Just before he threw up, the merry-go-round stopped and he went weightless. No longer spinning, he was suspended in warm air, and thank fuck for it. Inhaling deep, he felt his belly ease up and the tension in his arms and legs release, his muscles going lax.

And then his sight returned. Good God, even though his lids were down, he could see white light: The source was somewhere beneath him, piercing up through the floor he was supposedly on, his body carving out a pattern in the illumination.

Eddie's face appeared above his own.

The guy's mouth moved as if he were talking, and Vin didn't hear the words that were spoken so much as know them in his mind:

Take a deep breath and stay very still.

Vin tried to nod, but when Eddie shook his head, he just thought the word *yes* at the guy.

The crystal knife rose above Vin's chest, the weapon held steady in Eddie's big hands. As the white light hit it, a brilliant rainbow of color sparkled, everything from pinks and baby blues and pale yellows to bloodred and navy blue and deep amethyst exploding from its length.

Indecipherable words appeared in Vin's head as Eddie spoke faster and faster.

Bracing himself, Vin focused on the razor-sharp blade point.

It was going into his heart. He just knew it.

When the inevitable descent came, it was faster than a blink and slower than a century—and the impact was worse than he'd prepared for. The instant the dagger sank into Vin's flesh, he felt as if every nerve in his body transmitted the pain.

Then Eddie sliced him right open.

Vin screamed into the maelstrom as his body cleaved open at his breastbone, his spine straining as he contorted upward. He was vaguely aware of Eddie speaking words, and then the man's glowing hand reached inside the locus of the agony, making it so much worse.

Probing. Fisting. A great pulling.

Whatever Eddie was grabbing and yanking was holding on tight, and abruptly Vin couldn't breathe for the great pressure on his ribs and lungs. Gasping, he struggled to draw air down in the midst of it all.

He started to scream again. Which made no sense because he had no breath.

As the battle for extraction raged, Vin fought to hold on not for himself, but for Marie-Terese. He would not die in front of her. He would not die tonight in front of her. He would not—

But Eddie didn't let up and the thing didn't loosen and Vin started to fail. His heart went from pounding to tripping to failing to pump, and with the fibrillation came a numbing cold that overtook him. He tried to fight it, tried to will his body back into functioning, but there was no reserve left to call upon. Even as his mind and soul wanted to stay, his flesh was done.

Except then the evil loosened.

At first, there was just the slightest of slips, as if only one of the tendrils that clung to him snapped free. But then another broke, and another, and more in a bunch. And—

With a screeching tear, like metal was being torn apart, a blackness was lifted from him, taken out of him, torn free ... and his first thought was that he felt far too light in his body in its absence. His second was that he was still dying—

Vin was saved by the white light.

All at once, as if it knew how little time he had left, he was resuscitated, the illumination's blanketing warmth easing the pain, and then wiping it clean as if the torture had never existed. He soared free, light and transparent, indistinguishable from what surrounded him.

He wept in ecstatic relief and gratitude.

It was the first time in thirty-three years that he'd been alone in his own skin.

Jim's eyes had divided loyalties.

Every time a car rolled slowly down the street, he stared out the window. Any noise around the house? Creak of a tree? Breeze rattling the window? It was the same. He was constantly searching corners, waiting for Devina to come roaring in.

And yet the center of the room consumed him.

He'd never seen anything like it. From the moment the floor dropped free from Vin and that blast of white light shot up from nowhere, to the electric second when Eddie put the knife to use and then started pulling, it was all so incredible.

God, that knife.

It was the most beautiful thing Jim had ever seen: When the light had hit it, a child's spectrum of vivid colors had sprung forth, the hues so bright and clear, it was as if his eyes were young again and seeing them for the first time.

But the struggle . . . he'd been certain Vin was going to die. In the fulcrum of the glow, Eddie had stabbed the man and reached inside his chest and started yanking like he was trying to drag a car out of a swamp. And in response, Vin had screamed from a vast distance, the agony tearing out of his throat as his body had strained.

At that moment, Marie-Terese had lunged forward, but Jim had caught her, instinct telling him she couldn't get in the way of what was going on, no matter how dire things appeared. Interrupting was not in the playbook: This was surgery for the soul and the cancer had to come out. Even if the man died in the middle of it, the extraction attempt was the right course of action.

Jim held her as loosely as he could, and she ended up

against him, nails deep in his forearm as she watched, as helpless as he was to affect the outcome.

It was all about Eddie and Vin and whatever fate was going to roll out.

And then it happened. Eddie started to win the battle—what he was pulling on began to give way, first in increments, then with a final, exploding separation that landed the angel on his ass.

But there was no time for celebration.

As soon as whatever that black shit was got out of Vin, it was free in the air, a vicious-looking shadow that wafted loose—and immediately came gunning for Marie-Terese. Rippling through the air, it pulled itself together, darkened up like it was gathering strength, and faced off at the woman.

Jim shoved Marie-Terese behind him and forced her up against the wall. Working fast with the crystal gun, he popped the plug on its belly and poured what was inside all over her, until it was dripping off her nose and from the ends of her hair.

He wished he had a bucket of the shit.

Wheeling back around, he braced himself as the shadow hurled itself at them. Impact was not a party, the smoky nonentity registering like a thousand bee stings across his skin. Marie-Terese screamed—

No, it wasn't her. The thing screamed and splintered apart, looking like BB pellets that had been scattered across a floor.

Fucker re-formed, but it didn't take another shot. It boiled for the one window that didn't have salt on its sill and the shattering of glass was a shocker, the sound echoing throughout the house.

At that very same moment, the light in the circle sucked out of the room, and its exit was even louder, a sonic boom that made Jim's eardrums pop and the mirror over the dresser crack into pieces. Eddie was thrown back by the burst of energy and he slammed against the wall just as Vin was revealed on the floor, pale, shaky, covered with sweat.

As he curled over onto his side and drew his knees up to his chest, Marie-Terese broke free of Jim's hold and rushed to him.

"Vin?" She brushed the guy's hair back. "Oh, God, he's freezing cold. Give me the duvet."

Jim yanked the cover free from the bed and put it in her hands; then he went to check on Eddie, who seemed to be out cold. "You okay there, big man? Eddie?"

The guy jerked to attention and looked around as if he were momentarily lost. To his credit, though, even in his out-of-it state, the crystal dagger was locked in his fist, his knuckles white like the thing was going to have to be pried out of his grip with a pair of pliers.

His expression was not one of triumph.

When he tried to get up, Jim grabbed the guy under the armpits and helped hoist him off the floor and onto the bed. "You're not looking like this went okay."

Eddie took a couple of deep breaths. "He's clean . . . and nice move with soaking her."

"Figured it'd be more effective." Jim shifted that thick braid over the guy's shoulder and couldn't understand why Eddie seemed so disappointed. "I don't get it. What's the problem?"

Eddie focused on the busted window and shook his head. "This was too easy."

Shiiiiiiit.

If this had been a walk in the park, Jim wondered what in the hell a real fight looked like.

CHAPTER
39

Saul pulled into his driveway in a daze and put the cab in park. In the glow from the garage light, he lifted his eyes to the rearview mirror and tilted his head to the side. With his cut finger, he brushed at the bald spot near his ear and remembered being with the woman in the back of the cab.

They'd had sex.

It had been the first time since he'd been to prison ten years ago.

He'd liked it ... at least until the end. In the afterglow, as he'd gone lax beneath her, a strange, sickening lethargy had seeped into him, and he'd found himself not so much relaxed as trapped.

That was when she'd taken out the scissors. She'd moved so quickly he couldn't have stopped her even if he'd been alert: Snip of his hair, slice of his skin. Then she'd rubbed his blood in with what she'd taken from his head, dismounted from his hips and disappeared her hands under her skirt.

After that, she'd left him where she'd taken him: in the back of the taxi.

She hadn't even bothered to shut the door, and even though the cold had chilled him, it had been some time before he was able to reach over and pull the thing shut. After he zipped himself up, he gave in to the exhaustion, ignoring the squawking dispatcher and the fact that it wasn't all that bright for him to be so vulnerable downtown even in the middle of the day.

The dream while he'd slept had been horrifying, and in the dim light now, he yanked his head around and double-checked that there was no one in the backseat with him. Except of course there wasn't . . . he'd locked himself in the car the instant he'd gotten back behind the wheel.

God . . . the nightmare. In it, he'd been fucked by a de-caying monster who was and was not the woman who he'd been with. . . . and in the dream, he'd made some sort of agreement with her. Except he couldn't remember what he'd gotten in return for whatever he'd given.

His beloved . . . it had something to do with his beloved.

It had been dark by the time two young punks woke him up by opening the front doors of the taxi and rifling through his backpack and his jacket.

Of its own volition, his hand had shot forward and grabbed onto the ponytail of the one by the steering wheel. Snagging hard, he became aware that he was a hundred times stronger than he'd been before he'd slept. Stronger, focused. He felt like . . . a killing machine.

The kid on the other side of the taxi had taken one look into Saul's face, dropped the wallet in his hand, and disap-peared at a dead run.

Saul had snapped the neck of the one with the ponytail by dragging him halfway into the backseat and twisting his head around until there was a crack and a dead body.

He'd left the cooling corpse right on the ground next to where the cab had been parked. And looked up into a security camera.

What luck, though. The red light indicating the thing was on had not been blinking. So there was no record of him or the woman or the two boys.

Not luck, he'd heard a voice tell him. *Part of the bargain.*

And that was when it had come back to him: He had wanted to be free from prying eyes, to be able to do as he chose without worrying about being caught. No more hiding weapons, covering tracks, disguising himself, sneaking around.

And so it was done.

Getting in on the driver's side, he'd felt both a weight and an elation, and that was when he'd realized the engine had been on since the woman had left him. So why wasn't he dead from carbon monoxide? It was cold and the heater had been on the entire time.

Go home, he'd heard in his head.

As his hands had grasped the steering wheel, he'd instantly had his direction set by a powerful draw in the center of his chest: He needed to *go home.*

Hurry.

That was all he'd known and that was precisely what he did. He'd driven from downtown out toward the suburbs, going as fast as he could—whereas after his other killings he'd been as law-abiding as a preacher's wife.

Yet now, though, in spite of this odd power coursing through him, he felt stuck, an engine not in gear: All he could do was stare straight ahead.

On a dim back shelf of his mind, he was concerned that he wasn't worried about what he'd done for a third time in that alley. He should have left the cab off at dispatch and disappeared. Dreams were all well and good but they were fantasy, not reality. And everyone who murdered people could get caught—

Not you. Not anymore.

Go inside.

The thought struck him with the clarity of a bell rung on a clear dawn. Unlocking the doors, he got out and looked around, still having difficulty understanding the transformation he'd gone through. He was different in his own skin, and as good as it was, he felt like a lottery winner whose ticket had yet to be authenticated. What if this was taken away? What if something came up behind him and . . .

You don't worry about that. Go inside.

As he got out his house keys, he noticed that there was a truck parked in front of the house next door, and a fancy car in the driveway, but he paid them no attention. He had to *go inside*.

When he was standing in his front hall, he looked past the empty living room and into the kitchen that was littered with McDonald's bags and pizza boxes and empty Coke bottles. Now what? He was not hungry or thirsty and he was not tired and he couldn't for the life of him understand why he had to be in the house.

He waited.

Nothing came to him, so as he did every time he got home, he went upstairs.

The second he entered the bedroom, the marble statue of his woman energized him and focused him, and he rushed forward, falling to his knees in front of it. Cupping the perfect marble face, he felt his palms warm the cool stone.

And that was when the bargain came back to him, word for word.

The voice of the woman from the cab echoed through his head: *For a small price, you can have exactly what you want. I can tell you what you have to do to get her and keep her. And I protect what is mine. I won't let anything happen to you. Forever.*

You can have exactly what you want.

Kill her and she's yours.

"Yes," he said to the statue. "Yes . . . my love."

All he had to do was go over to that house of hers and get inside. He had to find a way to get close enough to Marie-Terese to—

The sound of a window shattering brought his head up. As the glass exploded out of the house next door, it was broken with such force that it pelted Saul's place, pinging off the aluminum siding in a *ra-ti-ta-ta*.

In the aftermath, and with contrasting silent grace, the drapery billowed out of the hole that was left behind as if the pressure inside were greater than outdoors—

His beloved was revealed to him.

In the illumination of a ceiling light, Marie-Terese's perfect face was drawn in lines of horror and fear as she looked at where the window had been. Her hair and her clothes were wet and there was no color in her cheeks—which made her look even more like the statue.

As he stared in wonder and joy, he didn't worry about being seen by her. As he was in darkness, he was invisible to her, and to the other two men who were with her.

Interesting ... one of them was from that hideous club. He'd been in that hallway beating up the pair of college boys Saul had killed back in the alley.

No time to waste. Go ... go ...

Saul jumped to his feet, jogged out of the bedroom and down the stairs—all the while marveling at the woman from his cab.

She had power. True power.

It was the work of a moment to dip into the taxi and get the gun from under the driver's seat.

Marie-Terese wrapped the duvet around Vin and pulled him into her arms. His body was an ice cube, nothing but a static object that threw off cold. And as she rubbed him, trying to get heat into his body, he wasn't helping. He was agitated—twitchy and jerking, almost as if he didn't know where he was or couldn't understand what had happened.

"Shh ... I'm right here," she said to him.

Evidently, the sound of her voice was exactly what he needed to hear, and he calmed down.

"Vin, I want you to lie against me." As she tugged him, he followed her prompting, easing into her lap and holding on to her. "Shh ... you're okay. I'm okay. ..."

As his face tucked into her side, she couldn't believe what she had seen and yet didn't doubt it had been real. She also got a clear sense that she had been aware of only part of what had actually happened.

Fortunately, Eddie had only acted out the stabbing, that see-through knife stopping with the point directly on Vin's breastbone. But the agony had been real for both men while they had both struggled. And then . . . well, she didn't know what went down next, really: Eddie reared back as if he'd pulled something out of Vin, and then Marie-Terese felt a sharp, ringing panic that was tied to nothing specific—at least at first.

That changed fast. She'd felt an evil spirit focus on her, and at the moment it did, Jim pushed her behind him and then doused her in a solution that smelled like the sea. As she sputtered, the evil seemed to splinter around her, and that was when the window shattered.

Vin rolled over in her arms and looked into her face. "You . . . truly okay?"

He could barely get the words out from between his chattering teeth.

"I'm fine."

"You're wet."

She pushed her damp hair back. "I think it saved me."

Eddie spoke up from over on the bed, his voice gravel. "It did. Jim made a good call with that."

The man nodded once, more focused on the rough shape his buddy was in rather than on any kind of compliment. "You sure we don't need to get you anything?" he asked Eddie.

"Adrian's the one we need to worry about. She didn't show and he's not here, and that means . . ."

Problems, Marie-Terese thought.

"Problems," Jim filled in. "So I'm just going to get a refill of the magic sauce."

As he headed for the bath, Vin let out a groan and tried to sit up.

"Here," she said, putting her arms around his torso and hefting his upper body off the floor. When he managed to hold himself upright, she yanked the duvet free from under his hip and wrapped it back around him.

He ran his hands through his hair, smoothing it down. "Am I done? Am I . . . free?"

Eddie got to his feet with a lurch. "Not entirely. Not until we get that diamond back."

"Can I help with that?"

"No, it's better to have one of us take care of it."

Vin nodded, and after a moment, he started to stand up. Even though he weighed so much more than she did, she helped him as best she could until he was standing on his own, and then she let him go so he could pace around.

When he went to get dressed, she didn't want to appear like a mother hen, so she headed over to look at the window that had been broken.

Staring at the damage, questions pinged around her head and scrambled together. The panes had been splintered completely, leaving nothing but stubs behind on the sashes, and she glanced outside. Down on the ground, there were bits and pieces of glass and wood, but nothing bigger than the size of a pen.

"Stay away from there," Eddie said, coming over and edging her out of the way with his huge body. "It's not sealed, which means—"

Eddie gasped and went for his own throat, like he'd been grabbed through the hole from behind. As he tipped backward, his head and shoulders started to fall through the opening and Marie-Terese lunged for him—only to get dragged along with him.

"The . . . knife . . ." Eddie gasped.

Everything went slow-motion as she called out over her shoulder. Thank God, Jim was already on it, racing in from the hall and going for the crystal knife that had been left on the bed. The instant the weapon got palmed, Eddie went to work, wrenching around and stabbing at something that was outside of the window.

Marie-Terese locked onto one of Eddie's legs as Jim bear-hugged the guy around the waist. While they worked together, Vin went for his gun on the dresser and spun around, pointing it at the tangle. She had faith he wasn't going to shoot unless he—

On the far side of the bedroom, through the open door, she caught sight of a man coming up the stairs. He was mounting them in silence and moving with relentless focus. As he turned his head, their eyes met..

Saul . . . from the prayer group. What was he doing—

The gun in his hand swung up and then around, pointing at her. "Beloved," he said with reverence. "Mine now and always."

The automatic weapon went off.

Vin shouted something, just as Jim threw his body in the way of the bullet: With the grace of an athlete, he sprang up into the air, putting his chest in the path of what was intended for her, his arms spread wide, his torso flat to the shooter so that he offered the greatest possible surface area to protect her.

As the sharp, loud sound echoed, Eddie fell through the window, tumbling from the room.

And then a second shot rang out.

CHAPTER
40

Vin threw off his lethargy the moment it became clear there was trouble over at the window. He'd been half-way into his pants when he heard the scrambling, and his first thought was for Marie-Terese—except she wasn't the one who appeared to be getting strangled. Jim was quick to respond, though, getting Eddie that crystal knife and then hanging on with every ounce of muscle he had. And Marie-Terese was right there to help, doing what she could to keep the man from being pulled out by God only knew what.

Vin's first thought was to go for the gun he'd left with his clothes and he followed up on it fast. Licking the safety off with his thumb, he leveled the muzzle at the mess of bodies at the window. He had no clue what the hell he could shoot at, so he held steady—

And then the expression on Marie-Terese's face abruptly changed from one of determination to shock as she focused on the doorway.

Someone else was in the house.

Vin pivoted on his bare feet and saw the vision he'd been given in his trance play out: A man with thinning blond hair was turning the corner at the head of the stairs and lifting a gun to point it straight into the bedroom. Yes . . . this was it. The trigger was going to be pulled and the bullet was going to travel through the air in the blink of an eye . . . and Marie-Terese was going to be struck.

"No!" Vin screamed as the shot went off.

From the corner of his eye, he saw Jim leap in front of her, the man's body blocking the lead that was meant for her by taking it in the chest, the impact carrying him back and knocking her down.

Vin's instinct was to go to her, but that was not the right move. Wheeling around with his gun, he knew that he had to make sure the intruder didn't get a second shot—it was the only thing he could do to improve the chance of people surviving.

Although he had the cold, deadly suspicion that Jim was down for count permanently.

Holding his weapon steady, Vin stepped into the door-way—and directly into the face of a man who was a good three inches shorter than he was.

It was a question of who pulled their trig first, and sur-prise worked in Vin's favor—the shooter had naively as-sumed that there were only three people in the room.

Vin didn't hesitate to squeeze out a round, right into the guy's heart, and the impact kicked the man's aim off and tightened his index finger at the same time. Which meant Vin took a slug in the shoulder.

Fortunately it was the left one.

As the intruder went down flat on his back and his weapon scattered away, Vin squared his muzzle off and pumped another round and another round and another round into the guy so there was no chance the fucker was going to be able to blink, much less lift a gun.

With each shot, the man jerked, arms and legs flopping like a puppet.

"Marie-Terese, are you hit?" Vin called out as the din faded.

"No . . . but oh, God . . . Jim's barely breathing and Eddie fell out of the window."

Blood dripped off Vin's free hand and onto the intruder's jeans as he stepped over the guy and kicked that gun all the way down the stairs. He still wasn't about to trust that the bastard was dead, though, so he trained his weapon on the paling face before him as he listened hard for more footsteps downstairs.

"Get your phone," Vin said to Marie-Terese. "Call nine-one-one."

"Already dialing," she replied.

He wanted to look over his shoulder and check her with his own eyes, but he wasn't taking any chances. There was no telling who else had come into the house, and there was still a shallow movement in the intruder's chest.

As seconds drifted into minutes, Vin totally approved of the way the color was leaving the unremarkable features of the man's face, but Christ . . . who was he? What was he?

Although if a bullet could stop him, he probably was just a human.

Marie-Terese's voice drifted across the room. "Yes, there's been a shooting at One-sixteen Crestwood Avenue. There are two men—three down. . . . We need an ambulance right away. Marie-Terese Boudreau. Yes . . . yes. Yes . . . no, it's not my residence—"

The lids of the intruder suddenly flipped open and Vin found himself staring into a pair of pale browns that were fixated on something other than whatever was in front of him. With a stiff twitch, those graying lips started to move.

"Noooooo . . ." The word was extended for the length of a horrified exhale, as if whatever he was seeing made nightmares seem like sitcoms.

With a gasp and a shudder, the guy passed into the hereafter, an expression of terror freezing on his face as a line of blood oozed out of the corner of his mouth.

Vin kicked those loose legs a couple of times and then he listened hard. He could hear wind whistling up the stairs, but there were no other sounds anywhere else.

He backed up slowly, gun swinging from left to right in

case somebody came up from down below or popped out of any of the doorways.

Inside the bedroom, he held his arm wide and Marie-Terese came forward for a hard hug. She was shaking, but she held on strong for the split second they were together.

"Can you do CPR on Jim?" he asked. "Or do you want to hold this gun on—"

"No, I'll take care of him." She went over to the man, knelt down and put her ear next to Jim's mouth. "He's still breathing, but it's not by much."

Whipping off her fleece, she wadded it up and put it to the bleeding wound on the front of the chest and pushed down while she took his pulse. "So faint . . . but it's beating so I can't do chest compressions. The ambulance is due in five minutes."

Which was forever in a situation like this.

"Don't shoot," came a groggy voice from downstairs. "It's just me."

"Eddie?" Vin called out. "Jim's hit!"

When Eddie appeared at the top of the stairs, he looked like roadkill, and as he limped forward, he glanced down at the intruder. "That's really dead. How's Jim?"

"Good," Marie-Terese whispered as she stroked the man's face. "Right, Jim? You're good and you're going to get fixed. You're going to make it just fine. . . ."

Vin put his gun down on the bed and knelt on the other side of Jim, mirroring Marie-Terese's position on the floor as she reached out to the fallen man.

"He saved me," she said, her fine hand stroking Jim's thick arm. "You saved me, Jim. I'd be dead without you. . . . Oh, God, Jim, you saved my life. . . ."

Vin ran his eyes over that big chest and didn't need a medical degree to know that the wound the man had taken was fatal. Jim was breathing in the same shallow way the intruder had been, and he was soon going to go the route the shooter had: His color was fading at an alarming rate, evidence of internal bleeding.

Shit, there was nothing they could do other than wait for the pros to come with their stretcher. CPR was not an option as long as Jim had a pulse and was breathing on his own, and pressure wasn't going to do shit for a torn artery.

For the first time in Vin's life, he started praying for the sound of sirens.

Jim had been shot before. And stabbed. Hanged once, too. He'd been injured in fights by fists and crowbars and jack-knives and boots. Even been impaled with a Montblanc pen.

In all of those situations, he'd known he was going to survive. No matter how much it had hurt, or how much he'd bled, or how vicious the weapon, he'd known his injuries weren't fatal.

And now he knew with the same certainty that the bullet in his chest had left in its wake the kind of tearing trail that was going to carry him to his royal reward.

Angel or no angel, he was dying.

Funny, it didn't hurt much. There was a sharp burning, sure, and he was having trouble catching his breath—which he took to mean either his lungs were starting to fill with blood, or his chest cavity was flooding out—but overall he was comfortable. Maybe a little cool, but mostly comfortable.

So he was clearly in shock.

Guess that little bullet had nicked an artery.

He opened his mouth on instinct only, not because he wanted to pray or beg for the medics to come faster: He was drowning in his own body and that was the long and short of it.

And it was not a bad outcome, really. Thanks to the Four Lads, he knew he'd be seeing his mother soon. And he hoped to meet up with the lovely blond girl who hadn't deserved to die as she had.

All that put him at peace.

Funny, as he pictured those English guys in their whites with their dog, he wished them well and felt sorry for them. Guess those angels had been wrong. He wasn't the answer to their problems—although at least he'd gotten Vin and Marie-Terese on the right track.

And it was strange to know, but it had turned out the crossroads had been his, not Vin's.

When he'd seen that gun muzzle up and all ready to rock-and-roll, his only thought had been about Vin and Marie-Terese. Saving her meant saving them both, and their love was worth so much more than one paltry life.

It was the first time he'd done that. The first time he'd not only been truly unselfish, but acted out of something other than anger or vengeance. And he'd never been more sure of anything, except the need to avenge his mother all those years ago.

Summoning his flagging strength, Jim focused his eyes and saw Marie-Terese and Vin bending over him. Vin had gripped his hand and was talking at him, the man's face intense to the point of distortion, his features pulling together, his eyes burning. Jim tried to concentrate and get his hearing to work, but sound was beyond him. Best guess was that the guy was telling him to hold on, ambulance on the way, hold on, ambulance coming. . . . *Oh, God, Jim, stay with us. . . .*

On the opposite side, Marie-Terese was silently crying, her beautiful eyes resplendent in her sorrow, her crystal tears falling off her cheeks and onto his chest. She had his other palm and was slowly rubbing his arm as if trying to warm him up.

He couldn't feel a thing, but as he watched her stroke him, he was touched.

Unfortunatley, he didn't have a lot of time left with them, and he didn't have the breath to speak . . . so he did the only thing he was able.

With the last of his strength, Jim brought their hands together, linking them over the pinhole in his chest that had changed everything for all three of them, holding the two halves of them so they were one.

As his vision receded, he looked at those fingers, the small and the large, woven among each other. In a rush, he knew for certain the future was going to be kind to them. The demon was gone from Vin and somehow those talismans were in the possession of Adrian. These two fine, broken people were going to heal each other and walk through the hours and days and years of their decades side by side, and it was right; it was good.

He'd done a good thing. After so many years of taking lives, he'd saved one that mattered. And two that counted.

At the crossroads, he'd chosen wisely.

Abruptly, Jim's chest seized up and he coughed hard, his mouth becoming wet. His next inhale was nothing but a gurgle, and his heart started to hopscotch. Not long now, not long at all.

He couldn't wait to see his mother. And he was surprised at how much what he had done put him at peace.

Just as red lights played across the ceiling—the sign that an ambulance had pulled into the driveway—Jim let out his last breath . . . and died with a smile on his lips.

CHAPTER
41

The ambulance ride was bumpy from the speed and bright from the flashing lights. The sirens, however, came on only at intersections.

Marie-Terese took this as a good sign.

Sitting on a built-in bench beside Vin, with one hand locked on a vertical stainless-steel bar to steady herself and the other tight to his warm palm, she figured if his condition were really dangerous, the rip-snorting, high-pitched stuff would be going constantly.

Or maybe she was just trying to placate herself.

As he lay on the gurney, Vin's eyes were closed and his face was pale, but he was holding on to her. And every time they went over a pothole, he winced, his lips pulling back off his white teeth—which had to mean he wasn't in deep shock or a coma. And that was good, right?

Compared to the downside potential.

She glanced over at the medic. The woman was concentrating on the screen of a portable EKG, and her expression gave nothing away.

Marie-Terese leaned to the side and tried to get a look at whatever readout the machine was giving . . . and all she saw was a white line making some sort of pattern against a black background. She had no clue what it meant.

Out the back window of the ambulance, she prayed to see more street lamps on the sidewalks . . . and buildings instead of strip malls or residential streets . . . and cars parked parallel to the curb.

Because that meant they were finally downtown.

It wasn't just for Vin's sake.

Shifting around and moving her butt forward on the seat, she was able to look through the front windshield, and she took solace in the fact that the ambulance ahead of them—which had Jim in it—still had its lights going. The medics had triaged both men, called for a second team, and treated Jim first—and she had stood out in the hall with Eddie as a portable defibrillator had been brought in and that wounded chest had been shocked once . . . twice. . . .

The sweetest words she'd ever heard had come from the man with the stethoscope: *I have a pulse.*

She hoped they were able to keep it going up in front. The idea that Jim would have to die to save her was nearly unbearable.

And as for Saul . . . he hadn't needed fast transport to the hospital. Plenty of time for him.

Good God . . . *Saul?*

He'd been all but invisible in those prayer group meetings, nothing but a quiet, balding man who had the sad-sack look of someone perpetually on the losing end of life's equation. She'd seen nothing from him to lead her to believe he was obsessed with her, but the trouble was . . . he was precisely the kind of man you wouldn't remember.

Thinking back to when she'd run into him at church the night before at confession, she wondered how many times she'd missed noticing him. After all, he'd been the first car to stop when she'd had that near miss in traffic after the service today. Which suggested he'd been right behind her.

How often had he followed her home? Had he come to the Iron Mask?

On a cold shiver, she wondered . . . had he killed those men she'd been with?

The whole thing didn't exactly make her glad for the kind of man her ex-husband had been. But she appreciated the precautions she'd taken because of Mark.

From out the front windshield, the offices of the *Caldwell Courier Journal* flew by and she squeezed Vin's hand. "Almost there."

His lids lifted. Those gray eyes that had first captivated her did the trick all over again: Staring into them, she felt as though she were tripping and falling and didn't have a clue where she was going to land.

Although that was no longer true, was it. She knew exactly the sort of man he was, and he was *not* the kind she had to look out for.

He was the man she needed in her life. Wanted in her life.

Leaning down to him, she smoothed his hair back, stroked his five-o'clock shadow, and looked into his eyes. "I love you," she said, bending down and kissing his lips. "I love you."

His hand cranked down on hers. "Love you . . . too."

Boy, that croaking voice lit her up from the inside. "Good. We're even then."

"We . . . are. . . ."

The ambulance bumped over something in the road and everything from the machines to the medic to Vin on the gurney got tossed up. As he sucked in a vicious hiss and squeezed his eyes shut, she went back to looking out the front window again, anxious to see the ambient glow of the St. Francis Hospital complex . . . hoping that somehow her making visual contact with their route would speed things along.

Come on . . . come on. . . .

All at once the ambulance up ahead put its red lights out and slowed down to the speed limit, and the one she and Vin were in caught up quickly . . . then passed its leader.

"Why did they slow down?" she demanded as the medic

repositioned the EKG monitor. "Their lights are off. *Why are they slowing down?*"

The shake of the head she got in response was not a surprise. It was a tragedy: You needed to rush only if the person were alive. Which was why no one had attended to Saul after he'd been pronounced dead.

Death left you with an eternity to deal with bodies. No hurry there.

Marie-Terese dragged in a breath, and as tears came to her eyes, she let go of the stable bar and brushed them away. The last thing she wanted was for Vin to crack his lids and see her upset.

"ETA two minutes," the driver called out from in front.

The medic picked up a chart. "Ma'am, I forgot to ask you. Are you his next of kin?"

Wiping her eyes, she pulled herself together for Vin's sake and knew right off there was no way in hell she was going to risk getting sidelined when it came to his care. Acquaintances and friends got only so far when it came to ER doctors and nurses.

"I'm his wife," she said.

The woman nodded and made a note. "And your name is?"

She didn't even pause. "Gretchen. Gretchen Capricio."

"You are a very lucky man."

Two hours later, those hell-yeah words were spoken to Vin as his admitting physician snapped off her bright blue surgical gloves and tossed the pair into an orange biohazard container.

She was so right. All it had taken was local anesthesia and some stitches to close up the entrance and the exit wounds. No bones busted up or tendons sliced or nerve damage. That bastard with the gun had hit nothing but meat, which was gross and a good call.

Vin had been really lucky.

Unfortunately, his response to the good news was to curl over and throw up into the pink bedpan next to his head. And the fact that he moved his torso made the pain in his shoulder go rock-star ... which made the vomiting worse ... which made the pain worse ... and around and around he went.

And yet still he had to agree with the woman in the scrubs. He was lucky. The luckiest bastard on the face of the planet.

"You cannot handle Demerol, however," she said.

Thanks for the newsflash, Vin thought. He'd been hurling since they'd given him the shot about thirty minutes ago.

After his latest bout of gagging lost its enthusiasm, he settled back against the pillow and closed his eyes. As a cool hand towel-wiped his mouth and his face, he smiled. Marie-Terese—Gretchen, actually—was still terrific with the terry cloth.

And God willing, she wouldn't have to put that skill set to use on him again anytime soon.

"I'm going to give you an antinausea injection," the doctor said, "and if the vomiting subsides, we can release you. Stitches need to be removed in ten days, but your internist can do that. We've given you a tetanus shot and I'll write you a prescription for oral antibiotics—but we have some samples here, and we've already given you one of them. Any questions?"

Vin opened his lids and looked not at the doctor, but at Gretchen. She loved him. She'd said so, in the ambulance. He'd heard the words from her very own mouth.

So nope, he didn't have any questions. As long as he knew she felt like that, he was good to go on pretty much everything else.

"Just shoot me up, Doc, so I can get the hell out of here."

The woman snapped on fresh gloves, uncapped a syringe and put the needle right into his vein. As she hit the plunger, he didn't feel a thing, which made the hurling almost worth it. "This should ease things immediately."

Vin held his breath, not really expecting—

Holy shit. The effect was lickety-split, as if his belly had been blanketed in a whole lot of whoa-nelly-easy-there-big-boy. On a shuddering breath, his entire body went loose, giving him a clear idea, as if the upchucking hadn't, of exactly how green he'd felt.

"Let's see if that holds," the doctor said, recapping the syringe and tucking it into an orange box. "Just rest here, and when I release you, we'll get you and your wife a cab."

He and his wife.

Vin brought Gretchen's hand up to his mouth and brushed her knuckles with a kiss. "Sound good to you?" he asked. "Honey?"

"Perfect." A smile lifted her lips. "As long as you're ready to go. Dear."

"I so am."

"All right, I'll be back to check on you." The doctor went over to the curtain that separated Vin's bay from the rest of the ER. "Listen, the CPD is asking to see you. I can tell them to contact you—"

"Send them in," Vin said. "No reason to wait."

"You sure?"

"What's the worst that can happen? I start throwing up again and use the guy's pockets instead of my bedpan? I'm willing to risk that."

"Okay, you got it. If it goes on too long, hit the nursing button and we'll intervene." The doctor nodded and swept the drape back. "Good luck."

As the curtain swung shut, Vin squeezed Gretchen's hand with urgency, because he didn't know how much time they had.

"I want you to tell me the truth."

"Always."

"What happened with Jim? Did he . . . ?"

The hard swallow she took before she answered told him everything, and to spare her from having to put out the words, he kissed her hand again. "Shh, it's all right. You don't have to say it—"

"He was your friend. I'm so sorry—"

"I don't know how to say this, so I'm just going to." Vin

rubbed the beating pulse at her wrist with his thumb. "I'm so glad you're still here. For your son. For me. Jim did an incredibly selfless, heroic thing, and as much as I wish he hadn't died because of it, I'm very grateful for what he did."

She dropped her head and nodded, her curling hair falling forward. As he drew circles over the fine bones of her wrist, he traced the glossy waves with his eyes. Jim's final action on earth had left one hell of a legacy, namely a life to be lived ... and a son who still had his mother ... and a lover whose heart hadn't been shattered by loss.

A fine legacy.

"He was a real man." Vin cleared his throat. "That one ... was a real man."

They sat in silence together, he flat on the gurney, she on a plastic chair, their hands linked tightly—just as the man who had saved her life had put them together over his chest.

On the other side of the gray-and-blue curtain, people rush-rush-rushed along, their voices overlapping, their shoes shuffling by, their shoulders brushing the drape and causing it to swing from the metal hooks it hung from.

He and Gretchen, on the other hand, were motionless.

Death did that to a person, Vin thought. Stopped them in their place in the midst of the great tumble and scramble of their life, isolating them in still silence. In the instant it took hold, it changed everything, but its effect was like that of a car slamming into a wall—what was inside kept on going because the shit didn't know better ... with the result being utter chaos: All the clothes the person had worn became some kind of history exhibit to be cleaned out by a weepy nearest-and-dearest ... and their magazine subscriptions and account reports and dental reminders went from "correspondence" to "junk mail" ... and the place where they lived went from being a home to a house.

Everything stopped ... and nothing was what it had been.

God, when the news hit that someone you knew died,

you got a small shot of what the deceased was getting a whole boatload of: You stopped short and pulled out of the business of life as the ringing of the bell resonated through your mind and your body. And because humans were a pain in the ass, usually the first thought was, *No, it can't be.*

Life, however, didn't come with a rewind button and it sure as fuck wasn't interested in opinions from the peanut gallery.

The curtain pulled back, revealing a stocky man with dark hair and dark eyes. "Vin diPietro?"

Vin jerked himself to attention. "Ah ... yeah, that's me."

The man stepped inside and took out a badge. "I'm Detective de la Cruz from Homicide. How you doing?"

"Haven't thrown up in about ten minutes."

"Well, good for you." He nodded to Gretchen and gave her a little bow. "I'm sorry we have to meet again so soon ... and under these circumstances. Now, can you guys give me a quick version of what happened? And listen, neither of you is under arrest—but if you'd rather talk with a lawyer present, I understand."

Mick Rhodes hadn't been called yet, and he'd no doubt advise against saying anything without him, but Vin was too tired to care—and anyway, it didn't hurt to be nominally cooperative when you'd acted within the bounds of the law.

Vin shook his head back and forth on the pillow. "No, it's fine, Detective. As for what went down ... we were upstairs in the bedroom with ..." For no good reason, an overriding instinct told him not to mention Eddie—one so strong that he felt powerless to resist it. "... with Jim."

The detective took out a little pad of paper and a pen, all Columbo-style. "What were you doing in the house? The neighbors said that usually there's no one in it."

"I own the place and I've decided to finally do it over for resale. I'm a real estate developer and Jim works ... worked ... for me. We were there discussing the project, you know, going through the rooms. . . . I guess I'd left the front door open and we were upstairs when it all happened." As the detective nodded and made notes in his pad, Vin gave him a chance to get it all down. "We were in the bedroom, talking, and the next thing I know I hear this gun go off. It happened so damn fast. . . . Jim jumped in front of her and took the bullet. . . . I was by the dresser with my back to the door, and I went for my piece—which, by the way, is registered and I have a license to carry. I shot the guy with the gun and he went down."

More notations in the pad. "You shot him a number of times."

"Yeah, I did. He wasn't getting a chance to let loose any more rounds."

The detective backed through his notebook, the inked-up pages making a crackling sound. When he looked up again, he smiled briefly. "Right, okay . . . so why don't you try it again and tell me the truth this time. Why were you in that house?"

"I told you—"

"There was salt poured everywhere and incense in the air and the window upstairs in that bedroom had been broken. The sink on the second floor was filled with some kind of solution, and there were empty bottles of things like hydrogen peroxide all over—and the circle drawn on the floor in the middle of that bedroom you were in was also a nice touch. Oh . . . and you were found with your shirt off and no shoes on, which seems like an odd wardrobe if you were gum-flapping about business. So . . . although I'm inclined to believe you about the shooting part, because I can trace the paths of bullets as well as the next guy, you're full of crap about the rest of it."

Right, pin-drop time.

"I think we should tell him the truth, honey," Gretchen said.

Vin looked over at her and wondered, Exactly which truth would that be, dear?

"Please do," the detective said. "And look, I'll tell you what I believe, if it'll help. The guy you killed was named

Eugene Locke, alias Saul Weaver. He's a convicted murderer who got out of prison about six months ago. He was renting the house next door and he was obsessed"—the detective nodded at Gretchen—"with you."

"This is what I can't understand ... why—" Gretchen stopped. "Wait a minute, how do you know that? What did you find at his house?"

The detective looked away from his notes, focusing on a middle ground. "The man had pictures of you."

"What kind of pictures," she asked in a flat tone.

As Vin rubbed her hand, the detective met her eyes. "Wide-lens, telephoto stuff."

"How many."

"A lot."

Gretchen's palm tightened against his. "You find anything else?"

"There was a statue upstairs. One that actually had been reported stolen from St. Patrick's Cathedral—"

"Oh, my God, the Mary Magdalene," Gretchen said. "I saw it was missing from the church."

"That's the one. And I'm not sure if you noticed or not, but she looks a lot like you."

Vin struggled with the urge to kill the guy all over again. "Could this Eugene ... Saul guy ... whatever his name was, be responsible for those deaths and beatings in the alleys?"

The detective flipped through his book. "Since he's dead, and therefore there's no chance of maligning his reputation ... I'll tell you that I think I can tie him to both incidents. Right now, the man who was wounded in the head last night is still hanging on. If he makes it, I believe he'll identify his attacker as having dark hair, because when we went through Locke's house, we found a men's brunet wig with fine traces of blood splattering on it. The CSIers are already running tests, and I believe that the residue is going to match one or all of our victims. We also have a shoe print from the first scene which happens to look a helluva lot like what Locke was wearing tonight.

"So, yeah, pulling this all together..." More with the flipping through, then another glance at Gretchen. "I'm thinking that Locke was targeting men you'd danced with or for at the club, and that explains those attacks. And it was a stroke of luck—or misfortune was more like it—that he happened to live in the house next to where you guys were tonight. Because he didn't know that place was yours, right?"

Vin shook his head. "I'd been there like one other time in the last month, and before that ... I can't recall. And I don't think he knew my name to search the real estate records. Besides, how long had he lived next door?"

"Since he was released from prison."

"Yeah, she and I didn't meet but ... three days ago."

De la Cruz made another note. "Okay, I've been candid. How about returning the favor ... ? You want to tell the truth about why you were there?"

Gretchen spoke up before Vin could. "Do you believe in ghosts, Detective?"

The man blinked a couple of times. "Ah ... I'm not sure."

"Vin's parents died in that house. And he does want to do it over. The problem is ... there's a bad spirit in it. Or was. We were trying to get it out."

Vin popped his brows. Holy crap. That was fantastic, he thought.

"Really?" the detective asked, his brown eyes going tennis-match between them.

"Really," Vin and Gretchen said together.

"No shit," the detective murmured.

"No shit," Vin replied. "The salt was supposed to create a barrier or some crap, and the incense was to clean the air. Listen, I'm not going to pretend I understand all of it...." Hell, he still wasn't clear on everything. "But I know what we did worked."

Because he felt different. He *was* different. He was just himself now.

De la Cruz flipped to a fresh page and wrote something. "You know, my grandmother used to be able to predict the weather. And there was a rocker up in her attic that moved by itself. What got thrown out the window?"

"Would you believe it broke on its own?" Vin answered.

De la Cruz glanced up. "I don't know."

"Well, it did."

"Guess whatever you did might really have worked."

"It did." Vin rubbed his eyes with his free hand until his shoulder let out a holler he couldn't ignore and he had to stop. "Let's fucking hope it keeps, though."

There was a pause and then De la Cruz looked at Gretchen. "I have a follow-up question for you, if you don't mind. You stated to the medics that your name is Gretchen Capricio, but I have it down as Marie-Terese Boudreau. Would you feel comfortable helping me out a little about that?"

Gretchen did a thorough explanation of her situation, and as she spoke, Vin stared at her beautiful face and wished he could take all the pain from the past and the stress from the present away from her. She had shadows in her eyes and under them, but as he'd come to expect, her voice was strong and her chin up.

Man, he was in love with her.

The detective was shaking his head as she finished up. "I'm really sorry about all that. And I understand completely—although I do wish you'd been up-front in the beginning with us."

"I was afraid of the press, mostly. My ex-husband's in prison, but his family connections are all over the country ... and some of them are in law enforcement. After what happened with my son, I don't trust anyone—even those people with badges."

"What made you decide to come clean tonight?"

Her eyes shifted to Vin. "Things are different and I'm leaving town. I'll still let you know where I am, but ... I have to get out of Caldwell."

"After all this, I understand it—although we're going to need to be able to reach you."

"And I'll come back anytime you need me."

"Okay. And look, I'll talk to my sergeant. Giving a false identity to the police is a crime, but under the circumstances . . ." He put his notebook away. "I also heard from the staff here that you told them you were his wife?"

"I wanted to stay with him."

De la Cruz smiled a little. "I did that once. My wife and I were dating and she sliced her finger open with a knife cutting up a salad for dinner. When I took her to the ER, I lied and told them we were married."

Gretchen lifted Vin's hand to her lips and kissed it briefly. "I'm glad you understand."

"I do. I really do." The detective nodded at Vin. "So you two just started dating?"

"Yeah."

"Guess your previous lady friend didn't like it, did she."

"Yeah . . . I had the ex-girlfriend from hell." Literally.

In a rush, Vin thought back to the mess his duplex had been left in and the lies Devina had told the police. "She's vicious, Detective. Worse than you can imagine. And I did not hit her, not once that night, not ever. My mother was abused by my father, and I don't pull shit like that. I'd walk out and leave everything I own behind before I ever struck a female."

The detective's eyes narrowed and that eagle stare locked on Vin. After a moment, the guy nodded. "Well, we'll see. I'm not handling that side of things because it's out of my department . . . but I wouldn't be surprised if they didn't find there was more going on, like a third party or something. I've looked into the faces of a lot of wife beaters and you're not one of their kind."

De la Cruz put his notebook and pen away and glanced at his watch. "Hey, check it out. Now you haven't thrown up in almost a half hour. That's a good sign—maybe they'll let you blow this Popsicle stand."

Vin extended his free hand even though his shoulder didn't appreciate it. "You're okay, Detective, you know that?"

A solid palm met Vin's and they shook. "And I hope you two are going to be all right. I'll be in touch."

After the guy left, the curtain flapped back down in place and Vin took a deep breath. "How long do you suppose I have to wait before I can go?"

"Let's give it another half an hour, and if they don't come to check on you, I'll go find that doctor."

"Okay."

The trouble was, being powerless and waiting like a good boy had never sat well. Within five minutes, he was getting ready to hit the nurse-call button, except then the curtain parted again.

"Perfect timing—" Vin frowned. Instead of a nurse or a doctor, it was Eddie, looking as grim as a guy who'd just lost a friend and fallen out of a second-floor window.

Go. Fig.

Vin's first instinct was to sit right up, but that didn't go over well at all. As his shoulder let out an opera-singer scream, he had to close his throat up to keep from vomiting all over the front of himself—but at least it wasn't from the Demerol.

As Gretchen lunged for a fresh bedpan and Eddie held up both of his palms in the universal language of whooooooooooooooa, Vin tottered on the edge of losing it.

Thank fuck the tide receded and his stomach eventually loosened up.

"Sorry 'bout that," he said roughly. "I'm having issues."

"No probs. No probs at all."

Vin breathed in through his nose and out through his mouth. "I'm sorry . . . about Jim."

Gretchen went up to Eddie and gripped the guy's massive upper arms. Standing in front of him, she was both tiny and fierce. "I owe him my life."

"Both our lives," Vin chimed in.

Eddie hugged her briefly and nodded once at Vin. Clearly, he was the type who controlled his emotions—which was something Vin could respect.

"I appreciate it. And now, why I've come." Eddie reached into his pocket, and when he brought out his palm, in the center of it was the diamond ring and the gold earring. "Adrian did what he had to and got them away from her. You're both completely free, and the way it works is you're now off-limits to her. You don't have to worry about Devina coming back. Just hold on to these, okay?"

As Gretchen took the pieces and hugged him again, Vin let her embrace say everything he wished he could, but didn't dare. He was getting a little choked up, and not because his stomach was rolling into another evac: Sometimes sharp gratitude had the same effect on the gut as nausea. The thing was, he just couldn't figure out what these men had gotten from helping him and Gretchen. Jim was dead, Eddie looked like shit, and fuck only knew what Adrian had done with Devina.

"You guys take care of yourselves, okay?" Eddie murmured, turning to leave. "I've got to go."

Vin cleared his throat. "About Jim . . . I'm not sure if you were planning on claiming his body, but I'd love to give him a proper burial. Nothing but the best. Straight up."

Eddie looked over his shoulder, his odd red-brown eyes grave. "That would be cool—I'll leave you in charge of him. And I'm sure he'd appreciate it."

Vin nodded once, the deal struck. "You want to know when and where? Can you give me your number?"

The guy recited some numerals, which Gretchen wrote down on a piece of paper.

"Text me with the details," Eddie said. "I'm not sure where I'll be. I'm taking off."

"You don't want to be seen by a doc?"

"No need to. I'm fine."

"Ah . . . okay. Take care. And thank you . . ." Vin let the words drift because he didn't know how to say what was in his heart.

Eddie smiled in an ancient way and held his hand up. "You don't have to say anything else. I feel you."

And then he was gone.

As the curtain flapped shut, Vin watched under its hem as those shitkickers turned to the right, took one step . . . and disappeared into thin air. Like they'd never been there in the first place.

Bringing his right palm to his face, Vin rubbed his eyes. "I think I'm hallucinating."

"Do you want me to get the doctor?" Gretchen came over, all worried. "I can use the nurse's button—"

"No, I'm okay. . . . Sorry, I think I'm just really overtired." For all he knew, the guy had simply moved over to the left and was now, at this very moment, striding out of the ER and into the night.

Vin tugged Gretchen down next to him. "I feel like it's over now. This whole thing."

Well, over except for the fact that his visions were back to stay—at least according to Eddie. But maybe that wasn't a bad thing. Maybe he could find some way of channeling them or using them for good.

With a frown, he realized he'd found a new purpose. Only this one would serve others, not himself.

Not a shabby outcome, all things considered.

Gretchen opened her hand and the jewelry, especially the diamond, gleamed. "If you don't mind, though, I'm going to put these in a safety-deposit box."

As she shoved them down deep into the pocket of her jeans, Vin nodded. "Yeah, let's not lose those again, shall we?"

"Nope. Never again."

CHAPTER
42

When the taxi pulled up in front of Gretchen's rental house, the light of dawn was breaking over Caldwell in a lovely wash of peach and golden yellow. The trip away from St. Francis had been a hell of a lot better than the one to the ER in the back of that ambulance, but it was clear to Gretchen that Vin was far from well. With his pale green, rigid face, he was obviously in pain, and mobility was going to be a problem with that arm of his in a sling. Plus he looked like a homeless man in the floppy shirt the hospital had given him, its wide-open collar showing off the super-white bandage that ran from the base of his neck all the way across one side of his chest.

"Next stop the Commodore, right?" the driver said over his shoulder.

"Yeah," Vin replied in an exhausted voice.

Gretchen stared out the window at her little house. The babysitter's car was parked in front on the street and there was a light on in the kitchen. Upstairs, Robbie's room was dark.

She didn't want Vin to go back to the duplex by himself.

She wasn't sure how Robbie would take to meeting him.

And she felt trapped between the two.

Turning to Vin, she searched his familiar, handsome features. He was talking to her ... patting her hand ... probably telling her to get some rest, take care of herself, call him when she was up. ...

"Please come in," she blurted. "Stay with me. You've just been shot and you need someone to look after you."

Vin stopped in midsentence and just stared at her. Which was precisely what the cabbie did in the rearview mirror. Then again, both the invitation and the gunshot part were no doubt equally surprising to each of the men, respectively.

"What about Robbie?" Vin asked.

Gretchen glanced up and met the driver's eyes. God, she wished there were some way of putting up a partition so the guy behind the wheel didn't hear all this.

"I'll introduce you to him and him to you. And we'll just go from there."

Vin's mouth tightened and she braced herself for a no. "Thank you ... I'd like to meet your son."

"Good," she whispered with a combination of relief and fear. "Let's go."

She paid the fare and got out of the cab first so she could help Vin—but he shook his head and grabbed the side of the taxi to pull himself up. Which was a good thing, considering the way the muscles in his forearm clenched. Given how much he weighed, she was more likely to fall on him than actually get him to his feet.

Once he was upright, she hitched herself under his good side, shut the door, and helped him up the front walk.

Instead of trying to find her keys, she knocked quietly and Quinesha opened the way immediately. "My lord, will you look at you two."

The woman stepped back and Gretchen got Vin over to the couch, where he didn't so much sit down as fall on the cushions—which led her to believe his knees gave out.

For long moments, everyone waited to see if he was going to need to be rushed to the bathroom.

When it seemed like he had himself under nominal control, Quinesha didn't ask a lot of questions. She just gave Gretchen one of her quick, hard hugs, asked if there was anything she could do, and hit the road when she was thank-you-but-no'd from the heart.

Gretchen locked the door up and put her purse down on the ratty wing chair by the TV. As Vin let his head fall back and his lids crash down, she was not surprised when he took a series of long, deep recovery breaths and held otherwise completely still.

"You want the bathroom?" she asked, hoping he didn't have to throw up again.

When he shook his head, she went into the kitchen, got a glass out of the cupboard, and filled it full of ice. Courtesy of her son, there were two things she always had in the house: ginger ale and saltines, also known as mother's cure-all. Even though Robbie was homeschooled, he played with other kids at the Y, and the sitters all had children who came down with flus and colds and stomach bugs.

A mom never knew when she might need the magic combo.

Cracking open a fresh can of Canada Dry, she poured the soda over the ice and watched the fizz go crazy and foam up right to the top of the glass. As she waited for things to settle, she got out a sleeve of the crackers and put a two-inch stack on a folded paper towel.

Just as she was topping off the glass again, she heard Vin's gravelly voice from the living room: "Hi."

Her first instinct was to rush in to reassure Robbie—but she knew if she made it look like there was a problem, she'd only make things more dramatic than they already were going to be. Picking up what she'd gotten for Vin, she forced herself to walk calmly into the living room.

Robbie's hair was sticking up in the back as it always did when he got out of bed, and his Spider-Man pj's made him look smaller than he really was because she'd purposely bought them two sizes bigger than he needed.

Standing just inside the room, he was focused on their guest, his eyes wary, but curious.

God . . . her heart was pounding and her throat was tight and the ice in the ginger ale was rattling from the way her hand shook.

"This is my friend Vin," she offered quietly.

Robbie glanced back at her and then refocused on the couch. "That's a big Band-Aid. You gots a cut?"

Vin nodded slowly. "I do."

"From what?"

Gretchen opened her mouth, but Vin got there first with an answer. "I fell down and hurt myself."

"That why you gots the sling, too?"

"Yeah."

"You don't look so hot."

"I don't feel so hot."

There was a long pause. And then Robbie took a step forward. "Can I look at your Band-Aid?"

"Yeah. Sure." Though it clearly cost him a lot of agony, Vin moved the strap of the sling off his shoulder and slowly unbuttoned his borrowed shirt. Peeling the cloth back, he exposed the padding and gauze and tape.

"Woooooooooow," Robbie said, walking all the way over and reaching out.

"Don't touch him, please," Gretchen said quickly. "He's hurting."

Robbie retracted his hand. "I'm sorry. You know . . . my mom's good at healing my cuts."

"Yeah?" Vin said roughly.

"Uh-huh." Robbie glanced over his shoulder. "See? She already gots the ginger ale." Dropping his voice down to a whisper, he added, "She always gives me ginger ale and saltines. I don't really like 'em all that much, but I usually feel better after I eat 'em."

Gretchen went over to the couch and put the crackers on the table next to Vin. "Here. This'll steady your stomach."

Vin took the glass and looked at Robbie. "You okay with me hanging on your couch for a little while? Truth is, I'm really tired and I need a place to rest."

"Yeah. You can stay here till you're all better." Her son put his hand out and introduced himself. "I'm Robbie."

Vin extended his good arm. "Nice to meet you, my man."

After they shook, Robbie smiled. "I have an idea, too."

As he headed out of the room, she said, "You want to get changed out of your pj's, please?"

"Yes, Mom."

It took every ounce of control for Gretchen not to do the whole snatch and hug thing as he passed by—but he was behaving as the man of the house, and seven-year-olds deserved to have their pride.

"You think that went okay?" Vin asked softly.

"I really do." She blinked fast and sat down next to him. "And please drink some of that."

Vin clasped her hand in a fast squeeze and then took a sip. "I don't think I'm up for the saltines."

"We can wait on those."

"Thank you . . . for letting me meet him."

"Thank you for being so good with him."

"I'll stay on the couch, okay?"

"Yup and we can do our lessons in the kitchen. I home-school him, and today's Monday."

"I love you," Vin said, turning his head to face her. "I love you so goddamn much it hurts."

She smiled and leaned in, kissing him. "That might just be your shoulder talking."

"No, it's closer to the center of my chest. I think . . . it's called the heart? Not sure, as I haven't had one before."

"I believe that would be the heart, yes."

There was a pause. "You still going to move into my farmhouse?"

"If it's still okay with you, yes."

"You mind having someone else in one of the guest rooms while you're there? You know, a fellow tenant? It's a big place, and there's this maid's room over the kitchen that he could use while you and Robbie have the whole run of the second floor. And I can vouch for the guy. He's neat and clean, quiet, respectful. Known him a long time. He's trying to get his life back together and is going to need a place to stay."

She stroked his face, and thought they hadn't known each other for all that long if you counted the hours ... but considering what they'd been through, it was as if everything needed to be measured in something like dog years. Or more.

"I think that would be great."

They kissed again quickly and he said, "If it doesn't work, I'll leave right away."

"Somehow I think it's going to be fine."

Vin smiled and sipped a little more. "I haven't had ginger ale in years."

"How's your stomach—"

Robbie came back down, still in his pj's. "Here, this'll help!"

As he held out his favorite Spider-Man comic book, Gretchen took the soda so that Vin could accept the gift.

"This looks really cool," Vin murmured as he put the comic on his lap and opened the first page.

"It'll take your mind off things." Robbie nodded as if speaking from decades of experience. "Sometimes when you hurt, you need distraction."

Distraction came out *discrackshion*.

"I gotta go get ready for school. You stay here. Drink that. Mom and I will check on you."

Robbie marched out of the room like he'd arranged everything.

And just like that, Vin was in like Flynn.

CHAPTER
43

Again with the fresh grass.

Although at least this time, Jim knew where the fuck he was.

As he opened his eyes and got a whole lot of bright green and fluffy, he turned his face to the side and took a clear, deep breath. His whole body hurt, not just where he'd taken the bullet, and he waited for things to quiet down a little before he attempted any flashy moves like . . . oh, lifting his head or some shit.

Guess this facedown business meant he was really dead—

A pair of perfectly polished white bucks overtook his visual field, and above the natty shoes, a set of linen slacks pressed with a knife edge hung with the perfect break at the ankles.

The bottom cuffs were jacked up sharply, and then Nigel knelt on his haunches. "How lovely to see you again. And no, you'll be going back down again. You have more missions ahead of you."

Jim groaned. "Am I going to have to die first before I come here every time? Because no offense, but for fuck's sake, I can just give you a cell phone to call."

"You did very well," Nigel said. The man . . . angel . . . whatever . . . extended his hand. "Very well indeed."

Jim gave the springy ground a shove and turned himself over. As he shook what was offered, the sky was so bright he blinked fast and let go quickly so he could rub his eyes.

Man . . . what a trip it all had been. But at least those two people were okay.

"You left out one crucial piece of information," he said to the angel. "The crossroads was mine, wasn't it. When that bullet went flying, the key choice in all this was mine, not Vin's."

"Yes, it was. When you chose to save her over yourself, that was the critical turning point."

Jim let his arms flop down at his sides. "It was a test."

"You passed, incidentally."

"Go, me."

Colin and the other two dandies came over, and all three of them were dressed as Nigel was, in pressed white slacks with cashmere sweaters that were peach and yellow and sky blue, respectively. Nigel's top half was done in coral.

"You guys ever wear camo?" Jim grunted as he propped himself up on his palms. "Or does that offend your sensibilities."

Colin knelt down and actually put his knees right on the grass—which suggested Heaven had Clorox bleach in its laundry room. "I'm rather proud of you, mate."

"As are we." Bertie stroked his wolfhound's head. "You succeeded marvelously."

"Marvelously indeed." As Byron nodded, his rose-colored glasses winked in the diffused light. "But then I knew you were going to choose wisely. All along, I was sure, yes, I was."

Jim focused on Colin. "What else are you guys hiding from me."

"I'm afraid things are on a need-to-know basis, dear boy."

Jim let his head fall back on his spine and he stared at

the milky blue sky that seemed at once miles away and close enough to touch. "You don't by any chance know a fucker named Matthias, do you."

As a soft breeze rolled on by and rustled through the blades of grass, the question went unanswered, so Jim struggled to get to his feet. When Bertie and Byron leaned in to help him, he put them off even though his ass was about as steady as a pencil standing on its eraser.

Jim knew what was next. Another assignment. Seven souls out there and he'd saved one . . . or was it two?

"How many more do I have to take care of?" he demanded.

Colin swept his arm over to the left. "See for yourself."

Jim frowned and looked to the castle. On the top of its towering wall, curling in the breeze, was a massive triangular flag in brilliant red. The thing was incredibly bright, as vivid as the green of the grass, and as it waltzed in the breeze, he was transfixed.

"That is why we wore pastels," Nigel said. "Your first flag of honor is unfurled and nothing save the grass of the earth here should rival it."

"That's for Vin?"

"Yes."

"What's going to happen to them?"

Byron spoke up. "They're going to live out their days in love, and when they come herein, they shall spend an eternity together in joy."

"Provided you don't cock things up with the other six," Colin interjected, getting up. "Or quit."

Jim leveled his finger at the guy like it was a gun. "I don't quit."

"We shall see . . . we shall see."

"You are such a prick."

Nigel nodded gravely. "He very much is."

"Because I am logical?" The angel didn't seem concerned at all—or *a'tall*, as he would say—with the label. "There is a point in every endeavor when one feels the burn of too many vertical steps. We have all been there ourselves and so have you. We shall just hope that when you reach that point—"

"I'm not going to quit, asshole. Don't you worry about me."

Nigel crossed his arms over his chest and stared flatly at Jim. "Now that Devina knows you and you've taken something from her, she's going to start targeting your weaknesses. This is going to get much harder and much more personal."

"The bitch can bring it on, how about that."

Colin grinned. "It is a bit of a shock we two don't get along better."

Byron cleared his throat. "I think we should all just take a moment to support Jim as opposed to challenging him more. He has done a wonderful, brave thing, and I for one am quite proud."

As Bertie started chiming in and Tarquin's tail wagged, Jim held out his palms. "I'm cool— Oh God, no hugging, no—"

Too late. Byron wrapped surprisingly strong arms around Jim and embraced him, and then Bertie was next, with Tarquin rising up and putting his paws on Jim's shoulders. The angels smelled good; he had to give them that— just like that smoke that had come from the cigars Eddie had lit up.

Fortunately, though, Nigel and Colin weren't the brothers-inside-arms types.

Sometimes you lucked out.

Funny, Jim was a little touched, though it wasn't like he'd admit it. And abruptly, he was also ready to go back into battle. That flag, that tangible symbol of success, was a serious motivator for some reason—maybe because in his old life headstones were how he measured whether he was getting the job done, and that waving banner was far more attractive and uplifting.

"Okay, here's the deal," he said to the group. "I've got something I need to do before my next case. I need to find a man before he gets killed for the wrong reasons. It's part of my old life and not the kind of thing I can walk away from."

Nigel smiled, his strangely beautiful eyes locking onto Jim's as if they saw everything. "Of course, you must do as you wish."

"So do I come back here after I'm done or . . . ?"

More of that all-knowing smile. "Simply take care of things."

"How do I get in touch with you?"

"Don't call upon us. We shall call upon you."

Jim cursed under his breath. "You sure you don't know Matthias?"

Colin spoke up. "You do realize that Devina can be anything and anybody. Men, women, children, certain animals. She is pervasive in her numerous forms."

"I'll keep that in mind."

"Trust no one."

Jim nodded at the angel. "Not a problem, I got plenty of experience with that shit. One thing, though . . . do you guys actually communicate with me through the TV or did I lose my damn mind?"

"Godspeed, James Heron," Nigel said, raising his palm. "You have proven yourself worthy against our enemy. Now do it again, you tough bastard."

Jim got one last look at the castle walls, and imagined his mother safely and happily on the far side of them. Then a blast of energy blew out of the angel's hand and he was scrambled down to his molecules and sent flying.

Hard. Cold.

Fuckin' ow.

Those were Jim's first thoughts when he woke up again, and opening his eyes, he got another load of milky, diffused light that seemed to come from no particular source. Which made him wonder if Nigel's flashy palm crap hadn't fucked up and landed him right back where he'd been.

Except the air wasn't fresh. And instead of a bed of springy grass, he felt like he was lying on a stretch of pavement—

As a sheet was whipped off his face, Jim nearly jumped out of his skin.

"Hey," Eddie said. "Ready to go?"

"Fuck!" He clutched his chest. "You want to scare me to death?"

"Little late for that."

Jim looked around. The room they were in had pale green tiles on the floor, walls, and ceiling and an entire bank of three-by-two-foot stainless-steel doors with meat-locker handles on them. Empty stainless-steel tables with hanging scales and rolling tables were arranged in orderly rows, and the sinks in the far corner were the size of bathtubs.

"I'm in the fucking *morgue*?"

"Well, yeah." The *duh* was implied.

"Jesus Christ . . ."

Jim sat up, and sure enough there was a body bag with an occupant two tables down, and a sheet-covered corpse with its feet sticking out from the end next door. "So they really do put toe tags on them, huh."

Eddie shrugged. "It's not like they can give their name or some shit."

With a curse, Jim swung his legs off the table he was on, and that was when he saw Adrian. The angel was standing just inside the room by the double doors and he was unusually self-contained: Typically a sprawler, he had his arms linked tightly across his chest and his feet were set right together. With his mouth nothing but a slash, and his skin the color of Kleenex, the guy stared at the tile floor, brows down, lashes dark against his pale cheeks.

He was hurting. Inside and out.

"I brought you some clothes," Eddie said. "And yes, I went back and got Dog. He's in our truck, happy as a little clam."

"So I'm dead?"

"As a doornail. That's the way it works."

"But I still get to keep Dog even though I'm ..." A stiff?

God, was there a politically correct word for the dead? he wondered. Or was it a case of, if you'd bit the big one, you didn't have to worry about politics?

"Yup, he's yours. Wherever you are, he'll be."

This was a momentous relief for some reason.

"So you want these threads?"

Jim looked at what was in Eddie's arms and then down at himself. His body seemed the same, big and muscular and solid. Eyes, nose and ears seemed to function just fine.

How the hell was this going to work?

"There'll be a better time and place to explain shit," Eddie said, holding out the clothes.

"No doubt." Jim took the jeans and the AC/DC T-shirt and the leather jacket. The boots were shitkickers. Socks were thick and white. And everything fit.

As he dressed, he kept glancing back at Adrian every now and again.

"Is he going to be all right?" Jim asked quietly.

"In a couple of days."

"Anything I can do?"

"Yup. Don't ask him about it."

"Roger that." After he did up the buckles on the boots, Jim pulled the jacket on over his shoulders. "Listen, how are we going to explain that I'm back from the dead? I mean, there's going to be a body missing—"

"No, there won't." Eddie pointed to the table Jim had been on and ... holy shit. It was his body. Lying there like a slab of beef, with gray skin and a bullet hole right in the center of the chest.

"Your probationary period is over," Eddie said as he tugged the sheet in place over the face. "There's no going back now."

Jim stared down at the peaks and valleys that contoured the shroud and decided he was really glad his mother wasn't alive to "mourn" him. Made shit much easier.

And now Matthias was off his back.

This made him smile briefly. "There are advantages to being dead and gone, aren't there."

"Sometimes, sometimes not. It just is what it is. Come on, let's blow this place."

Still staring down at his corpse, he said, "I'm going to go up to Boston for a little while. Not sure how long. The boys upstairs were cool with it."

"And we're going with you. Teams stick together."

"Even if it's not your fight?"

"Yup."

The idea of having his own backup was attractive. Three could definitely cover more ground than one, and God only knew how long it was going to take to find Matthias's target.

"Okay, cool."

At that moment, two white coats came in, both with coffee mugs in their hands and mouths that were flapping. Jim got ready to bolt behind something, anything—and then realized that whereas he could see the pair, and smell what they were drinking, and hear their Crocs across the tile floor, they were utterly unaware that there were three other people in the room with them.

Or not people, he supposed.

"You want to do the paperwork on that one?" the guy on the right said, nodding to Jim's body.

"Yup. And I have a name to call if no one claims him. It's . . . Vincent diPietro."

"Hey, he built my house."

"Oh?" The two put their mugs down on a desk and picked up clipboards with forms on them.

"Yeah, me and my wife are in that subdivision down by the river." The man walked over, lifted the sheet up off Jim's feet, and read the tag tied to his big toe.

"Must be nice."

"It is." He started to fill out the squares one by one. "But it was expensive. I'll be lucky if I can retire at the age of eighty."

Jim took a moment to say good-bye to himself—which was fucking weird, but also a relief: He'd been looking for a fresh start when he'd come to Caldwell, and man, had he gotten one. Everything was different now—who he was, what he was doing, who he was working for.

It was as if he had been reborn and the world was fresh once more.

As Jim left the morgue with his wingmen, he was curiously uplifted ... and totally ready to fight again. And he had a feeling that for the next couple of years, *Bring it on, bitch* was going to be his goddamn theme song.

And then he remembered.

"I need to go back to that warehouse," he told them out in the hall. "Now. I want the body of that girl."

Adrian's voice was little but a rasp. "It's gone. All of what was in there is gone."

Jim stopped in the middle of the corridor. As an orderly pushing a cartload full of sheets went through the three of them, literally, Jim felt nothing more than a shiver in his body—and maybe he would have done a hey-check-this-shit-out under different circumstances, but he was instantly obsessed and cared only about one thing.

"Where did Devina take her?" he demanded.

Adrian just shrugged, his eyes still locked on the floor, his piercings glowing darkly in the corridor's fluorescent lighting. "Wherever she wants. When I woke up on the floor in the middle of that place, it was empty."

"How'd she move the shit so fast? There was a lot of it."

"She has help. The kind that she can mobilize quick enough. I was chained or I would have—" The guy stopped himself. "It took 'em about two hours, I think. Maybe longer. I was kind of in and out at that point."

"And they removed the girl's body?"

Adrian nodded his head. "For disposal."

"How do they get rid of it?"

The angel started walking again, like he was finished with the conversating business for a while. "Same way anybody ditches one. They'll cut it up in pieces and bury it."

As Jim followed, the need for vengeance choked him up and his focus sharpened to the point of pain. He was going to need to find out more about the girl, her family, where her body ended up. And sooner or later he was going to take that innocent's death right out of Devina's hide.

Oh, yeah, things were gonna get personal, all right.

Real, bloody and personal.

Jim had a job to do.

Turn the page for an exclusive sneak
preview of the next thrilling instalment in
the Black Dagger Brotherhood series!

Lover Mine

Coming soon from Piatkus.

"Okay, I think we're done."

John felt a last dragging swipe on his shoulder and then the tattoo gun went silent. Sitting up from the rest he'd been curled against for the last two hours, he stretched his arms over his head and pulled his torso back into shape.

"Gimme a sec and I'll clean you up."

As the human male headed for a stainless-steel sink, John settled his weight on his spine once again, and let the tingling hum that stretched across his upper back reverberate through his whole body.

In the lull that followed, an odd memory came to him, one he hadn't thought of for years. It was from his days of living at Our Lady's orphanage, back when he hadn't known what he truly was. One of the benefactors of the place had been a rich man who owned a big house on the shores of Saranac Lake. Every summer, the kids had been invited to go up for a day and play on his football field-sized lawn and go for rides on his beautiful wooden boat and eat sandwiches and watermelon.

John had always gotten a sunburn. No matter how much goo they slathered on him, his skin had always burned to a crisp—until they finally relegated him to shade on the porch. Forced to wait things out on the sidelines, he'd watched the other boys and girls do their thing, listening to the laughter roll across the bright green grass, having his food brought to him and eating alone, witnessing the party instead of being a part of it.

Funny, his back felt now as his skin had then: tight and prickly, especially as the tattoo artist came back with a wet cloth and made circles over the fresh ink.

Man, John could remember dreading that annual ordeal at the lake. He'd wanted so badly to be with the others . . . although if he was honest, that had been less about what they were doing, and more because he was desperate to fit in. For fuck's sake, they could have been chewing on glass shards and bleeding down the front of their shirts and he still would have been all *sign-me-up*.

Those six hours on that porch with nothing but a comic book or maybe a fallen bird's nest to inspect and reinspect had seemed as long as months: Too much time to think and yearn. He'd always hoped to be adopted, and in lonely moments like that, the drive had consumed him. The thing was, even more than being one among the other little boys, he'd wanted a family—a real mother and a father, not just guardians who were paid to raise him.

He'd wanted to be owned. He'd wanted someone to say *you're mine*.

Of course, now that he knew what he was . . . now that he lived as a vampire among vampires, he understood that "owning" thing much more clearly. Sure, humans had a concept of family units and marriage and all that shit, but vampires were more like pack animals. Blood ties and matings were far more visceral and all-consuming.

As he thought about his younger, sadder self, his chest ached—although not because he wished he could reach back in time and tell that little kid that his parents were coming for him. Nope, he ached because the very thing he'd wanted had nearly destroyed him. His adoption had indeed come, but the "owning" hadn't stuck. Wellsie and Tohr had waltzed into his life, told him what he was and shown him a brief glimpse of home . . . and then disappeared.

So he could say categorically, it was far worse to have had and lost parents, then to have not had them at all.

Yeah, sure, Tohr was technically back in the Brotherhood's mansion, but to John he was ever away: Even though the guy was now saying the right things, too many takeoffs had occurred such that now that a landing might actually have happened, it was too late.

John was done with that whole Tohr thing.

"Here's a mirror. Check 'er out, my man."

John nodded a thank-you and went over to a full-lengther in the corner. As Blay came back in from his cigarette and Qhuinn emerged from behind the side room's curtain, John turned around and got a look-see at what was doing on his back.

It was exactly what he wanted. And the scrollwork was boss.

He nodded as he moved the hand mirror around, checking out every angle. God, it was kind of a shame that no one other than his boys were ever going to see this. The tat was spectacular.

Xhex's name was in his skin. Ever a part of him. 'Til death did his flesh decay off his bones.

No matter what happened next, whether he found her dead or alive, she would always be with him.

The sight of those four Old Language characters eased him. Which was more than he could say of anything else he'd tried. Drinking, working out to exhaustion, fighting *lessers* until they weren't the only ones bleeding . . . nothing gave him any peace.

These last two weeks since her abduction had been the longest of his life. And he'd had some pretty fucking long days before this shit.

Christ, to not know where she was. To not know what had happened to her. To have lost her . . . he felt as if he'd been mortally injured though his skin was intact and his arms and legs unbroken and his chest unpenetrated by bullet or blade.

She hadn't wanted him, true. She had shut him out, true. But here was the deal. After having become toxic over the rejection, it had dawned on him that although she didn't feel the same way he did, he could still own his own emotions.

He could still pledge his life to her. And kill to find her. And bring her home in whatever condition she was in— whether it was to heal her or bury her.

She was his. And the lack of reciprocation didn't change that reality. Even if he got her back just so she could live a life that didn't include him, that was okay. He just wanted her safe and alive.

Guess that was how he knew he really did love her.

John looked at the artist, put his hand over his heart and bowed deeply. As he rose from his position of gratitude, the man stuck his palm out.

"You're welcome—means a lot that you approve. Now let me cover it up with some wrap."

Except John signed and Blay translated, "Not necessary. He heals lightning quick."

"But it's going to need time to—"The tattoo artist leaned in and then frowned as he inspected where he'd worked.

Before the guy started asking questions, John stepped back and grabbed his shirt from Blay. The fact was, the ink they'd brought with them had been lifted from V's stash—which meant part of its composition included salt. So that name and those fabulous swirls were in John's skin permanently—and his skin had already recovered.

Which was one advantage of being a nearly pure-bred vampire.

While Blaylock handed over John's jacket, the woman Qhuinn had balled came out from behind that curtain and it was hard not to notice Blay's pained expression. As someone who also had their shorties in a pinch over the whole unrequited-love thing, John's first impulse was to reach out to his buddy, but he held off.

Sometimes all a guy had going for him was his dignity.

"The tat rocks," Qhuinn said.

As the woman nodded, she slipped a piece of paper into Qhuinn's back pocket, but John wanted to tell her not to get her hopes up. Once the guy had someone, that was it— kind of like his sex partners were disposable razors he used to shave off the edges of his aggression. Unfortunately said Kat von D look-alike had stars in her eyes.

"Call me," she whispered to him with a confidence that would fade as the days passed.

Qhuinn smiled a little. "Take care."

At the sound of the two words, Blay relaxed, his big shoulders easing up. In Qhuinn-landia, "Take care" was synonymous with "I'm never going to see, call or fuck you again."

On that note, John took out his wallet, which was stuffed with tons of bills and absolutely no identification, and peeled off four hundreds. Which was twice what the tat cost. As the artist started shaking his head and saying it was too much, John nodded at Qhuinn.

The two of them lifted their right palms at the humans, and then reached into those minds and covered up the memories of the last couple hours. Neither the artist nor the receptionist would have any concrete recollection of what had been done. At the most, they might have hazy dreams. At the least, they'd have a headache.

As the pair slipped into trances, John, Blay and Qhuinn walked out of the shop's door and into the shadows. They waited until the artist shook himself into focus, went over and flipped the lock . . . and then it was time to get back to business.

"Sal's?" Qhuinn asked, his voice a little lower than usual, evidence of postcoital satisfaction.

As Blay lit up a Dunhill, John nodded and signed, *They're expecting us.*

One after the other, his boys disappeared into the night, but John paused for a moment before ghosting out, his instincts ringing.

Looking left and right, his laser-sharp eyes scanned Trade Street. There were a lot of neon lights and a number of cars going by because it was only two a.m., but he wasn't interested in the lit parts.

The dark alleys were the thing.

Somebody was watching them.

He put his hand inside his leather jacket and closed his palm around his dagger's hilt. He had no problem killing the enemy, especially now when he knew damn well who had his female . . . and he truly hoped something that smelled like a week-old dead deer stepped up to him.

No such luck. Instead, his cell phone went off with a whistle—no doubt Qhuinn and/or Blay wondering where the fuck he was.

He waited a minute more and decided the information from the Shadows was more important than throwing down with whatever slayer was hanging around. Xhex was the focus. She was the only thing that mattered in his whole world.

Getting her home safe was the be-all and end-all.

With vengeance flowing thick in his veins, John dematerialized into thin air, leaving nothing of himself behind.

*Watch out for titles in the Black Dagger Brotherhood series
by J.R. Ward*

DARK LOVER

In the shadows of the night in Caldwell, New York,
there's a deadly turf war going on between vampires
and their slayers. There exists a secret band of brothers
like no other-six vampire warriors, defenders of
their race. Yet none of them relishes killing more
than Wrath, the blind leader of the Black Dagger
Brotherhood.

The only purebred vampire left on earth, Wrath has
a score to settle with the slayers who murdered his
parents centuries ago. But, when one of his most
trusted fighters is killed – leaving his half-breed
daughter unaware of his existence or her fate – Wrath
must usher her into the world of the undead – a world
beyond her wildest dreams . . .

978-0-7499-3818-5

LOVER ETERNAL

Within the brotherhood, Rhage is the vampire with the strongest appetites. He's the best fighter, the quickest to act on his impulses, and the most voracious lover – for inside him burns a ferocious curse cast by the Scribe Virgin. Possessed by this dark side, Rhage fears the times when his inner dragon is unleashed, making him a danger to everyone around him.

Mary Luce, a survivor of many hardships, is unwittingly thrown into the vampire world and reliant on Rhage's protection. With a life-threatening curse of her own, Mary is not looking for love. Her faith in miracles was lost years ago. But when Rhage's intense animal attraction turns into something more emotional, he knows that he must make Mary his alone. And while their enemies close in, Mary fights desperately to gain life eternal with the one she loves . . .

978-0-7499-3819-2

LOVER AWAKENED

A former blood slave, the vampire Zsadist, the most terrifying member of the Black Dagger Brotherhood, still bears the scars from a past filled with suffering and humiliation. Renowned for his unquenchable fury and sinister deeds, he is a savage feared by humans and vampires alike. Anger is his only companion, and terror is his only passion – until he rescues a beautiful aristocrat from the evil Lessening Society.

Bella is instantly entranced by the seething power Zsadist possesses. But even as their desire for one another begins to overtake them both, Zsadist's thirst for vengeance against Bella's tormentors drives him to the brink of madness. Now, Bella must help her lover overcome the wounds of his tortured past, and find a future with her . . .

978-0-7499-3823-9

LOVER
REVEALED

Butch O'Neal is a fighter by nature. A hard living,
ex-homicide cop, he's the only human ever to be
allowed in the inner circle of the Black Dagger
Brotherhood. And he wants to go even deeper into
the vampire world to engage in the turf war with the
lessers. He's got nothing to lose. His heart belongs to
a female vampire, an aristocratic beauty who's way out
of his league. If he can't have her, then at least he can
fight side by side with the Brothers . . .

Fate curses him with the very thing he wants. When
Butch sacrifices himself to save a civilian vampire from
the slayers, he falls prey to the darkest force in the war.
Left for dead, found by a miracle, the Brotherhood
calls on Marissa to bring him back, though even her
love may not be enough to save him . . .

978-0-7499-3822-2

LOVER UNBOUND

Dr Jane Whitcomb, leader of a cardiac trauma team, is about to leave the medical centre for the night when an emergency is brought in – a man with a gunshot wound to the heart. As she examines him, however, she begins to suspect that her dangerously sexy new patient is not entirely human.

One night, while he's still in recovery, this tattooed stranger reaches out to her. He seems soothed by her presence. And she is oddly captivated by his. She will soon learn that he is Vishous – V for short – the smartest vampire in the Black Dagger Brotherhood. But his tortured past has left him avoiding intimacy. It is against V's nature to let anyone see his vulnerable side. Except Jane. He has the oddest sense that she understands.

978-0-7499-3848-2